By Kiersten White

THE PARANORMALCY SERIES

Paranormalcy
Supernaturally
Endlessly

THE MIND GAMES SERIES

Mind Games
Perfect Lies

The Chaos of Stars
Illusions of Fate

THE AND I DARKEN TRILOGY

And I Darken
Now I Rise
Bright We Burn

The Dark Descent of Elizabeth Frankenstein

THE SLAYER SERIES

Slayer
Chosen

THE CAMELOT RISING TRILOGY

The Guinevere Deception
The Camelot Betrayal
The Excalibur Curse

Beanstalker and Other Hilarious Scarytales

THE SINISTER SUMMER SERIES

Wretched Waterpark
Vampiric Vacation
Camp Creepy
Menacing Manor
Haunted Holiday

Star Wars: Padawan
Hide
Mister Magic
Lucy Undying

LUCY UNDYING

LUCY UNDYING

A Dracula Novel

KIERSTEN WHITE

New York

Lucy Undying is a work of fiction. Names, places, and incidents either are products of the author's imagination or are used fictitiously. Any resemblance to actual events, locales, or persons, living or dead, is entirely coincidental.

Published in the United States by Del Rey, an imprint of
Random House, a division of
Penguin Random House LLC, New York.

Del Rey and the Circle colophon are registered trademarks
of Penguin Random House LLC.

Library of Congress Cataloging-in-Publication Data
Names: White, Kiersten, author.
Title: Lucy undying : a Dracula novel / Kiersten White.
Description: First edition. | New York : Del Rey, 2024.
Identifiers: LCCN 2024022765 (print) | LCCN 2024022766 (ebook) |
ISBN 9780593724408 (hardcover; acid-free paper) |
ISBN 9780593973806 (international edition) | ISBN 9780593724415 (ebook)
Subjects: LCGFT: Fantasy fiction. | Vampire fiction. | Novels.
Classification: LCC PS3623.H57854 L83 2024 (print) | LCC PS3623.H57854 (ebook) |
DDC 813/.6—dc23/eng/20240531
LC record available at https://lccn.loc.gov/2024022765
LC ebook record available at https://lccn.loc.gov/2024022766

Printed in the United States of America on acid-free paper

randomhousebooks.com

9 7 5 3 1 2 4 6 8

First Edition

Book design by Debbie Glasserman

For Tricia, whose patient enthusiasm gave me the confidence to know it was time, at last, for Lucy

LUCY UNDYING

1

Salt Lake City, January 10, 2025

DRACULA

It starts the moment you look out the window.

You don't see him through the glare of the night-dark glass. You just *look,* safe inside but flinging your soul outward.

Your features transform whenever someone speaks to you, but you drop your sweet smile as soon as they turn away—a girl who wears a disguise to survive. It surprises and intrigues him, so he follows when you walk outside.

The night caresses with a grasping cold. Your head is down as you hurry to get home, soft brown curls hiding your face, hands shoved in the pockets of your coat. Rushing for safety and warmth. So dull and predictable, just like everyone else.

Though he has infinite time—a vast and depthless pool of it, holding him in place while the world's currents drift around him—he no longer has any more time to waste here. He's ready at last to move on.

But.

Your steps slow as soon as you leave the pools of manufactured light. Your head drifts up, the curtain of your hair parts, and you gaze heavenward as though seeking the sun for warmth. The stars offer no such comfort. Theirs is a piercing, lifeless grace. You linger in the darkness and devour eternity with your eyes.

His own heart, stilled so long ago, seems to judder to life at the sight of you. You're *special.* He aches to make your strange blood his own, to take everything you were or are or could have been.

If others weren't watching, too, he might not have had the will to hold himself back. He loves the hunt, but you are a prize worth waiting for.

It doesn't matter how many times he's started this dance over the centuries, how many yous there have been. Because it feels new to him every time, when it's right. And every time, for him, there is only *you.* There has only ever been *you.*

He is Dracula, and you are young and lovely and vulnerable, and he knows exactly how this dance will end.

You will invite him in.

2

London, October 4, 2024

IRIS

Everything in London looks suitably old. Not in a run-down American way, but in a wearily ornate way. Like a grandma whose entire house is covered in plastic to preserve it in exactly the same state forever. England settled into "fussily impressive and obsessed with history" as its aesthetic and never changed. I admire the English for their commitment to it. The only thing *I've* ever been committed to is destroying my own family legacy.

I answer my phone without checking as I navigate out of the train station. Only one person ever calls me now, and I have to pick up so he doesn't get suspicious. "Dick. Seriously. Give me at least a day to settle in before you start trying to lawyer me back to America."

"Your mother," Dad says, his voice as cracked as the ancient sidewalk beneath my feet. I stop dead. A tourist bumps into my oversized backpack, cursing. I barely hear them.

"Dad? Dad, what's wrong?" I shout, both out of fear and so that he can hear me. My dad has always been an old man, nearing fifty when I was born, but he's gone downhill fast recently. The slide started years ago, though, when I opened a door that should have stayed shut. *My fault, my fault.*

His voice drops as though he's worried about being overheard. "She was here last night."

I put my free hand to my forehead. I don't know what hurts more—my head after the transatlantic flight and train ride into London, or my heart as I hear how scared and confused he is. I'm sorry to leave him alone, I really am, but—

But he abandoned me when I needed him most, didn't he? The only way he can make it up to me is by letting me go, whether he knows he's doing it or not. I can't feel guilty about it. He's in the nicest home money could buy, with the best staff, the best meals, and an upfront payment so large I can be assured he'll be safe and taken care of for the rest of his life. That's what we Goldamings do: slap some money on the problem and move on.

"Dad," I say. "Mom wasn't there last night. She's dead."

"She was beating against the window. She had red eyes and an evil smile. Please, Iris, you have to get me out of here. She knows where I am. You have to hide me or she'll get in."

I try to sound gentle, but I'm exhausted. "Mom couldn't have been at your window. Both because you're on the third floor, and because she's dead."

"I saw her, though. I saw—"

"I watched her die." Blood being pumped out as fast as she could produce it, her body consuming itself. I rub my arm, tiny bumps of scars hidden beneath my sleeves, thinking about tubes sucking, sucking, sucking the blood. "I'm sorry you couldn't come to the funeral, but I promise, we sealed her right up."

Maybe if he'd been healthy enough to travel to Miami, he'd be convinced. It still makes no sense why she was buried there when she lived and died in the desert West.

"But I saw—"

"She's gone, Dad. I promise." I don't tell him that I took a few minutes alone with the casket on the long flight to her custom mausoleum. I expected her waxen, bloodless face to haunt me. Instead, I keep returning to the memory as a comfort. She's *dead,* and I'm so close to being free.

"But she was here," Dad whimpers. "She told me to open the window and let her in. She'll be back tonight; I know she will." He sounds like a child, scared of the dark. But he never protected me from the darkness *or* from my mother.

I glance down the street, trying to get my bearings. All the buildings feel too close to each other, so there's no way to see where the sun is. "Tell your nurse to make sure the window's locked and close the drapes nice and tight. And if Mom comes back, tell her to fuck off. Bye." I hang up and immediately regret it. And then try my hardest not to regret it.

God, I'm never going to escape. No matter where I go, she follows me. Exhaustion radiates from my core, like if I don't sit down and dissociate right now, I might die. I have no idea what to expect when I get to the house, either. Will it be in good enough condition for me to stay there, or will I have to get a hotel? That bastard Robert Frost taunts me, my mind repeating, *The woods are lovely, dark and deep, but I have promises to keep, and miles to go before I sleep, and miles to go before I sleep.*

I guess it's "kilometers" here, though. Such a typically dry English joke, giving us their nonsense measurement system and then switching to metric themselves.

It's so tempting to find a hotel and sleep off the jet lag. Burrow into white sheets, be blissfully unconscious for a day or two. But I can't risk the delay. I can't be sure they aren't already following me. My beloved running-away-backpack straps dig into my shoulders, and I welcome the weight. It helps me focus. It reminds me why I'm here.

This is the only chance I'm ever going to get, and I won't blow it because I'm tired.

My phone rings again and this time I check before answering. "Can I just burn the house down and be done with the estate that way?"

Dick's voice is as dry as kindling. "That's arson, Miss Goldaming, and even in the UK it's quite illegal."

"What a hassle."

"You could always return home and address the responsibilities you have here."

I want to punch his voice in the mouth. My mother really outdid herself when she put Dick Cox in charge of executing her will. A name like that, he should be a world-renowned adult film star, not a pedantic attorney so relentless I'll never escape him.

"Don't want any of it. The responsibilities, the company, even the money. Once I sell the London and Whitby houses, we'll talk about getting me out of the rest."

"You will want it," Dickie says with bland assurance. "It's in your blood. And the blood is life."

I flinch at the hateful mantra. It feels like my mother, pinching me under the table so I'll sit up straight and smile. "In my case, the blood is my eventual death, so thanks for your continued insensitivity. Bye, Dickie." I hang up. Between my dad and Dick, I'm a walking panic attack. I thought I'd feel brave when I got here. Ready. Instead, I just feel haunted.

There's a café across the street. Coffee is my greatest ally; it will help me fight my jet lag, fight my blood, fight my past. I can do this. I look to the left and step into the street.

Three things happen at almost the same time:

A hand grabs my pack and yanks me so forcefully I fly backward through the air.

A black cab passes on my right within inches of mowing me down.

And I fall onto my ass, looking up at a stunning porcelain angel of a woman, golden head haloed by the sun, still holding the backpack strap she used to save my life.

3

May 6, 1890

JOURNAL OF LUCY WESTENRA

Mother's been in my room. I leave little traps for her everywhere, little ways that I'll know where she's been with her prying fingers and cutting eyes. But she didn't find my journal. Dear, dear Mother, who loves like a knife, slicing me into ever smaller pieces until I'm exactly the shape that pleases her the most.

Though this shape she cuts me into is pleasing all around. Doctor Seward has been by again. What business does he have doing house calls for my mother? He shouldn't be looking after a fussy woman convinced that every cough or sniffle is the plague. I wish he would tuck her into his big black bag along with his vials and bottles and take her to his sanitarium. She could complain all day and have him instead of me at her beck and call. But he loves sitting for tea after he listens to her heart and her ever-lengthening list of ailments. And all the while, he watches me over those glasses, tracking me more carefully than he tracks her pulse.

Sometimes I smile at him, as placidly as I imagine a saint would. What he doesn't know is I'm Saint Joan of Arc, waiting to take up a sword and make all of England cower before me.

But that's wishful thinking. I could no more wield a sword than Doctor Seward could inspire a young woman to blush. But as my mother taught me, if someone frightens you, make them love you. Then you will be in control.

If my mother's love is any indication, that's not true. I certainly don't control her. But I will not make an enemy, and I will pray Doctor Seward grows tired of my mother's complaints long before he grows tired of my face. He promised to come again next week and bring his friend from America, and I had to pretend to be thrilled at the prospect. I do not care for Doctor Seward—why should I care for his friend?

But oh! My dearest heart is coming today, and I think I will die of all the love I have in me, the flutters and the hopes and the absurd little dreams that always come when I know what the train is bringing. A respite. Someone who cares about me, who cares for me, who wants only my happiness.

FIE! A CURSE ON my earlier hopes. Arthur Holmwood and his flesh-colored mustache are coming instead. He sent a card asking to call on us this afternoon. I forgot he existed until he insisted on reminding me.

He picked up my glove at the opera last week and assumes he also picked up my heart. As if I would be so easily won! I have dozens of gloves. I could lose a glove a day for the next month and never miss a single one of them, just as I could lose a dozen of these exhausting men and never think of them again.

What a waste of a day. I'm all foul moods and tempers, the worse for having to hide them. I shall go crazy pretending to be happy. Then Mother will send me to the sanitarium and Doctor Seward can study me at his leisure. He would like that very much, I think. Perhaps that's why he's always lurking about. Waiting for me to crack into pieces so he can examine each of them.

Speaking of torments. Arthur Holmwood and his horrid lip caterpillar are here. My journal must go into hiding along with all my true feelings. Smile, Lucy! Time to pretend.

4

Boston, September 25, 2024

CLIENT TRANSCRIPT

Thank you for inviting me in, Vanessa. You didn't need to. Both because this is your office, not your home, so technically I don't need an invitation, but also because I wasn't going to kill you if you didn't.

It must have been upsetting, though, seeing me decapitate that other vampire in your parking lot. Are you sure *I* shouldn't be giving *you* therapy? No? Probably for the best. So kind of you, offering to listen to me. Therapy might be the only thing left that I've never done. How fun to be having a new experience!

Well then, to answer your questions in order of importance:

Yes, it's fine that you're recording this. I don't mind. All these endless years, and I have nothing to show for them. Might as well live on as a ghost in your phonograph, or whatever they call them now.

Yes, vampires are real, and yes, I'm one, and yes, that other vampire was trying her best to kill me, poor thing. She might have succeeded, too, had I not outrun all her friends.

I hope your neck doesn't hurt too much. The bleeding has stopped, at least. I'm sorry I didn't get her before she bit you, but please don't think too unkindly of her. She was basically a baby rattlesnake. All instinct and no control. You startled us, so she attacked. Which, again, I'm grateful for. They'd injured me enough already that I needed a little help, and you were an excellent accidental distraction.

And now to the other questions you peppered me with as I helped you back inside: *How is this possible? Why is this happening? Are there more of them out there? Who are you?* All valid things to wonder.

I'll start at the beginning. The beginning is, as all beginnings are, soaked in blood and shrouded in darkness. The end will be, too, but we'll get there together.

My name is Lucy Westenra, and this is my story.

5

London, October 4, 2024

IRIS

"American?" the angel asks, still clutching the strap she tore clean off while pulling me to safety. I'm turtled on the pavement, backpack keeping me off the ground but also making it impossible for me to get up. She holds out her free hand to help; her skin's warm and her fingers fit just right. I manage to awkwardly stand.

My heartbeat is an ocean pounding in my ears. Everything seems heightened and bright and loud. I almost died. Holy shit, I almost *died.* If I'd brought luggage instead of my old running-away-backpack, I might have. "What gave me away?" I ask.

"You have to look right here." She points down where, sure enough, "LOOK RIGHT" is painted directly on to the asphalt. "Also, sorry about this." She waves the narrow length of nylon that used to be my backpack's top strap.

"That's fine. I'll sew it on like a patch to commemorate the time I survived not looking right." I take it and shove it into my pocket to give myself something to do with my shaking hands. It's hard to tell how old my angel is, with her golden hair, flawless cream-colored skin, and small frame, though she carries herself with an assured confidence I can only describe as *not a teenager.* But she's such a slip of a thing, it's amazing she managed to yank me that hard. "I'm glad you're stronger than you look."

"Adrenaline." Her smile's nearly as brilliant as the sun. But this is London, so it's not hard to rival the sun for brightness. Still, I feel myself starting to go stupid and fuzzy, the way I always do when meeting gorgeous women. Or maybe it's just my body, still flooded with that same adrenaline.

"Right. Wow. Welcome to England, I guess."

She laughs, and it's like champagne flutes being chimed together. Fizzy and bright and crystalline all at once. If I'd known they had women this beautiful here, I'd have gone to Oxford instead of Salem State. Mom would have been *thrilled* to pull strings and get me in. Even happier to pay for it. After all, whatever she financed, she owned.

Stay dead, Mom. Let me enjoy a beautiful face in peace. All the other beautiful faces my mother got her claws into flash in my mind, and my throat aches with pent-up emotion. Maybe this time. Maybe with Mom dead, with Goldaming Life far away . . .

My angel bends down and retrieves a spilled to-go cup. Her drink splattered on the sidewalk so I wouldn't be. Which gives me an opening.

"Can I buy you a new coffee—tea, I guess—to thank you for saving my life?" I gesture at the café that nearly got me killed.

"Surely your life is worth more than a cup of tea." Her lips, rosebud pink and promisingly full, purse in a teasing smile. She knows I'm trying to pick her up. Am I that obvious?

I'm that obvious. I can't stop staring at her. I give up on being coy and let myself smile as big and goofily as my body wants me to. "Depends on who you ask."

That earns me another laugh. But then her head tilts and something closes off in her dark blue eyes. She's still smiling, but I realize now what it is that makes it clear she's not a teenager. It's not confidence; it's *exhaustion*. Beneath that perfect skin and beautiful face, she's more worn down than most teenagers could ever understand being.

"Sorry, my little cabbage," she says, and my soaring hopes plummet back to earth. "I'm afraid I'm very late."

Right. She was coming from the train station, too. Clearly in transit, and here I am, trying to divert her. I shove my hands back in my pockets and shrug. "Another time, then."

"Another time." Her smile blooms from bud into a full rose, and I wish she would stay. Distract me from everything I have to do. "Until then . . ." She leans close enough that my heart picks up again—she's flirting, too—and she whispers, "*Look right.*"

I laugh, half because it's funny and half to release the tension of having her close enough to kiss. She glides down the sidewalk, weaving her way through the masses trying to interpret their phone map apps. When she reaches the corner, she glances over her shoulder at me. I will her to come back. To decide to be even later than she already is. I'll be her little cabbage. I'll be whatever she needs me to be for a few hours until I can't pretend my life away anymore.

Instead, she disappears, swallowed by the crowd.

"Real smooth, Iris," I mutter to myself. Just as well. It would be like painting a target on her back, and she doesn't deserve that. The hairs on my neck prickle. I refuse to look over my shoulder to check if someone is watching me.

The sooner I get going, the sooner I can actually get going. I'm so close. A few more weeks and then I can leave my mother's fucking cult behind forever. I'll be where they expect me to be until the moment I never am again.

"Your precious blood," someone says beside me.

I jump into the street without looking. I'm three blocks away before I stop running, gasping for breath. My lungs burn. So does my elbow, stinging and raw. It's bleeding through my sleeve. I must have hurt it when I fell, but didn't notice because I was so besotted with my angel. Whoever commented on my blood was pointing out that I was hurt. That was it, nothing else.

I tell myself that, but I don't believe it. I know better by now. It's *always* something else. Pressing a hand against the wound, I look left *and* right *and* behind myself, scurrying deeper into London as if a new city could ever hide me.

6

Boston, September 25, 2024

CLIENT TRANSCRIPT

I was born in 1871, which makes me— What year is it? Doesn't matter. Math is awfully tedious. Besides, you get less precious about age when all the years stretch behind and before you, infinite, empty, marking neither the passage of time nor a march toward death. Endless night without the hope of a dawn. But also, I know I look amazing for my age.

My first birth was hardly noteworthy: a tiny squall in a world that demanded girls be silent and still. I don't care to think about that time, and it's not what you're interested in. You want what came in the second birth, where I emerged from the womb of life and the cavity of death as something not quite living, but certainly not dead.

If you've never woken up in your own coffin, I cannot say I recommend the experience. Darkness and pain and thirst—devastating thirst, like my entire body was parched and I would die if I didn't do something to soothe it. I was closed in on all sides, certain there were red eyes in the black with me, teeth caressing my neck. I screamed and screamed and no one answered. Every spinning particle of dust that made up my body wanted to be somewhere, anywhere else.

And then I was. I found myself standing outside a mausoleum. If you had asked me my name, I wouldn't have known it. We all lose that in the space between dying and waking. We lose most everything then.

Have you ever gone to sleep certain the world worked in predictable ways, and the next day woken up to find everything changed? Everything rendered absurd and meaningless such that you didn't know whether to scream or laugh and were afraid if you chose to do either, you could never stop?

Laughter wasn't really an option. My entire existence was one anguished scream, even now that I was free from my confinement. My throat was raw from thirst. I didn't know exactly what I needed, but I *had* to drink something immediately.

Didn't he know I was here? Didn't he know I was hungry and terrified? I felt like he was near. Over my shoulder, in the shadows. I thought he would appear, and if not help me—I was not so naïve, even then—at least give some sense back to the world. Even not knowing who I was, barely remembering what I had been before becoming this creature filled with panic and need, I remembered Dracula.

He had wanted me. He had claimed me as his own. And yet I was alone. Not for long, though. Dracula's brides were already on my trail. And not just them. There were so many like me out there, waiting. So many I'd meet and love and betray and hunt and kill.

Sometimes I feel like I never left that cemetery. Like I'm still standing there, screaming, waiting for Dracula.

Oh, dear. You're lost. I can see it in your face. I know, because I've been lost for so long. You get used to it. Time isn't a line. It's a bottomless pit we throw more and more of ourselves into until we're swallowed completely. Everything is still happening, has never happened, will always be happening, hasn't happened yet. I walk with the ghosts of everyone I've ever been, and I don't know which I am, or if I'm one of the dead that haunts me.

Stories are hauntings, aren't they? The ghosts we carry with us everywhere. I'll try to tell you my stories in order. Build a house for you where all my ghosts can be contained and haunt you in a way you can make sense of.

You're already in the house. You don't know how you got inside. All you know is there's no way out, only deeper in. And behind the next door is a bride. She feels like velvet and smells like sex and tastes like blood.

So much blood.

7

May 10, 1890

JOURNAL OF LUCY WESTENRA

I cannot decide whether Quincey Morris is simple, or simply American. I wish this cowboy and Doctor Seward would not inflict themselves upon me. The dreadful stories they share! If I have to keep smiling and act amazed that the brave, strong men used weapons to kill some poor creature, my teeth will break from all the gnashing I do.

How is it brave to go against an animal while wielding a gun? Perhaps if they bested a buffalo in hand-to-hoof combat, or wrestled a wolf into submission, I would be impressed. No. I would root for the wolf. To be a wolf, sliding silent and unseen through the wilderness . . . I always imagine what it would feel like to be a falcon, a wolf, a tiger. But Mother calls me her little dove, and Mina calls me her pet. Alas, no fierce and wild predatory life for me. I am a kept and coddled thing. But that makes me safe from the guns of Doctor Seward and Mister Morris.

Another aggravation? I can only understand a fraction of what Mister Morris says. His cowboy turns of phrase are bewildering. Does no one make sense in America? And he speaks so slowly, as if I were a simpleton instead of him.

I'm being unfair. He doesn't seem unkind. But now I've learned that Arthur Holmwood and the omnipresent doctor and the earnestly incomprehensible cowboy are allied in brotherhood and friendship. Arthur will be joining them on their next visit! Does every swaggering boastful man in the world know one another? I feel beset on all sides. Or like they are hunting prey together, and I'm the bumbling creature they have in their sights.

This might even be a relief. I've lived in fear of a proposal from Doctor Seward, Arthur Holmwood is determined to court me, and even Quincey Morris seems keen to occupy my time and attention. But if all three are such dear friends, then surely none of them can pursue me without permission from the others.

I cannot imagine Arthur, elegant and assured and entitled, relinquishing a claim on anything. Nor can I imagine the doctor and his cold, dead eyes willingly looking elsewhere. Nor can I imagine the Texan giving up a hunt once he has found his prey.

Perhaps they will kill each other! Then I can prettily mourn them and be free. I do quite like the drama of black lace. I would look lovely, pretending to cry over their graves as my darling held me close.

I have hidden sharp teeth after all, daydreaming the deaths of three perfectly fine men. I should repent. But repentance never seems to take with me. Still, no wishes for the men's deaths. The best I can hope for is that they grow tired of me. I find myself deeply tiresome in their company. Surely they will come to find my performance tiresome, too.

No need to think of them further. Mother has entombed herself in bed today and all my men are off somewhere drinking and smoking together, so I'm free. I will write my darling and await a reply, and then practice my best listening faces for when Mother awakes or my tormentors return. I've been slipping lately, and Mother has noticed. I would prefer she not pay more attention to me.

I miss school. I miss learning. I miss having something to do with my time, knowing what was expected of me and earning smiles and praise. Mother tells me I will be happier when I'm a wife and mother. She certainly doesn't seem happy being a mother. And being a wife ended in disaster for her.

I do wish for a life where I'm happy, but whenever I try to imagine it, I see myself on the cliffs, walking arm in arm with my darling, laughing.

Why can I not have that future? Why must maidens become mothers? Why must I marry at all? I have never felt more loved or taken care of than when I was young and guided and taught by someone who truly cared about me. Take me back to those days, sharp brown eyes looking at me over my book, whispered secrets and an entire shared world, just the two of us.

Mother calls. My daily taste of freedom is over. Perhaps Mister

Morris will teach her his cowboy rope tricks, and she can keep me close even more efficiently.

If I can survive until Mina comes next week, I'll have so many funny stories for her. That's what I'll do. I'll take all my pain and aggravation, wrap it neatly with a bright bow, and turn it into something to make her laugh.

8

London, October 4, 2024

IRIS

I discover two things while getting my keys and legal documents. The first is that, in the UK, lawyers are called solicitors. The second is that, regardless of what they're called, my mother had a type when it came to legal representation. It's not just the fact that Albert Fallis also has a lewd-adjacent name. There's something eager and possessive in the way he speaks to me, a malicious twinkle in his eye, like he knows a secret I don't.

Joke's on him. I'm the one with a secret neither he nor Dickie Cox will find out about until it's too late.

"So lovely to meet the newest Goldaming. Such a legacy." He taps his fingers against his thumbs as though pinching the air between them. He's shelled in layers of tweed with a scarf so large he could retreat into it if threatened. A pale white hermit crab of a human.

The whole office is wood paneled, from the floors to the ceiling. It's as dim as twilight and so dusty my allergies are already declaring war. Albert looks proud, gesturing around his claustrophobic box of an office. "I have more than a century of work with your family here in this very room."

"Wow," I say, nursing my coffee. "You look great for your age."

His eyes disappear beneath bushy gray eyebrows in a deep scowl. "Not me, personally. I mean my office. We've served your family as solicitors for generations. With *respect* and *dignity*." He even talks like he's pinching me. I'll bet he'd love to leave angry red welts on my arms beneath my sleeves where no one could see them.

I lean back in a stiff leather seat. It's so low that my shoulders barely come up to the height of Albert's desk. He isn't a tall man, but he's positioned himself as the biggest person in the room. I really do feel like a kid, staring up at him.

I hated being a kid, and now I hate Albert, too. I'm sure there are good lawyers in the world somewhere, but it's little surprise my mother only employed creeps.

Leaning back farther in my chair, I take up as much space as I can, knees wide and unladylike. "I'll take the keys to the London house, the Whitby house, and all the legal documents for both. Now."

He blinks at me for several seconds before speaking. "The Whitby house is being let out as a holiday rental; we'll have to check with the manager if it's available to visit."

My heart sinks. If it's a vacation rental, odds are there's nothing valuable there I can sell for quick cash. The revenue is probably folded into my mother's strategically scattered bank accounts and investments. Dickie has an iron grasp on those, and I'm not willing to do what I have to in order to access them. I resist the urge to rub my arms, the scent of disinfectant a ghost haunting my sinuses forever.

"As for Hillingham," Albert continues, "since it's not far, I thought I would take you there, help you—"

"It belongs to me, right? It's *mine.*"

"Yes." His narrowed eyes make it clear he wishes he could answer differently. "The house is willed to the Goldaming line in perpetuity, and you are the only heir."

"I'll take the paperwork and the keys to both properties, then. Call me when I can see the Whitby house." It's his turn to look up at me. I stand and raise an eyebrow, coldly impatient. It's easy to demand others bend to my will. I just pretend I'm my mother, a carefully honed impression that's served me well for many years.

"Right, y-yes," he stutters, patting the front of his suit coat until he finds a key. He unlocks one of the drawers in his desk and pulls out two sets of keys, which he places in front of me before scuttling to the wall of files. None of them are marked. He goes to the fourth row, seventh drawer, with no hesitation. Maybe he really has worked here for more than a century. The interior of the drawer brims with neatly sorted documents. Most of them are yellowed and brittle with age, but he skips those in favor of two sheaves of paper near the back. They're still white, so recently printed I can practically smell the ink.

He closes the drawer, sealing away the history of my family and these houses. I have the oddest impulse to ask him to give me all of it. But what good are decades of documents to me? Can't very well sell those. Besides, I don't want to invest in my family tree. I want to prune my branch off forever.

He stares down at the deeds, stroking them as though they're precious to him. "It all started with this house, you know. The first time we worked with Lord Goldaming. It was his patronage that allowed our office to survive all this time, to grow into what we are now."

"And what is the office now?" I ask. A lightless box? An absolute coffin of a workplace?

He beams at me. "The protectors of legacy." If I thought his scowl was unpleasant, nothing prepared me for his smile. His eyes have the same grasping pinch as his fingers, gaze reaching hungrily toward me.

"Cool," I say with as much enthusiasm as I can manage, which is none at all. I take the papers from him—his crab fingers briefly spasm shut around them, but then he releases—and swipe the keys from the desk before he can stop me.

"Always an honor meeting Lord Goldaming's blood," he calls as I turn my back and hurry from the room. "After all, the blood is—"

I slam the door shut behind myself before he can finish the phrase.

9

Boston, September 25, 2024

CLIENT TRANSCRIPT

Dracula usually kept three brides, but they lost one in transit. I imagine she's still wandering around Europe somewhere, trying to find her way to London. Or maybe I ended her existence at some point without realizing it. Doesn't matter.

Although I never knew their names—they didn't know them, either—for the sake of clarity we'll call the two brides I met Raven and Dove. Raven had long, thick hair so black it swallowed all light, and Dove's hair was so ephemeral and white it floated around her like a cloud.

Free from my mausoleum, I stood frozen in the cemetery. It was night, but like no night I had ever known. The air swirled with sound and scent, as if all my senses had merged into one. Had rotting roses always shimmered like that? Had birds always flown with such a clatter of wings and creaking feathers? Had the presence of the small creeping things of the earth really been a secret to me, when now they announced themselves with such obvious heat?

Heat. I needed heat. I was so brutally cold. I blurred in and out of myself, whole sections of the cemetery appearing and disappearing along with my consciousness. Somewhere close by, there was heat. I let out a cry as my teeth grew into sharp points with an aching pain close to pleasure. And then my teeth found the heat, and I lost myself to the sheer animal joy of satisfying a need.

I still don't know who I killed. I'll never know. When I think about what I did that night, I can feel the space where I should carry guilt, but there's nothing there. I wasn't a person yet—or at least, as much a person as I'm capable of being now. I was merely a squall, a newborn once more.

I sat on the ground, shivering in ecstasy, marveling as the heat of another life spread through my body. I hadn't even remembered I *had* a body until then. I had only been my senses, and then my teeth. I stared at my hands, amazed at how small and white they were. And my neck—I kept touching my neck. There was nothing there, but I could *sense* those twin icy points, the holes where I had been drawn out of myself. Where I'd been removed. How had I gotten back in?

The brides found me there. I would have imprinted on anything that touched me gently that night, a duckling in their confident thrall. Raven hummed and stroked my hair as I trembled. Dove cooed at me, exclaiming over how small I was, how pretty, how new. They coaxed me back to my mausoleum.

I was as starving for loving touch as I had been for blood. A flaw that led me here. But we aren't to that story yet.

Being with them felt like . . . Do you remember the first day you realized you could be the same woman on the inside *and* on the outside? That the *you* who had always nestled beneath, hidden and trapped, the you that had always been there, could be the *only* you?

You know who you are. You claim the woman you are and celebrate her. I wish I had been able to do that during my life, too.

But the pretty idiot I once was had died alone and afraid and didn't understand how she felt and could never say what she longed for. What she wanted.

Meanwhile, this new pretty idiot I had become, freshly risen from the grave with someone else's blood coursing through her? *She* knew what she wanted. I let Raven kiss me and Dove pet me. I felt flush with possibility. I didn't know what or who I was anymore—and I quickly realized that meant I could be anything. Anyone. I could do whatever I desired, and who could tell me no? Who could say what was wrong, what was wicked, what was unnatural, when everything simply *was*?

I don't regret what the brides and I did that night and others. I don't regret losing myself in the rush and thrill of sensation. Letting myself *want*. I didn't love the brides and they certainly didn't love me, but at least there was finally one thing I understood about myself when everything I knew in the world had come undone:

Breasts really are fantastic.

I mean, just the best. Absolutely divine. I could live for a thousand more years and never tire of them.

So that night I also discovered hands and tongues and teeth and a thousand surprising things to do with them. At the time I thought all those parts of me Raven was finding were entirely new and came with being a vampire. That was how little I'd been educated about the facts of life. It took me too long to realize I could always have felt those things. They didn't have to be tied to blood and death and violence. They could have been based in love and sweetness and tenderness.

Love was never my destiny, though.

For a few days we slept tangled and inseparable in my mausoleum, and for a few nights we prowled the darkness, searching only for heat we could steal. Raven hunted with me, but Dove slipped away on her own. Dove always met us before dawn, though, so we could seal ourselves inside my mausoleum once again.

When it comes to healing, or regenerating, or merely building up strength, blood is good for a vampire. But sleep is even better—especially a deep mindless undreaming rest in your own grave dirt, but any unhallowed ground will do.

Because Dracula had turned each of us into vampires, Dove and Raven could use my grave dirt and find nearly the same level of restoration as they had in their own.

But sleeping in your own grave dirt isn't the only way to find rest. My mausoleum feels like home, the way you sleep better in your own bed than anywhere else, but I can nearly always find somewhere good enough. Old blood helps, whether freely or violently spilled into the dirt. Makes it nourishing, like vampire fertilizer. A battleground, a plague pit, or some other hasty receptacle is best. Cemeteries aren't actually good at all.

It's not because of the sacred ground nonsense. Don't take that concept as proof God is real. I rather think I exist as proof in the opposite direction. And if not me, certainly Dracula is evidence there's no larger plan, no benevolent protector watching out for precious children.

No, the real reason is that cemeteries, especially modern ones, are filled with chemical-tainted bodies with almost no blood at all.

I haven't thought of my own mausoleum since I left it the last time. But back then it was my home, one I happily shared with Raven and

Dove. I was always eager to get back to it. Sunlight was a cage. We could survive with the rays of the sun beating down on us, but we were trapped by it. Unable to change form, sapped of much of our strength. Raven warned me to avoid it at all costs.

One night, though, I hesitated. While I still didn't have much of myself back—I couldn't have told you my name or my address, or even told you what my mother looked like, though she'd died nearly the same time I had—I still held on to one thing: I wanted to see my darling.

"I have to go home," I said to Raven. "Can you help me find it?"

Raven stroked my hair. Then she pulled it, yanking my head back. She traced a single sharp nail along the line of my throat. "Pretty thing," she said. "Silly thing. You can never go back. You forget whose bride you are now."

She dragged me toward my mausoleum, but something made her freeze. She hissed and disappeared into the night. I kept going. People were waiting at my resting place. I could feel their heat radiating outward.

I arrived to find four men. It wasn't their faces I recognized—I had lost those, in the space between dying and waking. But I knew the scent of their blood. Traces of it lingered in my body. How had I come to possess their blood, when I'd never tasted them?

One had a growth of pale hair above his lip, as though someone was trying to sweep away whatever came out of his mouth. "Lucy?" he asked.

My name! I was Lucy! Or at least, I had been. More names came to me in a sudden spilling rush. Memories are like that, now. Trapped behind a dam, waiting for the right crack to give way.

"Arthur!" I said.

He'd been my fiancé. There with the doctor, the cowboy, and the old Dutch man. All waiting for me. Longing for me, just as they had before I changed.

Flush with blood and full of secrets, knowing at last the pleasures I had been denied my whole life, I opened my arms. I hadn't wanted my fiancé before, but he was warm. I would teach him such things. I would teach them all such things. They had tried to save me, in their own foolish way. I wanted to let them know it was okay. *I* was okay.

Better than okay. I had been good at showing them what they

wanted to see. Now I showed them what they had always secretly hoped for from me. What they still hoped for, based on the blood rushing to their extremities. I was finally unbound, and hungrily curious. Affectionate, even. They were such breakable, mortal things, these four men who had altered the course of my life and death. I'd be careful with them.

"Come here," I said with a laugh. "It's all right. I'll kiss you all, and tell you my secrets, and we can at last know one another truly."

And do you know what they did, when I, the object of their mutual affection and lust, revealed myself ready at last to embrace them on my own terms? They recoiled in disgust and horror.

For so long I thought it was because I was a vampire. But I've been with enough people to know I'm not horrifying. Quite the opposite. My teeth weren't even out. No, what disgusted them was that they had no power over me. I no longer fit their ideal of a virgin waiting for them to claim me. *That* was what repulsed them. *That* was what they found monstrous.

I wasn't theirs anymore, and I never could be again.

Naturally, violence came next.

10

London, October 4, 2024

IRIS

Still convinced I'm being followed, I opt for a cab rather than the Tube. At least then I can slump and zone out.

"Where to, miss?" the driver asks. He has warm brown skin and a fantastic, sculpted black beard. I'd put him in his thirties, but I'm bad at guessing ages.

I glance down at my documents. "Hillingham?"

He enters it in his phone and frowns. "Nothing's coming up."

I look closer. "Oh, no, sorry. Haverstock Hill?" I show him the address.

"Right, close to Hampstead, near the old zoo. I know the area; my husband has a restaurant nearby." He gives me the look all queer people share when we find one another. I instantly feel safer. And glad that my multitude of rainbow backpack patches—leftovers from my teen years, trying to make my family recognize my queerness—made him feel comfortable enough to mention his husband. Maybe it's biased of me to inherently trust other queer people, but I do.

"Glad one of us knows where we're going," I say. "And glad it's the one of us who's driving. What's Hillingham, then, if it's not a street?"

He shrugs. "Could be the neighborhood, could be the house itself. It's an old area with loads of historical mansions. Most used to have their own names."

"Seems a bit pretentious."

"Welcome to upper-class London." He laughs, the sound brassy and bright, and I laugh with him. For once I don't worry that he's secretly working for my mother or spying on me. Goldaming Life is one of those subtly bigoted groups, despite their glossily diverse brochures. No one in power there is anything other than white and straight.

He pulls into the street. "I'm Rahul."

"Iris." I relax into my seat, letting the neighborhoods blur together. Part of me wants to take it all in, since I'll never come back. But I'm too tired to care. London is a means to an end.

"Here for business or fun?" Rahul asks, and I'm glad he didn't say "pleasure." That phrase has always creeped me out.

"Business, I guess. My mom died. I'm sorting out her estate."

"Oh, I'm sorry."

"Don't be. I'm not."

He glances in the rearview mirror in surprise, then shrugs. "My mum's the best, but my husband's mum was awful. More relief than grief when she passed."

"May they rest in silence." I hold up my coffee cup like it's a toast, then go to take a sip only to find it empty. It feels like karma for speaking ill of the dead, but why should I value that wretched woman just because she's gone?

"Was your mum a Londoner?" he asks as we enter residential areas. The deeper we get, the fancier the houses. The street is lined with row homes, shared walls between them, each four stories tall and a delicious variety of cheery pastels. Thirty-one flavors of paint. I wonder how the car's suspension can handle the cobbled road. Kudos to London for refusing to make concessions to little things like modernity.

I raise my voice to be heard over the clattering tires. "American. I don't think she ever even visited the UK. I have no idea why she still owned this house."

"Should be worth a mint if you decide to sell."

"You in the market?"

He laughs again. "Can't afford a house pretentious enough to have its own name."

"Fair. Plus it'd be like adopting a pet someone else had already named. What if you wanted to call the house Cuddles, instead?"

"And it would only answer to the old name. Tragic."

I like Rahul. Maybe I'll just *give* him the house on my way out. Then again, that would draw him into Dickie's orbit. Albert's, too. Rahul seems lovely; I don't want to do that to him.

Rahul carefully navigates roads that predate automobile traffic, twisting and winding into what I assume are the aforementioned Haverstock Hills. The houses get bigger, no longer built shoulder to shoulder, but instead sitting regal and chilly on their own lots. Gone are the pinks and blues and yellows; everything is ash gray, rust red, or chalk white. At last Rahul pulls to a stop in front of an actual mansion.

He lets out a suitably impressed breath. "Yeah, that house is *not* going to answer to the name Cuddles. Wait. Wait! I think this is the wolf house!"

"The wolf house?" I ask, intrigued and alarmed.

"Bit of a local legend. Ages ago a wolf escaped from the zoo, jumped through a window into a house, scared a woman to death, and then went back to the zoo."

"Really? That actually happened?"

"I mean, I did say legend. And I'm not positive it's this house. But this feels like a house a wolf would decide to attack, know what I mean?"

I do know what he means.

A wrought iron gate has the name "Hillingham" written out in an arc. It cuts into the sky like barbed wire, more a warning than a welcome. The house looks about as warm. It's bone white, but the white of bones that have been left to decay, with great gashes of black blooming between its boards. The roof, a gray so dark not even the looming clouds can compete, looks intact. As are the windows, from what I can see. I should have asked more about the condition before demanding the keys.

"You staying here?" Rahul eyes the place dubiously, unwilling to ease the car closer to the locked gate. I don't blame him. Not only because the gate looks threatening, but also because it's old. I'd feel awful if it collapsed onto Rahul's tidy cab.

"Maybe." I'm tempted to ask him to drive me to the nearest hotel. But no. I can't delay. I brace myself and nod. "Yeah," I correct. "I'm staying here. Assuming there are no wolves and that it isn't a total health hazard. Can't afford anywhere else."

"Mum left you houses but no cash? That's a proper British tradition. Sure you aren't a lady?"

I laugh. "Might have been, back in the day. Definitely not a lady now; ask anyone who knows me."

He grins and holds out a card. "Give me a call if you need a car again, yeah? Or if you get inside and there's wolves, but more importantly if there's mold or fungus. I played *The Last of Us;* no one should breathe that shite in."

I tuck his card into my wallet and then pay him. I'm hyperaware every time I use my credit card that Dickie can probably track it somehow, but this charge makes sense with the story I gave him. "I promise not to start a zombie apocalypse."

"Good. And I mean it—call if you need to get away. Or if you need food." He hands me another card, this time for a restaurant called Haverstock Himalayan. Then he glances back at the mansion that's my one desperate gamble for freedom. His eyes narrow. "This house feels . . . off."

"So, you're saying you *don't* want to buy it from me."

"I've never worried that my flat wants to eat me alive. Can't say the same for this place."

"Maybe that's why my mom owns it. She loves vicious things." I correct myself. "Loved, I guess."

Rahul waves goodbye. "It was nice to meet you, Iris."

"You, too." I smile, meaning it, and get out of the car. He watches as I take the estate keys out. Even though they were in my pocket, they still feel cold. Heavier than is reasonable, too. The gate key isn't hard to pick out. It's ornate iron, black with age, large and heavy enough to double as a weapon in a pinch. I don't know what to hope for. Maybe that the key won't work and I won't be able to get in.

The key turns with barely a whisper. The gate swings open as though it's been waiting for me this whole time. I check for a spring mechanism, but there's nothing. Maybe it's the angle of the drive. Either way, the effect is . . . unnerving.

I give Rahul a thumbs-up. He answers with a pained smile, then pulls away. I wish I had asked him to stay until I was inside, but odds are if the gate key works, the house key will, too. And I have his number. I only feel mildly pathetic that right now kind Rahul, a cabdriver I spent thirty minutes with, feels like my only lifeline.

If only I'd gotten the angel's number. Then I could have had two whole friends in London. Alas.

As soon as Rahul's cab is out of sight, I turn back to the house. The front yard looks like opulence turned to neglect, though "yard" feels like the wrong word for an ancient mansion. Maybe "grounds"? That sounds vaguely British. The rosebushes have grown tall and straggly, years' worth of thorns petrified beneath a few desperate blooms. The hedges are similar, long ago having defied the neat boxy bounds they'd been designed for. A few steps in and I already feel sealed off from the street. I look back to make sure I can still get out if I want to. I should close the gate and relock everything behind myself, but I'd almost welcome a burglar. We could explore the house together, and they could advise me on what moves fast and for the most money.

I walk up the cracked flagstone path. There's a fountain with green sludge pooled in the bottom, a water-stained stone bench mostly hidden beneath a weeping tree, and a statue so eroded by time and weather it has no discernible features. Or maybe it was always intended to be an expression of exhausted despair?

I pat it as I ease by. "I feel you, babe."

No one has lived at Hillingham in a long, long time. That gives me some hope. The less things have been messed with inside, the more likely there are valuables. Heavy drapes and heavier dust obscure any hint as to what's beyond the rippling, thick glass of the front windows. I resign myself to suspense and climb the porch steps.

The craftsmanship is solid; nothing seems precarious. The front entrance is a double door, carved with elaborate swirls and set with impenetrably dark stained-glass panels. There's also a decidedly unwelcoming door knocker: an iron ring hanging from the mouth of a baleful wolf's head. I half suspect if I tried to use it, the wolf would bite me.

Besides, I never knock on a door I know no one's behind. It's asking for something unexpected to answer. Superstitious, yes, but superstition has served me okay in the past.

Instead of knocking, I choose from the three remaining keys. One is a modern key, which I assume will be for the rental in Whitby. One is a small, unassuming key, simple in design and old-looking. The last key matches the door, heavy and ornate. Once again, it turns with barely any effort. Despite all the disrepair here, someone has taken pains to make certain the keys still work. I take a deep breath and reach for the doorknob. But I don't have a chance to turn it before the door swings silently open on its own.

"Don't you know you should never invite a stranger inside?" I whisper as I cross the threshold.

11

May 12, 1890

JOURNAL OF LUCY WESTENRA

My trio of hunters have begun to divide, but not in the ways I hoped.

I'm reminded of the magic show Mina and I went to once. Every time the magician reached into his hat, somehow there was another rabbit inside. Every time the maid summons me, somehow there's another man calling. And then I must perform my own magic. Look at the Magnificent Lucy, conjuring a delighted face out of thin air! Marvel at her disappearing act: The real Lucy—poof!—is gone, replaced by a smiling, nodding, giggling doll, the perfect companion!

I've been doing that magic trick for years, though. It keeps Mother happy.

Today my caller was the cowboy, Quincey Morris. He just showed up on our doorstep. Mother barely hid her outrage at the lack of manners. She berated *me* afterward. As if I had invited him! As if the very things that attract him were not relentlessly forced upon me by *her.* If she'd let me be my silly, unpleasant, wicked self, we'd have far fewer gentleman callers.

I was surprised to see Quincey alone, though. (I know I should think of him as Mister Morris, but it feels absurd to be formal with such an informal man. If anything, I think of him as the cowboy.) He's never visited without Doctor Seward. Quincey said Doctor Seward was busy with a patient today. But I've been reading detective stories, and I cleverly noticed a key detail: Mister Morris was not using Doctor Seward's cab, but rather a rented one. Therefore, I suspect that Doctor Seward is unaware of his friend's location. Intrigue!

But really, it was not so bad. At least listening to Quincey as he talks in my direction is easier than enduring Mother. He never criticizes me, never pinches me, never cries and says I'm all he has in the world and if I leave him he'll die.

I think he truly loves the animals he hunts; perhaps, then, he truly loves me. Or could come to. I would be his English rose, plucked from my home and toured around America for display, like the upsetting wax figures in the tent next to the magician. (We didn't stay long there. Fake people, dragged out and set up whenever anyone wished to look at them. I felt far too much kinship for my liking.) Would Quincey want me to be demure and proper in order to surprise his rough and rowdy American friends? Or would he want me to acclimate? To hunt by his side, riding wild across the American West?

For all my dreams of being a predator, I don't think I would like it. I'm a creature of habits and comfort. Sleeping under the stars sounds romantic until one considers the lack of proper baths and toilets.

Once I get past how difficult it is to wait for Quincey to finish a single dawdling, drawling sentence, he's harmless. He would be kind to me, I think, or at least indifferent in a pleasant way. And he would take me far, far away from Mother. Imagine if my darling came with us! We could explore America together and have such wonderful adventures with Quincey as our heroic cowboy guide.

Oh, but what if he wanted to marry me and stay in England? I would die of humiliation. I could better handle being the object of spectacle than being on the arm of spectacle. If he couldn't make me thrillingly rough like the American wilderness, I certainly couldn't make him viciously polite like British society.

I nearly forgot the best part of his visit! When he was leaving, he shook my hand. He actually shook it! I could not help a burst of laughter. He was not offended at all. I wish I could have him as a friend. If we could be honest with each other, we'd get along very well indeed. But I'm not allowed to have friends like Quincey Morris.

Why would his friendship reflect poorly on me, while it makes Doctor Seward more interesting to society? If Arthur Holmwood can be friends with Mister Morris, why can I not?

Arthur. He is everything a man of his station should be. And if I were everything a woman of my wealth and status should be, we would make a perfect pair.

Arthur's as handsome as he is charming and pleasant, if one can stop wondering what that dreadful pale mustache would feel like pressed against one's own face. If Quincey Morris baffles me and Doctor Seward unnerves me, Arthur merely breaks my heart. Another magic trick. Arthur holds up a mirror and in it I can see what the world sees. Exactly who I ought to be, who I should be. Who I can never be.

~~It always leaves me wondering what is so broken and strange inside me that I imagine a life with Arthur and it makes me want to follow my father's steps into the night, never to~~

I'm getting maudlin. Perhaps I should have Quincey back to regale me with more tales of absurd heroics. Wrestling an alligator, or challenging a buffalo to a fistfight. I'll write and ask him to call on me again. Mother hates the crass American, but until she has figured out whether he is wealthy or simply connected to wealthy men, she'll be polite and allow him to visit.

But, oh! Three days! Three days until I am reunited with the only person I wish to see on my doorstep. My darling, my darling, coming to me.

12

Boston, September 25, 2024

CLIENT TRANSCRIPT

There I was, offering myself to four men who had always wanted me. Anger and horror warred on their faces. Anger won. They held up crucifixes in an attempt to banish me, but also as condemnation.

The most humiliating part of their rejection was that I didn't actually want any of them. Not in that way. I was just cold and confused and always so very, very thirsty. And Arthur had given me back my name. It was more than either of the brides had, and I was grateful. I still am.

I let them drive me away. It was not the crosses, but the looks on their faces. Was I really that horrifying? I retreated into my mausoleum. I tried to remember how they had looked at me before. I said my name out loud, pulled it on like a dress, but it didn't fit quite the same way it used to. As though I had grown and shrunk at the same time.

Raven appeared next to me, pulling me close. "That is why you can never go home." She caressed me, giving me the physical intimacy I had been ravenous for long before I woke up in this dark place. "They think you're a monster now. They'll kill you."

Maybe they were right. I hadn't considered it before then, lost in the hunger and new sensations. The relief of plunging my teeth into a neck, the burst of feelings built by Raven's fingers or tongue, the way I could smell and see and *feel* the night around me. I had been ruled entirely by my senses up until then, but now I was forced to think. All the next day as the sun made its relentless trek across the sky, I thought about the things I'd been doing with Raven and Dove.

Not the sex—I didn't feel guilty for that, and I still don't—but the killing. Is it murder when a wolf sinks its teeth into a rabbit? When a hawk snatches a mouse? Where is the line between murder and survival?

I didn't know then. I still don't. I have lines I won't cross; many of us do. Not all of us, as you'll see.

The simple ease of my newborn existence was gone, though. Everything was wrong and right and neither. I didn't want to be a bride alongside Raven and Dove anymore. Their spell over me was broken. I needed someone else to tell me what to do, and I knew exactly who that was now. With my own name, I'd remembered one other: Mina.

Mina had always been so good at taking charge of me. I knew if I could find her, she would lecture me about how being an undead creature of the night simply wasn't becoming of a young woman of my station, she would *tsk* over how silly I was being, and she would set me right. I really believed in that moment that she could fix everything. As soon as the sun set, I was ready to go.

"Stop that," Raven said. She held me back, her fingers a manacle around my wrist. I had begun drifting away on a shaft of moonlight. She often had to remind me to hold my human form.

Oh. That requires explanation. The sun binds us to what we are when it rises, so we can't change our shape then. It's crucial to have a body when dawn arrives. Being able to turn into moonlight or mist is all very well and good until you're stuck that way under the brutal rays of the sun. I once lost months because I forgot to change back in time and got scattered by daylight.

We can change into animals, too. I've been a fox and a bird and a moth, but I don't enjoy animal form. I was always good at moonlight, though, because moonlight isn't real, either. It's just a wan reflection of something else's light.

Raven didn't understand why I liked being nothing sometimes. Most vampires I've met hate abandoning their human forms, afraid they'll get stuck or trapped. But this body was always both boon and curse. I like that I have the power to leave it at will. Even with the risks.

There's a lot you can do as a vampire if you aren't afraid of consequences. For example, vampires are petrified of running water. We get denser every year, time compressing us tighter and tighter. Like coal into a diamond. All this to say, we sink. Fast. Under water there's no hallowed ground, no warmth to steal or borrow, so all our strength is sapped. We're stuck, forever starving without the hope of the release of death. It's a vampire's hell.

I cross water all the time. If I sink, I sink. I probably deserve to, but it hasn't happened yet.

Ah, Vanessa. I can see in your expression that you want some rational explanation for all of this. Why does the sun bind us? How can I change into moonlight? How can I move and think and feel without being alive?

But I'll ask, why do you dream? Why do you look at the ocean and feel awe? Where does love come from, and why does it feel so much like fear? There might be reasons for all those things, but do you need to know the reasons? Will that help you feel any of those things?

Don't try to make sense of what I am. You never will. I never have.

Let's get back to the story. In the cemetery where my first life was buried, Raven was still holding on to me. "I want to play a game," she said. "You owe me that, don't you? For welcoming you into the world? For taking such good care of you?"

Though I have confessed to multiple murders already, it's important to me that two things are perfectly clear:

The first is that I had no idea what Raven's game would result in. I didn't understand her yet. I do now, which is why I left her alive the last time we met. She deserves that torment far more than she deserves death.

The second is that I never knew what Dove had been doing as she skipped away from us each night, singing and cheerful. I had no inkling.

Dove hadn't left us yet, but she had that faraway, vacant look that meant she was about to.

"Isn't our new sister pretty?" Raven said to Dove, toying with my hair. "Dracula likes Lucy best right now. I think he'd like you best if you looked more like Lucy. I think *everyone* would like you best if you looked more like Lucy."

Dove stared blankly at me. Something was missing behind her eyes. If it's possible to see a soul, Dove didn't have one. As I watched, her hair changed from a white nimbus to dark, silky gold. Her features shifted subtly, too, until she could have been my sister. Then she skipped away into the darkness, singing a lullaby.

Raven's laugh was as rough as a cat's tongue rasping against my skin, and I was easy to lead away into the cemetery. What was one more night of hunting and sex? When it was nearly time to sleep, though, instead of rushing us toward my mausoleum, she held back. "Watch," she said, tucking us into the shadow of a looming tree. "The game, remember? It's nearly over."

I had forgotten about Raven's game, because it didn't interest me. But something else caught my attention. The men from the night before—my fiancé, the doctor, the cowboy, and the old Dutch man—came tromping righteously by and stood outside my mausoleum, barring the entrance.

They didn't notice us watching. A low growl escaped me. Raven petted my hair, soothing me. "Look," she whispered. "Our sister is back."

Dove danced and twirled her way toward the mausoleum, clutching something to her chest. It was about half her size, a bundle wrapped in a blanket. Before I could see what it was, Raven turned my head and kissed me. She quivered with excitement, as mirthful as I'd ever seen her. I could feel her smiling against my lips. I wanted to be happy, too, but I didn't know what we were happy about.

"Wait," Raven whispered. "It's going to be divine. The most perfect joke."

Dove paused in front of the men, confused. She still looked so much like me she could have been my sister. Then she dropped what she was carrying and darted past them, sliding across the darkness through the cracks in the door. She was safe inside. But the door didn't hold the men back.

Doors never did keep them from me. A memory, fleeting and impossible to hold, of each of those men on my doorstep. Each holding flowers and promises. Each smiling. Each entering regardless of what I wanted.

They did not smile now. They held only weapons and crucifixes as they followed Dove inside.

"We should—" I started, but Raven put her hand over my mouth. She squeezed tightly, fingernails cutting my cheeks.

"We need to get closer," she whispered. We slipped through the darkness, right past the door they'd left ajar behind themselves, and joined the shadows in the back corner of the mausoleum. The men were so focused on their task, they never even noticed we were there. I would have screamed, or run, or intervened, but Raven held me as tight and silent as the night holds the earth.

And so we watched as it became clear that my fiancé—the man who had promised me he'd take care of me forever, the man who claimed to love me, the man who had tried so hard alongside his friends to save my mortal body—*couldn't tell the difference between Dove and me.*

He stabbed her through the heart, kissed her lifeless lips, and then proceeded to cut off her head.

13

London, October 4, 2024

IRIS

The front door of Hillingham doesn't latch. I have to use the dead bolt in order to keep it shut, which explains the spooky introduction. Not haunted, just old. And . . . kind of shitty.

I'd hoped for a set of silver dishes, or a convenient chest full of jewelry. Those hopes seem highly unlikely given the condition of things. I dig through my backpack for an extra shirt and tie it over my nose and mouth. I'll need more allergy meds just to survive this place. As if my immune system wasn't already haywire enough, but at least the unseasonably warm fall weather means the house isn't too chilly. Cold is the true enemy when it comes to my blood.

I wander the main floor, opening what windows I can. Most are sealed shut, and the thick glass gives the light a strange underwater quality. I keep trying to clear my ears, but they're not the problem. This tomb of a house is. Muffled quiet presses in all around me. Even the wood floors are surprisingly noiseless beneath my feet. It's not that the house doesn't want to be disturbed, it's that it *refuses* to be disturbed. If there's a ghost here, it's me.

Spooked by the thought, I stomp. I clatter and bang and make noise to announce myself. It doesn't help much, but pretending not to be afraid goes a long way in making me feel brave.

I sing the lyrics of some of my favorite modern poets—the Beastie Boys, memorized in high school to annoy my mother—as I explore a sitting room, a dining room, a library-slash-den, and a kitchen in the back. They're all unpicked over, perfectly preserved. So much *stuff,* but none of it is valuable in a gold-or-gems sort of way.

My heart sinks further as I wander. I have no idea what any of this junk might be worth. Maybe nothing. Or maybe that chair with the hand-carved wooden frame is priceless, and the bookshelves are filled with first editions, and I'm sitting on a gold mine. But if I don't know, how can I figure out what to sell?

The kitchen is bleak, too. The stove is a hulking metal monstrosity, complete with overhanging brick cave. It's an actual antique. And not an exciting, *maybe I can pawn it* antique. A frustrating, *how can I live here if I can't figure out how to light the stove without burning the whole place down* antique. I'm sure it was the height of luxury at the turn of the century, but it's the wrong century turn for my immediate needs. I'm a 2000s girl, not a 1900s one. 1800s? I don't know how old this house is. I check the paperwork, but it's impossible to decipher. Should have asked for the whole file.

I slump in a sturdy chair at a round wooden table, the only items of furniture in the house that seem welcoming. Maybe because this kitchen was never meant for the inhabitants, only the servants. It feels accessible.

Even though she was American, I picture my girl Emily Dickinson sitting at this table, baking in this kitchen, scribbling poems on the back of cake recipes. It makes it all feel a little more hopeful to me, or at least a little less depressing. Hope is a thing with feathers, but the only thing this kitchen needs feathers for is a good feather duster.

I check my phone, which shows me my other problem as a 2000s girl. Almost no reception. Zero nearby Wi-Fi signals I can mooch off. My sense of being underwater gets even stronger, not helped by the fact that I can barely breathe through my shirt filter.

This whole idea was impulsive. Stupid. Futile, like all my other attempts at escape and independence. My mother reaches out for me from beyond the grave, her fingernails extending into claws, her grasp tightening. Maybe that's what Dad meant when he called. Even sealed in her coffin, my mother is inescapable.

Another Emily Dickinson poem I carry in my head: *The things that never can come back are several—childhood, some forms of hope, the dead . . .*

I repeat it to myself as a litany, but I don't believe it. Not really. Because I know full well that *anything* can come back; it just never comes back right.

But I took care of my mother. I'll take care of this, too. I stand resolutely, leaving my bag on the table. There are a few more doors down here I haven't checked yet.

Door number one is at the back of the kitchen. It leads to a pitch-dark set of claustrophobic servants' stairs I immediately vow to never set foot on. They're a broken neck waiting to happen.

Door number two is a pantry, filled with the detritus of decades gone by. A few empty crates, a disintegrating broom, some alarmingly half-full bottles. Nothing in there worth pawning, unless pawnshops are into generations of bespoke mold. Actually, bespoke, bio-targeted mold sounds like something my mom would sell in her idiotic wellness cult.

There's a back way out through the kitchen, but the door has swollen so much with age and moisture that I can't budge it. Probably a fire hazard, but what in this place isn't?

The last door in the kitchen leads to the hallway that connects the front of the house, the stairs, and the study. There's a door hidden in the darkness of the hall back here I didn't notice before.

The knob won't turn. None of the other interior doors were locked; why is this one? My hope gaining feathers once more, I pull out the littlest key in my key collection. This lock hasn't been kept in good working order like the others. The knob shrieks as though in pain when I turn it. Like the kitchen exit, age has warped the door. Unlike the kitchen exit, I *need* this one to open.

I shove my shoulder against the wood, and it bursts loose. My momentum carries me inside. One of the windows is boarded up, air whistling mournfully through the cracks in the planks. A new scent invades my sinuses. It's a hint of animal musk. Maybe something living has taken up residence here? Or maybe the wolf never left . . .

Between the boarded-up window and the dirty glass, I can barely see. I sweep my phone's flashlight over the floor, but there's no evidence of nests or burrows. Nothing furred, feathered, or fanged. I check the walls, too, just in case. My light catches on the edges of broken glass where windowpanes used to be. Odd that this window wasn't replaced, since the state of the boards makes it clear the breaking happened ages ago. Maybe there *was* some weird grain of truth to Rahul's urban legend.

Satisfied I'm not adding rabies to the list of diseases this house might expose me to, I relax and look around. There's a delicate vanity with a blackened mirror against the far wall. A brass headboard, dull and tarnished with age, looms over a hastily made bed. I touch the lacy bedspread material and it disintegrates between my fingers. The mattress is sunken in a perfect body shape, like it's holding someone's spot, still waiting for them to return. There's a bench seat beneath the missing window, stacked with a pile of forgotten books so old and moldy they've fused into a single entity. Who sat there, looking out at the garden? What did they hope and dream about?

And did they own anything valuable I can easily sell?

I step toward the vanity, crossing my fingers that jewelry got locked in this room. Glass crunches underfoot and I hop away. Despite the thick soles of my trusty Docs, I can't afford to get cut. I have to keep my promise to Rahul not to be ground zero of a zombie apocalypse.

When I flash my light down to check for more shards, there isn't any glass. I *know* I felt it, though. I crouch down and shine the light closer to the dull wooden floorboards. There's a glimmer of reflection from beneath the floor. The glass I'd stepped on has fallen through, which means a loose plank. I feel around its edges and am rewarded when the whole board wiggles like a tooth ready to be yanked.

"Jackpot," I whisper. I ease the board up to find a nest. But this is a nest of secrets, and in the center is a carefully wrapped object. *Jewelry,* I think. *Please be jewelry.* I do a quick spider check and then reach in and retrieve my bounty. It's a box, solid, wrapped in oiled cloth to keep out the damp. Whatever's inside, someone took great care to protect it and to hide it.

Freedom. Freedom's inside. I carry it back to the kitchen table and set it reverently down. Beneath the cloth is a simple but elegant wooden box, still polished, the metal latch bright. I ease it open.

It's . . . a book. I cross my fingers for a first-edition Dickens, or, I don't know, a handwritten Shakespeare folio. Something. Anything.

Instead, on the inside cover I find loopy cursive handwriting declaring it the property of one Lucy Westenra. It's a girl's secret *diary.* I wasn't wrong. I found something secret and precious. But also utterly valueless.

A claw scrapes down the window. I stumble up and grab my chair, ready to swing. But it's just one of the overgrown bushes. Not my mother returned from the grave, laughing at my slaughtered hopes.

"Fuck you, Mom," I say, shoving the box into the center of the table and getting back to work.

14

Boston, September 25, 2024

CLIENT TRANSCRIPT

There's no elegant or easy way to cut off someone's head.

It's a gruesomely tedious process. Layers of skin and tendon, to say nothing of the throat—hardly a minor obstacle. And then the spine. Arthur had to change tools at that point, a sheen of panicked sweat dripping down his face so it almost looked like tears.

But he wasn't crying.

When at last he'd managed to remove Dove's head, he at least had the decency to retire outside and vomit for a while. The old Dutch pervert stuffed Dove's mouth with garlic, patted her hand, and sighed in bitter regret. While staring at her breasts, now mutilated by the blade between them.

I trembled, hidden in the darkness. If Raven hadn't played her trick, that would have been *my* head laboriously cut off. I had died once; I didn't want to again. I wanted to exist. I wanted to be real.

The men, satisfied that their holy work was done, left my mausoleum. I sat on the floor to weep for poor Dove. Then I heard the men outside exclaiming. Unable to resist, still angry at what they'd done, I slipped out after them.

They'd found what Dove dropped. The little bundle she had been cradling? It was a toddler. The old Dutch man picked him up, and I followed them at a distance. They never once looked over their shoulders. Men! No danger for them simply by existing in the world.

I wanted to know if the child was alive or dead. It felt crucial. All this time, sheltered by my mausoleum, Dove had been hunting children. My very soul felt oily and contaminated. Imagine my surprise, though, when the men simply left the child on the pavement outside the cemetery.

The sun was rising. Despite all Raven's warnings, I didn't care. I crouched by the little bundle. He was pale and held in an unnatural sleep, but he was breathing. Doubtless those brave, stalwart men didn't want to answer the questions that would be asked should they show up at a hospital with a child in this state. I picked him up and carried him gently, wishing I could provide him with some warmth.

The sun was unpleasant but bearable. Raven made it sound deadly, but it just made me feel slow and vulnerable and weak. Much like I had been in life, so hardly a surprise. But a stark contrast now that I knew what it was to have power.

I found a bakery and stepped inside. It was warm, and I could hear the bakers in the back. The child would be safe. I laid him gently on the floor where he'd be impossible to miss. I wished I could have done more. But he was alive, and Dove was ended, and it would have to be enough.

I couldn't believe what she had done. I still can't. For the record, killing children is taboo even among vampires. Distasteful. Both figuratively and literally. Much like wine, blood is best when it's fully matured.

There's a theory I have of vampirism, though, having met so many of our kind. What we held in our hearts the moment we died doesn't change. It never leaves us. We're not just preserved in body, we're crystallized in soul and mind. Frozen.

"How could she do that?" I asked Raven a few nights later. I was sitting on top of my mausoleum, looking out over the cemetery, which had seemed so infinite and bold and full of newness. Now it looked small and sad and lifeless.

"I never asked." Raven wrinkled her nose in distaste. "Our husband didn't mind her peculiar diet, so it was never a problem. She always was a bit off, though. When she came to us, she had just lost her only child and was more than half mad."

Dove had died at the height of her despair as a grieving mother. I wondered later if that was what crystallized in her. If she froze at a moment of such agony that all she could do was inflict it on others. If she was compelled to mete out the same trauma, the same loss, to every mother she could. A twisted way of looking for reflections to understand her grief.

Raven had already moved on, even though they'd been together for more than a hundred years. "Why he picked her, I'll never understand. But he'll like you. You'll hold his interest. You're much prettier. We'll be so happy together, once he comes back to us!" There was a frantic edge to her voice as she scanned the borders of the cemetery.

I was watching for someone, too. My four would-be murderers never came back to memorialize or mourn me. Not once. But they weren't who I was waiting for anyway. I had no use for my fiancé, the doctor, the cowboy, and the old Dutch man.

That sounds like the setup for a joke! A lord, a doctor, a cowboy, and an old Dutch pervert walk into a mausoleum. "Hey, you cut the line," the vampire bouncer says.

"We're trying to get ahead," my fiancé answers.

Get it? A head? Okay, not my best punch line. The other I thought of was *very* dirty, and I didn't want to shock you. I can see you're still upset about Dove.

Anyhow, those four men's brutal efficiency in ending what they thought was my afterlife *had* defeated me in a way. Raven had been right: I could never go home. I had no home, not anymore. There was no one who would see me as a miracle instead of an abomination. At least not among the men. And I didn't know how to find Mina. I wandered London day and night, trying to feel out old familiar paths even though nothing looked the same to my changed eyes. Eventually, I found the flat where she'd lived. It was empty. I'd forgotten—she'd married.

But I remembered something else then, walking those streets, looking for Mina. I remembered *why* I'd died.

I desperately needed to find Dracula, too. To make certain that my death had been worth it. That I really had taken Mina's place, and that she was safe. I needed Mina or I needed Dracula, and somehow finding Dracula felt less threatening. I already knew what he was, and he already knew what I was—exactly what he'd made me.

But if I found Mina and she rejected me? If she recoiled, or was scared, or wanted me ended? It would have broken me. Shattered my crystallized heart forever.

Mina and Dracula. Dracula and Mina. In a way, they're the poles of my existence. The axis I spin on. My death, and my life. And me in between, turning and turning and never getting anywhere.

I wanted to find Dracula for another reason, too. I had so many questions I couldn't even put into words. Sometimes it felt as though I were one giant question, flinging myself in desperation at an uncaring universe.

It seemed inevitable that he would come for me. Dracula had made me this on purpose. And if he did it with purpose, there had to be a reason. I wanted to know what the reason was. That question burned in me, nearly as brightly as my need for Mina.

"Where is he?" I demanded of Raven. "I have to find him."

She hissed in annoyance. She needed him as much as or more than I did.

I think now he'd never invited her to come with him to London. I think he meant to leave her and his other brides behind forever in his castle in Transylvania. She followed him, because without him, who was she?

I understand Raven. She was my first mirror in a world where mirrors could no longer reflect what I had become.

But I couldn't keep waiting there with her. She was tiring of me as quickly as I was of her, and I couldn't rest while Mina was out there. Not until I knew she was truly safe. Unfortunately, I said as much to Raven. "Please. I have to make sure Dracula doesn't hurt my friend. And I need to speak with him so I can understand who I am."

Raven, ever clever, ever the loyal bride, devised another game to play. This time, I was the victim, though it would take crossing the world to realize it.

May 16, 1890

JOURNAL OF LUCY WESTENRA

My hopes that all Doctor Seward's visits would include Quincey Morris, who is at least distracting and tolerable, have been thoroughly dashed.

He—the doctor, with no Texan in tow—arrived early this morning, bearing his doctor's bag and also flowers. I wanted neither. With barely an examination, he told Mother that the condition of her heart was "precarious" and she had best retreat to her bed. Then he insisted on taking me on a walk about the park because my color was "off." As though I am a pampered pet and must not be allowed outside without a leash and minder.

I resolved to endure it as best I could. There is nothing outright beastly about the doctor. Mother certainly likes him. I do feel I'm being unfair to him at times. It's not his fault that his hair looks like a patch of dying grass, or that his breath has the strangest smell of antiseptic, or that he speaks in a monotone so droning I can feel it in my teeth. I can be indifferent to all those things. But spending time with him is like being under observation. I am more specimen than a person. I would so love to be a person sometimes.

The day was beautiful, though, and despite the company I enjoyed the walk.

Doctor Seward stopped. "You should sit," he said to me, pointing to a bench. I informed him that I would like to continue walking. He insisted I sit, so I sat. Perhaps I *am* a pampered pet, and a well-trained one at that. Mother has taught me it's always better to do as I'm told; it's not worth the fight.

Doctor Seward's face became even graver than usual. The light caught on his glasses so that his eyes appeared to be two half-moons of brilliant white, impassive light, burning down at me.

"Your mother is dying," he said.

How does one respond when calmly informed of such a thing? My etiquette lessons never included this. I said the first thing that came to mind, which was the wrong thing. I should never say what's actually on my mind. I know better.

"How long will it take?" I asked. His eyebrows raised in surprise and perhaps alarm, so I pulled out my kerchief and hid my face, feigning upset. Was I feigning? It is upsetting. But at the moment I only wanted information. Everyone's always keeping the truth from me for my own protection.

"I can see you're overcome with emotion," Doctor Seward said, which proves that while he can watch me all he wants, he doesn't see anything. "Here, this will calm you." He held out a vile little vial. He's always offering me laudanum drops, or other things in powders or pills. I never take them. I can only be myself in my own thoughts; why would I let something else influence those thoughts?

"No," I demurred. "I must stay strong for Mother."

He droned some nonsense about my own tender and excitable nerves needing care, relentlessly pushing the laudanum on me until at last I accepted. I slipped behind a tree as though modest and fearful of being observed—though laudanum drops are hardly a shocking matter among women of my station—then poured half the bottle into my handkerchief.

Doctor Seward seemed satisfied after that, assured my womanly hysterics would not inconvenience him. I moved as if in a daze while he walked me home—not because I was pretending to have taken his laudanum, but because I was actually in a daze.

Mother is dying. I still cannot force my mind to accept the information. Mother is everywhere; Mother is infinite. Mother is the gravity of my whole life, keeping me chained to the earth, forever revolving around her. What will happen when gravity ceases its terrible tyranny? Will I float away? Will I shed my mortal coil and become nothing but light and happiness? Or will I be condemned to hell for these very thoughts?

(I do not believe in hell, I think. It feels too much like something

Mother would invent to keep me in line. Fire and brimstone and eternal torment to deal with if I'm not a perfect doll who can marry well! Though marrying any man I know seems about as close to eternal torment as I can imagine.)

I was in a state of frantic confusion when I arrived home, ready to write a letter to Mina, begging her to come over. I burst into tears upon finding Arthur Holmwood in the sitting room waiting for me, instead.

"My mother is dying," I said, hoping he would excuse himself out of shame for my hysterics.

To my surprise, he rose from the sofa and took my hands in his. Genuine concern creased his brow. He looked at me like I was a person, rather than a silly girl.

"I'm so sorry, Miss Westenra. Please, come, sit. Would you like to talk about it?"

No one ever asks me what I'd like. Perhaps I've been too harsh in my judgment of Arthur. I babbled some of my fears—how long it might take, whether she would suffer very much. He generously assumed that I was afraid for her, rather than afraid of how badly this would increase my burdens. But he listened with gentle patience as I came to the end of my fears and was faced with the reality of the moment.

"Perhaps we should consult a specialist," I said, reluctantly.

He patted my hand, mustache pursing thoughtfully over his thin lips. "That's certainly an option. But I worry. She likes Doctor Seward so much. Would it upset her to introduce someone new?"

"It would upset her. You're right, it might do more harm than good. We must avoid upsetting her at all costs." I was relieved he agreed with me. ~~I am certainly going to hell for my feelings, but I do not want someone who might make her live another five, ten years. I cannot pretend it is out of concern for prolonging her suffering, only out of concern for my own.~~

He nodded, immediately trusting my assessment. It was nice to be listened to. "In that case, allow me to bring in a solicitor to make certain all your mother's affairs are in order. This is a perilous time for a young woman. We must secure all your inheritances so no distant, predatory relations swoop in and take advantage."

I had not thought of that. In truth, we've always had so much money that I'm careless and unaware of the cost of living, a fact Mina has often pointed out to me. I readily agreed to Arthur's offer, grateful that he understands these things and is willing to help.

I've softened toward him. I should be more generous in my judgments of others. After all, I've only known Arthur for a month. Surely if he does not really know me, I do not really know him, either. He could be a friend. And I have so few people in my life who care to protect me. Perhaps I can be a good friend to him, too, and convince him to shave his silly mustache. But gently, so as not to hurt his feelings by pointing out how much it looks like the clippings from a dog's coat.

Now I am as tired as I have ever been. Mother is in bed at last, none the wiser for what Doctor Seward told me. Part of me wants her to know what's coming for her. But then she holds my hand so tightly and says I'm her whole world, her heart outside of her body, and I feel ashamed of my secret dark resentment.

If Mother is dying, I can make her happy for what time she has left, and I can let Arthur help. It will not kill me.

16

London, October 4, 2024

IRIS

The second floor of Hillingham is bedrooms and the third floor is servants' quarters. There's a hatch in the third-floor ceiling that probably leads to an attic. I don't want to deal with that yet; my allergies can't handle it.

If I had a few months, I could appraise everything in the house. There's probably a decent amount of money to be made. But I don't have a few months. I *also* don't have a single piece of jewelry or an ounce of silver or gold. Why have a mansion if you don't stuff it full of easily pawned goods? It was super selfish of the last inhabitants.

I've discovered something else upsetting about the house: There are no light switches or electrical outlets. I wanted to find a time capsule, but I didn't actually want to travel back in time. At least there are toilets, bathtubs, and sinks, and miraculously the water works. I let one of the sinks run for several minutes to clear the pipes. It seems safe. Ish. At least I can wash up, which is a relief after the flights and the dust.

One of the bedrooms on the second floor, with dark greens walls and heavy furniture, has the anonymously fussy quality of someone trying to impress a stranger. It's as good as any of the others. I tear down the drapes and force the window open. There are no screens, but bugs are welcome to come in as long as fresh air does, too. The bed is creaky and hard, but usable. Assuming I can get some new bedding. Towels, too. Toilet paper. And bottled water, because I definitely don't trust these pipes.

This house had better pay off. It's costing me more than I can afford to spare. On paper I'm heir to a vast empire and an enormous fortune, but I won't touch money from Goldaming Life. It's all poison. I only have my meager barista savings, and I'm going to blow through it fast if I can't find things to sell.

I abandon the second story. It's down to the first-floor art and furniture for quick cash. Maybe the books. Surely old books will have a market in England, right?

I decide to make the den (or library or study or whatever this room is called in a mansion) my headquarters. There's a sofa that, while not comfortable, doesn't feel like it will break or impale me when I sit on it. The windows are more or less hedge-free, so there's a decent amount of light and air now that I've pried them open. I can almost breathe without my shirt filter. Plus, with all the built-in bookshelves and cupboards, there's almost no moldy wallpaper, which is about as aesthetically pleasing as the house gets.

I desperately need to sleep and eat, but I'm afraid if I stop, I'll get overwhelmed and not be able to start again. I try the cupboards first, but they're all locked. Hoping I'll find a key eventually, I pull every book off the shelves, separating them into titles I recognize and titles I don't. The second pile is, unfortunately, much larger. There are some ancient liquor bottles on a cart, which I carefully move to the kitchen. Not because I dare drink the amber liquid still stalwartly clinging to the bottom, but because the cut crystal decanters look like they could be worth something. Maybe the cart itself is.

And, in a small victory, beneath one of the bottles is a tiny key the exact right size for the cupboards.

I trace the little key as I eat a granola bar from my backpack and sip some water. Until I open the cupboards, anything could be in there. Schrödinger's jackpot—I both have and do not have money, as long as I don't look.

"Come on, Schrödinger," I whisper as I crouch in front of the first set of doors. I open them and find a deflated ball, several wooden figures, and some blocks. I hold a bluntly carved horse and imagine the child who lived in this house. Everything here would have made it clear that children were merely tolerated, not celebrated. The furniture is stiff and unwelcoming, the beds formal and large enough to get lost in. Even the toys were locked behind a door. A child would have needed permission just to play.

But I'm projecting. Maybe a grandmother lived here, and she stored toys for when her beloved grandchildren visited. Or maybe someone desperately wanted a child and bought toys in an act of hope, then locked them away when they were too painful a reminder of dashed dreams.

This house holds so many stories, and I'll never know any of them. That's okay, though. Some stories are best left unknown.

I put the horse onto one of the now-empty bookshelves and move on. The next cupboard has more alcohol, still in the original bottles. I move them into the kitchen. Rich people buy weird shit, as I well know. We had a whole room in the house dedicated to old pharmacological instruments and concoctions. Enough belladonna and mercury-based products to kill someone. That's not how I did it, though. Too obvious.

My earlier suspicion that a child lived in this cold, unwelcoming house is confirmed by the next two cupboards. More books, most of them children's workbooks and early readers. I try not to notice the clumsy handwriting, the personality infused into doodles of cats along the margins. I don't want to imagine the child who grew up here, wonder whether they were happy, whether they felt safe, if their bedroom held unknowable terrors in floating closets.

Another cupboard contains stacks of watercolors. They're unframed, amateur work, but I find them charming. There's a certain sly mockery to the exaggeration of the portrait work, particularly a sour-looking older woman. There are also several paintings of a dark-haired, dark-eyed young woman. I pause on them. They're done with so much more care and detail than any of the others. The subject is plain, with nothing remarkable about her face, but the artist has rendered her luminous. There are dozens of studies of her eyes and her hands, an obsessive quality to them I recognize. I've been in love, too.

I don't bother going through all of them. None of the paintings are signed, but if I'm charmed by them, someone else might be. I set them carefully on the desk where nothing will disturb them.

I've almost moved on to the next cupboard when I notice something strange. The painting cupboard isn't as deep as the others. I push against the back. A false panel! Without any attempt at caution, I pry and tug until it comes free. It was hiding a squat black safe. The silver dial and handle are tarnished but still the most beautiful things I've ever seen.

"Oh, thank god," I whisper, nearly in tears. I won't have to spend precious time trying to discreetly sell furniture and paintings. I can cash out and run.

But then it hits me: I'm excited about a locked box intended to keep everyone but the owner out. And I might be the owner of this house now, but nothing is mine. Nothing has ever been mine. Not the houses, or the money, or even my own body. And not my future, still.

I sit back on my ass and let my head hang in defeat. Mom was right. I'm never going to win this fight. I might as well surrender.

17

May 18, 1890

JOURNAL OF LUCY WESTENRA

I couldn't sleep at all last night. Not out of grief or fear like a good daughter would have been feeling, but because as soon as I lay in bed I was overcome with all the possibilities on my horizon. As Arthur so astutely pointed out, I am a young woman of tremendous means. And though Mother has always treated our money as an obligation, as something that demands we behave in certain ways and do certain things and never step outside the cage we have made for ourselves, I know differently. Mina tells me money is freedom. Money means getting to make choices, not being chained to circumstances. She tried to help me understand. She must have been so frustrated with how silly I was, how spoiled.

But the money has never been mine. First it was Father's, and then it was Mother's. But when it is mine . . .

Everything will be better. I'll be free. Without Mother, my darling and I can run away together. Or we won't even need to do that! We can live in Whitby, walk barefoot along the rocky shore, laugh at censure, turn up our noses at society. We'll have the money for it, and what if others find us queer? The difference between a lunatic and an eccentric is always money, is it not?

We will be happy forever. Mother's death will at last give me the freedom I need, and then we can build a world that's just the two of us. I can't wait until next week, when my darling is here and I can divulge my plans. The way we can at last be together forever.

My darling! My Mina and I.

18

Boston, September 25, 2024
CLIENT TRANSCRIPT

The night after I told Raven I had to see Dracula to make certain Mina was safe, she left me with a promise to come back with information. And come back she did, beaming and flush.

"Wonderful news! Dracula is waiting for you in Liaoning," she said. "That's in China. I assume you can find your way there. I've never been one much for travel planning. I'd go with you, but it's so much water." She shuddered, a ripple of genuine loathing contorting her face.

I was naïve, but not a total fool. "I thought he was in London still."

"I thought so, too! But tonight I found one of his familiars, a horrid little thing named Renfield. He told me that Dracula hasn't come for us because he found passage to Liaoning, where he's been meaning to take care of important business. I've no idea how long he'll be. And you seem desperate to speak to him as soon as possible. When you find him, tell him I'm returning to our castle. I'll be waiting for you both there, preparing everything to welcome you." She kissed me. Her first kiss had thrilled me, but this one felt like a period at the end of our sentence. I was fine with that.

I didn't ask any more questions, because I didn't want Raven guessing I had no intention of living in Dracula's castle with her. I held no love for her, but I still felt sorry for betraying her like that when she'd done so much to settle me into this dark new world. She'd saved me, after all, giving the men Dove in my place.

I knew Mina was safe, if Dracula was in China. But I still wanted to go to him. I was lost. It's hard to explain how new I was then. I was desperate for anyone to tell me what to do, how to exist. I held no love for Dracula—what little I remembered of my long, tortured death made me glad I didn't recall more—but he had taken great pains to usher me into this strange afterlife. I wanted to know *why.* There had to be a plan, some reason for what he'd done.

I was looking for a higher purpose, and in my world, Dracula was both devil and god. Destroyer and creator. And I had to get answers. I think part of me hoped he . . .

Well, part of me hoped he wanted me still. His wanting me was the reason for all this. Maybe, now that I was on the other side of life, I'd discover kindness, affection, even love. Maybe everything he'd put me through had been so he could grant me immortality, because he couldn't bear to see me grow old, wither, and die like my mother.

I can see your expression, Vanessa. You're not as good at a neutral face as you think you are. I didn't want Dracula's love. I wanted love, period. *Any* love. And he seemed most likely to offer it to me, after what he'd done to keep me.

But in order to confront Dracula, I had to get to China. I'd never been farther than Paris, and that was during my life when other people took care of everything. How was I supposed to make my way across the world alone? I wished desperately that I could ask Mina for help. She had a mind for logistics, and always told me how good she was at managing train schedules.

Unfortunately, I wasn't strategic about my travel plans. Time was slippery, then and now. Sometimes a moment feels like an eternity, and sometimes taking a boat to France and then walking across all of Europe feels as rote and simple as . . . hmm. I forget what things were rote and simple when I was alive. Oh! Calling on my mother's acquaintances. Something to be endured and accomplished, requiring very little thought.

At night I could cover a tremendous amount of distance, provided I'd had a good rest and enough blood. It was surprisingly nice, walking across the world and being unafraid. Now *I* was the threat in the darkness. I was the thing with freedom and teeth.

My favorite ploy was pretending to be in distress. Someone always stopped for me. If they were sincere about helping me, I rode with them for a while and left them in peace. And if they hoped to prey on me, well. It didn't work out for them, and I had a meal.

Eventually I found a port with a boat heading to Liaoning. I tucked myself into the darkness between beams in the hold. Like a spider's egg sac, hidden and waiting to burst free.

There was nothing else to do for the journey but learn Mandarin as I listened to the sailors. They were great storytellers. I still think about them. We spent so much time together. They taught me a language, and also the delicate art of the dirty joke. Best tutors I ever had. I didn't feed on any of them, both because it felt too risky and because it felt cruel when they had no chance at escape.

When at last we arrived in Liaoning, I was as thin as late morning fog and burning away just as quickly. Aside from starving myself, I'd had no real sleep. It was my first experience with prolonged deprivation.

It would have been hard to focus even if I'd been at my best. There were so many new scents, a riot of signals crashing through my head like a train derailment. Ports are murder on heightened senses. Wood and water and fish and rust and rot, but also so many people living and sweating and coming and going. The night pulsed with unfamiliar blood, and my whole body growled in ravenous response.

I don't hunt when I'm like that. It makes me sloppy and careless, and therefore dangerous. I got sloppy and careless tonight. That's how I ended up in your parking lot, fighting for both our lives. Though this time I wasn't ravenous for blood, merely . . . tenderness? Release? Relief?

Obviously, I found none of those. But that's the danger of giving in to strong desires as a vampire. The part of me that's *me* goes away.

Anyhow, in Liaoning, having reached my goal but with no idea what to do next, I stood in the middle of the pier, bedraggled and half mad, staring with wild eyes at nothing. A man took my arm. He moved with furtive urgency, dragging me along in his wake.

"I have a place where you can rest," he whispered. There was something strange about him. He was human, but there was blood in him that wasn't his own. I let myself be tugged away from the pier and into the darkness.

19

London, October 4, 2024

IRIS

I glare at the safe as though I can open it by sheer loathing. I could pay someone to crack it, but I'd have to use my family credit card. Might as well just text Dickie directly and tell him I'm up to something.

A stupid thought possesses me. My mother used the same code for everything. Security system, phone, ATM pin. She had no idea I knew, and I only used it during the most desperate occasions. Both times it paid off.

This safe looks seriously old, and I don't know if my mother ever visited Hillingham, but she did technically own it. "Eight." I turn the knob, the clicking beneath my fingers like the scuttling of insect legs. "Eight. Eighteen. Ninety." Already certain of defeat, I grab the handle and pull.

The safe opens.

"Holy shit," I whisper. And then I shout. "Holy shit! I beat you! I *beat* you!" I point triumphantly at the safe, but it doesn't respond to my trash talking. It doesn't need to. As usual, the joke's on me. Inside is nothing but papers. I flip through them frantically. Letters, ancient contracts and legal documents, more letters, pages and pages of handwritten notes, and, in an identical leather book filled with identical loopy cursive . . .

"Another fucking journal?" I fling myself backward. The seam of the ancient rug digs into my spine as I stare up at the cracked plaster ceiling. Journals in the floor, journals in the safe. Did that girl really think anyone cared about what she thought? I could have disabused her of that notion.

When you're a girl in a house like this, no one cares what you think, or how you feel, or what you dream about. *No one.* They only care what you can do for them.

It's several minutes before I muster the will to sit up again. I should probably wash my hands or put on special gloves before handling antique books, but I can't care. I skim through the pages of the new journal. It looks like the same handwriting as the floor volume. Sure enough, in the front I find the name Lucy Westenra again. She'd better have the juiciest stories ever. Or, ideally, detailed instructions on where to find all the jewelry in the house.

Then I notice a cat drawn in the margin, a slinking, sly creature climbing along her words like they're a playground. It's a mature version of the drawing in the child's workbooks.

Lucy was the girl who grew up in this cold house with her toys locked away. I'm instantly intrigued. I wonder if she's the subject of those paintings, too? Are those her piercing, intelligent brown eyes, staring at me from the past?

"Nope." I shut the book emphatically. I don't have time for the problems of someone who lived more than a century ago. I don't even have time for my own problems.

I return the journal and papers to the safe, then retrieve the other journal from the kitchen and add it to the stack. It feels right to reunite them. I lock them up and, in a burst of paranoia, replace the false back of the cabinet. Maybe I'm wrong and they're valuable. Until I know for sure, I'll be careful.

Or maybe I'll leave them locked up forever. Lucy went to great pains to hide her floor journal. I'd hate to betray her and her playful cats.

Defeated, I step outside. The relief is instantaneous. For such a large structure, Hillingham is remarkably claustrophobic. The solitude is oppressive but somehow I still feel observed. Maybe it's the wallpaper—a peacock feather design like hundreds of eyes watching my every move. A dead house, reporting back to my dead mother.

I walk to clear my head and my sinuses, gawking at the opulent houses peppering the street. They're old like Hillingham, but fully wired for electricity and other newfangled marvels like that. I'll bet they even have Wi-Fi. Half a block away—which is nearly a mile, this neighborhood is so spacious—I finally have enough bars on my phone to use data.

I've got to sell things quickly and quietly, and I can't do that until I know what's worth money. A quick online search for antiques dealers is overwhelming, though. There are so many in London. Proximity is probably best, given that I don't have a car. I pull up my map app and zoom in on the area. Before I can target the search, I spot something surprising and promising—a local history museum.

Surely a museum would know what art and furniture in the house is worthwhile! And surely a museum would give me that information for free . . .

I dial the number. It rings and rings before going to voicemail. "Hi," I say, "my name's Iris Goldaming. I just took possession of Hillingham. It's a mansion. In Haverstock Hill. Anyway, I'm calling because the house hasn't been occupied or even touched in like a hundred years or more." Shit, I sound *so* American. They're probably rolling their eyes. "It's basically a time capsule. Anyway, I was hoping someone from the museum could help me know if there's any, uh, historical value? To the furniture or paintings or books? I wouldn't want to accidentally throw out some priceless antique." I laugh lightly like it's not a matter of survival, merely curiosity. "So, give me a call if you're interested, or you know of anyone who might be able to help me out. Thanks."

I leave my number, then hang up. Feeling good about this potential development, the next order of business is finding food. But I don't need to look for a restaurant—I already have the perfect option. No bad day can't be improved with Himalayan and Indian food. To my surprise, Rahul himself answers when I call his husband's place.

"You need rescuing already?" Rahul asks, recognizing my voice, or more likely my accent.

"No, I need butter chicken. And naan. And a side of roasted garlic. And a battery-powered lantern, a sleeping bag, a pillow, a towel, and toilet paper. But I'm assuming you only offer the first three."

Rahul laughs. "Actually, I'm off to the shops right now. If you want, I can pick up your whole order and have it dropped off. I've been worried about you."

My impulse is to protest, but kindness is rare and always worth accepting. "Thank you. That's genuinely amazing of you. I'll pay cash for everything. Unless you want to barter. An exchange of goods: one alarmingly dire house for an extra side of naan?"

"How about we stick with cash for now. The naan market fluctuates wildly and I can't be sure I'm getting the better end of that deal."

"Fair enough." I walk back to the house feeling lighter. Delicious food is coming, the museum lead might pan out, and at least I won't be stuck in the dark tonight. Plus, I've done a search on London zoo escapes and I think Rahul was right about the wolf. Which oddly makes me like Hillingham a bit more.

But my affection doesn't last long. Hillingham rises like a schoolyard bully waiting for me to show weakness. I linger on the street, unwilling to go back in. I really should find a hotel. Suck it up and use the credit card Dickie gave me. That would be an understandable expense, one that wouldn't raise red flags.

But using the company credit card feels like acceptance. The first silken strand of Goldaming Life's web snaring me until I'm wrapped so tightly I can never break free.

Besides, staying in a house without electricity will be like all the camping trips Mom and Dad never took me on. It's an adventure. The last challenge before freedom. I killed to get out; what's a little discomfort to stay that way?

A car drives by, slowing as it passes me. The neighbors are probably ready to call the cops, wondering who's creeping around Hillingham. I hurry inside as my phone dings with a message from an unknown number. It's a photo, which is taking forever to load. Must be from Rahul, asking about my supply preferences. Response is impossible as a single pathetic bar of reception flickers in and out of existence. I'm sure he'll figure it out.

Since I'm going to see another human being again soon, I head to the bathroom. My sink wash from before didn't include my hair, so I quickly soap it clean by leaning over the side of the tub and ducking my head under the faucet. The tub is clawfoot, cast-iron, in good shape. Maybe I can sell it.

My whole body goes tense from the discomfort of frigidly cold water. Cold is an instant anxiety trigger. I pick up my phone hoping Rahul's message came through, but the photo takes me a few seconds to process. Not from Rahul, after all.

It's the back of me, staring up at Hillingham. Taken mere minutes ago.

Those fuckers. Those absolute *fuckers.* I try to call Dickie, but whatever atmospheric anomaly gave me a single bar is gone again. I scream at my phone, then throw it across the bathroom.

Drying my hair with my old shirt, I drag on something clean. I'm coming down the stairs, shivering and paranoid, when I see a shadow lurking beyond the stained glass of the front door.

I leap the last few steps, unlock the door, and fling it open. "If you think you can scare me into—"

I stop dead, face-to-face with my angel from the train station.

20

Boston, September 25, 2024

CLIENT TRANSCRIPT

There was something hollow about the stranger tugging me away from the Liaoning port. His skin, hair, and eyes had the bleached quality of dead coral, and I tried not to shudder as his skeletal fingers tugged my arm.

Dracula almost never fed off men—his type is young and female and full of promise. But he'd still figured out how to use them. Like Raven's contact in London, this man was one of Dracula's familiars. Gaunt, gray men, lingering in the space between life and death, neither fully human nor infected enough to become vampires. The blood in his belly wasn't a matter of survival; the familiar chose to drink blood to feel closer to his master. I didn't know any of this at the time. All I knew was I needed help, and he seemed to be offering it.

There was enough variety of sailors at the port that he didn't stand out, but I definitely did. And starving as I was, I couldn't change my appearance. I needed to feed so I could be what people expected when they looked at me. As you know, a woman is always in danger if she doesn't show the world what they expect to see. Even a vampire woman.

"Blood," I moaned through cracked lips.

"Yes, yes, come on, quickly."

There was an urgency to his movements that I didn't like. It wasn't purposeful and assured. He dragged me, creeping from shadow to shadow, constantly looking over his shoulder.

His manner was possessive. It was the way rats grab bits of food, every sense on alert as they rush to get their prize to safety where they can consume it at their leisure. I was his prize. But I would never be a man's meal again.

I leapt onto his back. My knee cracked his spine in half as I bit through his throat and tried to drink. His blood was *foul*. Like spoiled milk. Even thinking of the taste now makes me gag. I couldn't stop, though; I was too desperate. There was fresher blood inside him, uncorrupted by the poison in his veins. I made a mess of pulling out his stomach, but I managed not to puncture it.

Oh, the look on your face. I'm sorry, I don't mean to laugh. If it makes you feel better, think of it like a juice pouch. At least it was fresher than his own blood. And it was enough to clear some of the fog. I could at last think.

I was crouched in a dark alley between two warehouses that stank of fish and salt. I could hear heartbeats all around me, smell the rich, complex scents of their late suppers. All while that *thing's* supper seeped, repulsive but replenishing, through my stomach and into my veins.

Mina would have chided me. *Look at that mess! Always acting without thinking!* In my defense, I was only a few months undead. But imaginary Mina was right. Aside from the gore, I'd made a mess of the whole situation—I'd ripped out his throat *before* talking to him. Now he couldn't answer any of my questions.

He lay there, surrounded by trash and his own pale, flaccid intestines, hands uselessly scrabbling to put them back in. Dracula had granted him some small measure of power and strength, so he wasn't dead yet. But he wasn't going to recover anytime soon, if ever.

I searched his pockets. Of all the things he could have been doing with his life, he'd bound himself to a vampire and lurked alone here, wearing the most atrocious, reeking, ill-fitting clothes! The least he could have done was take advantage of the incredible textiles being traded. So many beautiful things in the world, and he cared about none of them.

His hideous jacket held an envelope, several knives, and a tool that looked like a sharp-tipped metal straw. I removed the envelope and set it aside, but my mind was stuck on Mina and how disappointed she'd be in me. She hated when I left things undone. Embroidery unfinished, letters half written, paintings abandoned. For all I knew, the familiar didn't deserve to suffer. I erred on the side of compassion. I wasn't certain whether he'd turn into a vampire after death. Given what I'd done to him, I preferred he not be able to come back.

I had learned my lesson from watching Arthur laboriously hack away at Dove. I laid the familiar's sharpest knife flat against his neck—which was difficult, because I had to keep slapping away his scrabbling hands—and then slammed a brick down into it. My method severed everything at once. Awful, but efficient. He was dead, permanently.

I pushed the remains into a corner of the alley with the rest of the heaped trash. He blended right in. Then I sat and thought of Mina and had a nice, self-indulgent cry. Sometimes a girl finds herself alone at the feet of an unknown land, covered in grime, having just decapitated a stranger, and it's all too much.

Once I calmed, I remembered the letter. I opened the envelope and scanned the writing. I shot a regretful grimace at the remains of the hollow man. He *had* been dragging me away, yes. But not to devour me.

I assumed the letter was from Raven. It sounded like her. She opened with a plea for any news of Dracula, and then warned the familiar to be on the lookout for me. "She's young and stupid," Raven wrote, "but because she's Dracula's, he can safely rest wherever she leaves a victim. If she fills some graves for our master to sleep in, at last he'll have a foothold in the East. We'll both be rewarded with his love. Help her. Lie to her. Do whatever you must to encourage her to kill as many as she can before they find and destroy her."

I threw the letter on top of the man's bloody remains. I felt as fragile as spiders' thread, a few strands strung hopefully between branches, never strong enough to catch anything.

I had been sent across the world as a plague rat. My job was to make corpses and plant them in the ground like flags of conquest, each a safe place for Dracula to rest. Because he had infected me, any vampire or grave I created was his by default, too. A pyramid of death, with Dracula always at the top.

A devastating lethargy came over me. All that time, all that travel, pointless. Meaningless. Done in unknowing service of Dracula, who had abandoned me. Tricked by his bride and further than ever from any answers or purpose. *Where was he?*

I lugged the remains of the familiar to the harbor and unceremoniously dumped his pieces into the water. No grave for him meant no grave for Dracula. No triumph for Raven. They could have my mausoleum; I wouldn't give them anywhere else safe to rest.

I drifted until I was out of the inhabited spaces, up into the hills. It was beautiful, rolling land curved lovingly around a crystal harbor. All those shacks and buildings looked like barnacles from this far, clinging to the edges of uncaring forces. I admired their tenacity, their industry, their humanity. And I needed to remove myself from it so I wouldn't unhallow any ground for Dracula.

I sat on a rock. I was too tired to go on, too sad and betrayed. I didn't stand as I heard footsteps approaching. Not even when those footsteps had no accompanying heartbeat. I had failed yet again, undertaken a task without thought or planning and doomed to failure, just like Mina had always cautioned me against.

I was so very, very far from her, and I realized for the first time that I always would be. So when the other vampire grasped my neck, I did nothing.

I was ready to die, again.

21

May 19, 1890

JOURNAL OF LUCY WESTENRA

Mina is engaged.

I suppose this is punishment for my callous attitude toward Mother's failing health.

I met Mina over tea at the Rose and Thorn Inn, brimming with excitement to tell her that her worries about money and employment were forever ended. No more a governess or schoolmistress! No longer forced to guide graceless youths such as myself into a graceful and secure future denied to her!

It was all planned out in my head. I would remind her of our long walks, when she'd listen as I confessed my darkest secrets, then press her lips to mine to seal the darkness between the two of us, where it would never get out. I've thought of those kisses so often. Sometimes it feels as though my whole soul was sealed between us. But I wasn't going to tell her that. I was just going to remind her of that happy intimacy before giving her this last, best secret: that I was free, and she would be free with me. ~~And then we would press our lips together again, but linger there, and~~

It breaks my heart now, thinking of this morning. All the hope in my heart as I told Mina I had news. She held up a hand, begging to go first.

"I am engaged to Jonathan Harker." She presented it as she would have a lesson in geography. Here is Europe, here is Asia, here is the shattered remnant of Lucy's dreams, and here is Africa.

"Who?" I asked.

"I told you about him," she said. "Jonathan Harker. He works as a solicitor—well, he will be one soon—for a wealthy man. Mister Hawkins has a tremendous estate and he looks on Jonathan as a son."

"Jonathan?" I asked again, my mind spinning. I felt as I did last year when I got into Mother's liquor cabinet trying to soothe myself after what my art teacher did. Everything was too fast and too loud and too confusing. "Wait, not that man who picked you up from my house two months ago! The one who was all forehead and no personality?" I should not have said any of that, even if it was true.

Mina's eyes flared. "We cannot all be pursued by charming, handsome lords!" she snapped.

Immediately I burst into tears and apologized, and Mina forgave me, as she always does when I'm rotten, which is often. I asked how she knew about Arthur Holmwood. She blinked prettily at me before saying, "Who?" And then she went on to reassure me. "I understand you're upset because you want me to be happy, but I'm quite certain I can secure a future through Jonathan."

"I do want you to be happy!" I insisted. "But I thought I could help you, by—"

Mina shook her head. "How could you help me? You'll have a husband of your own soon and have no use for me. Besides, *I'm* the one who's taken care of *you* all these years we've known each other. I take care of everything."

I grasped her hand, eager for reconciliation, still spinning from this news. "Of course you do. You're the most capable, clever woman I've ever known."

She looked away, as she always does when she's confident that I will accept whatever point she's making. She never looks at me for approval; why should she? Mina is steady and wise, and I am a silly, stupid girl who came to tea hoping for secrets and kisses.

"Trust that I will make the future I deserve," she said.

"No one could deserve you, though! You're too good for anyone. We should run away to Whitby and be happy forever. You shouldn't have to marry if you don't want to." I said it lightly, but my soul was reaching out, trying to hold her with me.

Admit you don't want to get married, I prayed in my mind to Mina, because I knew God wasn't listening and didn't care. *See a future where the two of us are all we need,* I prayed. All while smiling so she wouldn't see how desperate I was.

Mina patted my hand. "My sweet, silly pet. Jonathan is a catch for a penniless schoolmistress like me. I have only my own mind and work ethic to recommend me. Unlike you, I can never be an angelically beautiful heiress."

My fingers twitched up, catching hers, linking as though I could chain her to me. "That's not all you have!" I listed her many, many qualities, which I hold in my heart at all times.

She seemed soothed, and by the end of tea I was almost able to pretend to be happy for her. I acted how a dutiful friend would, and asked how he had proposed (via a long-winded and terribly dull letter) and when they intended to marry (as soon as he got back from a terribly dull trip to help a European count finish buying property in London) and where they would live (she smiled and said she was still working on that, but I suspect somewhere terribly dull).

As I paid our bill, Mina looked at me with pursed lips, the same way she looked at any problem. "The only thing keeping me from perfect contentedness is you."

My heart dared to hope one last time. She loved me too much to ever marry and be separated from me. I could tell her my plan to save us both.

And then my heart was reminded what a fool it is and always has been.

She nodded as though answering a question I hadn't asked. "You will find love before the end of the year. You'll be married, and then I won't have to worry about you anymore and my happiness will be complete. Promise me that you'll find a good match. Someone to take care of you when I'm too busy being a wife."

I promised her, because I had to, because she's my Mina. Mine no longer, though.

I cannot write any more. My heart feels as desolate as a fog-choked horizon. Neither sea nor sky nor sun visible, only blank gray forever.

22

London, October 4, 2024

IRIS

My angel's blue eyes are wide with shock. "What are *you* doing here?" she asks, taking a step back from the open front door.

"Oh, wait," I say, slapping my forehead. For a moment I was paranoid she was one of *them*. But knocking politely on the door isn't Goldaming Life's style, and there's a far more likely explanation for her appearance. "Do you work for Rahul? Are you my butter chicken?"

She looks even more confused. And, ever observant, I finally clock that she's only holding a to-go cup of tea. "Butter chicken?" she asks. "Is that . . . a pet name?"

I laugh, because I don't know what else to do. This is all too baffling and wonderful and strange. "You did call me a little cabbage, if I recall." I do recall. I recall every second she's been in my life. "But no. I'm expecting food delivery, among other things. That's not you?"

"Not me. I'm here for Hillingham."

Then it *actually* clicks. I made two phone calls. "The museum! To help me look at things in the house! Wow, you got here fast."

Her rosebud lips—I've never wanted to garden so badly in my life—purse in a smile. "Sorry. I should have called first. I know it's unprofessional to be overeager, but I didn't want to waste any time getting into Hillingham. I had no idea *you'd* be here, though. I see you managed to make it safely even without my help." She's teasing me. It's agony. We already have inside jokes, why can't we already be girlfriends?

"Thanks to your advice, I looked right so hard my neck will never recover." I twitch and earn a small laugh. But I was cagey in my phone message to the museum. I'd better be up front. I don't want to hurt her. "I can't pay you for appraisal services. At least not right now."

Her eyes go past me, searching the interior like she's about to pounce. She *really* wants to get inside. I know that fevered look. It's how I felt visiting Amherst and touring Emily Dickinson's home. Or how I felt listening to the newest boygenius album the second it was available. This house is one hundred percent my angel's shit.

"No charge," she says. "I'm just eager to see it. My specialty is the late nineteenth century. It was a time of so much transformation. And I believe it was the last time this house was inhabited."

"You know about Hillingham?"

"Yeah. I know a lot about this whole neighborhood." She gives me a sheepish smile and shrugs, her hair shifting with the movement. The way it catches the late afternoon sun behind her, I notice it's red, not gold. The shade's a vibrant, rich color, so many tones blending and shimmering around one another.

I resist the urge to put a self-conscious hand to my own soaking wet hair. It's dyed a shade of bottle black I've used since I was fifteen. I call it Piss Off Your Mother Charcoal.

"I'm Elle, by the way," my angel says.

"Iris. But you already knew that."

She nods, waiting for an invitation inside. After a few awkward seconds, her smile drops a bit. "Am I—should I . . . I'll just come in then, yeah?" She steps past me into the entry.

I let out a relieved breath and nod. "Yeah."

Elle's smile twists, puzzled. "Do Americans not invite people inside?"

"Family custom. We never invite someone in unless they've already been inside." I learned that the hard way as a six-year-old, when I invited a man in because he scared me so badly I was afraid not to. I have only a few memories from that night. His red eyes. The sound as my father hit the wall. The way my mother stood calmly, just out of reach in the darkness.

I have lots of memories of what happened after, though. My new bedroom was so big it echoed, with soaring ceilings that slanted down to an alcove, always sliding my eyes toward two closet doors set up off the floor, too high for me to reach the knobs. Not that I ever wanted to.

The doors moved every night as I tried to stay awake, the wood breathing in and out, waiting for me to fall asleep so the darkness held inside could devour me.

Anyway, learned that lesson. No invitations.

Elle's delicate eyebrows draw close, creating two perfectly symmetrical lines between them. "That's a *really* odd custom."

"You have no idea how odd my family is. So, the house." I gesture. From the entry, we can see the stairs with hand-carved wood railings I wish I could sell, the hallway leading to the den, locked bedroom, and kitchen, and finally the opening to the sitting room or whatever it's called. The house I grew up in was palatial, but designed like a modern art gallery, sleek and white and forbidding. There weren't rooms so much as spaces, almost all of which were off-limits. Any useful or necessary thing like a kitchen or bathrooms or bedrooms were hidden in the back, as though human needs were something shameful.

"It really was frozen in time, wasn't it?" Elle's voice is low, like she doesn't want to disturb the house. I understand the impulse. There's a sense of something sleeping here. I had the opposite reaction, demanding it wake up and acknowledge me. I'm not good at respecting monsters.

I'd love to impress Elle and pretend I'm here for the history, too. But I can't abandon my plan, no matter how prismatic her hair or dark blue her eyes or kissable her smile. "Listen. Not to be crass, but I need money. If there's anything in the house that seems especially museum-worthy, you're welcome to take it for display. But I'm looking for valuable items I can sell quickly."

Her nod in response is thoughtful as opposed to judgmental, which is a relief. "Are you clearing out the property to sell? It's a great location."

"My focus is smaller items I can liquidate immediately."

Elle smiles wryly, but she takes a step toward the still-open door. "You're *sure* you own this house? I'm not helping you commit a crime?"

I let out a shocked burst of a laugh. Mom called it my donkey bray. I cover my mouth self-consciously. "No. God, no, sorry. If I were asking you to commit a crime with me, I'd come up with something much more exciting. And that involved considerably less dust."

"Such as?"

"High-profile assassination? Corporate espionage? Some sort of hilarious protest graffiti? I'm not sure. But I *am* sure I own the house and everything in it. This place has been in my family for generations. I have proof." I duck into the den and grab the papers I got from my crabby solicitor, then hand them to her. "Here."

She glances over them, setting her cup of tea on the stairs. "Goldaming?"

Fuck. The weight in her tone makes me certain she knows about Goldaming Life. I can't answer questions about it. Not now, not with Elle. I want to keep things breezy and fun. Flirty, ideally. "Yup. Iris Goldaming, like I said in the phone message."

She snaps. "Oh, right! That's where I know it from. Ha."

Thank god. I don't have to explain my mother's multilevel marketing empire. And if Elle hasn't heard of it, she's definitely not a member. If she'd excitedly told me she was walking the Gold Path and asked what gates I'd been through, I'd have thrown up all over her, which is the opposite of flirty.

Elle sets the papers on a side table near the door, then holds out her hand. It's warm and fits perfectly in mine, just like I remembered. We shake. "We're in business, then," she says. "Legal business. Maybe a dash of crime, though, if you come up with a sexy enough one." Then she's already moving on into the sitting room. Even the *word* "sexy" coming out of her lips gives me a rush of that good low warmth.

Calm your tits, calm your tits, I sing in my head. Be cool for once in my life.

I close the front door and lock it. "Does it feel like you're underwater in here? Like you're sealed away from the rest of the world? But not in a safe and cozy way? In a way where you're . . ."

"Trapped?" Elle's considering me with her head tilted. "I think houses hold their history, built up over decades. Like dust." She runs her fingers along the old piano framed in the bay window, then stares at the marks left behind. "All those stories are still here, even if no one knows them anymore. It's not surprising that Hillingham doesn't feel friendly to you. It has a strange and sordid past."

"You know about it?"

"Everyone does. It's locally notorious."

I sit on the edge of the stairs. "Do tell!"

Elle leans against the arched entry to the sitting room. "I might have oversold it a bit. It's mostly just the deaths."

"Oh, is that all?" I let out a choked laugh. "Please elaborate."

"The last family to live here—I could be wrong, I'd need to look at local records and I didn't have time before I came over—all met tragic ends. The father used to sleepwalk. He wandered out one night and never returned."

"God," I mutter. "That's bleak."

"Then the mother and daughter died on the same night."

"Wait," I say, holding up a hand. "How did they die?"

"I'm not entirely sure." Elle shrugs.

"Elle. *Elle.* I think I know how they died! Or at least how the mother died. It was the wolf!"

"*What?* There are wolves here? I didn't think there were wolves in England at all anymore, much less in London."

"Yes, but only because we're near the zoo." I wink at her, then make my voice serious and informative, like a docent leading a museum tour. Only instead of actual research, I have what the internet told me in three minutes of searching. "In the 1890s, a wolf escaped its enclosure. A whole day passed before they noticed it was missing. They'd barely begun searching for it when it appeared once more, pacing outside the gate as though impatient to be let back in. No one knew where it had been, how it got out, or why it came back. But the rumor—and this is unsubstantiated, something of an urban legend passed around schoolyards—was that it jumped through a window and frightened a woman to death. A window *in this very house*." I pause for dramatic effect, eyes wide, then point down the hallway. "Do you want to see the Wolf Window of Hillingham House?"

"Okay," she says, her smile dubious as she follows me to the bedroom.

"I relocked the door, in case the room was infested. With rodents, not with wolves. But maybe with wolves." I open it and gesture toward the boarded-up window. "See? The window's still broken! They never fixed it!"

Elle stays on the threshold of the room, looking in. "Huh. It's odd that they wouldn't repair the window, isn't it?"

"And this is the only bedroom anyone locked up. It could have been because of the wolf attack, right? They were afraid it would come back. Did we just prove an urban legend?"

She seems unmoved, her eyes lingering on the window. "Maybe. Can't exactly sell the story for quick cash though, can we?"

My excitement sputters out. "Right. Dammit. I keep getting caught up in the history."

"It's hard not to. History is stories, and we all live on stories."

"Still, it might make a good photo display for the museum. Pair it with the local legends and any historical documents you could find. And I do mean 'you' in this case, because historical research is literally your job, not mine. I'm just the girl who unlocks the door."

That earns me a smile at last. We're standing so close. I want to touch the creamy sweater hanging off Elle's shoulder, see if it's as soft as it looks. I want to lean even closer and breathe in, see if she smells as good as she looks. But more than that, I want to ask Elle what her story is, unearth all the things that make her who she is. I want to know everything about her.

There's a hurried knock at the front door, a frantic staccato demand. It's a desperate knock, not a threatening one. I rush down the hall and throw open the door. Rahul is there with a tall, bald man, their arms full of stuff, both looking over their shoulders. They push past me without waiting for an invitation inside.

"Close it, close it!" Rahul says.

A fox runs straight at us in an orange blur. I brace myself, but it stops dead on the steps. Just short of the doorway. It stays there, locked in place, teeth bared and yellow eyes fixed on me. Then it turns and calmly walks into the hedges.

As Rahul and his husband exclaim over what strange fox behavior that was, I close the door and lock it. I press my forehead against the glass, willing my heart to calm down. Willing myself to be able to react normally, to pretend I'm as surprised and confused as they are.

But the fox was another reminder. I'm not safe here. I can't forget it.

23

May 20, 1890

JOURNAL OF LUCY WESTENRA

It was all silly of me. I'm hardly better than a child, as Mina often chides me. Running away to spend all our days on holiday in Whitby? Why would someone as smart and determined as Mina waste her life that way? I'm ashamed of the flight of fancy that led me to ever dream of it.

The things I imagined for our future fill my heart with confusion. I can't write the whole of them, even here. There's something wrong inside me. Something queer and sideways, which is why I pretend, always, with everyone. I need to kill that thing. I'll find a way to be what Mina wants me to be. If it's what she needs for her own happiness, I'll make it happen.

But after all my foolish hopes were burst, everything is exhausting and fraught. Mother has been in here again, snooping. I found her bent over my bed, checking beneath it. I know she caught sight of my journal. She asked about the ink marks on my fingers. I told her I've been writing ever so many letters.

I can be cleverer than that, though. I've read enough detective novels to know it's always necessary to throw bloodhounds off a scent. I went into town this afternoon while Mother was sleeping and purchased an identically bound journal. I'll fill it with pretty lies, the Lucy she expects and demands to see, then leave it out where she can "find" it.

Then the true Lucy, the one sealed in the darkness between lips, the one who is so wrong even I don't understand her sometimes, can stay safe and hidden.

24

Boston, September 25, 2024

CLIENT TRANSCRIPT

Sorry, did I stop talking? Sometimes I get lost in memories. That moment in China when I was so tired and lost and ready to be done with it all. It feels like I'm still there, or there again. Like I never escaped that feeling, I just managed to ignore it for a while.

But we're about to meet the Queen!

In my mind, she's the color red. Red silk, red lips. Red eyes that night she found me, flashing with violence and death. But also red for good luck, red for the truest blood from the heart, red as both warning and embrace.

She had me on the ground with her hands around my throat before I could move. Each of her fingers was capped in golden blades, razor claws both deadly and breathtaking.

"Breathtaking." That's a funny word for me to use, since I don't need to breathe. It's fascinating, how many figures of speech are intimately tied to the systems running through our bodies keeping us alive. Mortality is what binds us to one another, the most intimately, universally shared experience.

It's a lonely thing to be cut off from mortality. Even the simplest phrases become complicated existential questions. If I don't need to breathe, can my breath still be taken away?

If it can, the Queen would have done it. She leaned close to my face, her painted white beauty filling my entire vision. It was like being threatened by the moon itself.

"Tell me whose blood I smell on you and where the body is," she said. Not a question—a demand. She never spoke in questions. The

Queen ruled her land with absolute authority. "I will never allow one of Dracula's vampires to claim unhallowed ground here."

Her bladed fingers were placed precisely over my spine, ready to sever it. But though I had been ready for an ending, I was now desperately curious about the Queen. And perhaps I was a little in love already. I always responded well to demanding women; something in me was forever eager to please them.

"I killed Dracula's familiar," I answered, as calm as she was furious. I'd been taught the safest tactic was to only tell people what they expected and wanted to hear. But I felt truth was my best play. It was my only play, really. "After I cut off his head, I threw him into the harbor. There will never be grave dirt for anyone to rest in. I didn't come here to serve Dracula; I came here to *find* him."

She spat on the ground next to my face. What a show of power! Our fluids have to be consciously, actively replaced, so for her to waste saliva simply to show me her disdain? Not only was she in charge, she had a vast supply of blood, and she wanted me to know it.

I understood none of that nuance at the time. I was still impressed, though. I didn't move, didn't try to fight her or flee. I was ever an obedient victim.

The frenzy faded from her eyes, and she stood. "Because you found one of Dracula's familiars who had managed to hide from me, I will not kill you." I was able to take in her clothes for the first time. She was robed in richly embroidered layers of silk, everything elegant and formal and structured. But her sash had been pushed out of place while attacking me, and some of the jewels and chains in her hair were askew. She gestured toward them.

I stared stupidly up at her. She held out her hands, giving me a clear view of the deadly pieces on her fingers. Then she clicked the blades together impatiently. "Attend to me, little fool."

She couldn't get her own clothes and accessories back in order herself. She'd fused the gold to her bones, making her fingers into permanent weapons. A threat, yes, but also a demonstration of her status. She never needed to use her fingers for anything else. I learned later she *never* shifted from her human form, refusing to surrender her body for anything or anyone.

I stood, brushing my hands on my skirt to clean them. If I'd ruined something of the Queen's, be it silk dress or leopard pet, she probably would have killed me without a thought. Then I carefully adjusted the pins and chains in her hair. I wasn't certain how everything was supposed to settle with her elaborate clothing. Each fold and drape had a precise placement, but I did the best I could.

She flicked her eyes down and gave a curt nod. Then *she* looked at *me* properly for the first time. Her nose, broad and perfect, wrinkled ever so slightly in disgust.

It hurt far more than her attack had. I'd always prided myself on being not just beautiful, but *lovely*. To be judged for my appearance after such an arduous, exhausting journey? Shame burned inside my chest. Presenting a picture of ideal feminine grace was one of the few strengths I'd had in life. It helped control the way people saw me and gave me some small measure of power. I had neither control nor power now.

Maybe that was why she took pity on me. She gestured sharply, then began walking. I followed a few steps behind. She led me deeper into the rocky, scrubby hills, until we dipped into a hidden verdant valley. A natural spring burbled cheerily past, but I couldn't look away from our destination.

I had never seen such an enchanting building. There were three levels of roof, all dark green, angling sharply down before swooping outward, much like the Queen's voluminous sleeves. Bold red pillars supported the roofs. The walls of the house were the same red, with gold accents and white trim. The peaks and edges of the roof were spiked, fanged like their Queen. Light winked behind windows, where elaborately carved screens turned even privacy into something elegant and beautiful.

As we approached, towering bronze double doors opened. Two women—girls, really—bowed as we passed through into an inner courtyard. Though it was cultivated with geometric precision and filled with carefully tended greenery, something was strange.

"None of the plants smell strongly," I pointed out. I had learned in my outings from the cemetery that gardens are overwhelming. What might register as vaguely pleasant to you attacks our senses. It makes it difficult to catch any other scents, which is a bit like walking around with an infant screaming in your ear, or flashing strobe lights aimed right at you.

I've never minded strong smells; it's nice to have something tugging on my nose other than blood. But most vampires can't abide them.

"This was once a summer palace for an emperor. Now it is my stronghold. Everything here exists for my pleasure, and to further my work," she said by way of explanation. When she said it, one clawed hand gestured outward toward the edges of the courtyard, where a group of girls were sparring with wickedly sharp blades. They stopped and bowed when they saw her.

A dozen other girls and women came out to silently greet her. I thought they were servants, but a closer look revealed flashes of gold, jade, pearl, and expertly carved polished stones. Everyone was wearing silk and a museum display's worth of wealth and treasure.

The Queen tapped two of her finger blades together. The women dispersed, disappearing through doors and behind screens, and the sparring group went right back to it. I could smell blood. They weren't practicing with dull weapons.

I had so many questions. I'd been living in my mausoleum with Raven, scraping together an existence. I hadn't been aware hidden palaces were an option.

The Queen continued, passing through a set of double doors ahead of us, smaller bronze siblings to the front gate. I followed her into a sitting room. The floor was sunken, strewn with pillows. Everything was green and blue, perfectly contrasting with the Queen in her resplendent red. Overlooking the sunken floor was a gilded throne, the back sculpted with a dragon holding the sun. When the Queen sat, she was haloed by the sun, wearing it as a crown.

She held out a hand. One of the girls appeared, rushing forward to place a jade goblet there. With her free hand, the Queen stroked the girl's cheek, a caress light enough to avoid cutting her. The girl closed her eyes, in fear or ecstasy or both. She murmured gratitude, and then left us.

The goblet was filled with blood. Fresh blood, that much I could smell. But there was an oddness to it. It was a blend, a little taken from each of the girls and women who lived in the compound. The Queen never drank directly from any of them, and they all contributed daily to keep her fed. As a rule, the Queen never killed, which meant she never created a body that could be buried.

"I have never let him or any other vampire into China," she said without preamble. "I guard every port. My girls are rescued from violence and predators, brought safely here. They're given tools and training, then sent out as spies and assassins to destroy vampires and their servants. Every few years Dracula tries again to make a safe place for himself here so he can infect my land. He never will."

"What about you?" I asked. "How did he attack you?"

"I was murdered and buried in Europe, far from my home." Her eyes went soft and distant. "I can feel it out there, still. My grave. Unmarked. Anonymous. I defy it, as I defied him. He was too wedded to comfort and strength; he could never come to my land without a guarantee of both. I am the first and last defense, an immovable wall barring him from all of China. Blood alone gives me strength, and it is enough." She tilted her chin up, and she was glorious. I admired her for her power and resolve.

I still do, despite everything.

Awed, I sat at her feet and gazed up at her in a stupor of exhaustion and adoration.

"Look what you made here," I said. Or something equally inane. I was mixing Mandarin and English, my thoughts bubbling and flowing as quickly as the spring outside, impossible to grasp. All I could feel was how much I wanted what they had.

Not what *she* had. What the girls and women who lived there had. A safe home. Beautiful things. But also someone in charge. Someone to protect them, someone to tell them what to do, someone to make sense of the world for them. I missed Mina so much; it was the same as thirst, clawing agonizingly through my veins, itching in every part of me.

"So you came here looking for Dracula, and now you are lost," the Queen said.

"Do you know where to find him?" If her questions always sounded like commands, my questions sounded like pleas. I was ashamed of my weakness in front of her.

"Tell me why you wish to find him."

It took me a long time to answer, to form into words what I hadn't fully understood until then. I could have explained that I was worried about Mina. That I wanted to make sure Dracula was far away from her. That I needed proof that my sacrifice had been worth it.

But that wasn't it. Not entirely. I tried to articulate what my questions were, for both our sakes. "Dracula took me with such focus and determination and care. So much struggle to make certain I'd become like him rather than simply dying. I want to know why. But he's never appeared to me again. And I'm afraid for the safety of someone I love. I don't know where he is, and I don't know where she is, either."

Because that was another upsetting truth: All those days and nights Raven spent watching for Dracula, I had kept watch, too. Mina never visited my resting place. Maybe she couldn't. Maybe Dracula was stalking her, and she was in danger. Or maybe the men who hadn't saved me had figured out the simplest thing to do was take Mina far away from Dracula's thirst.

Either way, finding him would give me answers to more than just Mina's fate.

The Queen gazed down at me. She was an altar I could have worshipped at. Her blades tapped against the arm of her chair. But there was a crack in the perfectly sculpted expanse of her face. A hint of the same pain I felt, the same loss. The same abandonment. "You will never have your answer. Dracula is dead."

"What? When? How?" I couldn't imagine anything killing Dracula. He seemed as inevitable as nightfall, as inescapable as winter.

"I have spies in Europe, too, watching his castle. They brought news a week ago. He was killed by men who chased him from London to Transylvania. He finally tried to take a woman whom men actually cared about."

"Who?" I asked, my throat tight, my fingers clenched into clawed fists. But I already knew the answer. Why had Raven been distracting me? Why had she scared me away from trying to go home and find Mina? Why had she sent me here?

Because Raven was always a bride. She always served Dracula. And she was doing whatever she could to keep me from protecting his next chosen victim.

When I was still alive, I'd put myself between Dracula and Mina to protect her. And he'd still tried to take her. My sacrifice had been worth nothing.

But that wasn't quite true. The men who failed to save me had managed to save her. Maybe because of what they'd learned from their failures. And if Dracula was dead, that meant Mina was safe, and I was . . .

What was I?

I should have been happy. Mina's safety was what I had given myself up for. It was what I wanted.

Almost what I wanted. Because in that desperate, aching, eternal *hunger* that plagued me even before I awoke in my casket, I had always imagined my future with Mina. Now I couldn't return home. Not ever. Because if I went back to Mina, *I'd* be the threat.

I didn't know if I could resist drawing her to me, pressing my lips to her white neck, devouring her in death like I had never been able to in life.

The Queen had no idea what was happening inside my head. She sipped from her goblet, watching me. "I was going to kill you to send a message, but there is no one left worth sending a message to. Dracula is dead. His brides will wither and waste without him. And no one cares about you."

The Queen was right about that. I would drift into the darkness, become one with it, cease being Lucy and exist as the night itself. Eternal and alone.

Or maybe . . . maybe I could stay here. Exchange a governess for a queen. Pour my desperate need to love and be loved into her. She seemed worthy of it.

The Queen tapped one metal-capped finger against her goblet as a summoning bell. "This land is mine. I am safe, and all the girls in my care are safe, too. No one can harm us. And now that you are here, no one will harm you, either."

She smiled at last, and that was when I should have known I'd stepped into a trap.

25

London, October 4, 2024

IRIS

I eat dinner with Rahul and his handsome husband, Anthony, while Elle fiddles with the stove.

"I've seen one of these stoves before." Elle's voice echoes. She's bent over, head practically shoved inside. "I never had to use it, though. But I bet I can figure it out. I have an affinity for old things."

I want to help her, or even just watch her, but I can't get up from the table while there's any remaining food. "Oh my god, Anthony, this is all so good."

He beams. He's a big dude, tall and broad and thick, but so warm that his bigness translates as comforting instead of intimidating. "Thank you. I wasn't sure about your spice tolerance, so we went easy."

"Embarrassingly low, but I promise I'm working on it. Are you sure you don't want some, Elle?" Soon there won't be any left. It's the best butter chicken I've ever tasted, sweet and savory at once, the chicken perfectly tender. I soak up more of the sauce with the rice and scoop with my naan, shoveling it all in, not even trying to be a little dignified.

"I ate before I came. And I have so many food allergies. Milk, nuts, eggs, corn, soy, rice—it's a whole grocery list. I basically can't eat anything I don't make myself."

"If you want to try, though, give me the list," Anthony says confidently. "I can work with it, I promise. My sister's allergic to shellfish, so we're careful with cross-contamination."

Elle's head is fully inside the oven now. "Deal," she says, her voice echoing metallically.

Rahul leans back in his chair. The supplies they brought me are piled in the corner. I've already paid them, but I feel like I still owe them. Rahul and Anthony had no reason to go out of their way to be nice to me, but they did. Already, I'm hatching a devious plan to thank Rahul and Anthony *and* stick it to Goldaming Life.

"I've never seen a fox behave that way," Rahul continues, still fixated on the fox. *Foxated.* "They can be pests, sure, but never aggressive like that."

"And it was so big." Anthony holds out his enormous hands to demonstrate.

"Could be rabid." Rahul frowns toward the front of the house. "You should call Animal Care and Control."

I gesture to the useless brick on the table. "Would if my phone had any service here. Anyway," I say, desperate to change the subject, "I'm sure it's just territorial. It's had this property to itself for a lifetime. Generations of its fox ancestors have lived and died here. We're the invasive species, not it."

Anthony slings an arm around Rahul. "Don't worry, love. I'll protect you on our way back to the car. I'm the only fox allowed to bite you." He snaps his teeth and Rahul boos, but can't hide his smile. There's an ease of affection between them that makes my whole core ache with hollowness. No amount of delicious food could fill that void. I want to keep watching them, to soak them in. None of the adults in my life modeled supportive and loving relationships. I'm always drawn to people like Rahul and Anthony, as if proximity to healthy love will infect me with the ability to experience the same.

"Maybe it was a fox that jumped through the window, not a wolf," I say, before they notice my besotted gaze.

"A wolf?" Anthony asks. "What wolf?"

"He didn't grow up around here. I never told him the story," Rahul says.

"Let me!" I clap my hands, turn on my show-person voice. It's perfectly pitched and crafted to command an audience. All those public speaking classes my mom made me take are good for something, at least. "One hundred and thirty years ago, a wolf escaped from the zoo. Unhappy with merely running away or hunting unfortunate house pets, it prowled through the neighborhoods, searching. Seeking. Until it found *this* house, jumped through a bedroom window, literally scared a woman to death, and then, mission accomplished, went right back to the zoo."

Anthony looks appropriately horrified. "That's quite the field trip."

"Do we think the Victorians trained wolves as assassins?" Rahul scratches his beard thoughtfully. "Wait, was that the Victorian era? Edwardian? I can't keep them straight."

"Where are you from, Elle?" Anthony asks. "I grew up in Redbridge. East London," he clarifies for my sake, which is useless because I have no idea what part of London we're in now anyway.

We all look at Elle and she straightens, leaning against the stove. Her slouchy, soft sweater has remained remarkably white, but there's a smear of ash along her cheekbone. I want nothing more than to cross the kitchen and wipe it away with my thumb. Maybe linger on those apple cheeks. Maybe trace my thumb down and press it against her lips. Maybe . . .

Elle gestures vaguely toward the neighborhood around us. "I'm from here."

"I *must* ask," Anthony says, "and I apologize for how rude it is, but if you're working at the museum, you've at least finished university, right? How old *are* you?"

Elle's lips twist in a sly smile that transforms her face from cherubic to painfully sexy. "Not a teenager, Anthony. But yesterday I was wearing an oversized jumper and a cap, and the café server offered me a children's menu."

"No!" I say.

She laughs. "It doesn't bother me. I like that people assume I'm younger than I am. It makes them underestimate me."

Anthony seems satisfied. "Okay, so if I bring wine the next time we all hang out, I'm not going to get in trouble for corrupting a minor?"

Elle's laugh is less chiming than it is deliciously wicked. "There's *nothing* any of you could do to corrupt me at this point."

I'm both thrilled that Anthony is already planning a future hangout and also desperate to get Elle to talk more on the subject of corruption, but Rahul stands and holds out a hand to Anthony. "We should get a wiggle on and relieve your sister at the restaurant."

"Who knew this job would require so much cooking?" Anthony stands, too, then squeezes my shoulder in goodbye. I don't want them to leave. They make the whole house feel warmer, more alive. I'm forever craving warmth, the need for it scarred onto both my soul and body.

"Call if the foxes get too frisky, or if a wolf pays a visit," Rahul says.

"You'll come save me?"

"God, no," Anthony answers. "But we'll cater the funeral for a discount."

"Only a small discount, though," Rahul points out. "We're trying to save money."

"In that case, charge my estate triple. I'll be dead, what do I care?"

I follow Anthony and Rahul to the front of the house. Elle comes, too, much to my disappointment. I don't want to be here alone, but I've only just met the three of them. I can't exactly ask them to have a slumber party in an ancient, decrepit house with no electricity, cell service, or hot water.

This afternoon made me realize how long it's been since I got to hang out with people, though. People who like me because they're cool and kind. People my mother can't bribe to stop talking to me.

I wave to Anthony and Rahul as they sprint for the gate to the street. They're both laughing at the silliness of it, but they aren't kidding around with how fast they're moving. They're spooked by the fox. They have good sense.

I shouldn't let them come by again; not while I'm still here. I might want to be infected with their love, but the reality is I'm far more likely to infect their lives with my poison.

Elle lingers behind me, leaning against the banister. It's not fair that I'm exposing her to Goldaming Life's tentacles, either. But I'm selfish. I need her help, and I want her company.

Besides, I don't think anything bad will happen. It'll just be for a couple weeks. Surely that won't be long enough to ruin her life. The most likely scenario is nothing happens and she never even hears about Goldaming Life. The next most likely scenario is she gets a windfall payout to stop talking to me. But the third most likely scenario . . .

God. I'm a monster, just like my mother. Putting Elle in a situation she can't possibly understand or consent to. I open my mouth to tell her not to come back, that I've changed my mind about the whole thing. Instead, I find myself saying, "See you in the morning?"

Her face shifts with subtle surprise. For a moment I'm afraid she's not planning on coming back. But it's something even more upsetting:

She wasn't ready to leave yet. Before I can correct myself, she walks past me. It's all I can do not to reach out and spin her into my arms. Tell her she should stay.

Tell her she should leave and never come back.

Elle looks over her shoulder at me. The turmoil on my face must be obvious, because she smiles in amusement. It's baffling how she transforms with a simple twitch of her lips or quirk of her eyebrows. No wonder people can't peg her age. I swear she's a different person from one breath to the next, and I want to know them all.

"In the morning, then," she says. "I'll do some research tonight and we'll get you that cash as soon as possible." She glances up at Hillingham. I'm in the house's throat, and as soon as I close the door, I'll be swallowed again. It's like she can sense it, too. "Be careful."

"Of wolves?"

"And foxes, apparently."

I give her my best *No worries* smile. It's well-practiced, one of the many looks I honed through endless sessions in front of a mirror. I have a whole repertoire of them. The *No worries.* The *Who, me?* The *I'm totally fine with what's happening here and not screaming inside.* And, my specialty, the *I'm absolutely listening to what you're telling me and I definitely agree.* That one got a lot of use convincing Dickie to let me come here.

Elle hesitates, like she isn't buying my reassurances. I'm touched by her concern, but it also sets off alarm bells. She can't afford to care about me. I make a joke, my other go-to. "My only danger tonight will be hypothermia from taking a cold bath." It's a lie on so many levels, because there's danger around me and even inside me, all the time.

I feel like I've won a prize, though, when Elle laughs. "I'll bring a fix for that in the morning."

"A water heater?" I ask.

"Even I have my limits." She waves and strolls into the twilight, unconcerned about fox attacks. I watch until she disappears through the gate, swallowed up by the hedges that block the house from view.

The sigh that escapes my lips is so pathetic I can't stand myself. Lord Byron is ringing through my head—*She walks in beauty, like the night.* He was an absolute bastard, and so am I for wanting Elle.

Though I had scouted out a bedroom, I opt to set up my bed on the den rug. It feels safer here—more potential exits. But the sleeping bag provides almost no padding between my bones and the boards. I'm paranoid that I'm going to get too cold, like the night air is death creeping closer, flowing sinister and ready through my veins. There's no way I'm sleeping tonight.

As usual, I'm wrong. Foxes with razor teeth pull Rahul and Anthony into the hedges; wolves jump through the window and scream at me in my mother's voice; Elle lies down on that disturbing bed in the back bedroom, then is slowly folded into it, all while looking at me with the saddest eyes.

I wake with a start from that one. The quiet acceptance in her gaze, as though she knew it would always end that way, haunts me right out of slumber. My relief at being awake quickly turns to dread, though. I can't move. *I can't move.*

Sleep paralysis has plagued me ever since I moved into that bedroom with the monster closets. I try my breathing and counting exercises. I wait anxiously for my body to catch up to my brain. But I still can't move. All I can do is stare at where the moonlight is streaming in through the window. No. That's wrong. The moonlight is streaming *out.* My eyes can barely process the wrongness of it, but the moonlight is moving of its own accord. It's slipping away, dimming as it pours back through the window I left cracked open.

I let out a whimper. Everything freezes. The moonlight, the dust motes, the air itself. Like the whole house is holding its breath. It's realized I'm awake, and that I know it's awake, too.

I squeeze my eyes shut. When I open them again, the room is empty once more and I can move.

I sit up, freezing, heart racing. I can't be cold, I can't get cold, but the cold is always waiting for me, ready to kill me the way it killed my mother. Maybe it's her. Maybe my dad was right. Maybe she's come back to get her revenge.

I stumble to the window, slamming it shut. Then I grab my lantern and check the whole house, room by room. All the doors are locked, all the windows shut. Not a fox, a wolf, a dead mother, or an anthropomorphic moonbeam in sight.

When at last I return to the den, I know I'm alone. I can feel it, because it's such a change from the sensation I had when I woke up.

But I don't like this new feeling, either. Without my phone, there's no way to distract myself. No shows to watch and lose myself in, no mindless scrolling. Just the cold and the fear and my own past creeping in the darkness.

I wish I could call Elle. That we could talk about nothing, fill the silence and the loneliness with each other's voices. Instead, I open the safe and grab the floor journal. It seems like it has more potential to be interesting than the other one. I'll take cleverly hidden over officially locked up any day. I've been both, and I definitely preferred hidden.

Then I curl up to live someone else's life for a while. It's got to be less of a nightmare than my own.

26

Boston, September 25, 2024

CLIENT TRANSCRIPT

You look surprised that the Queen trapped me instead of helping me, Vanessa. You're forgetting this is a story about vampires. And while vampires can be many things, they're never *nice.* No more than a falcon is nice, or a snake, or a spider.

But it's okay that you forgot. I forgot, too. She was so beautiful and elegant and commanding. I don't know if it was a particular vampiric power of hers or if I was just easily dazzled, but I was completely under her sway.

"You can be useful," she said, "as long as you never defy me or break my rules." I agreed readily. I wanted to be useful. I wanted to be anything at all. Dracula was dead, Mina was safe, and I had to stay away forever to keep her that way.

I joined the training. Though the Queen's girls lacked my vampiric strength, they had studied the few ways to kill my kind. I learned about anatomy: the fastest way to a heart, better methods of decapitation than my fiancé or I had used. Mostly I learned this by being their new practice dummy. They could stab me without killing me. It's quite the sensation, feeling a blade punch between your ribs. I'd always twisted myself into unpleasant shapes in order to be accepted. Pincushion was a new one, though.

I also learned how to recognize the signs of someone being fed on by a vampire. The point at which it was too late to save them. The ways to kill them and make certain they never came back.

The Queen didn't do any of this teaching herself, of course. I barely saw her. On the rare occasions she walked through the courtyard, everyone went still and silent with reverence. I pretended to do it, too, but I didn't feel the same way toward her. I wanted to get to know her.

I wanted to get to know *everyone* there, but they refused to talk to me outside of training. It made sense. They'd spent their whole lives hunting and fighting my kind to keep their land free of us. Why should they trust me, even if their Queen allowed me to stay?

I spent as much time as I could patrolling. The Queen had a pair of leopards—did I mention the leopards? She was so fucking cool back then. They prowled the valley and surrounding hills, and I stalked them. They tolerated me much the same as the rest of the Queen's subjects did. Barely, and at a distance.

I'd hoped by inviting me to stay, the Queen saw me as a potential companion or friend. But I'd been at the palace for over a month, and she still hadn't said a word to me, and made it clear I was not invited to speak to her, either. I could feel her, though. Watching. Whether in approval or to make sure I didn't step out of line I couldn't say.

She needn't have bothered monitoring me. I would have sooner clawed out my own throat than bite any of those girls. There was something sad and . . . not old, but weary, about even the youngest of them. They were tidy and quiet and devoted to their tasks, but so many of them had visible scars, and I suspected all of them had scars I could not see.

One afternoon, however, they seemed a bit rowdier. The sound of laughter rang through the usually silent courtyard. It woke me from my partial sleep. I still don't know how the Queen managed to fully rest there. She kept everything so meticulously clean, there wasn't even blood-soaked dirt from the leopards' hunting.

I crept close to the sound of happiness, drawn like a moth to a flame. I had learned a lot in my month at the Queen's palace, but I hadn't had much fun. I desperately missed fun.

"Come out, little vampire," called one of them, as lean as a whip and deadly with blades. I hadn't been able to sneak up on them, tired as I was and bound by daylight. "It's okay. She's gone for a while."

I emerged from behind a pillar. The girls were lounging around the garden, sharing a bottle of wine. I hadn't smelled alcohol once while I'd been here. The one who called out to me patted a stone next to herself.

I sat, delighted. "I'm sorry," I said. "I don't know any of your names." We never used them during training.

She laughed. "Neither does our Queen. She calls me Knife, for obvious reasons. Most of us you train with are named Knife, actually. The girls who are no good for sending out she calls Pearl. Unless she really likes you, and then your name is Jade."

A small woman who was missing her right arm nodded, taking a deep drink. "Pearl," she repeated. Several others raised their hands.

That didn't seem right. The Queen loved her girls. Why wouldn't she know their names? "Where is she?" I hadn't seen her leave since I arrived.

"Out getting supplies," Pearl answered.

"Food?" I asked.

Pearl laughed. "We can get food on our own. She's bringing in a new load of us." She gestured around the courtyard.

Knife nodded. "She goes out once or twice a year to rescue new girls. Whenever she hears of any who need saving, or whenever she needs to replace the ones she loses."

"You mean if any of you decide to leave?"

Pearl gave me a look as cutting as Knife's name. "Leaving is not an option."

"Just ask Jade," a young woman whose hair flowed down her back like a jet waterfall muttered.

Knife hissed.

"Who's Jade?" I looked around.

Knife stood, authority and warning in her voice. "Jade's dead, along with the lover she was stupid enough to take. Everything we have we owe to our Queen, and Jade forgot that. The new girls our Queen brings will love her as we do. And we'll teach them the rules of that love."

"But—" Pearl started. Knife cut her off.

"Remember where you came from. Remember what she's given us."

Pearl closed her eyes and nodded with a sigh. "I remember."

"Good. Now pass the wine. We need to drink as much as we can right now so it's out of our systems before she gets back." Knife lifted the bottle with a laugh, trying to tease the tone back to rebelliously playful, but the atmosphere had shifted. No one seemed light or playful anymore. They drank as though it were a chore.

Once most of them had fallen asleep in the heavy late afternoon heat, I cornered Knife.

"You're prisoners here," I said. I should have seen it from the start. They were safe, yes, but it was the safety of a cage, not a refuge. Trickles of memory from my life were pooling in my mind. I knew what it was to have comfort and protection but no say in your future.

"It's better than where I came from," Knife said. She was lying on her stomach, trailing her fingers through a pond, letting them linger where curious fish came to nibble. "But you should leave now, while you still can."

Her words stuck between my ribs, much like her blade often did, and they found just as quick a path to my heart.

I went to the gate without thinking. Would I have left then? I'm still not sure. It wasn't an option. The Queen had gone, but her loyal servants were lounging on either side of the pathway out, watching me with their enormous golden eyes. Without the cover of night, I couldn't change form, and I knew enough from trailing them during their hunts that I couldn't beat two leopards in my exhausted state.

Besides which, I love cats. Of all sizes. I didn't have it in me to hurt them.

I turned around. But instead of creeping back to the dim closet I'd been given, I ventured somewhere forbidden: the Queen's own bedroom. Maybe that's where my affinity with cats comes from—my curiosity, which has nearly gotten me killed on many occasions.

I'd expected opulence. Instead, behind her throne chamber, I found a room not much larger than my own. There was a simple mat on the floor, a few rolls of tattered gray silk that looked more like strips for binding wounds than finery, and a chest.

I opened the chest. It held oddly shaped shoes that couldn't possibly fit anyone's feet, a simple jade hairpin, and a few brittle sheets of paper.

I pulled them out. Painted in grossly exaggerated simplicity, the Queen stared back at me. It was a flyer, advertising a show in which the Queen herself was the attraction. The words blurred in front of my eyes, violence and cruelty evident in the spectacle they presented her as. More than a hundred years earlier, she'd been toured around Europe as an oddity—as a *display.*

A bell rang. Clutching one of the papers in my hand, I walked numbly back to the courtyard. The girls had done their best to recover, standing in neat lines as the Queen entered, pulling a cart behind herself. Only she could have looked regal and aloof doing that. The cart was filled with half a dozen girls, as young as toddlers and as old as teens. They were in rough shape. Not from anything the Queen had done—this was clearly the result of lifetimes of abuse.

The Queen's knives and pearls hurried forward and took the girls into the room they all shared. I knew they'd get the care they deserved. They'd be healed, as much as possible. And they'd accept this life and stay, indebted to the only being who ever tried to help them.

I finally understood the Queen.

She found and saved those girls because they were representations of who she had been. The girl no one protected. The girl who was merely an object for others. That was the core of the Queen, the thing inside her that became a bottomless pit of need. We're all driven by our needs, different ones for each of us, something older, deeper, stranger than blood.

Her desire was to protect the memory of a girl who had been stolen and abused. She dressed her collection in silk and jewels, trained them, and made certain that they never wanted for anything. She saved them from their pasts, but she alone decided their future.

She glanced at me and saw immediately what I held. Then she gestured with one clawed finger. I followed her into her sitting room, and then past it. She led me down stairs carved into the earth. And as she walked, her steps ginger with remembered pain, she talked.

"That was who I was when he found me. I do not remember what city I was in. They never told me. After the audience—those who paid extra to touch my bound, mutilated feet, those who paid extra to touch everything else—had gone, the man who owned me was locking me up for the night. But he failed to notice I'd stolen a blade. I plunged it into his eye, and then into his stomach, over and over. When I turned around, covered in blood, at last free, Dracula was waiting." She paused, looking over her shoulder at me. It was as dark as a moonless night on the stairs, but we could both see just fine. Her smile glowed like the memory of joy. "I leapt and bit him before he bit me. I went right for his throat. I think he never meant for me to be a vampire, but I woke up in a shallow grave thanks to my ferocity. And I have made him pay for it ever since."

I wished I could be like her. I wished I had a story like hers, where she died fighting, where she never gave in. But I also needed her to see what she was really doing here. "You have to give them their freedom, too," I said.

As though she hadn't heard me, she continued down the stairs. "You are the only living creature besides Dracula who knows any of my story now."

My heart swelled. We were finally connecting. She trusted me. We could work together to make a better life for her girls, and then—

She whipped around and snapped my neck.

May 22, 1890

JOURNAL OF LUCY WESTENRA

I am a creature entirely miserable. I should try to repent, but I don't know what to repent of, or why. I cannot bring myself to care about or trust in a distant God, fickle and unreachable and unknowable. ~~Didn't I already have that in my father?~~

We can add blasphemy to my list of sins, because I do not give two figs about God.

Mina has written. Raptures about dear, dreadfully boring Jonathan. She asks about Arthur—how she heard he has still been calling on me, I don't know. I certainly didn't tell her any more about him. Why would I have wasted any of my time with Mina talking about Arthur? But town is filled with gossips. Mina has her heart set on us both being brides, and she's made it clear who she thinks my groom should be.

Maybe this is how I fix the strangeness in my soul. I can pretend to be in love with Arthur as well as I pretend everything else. He's made himself useful. Not only is he helping Mother sort out the legalities of our estate, but he also endures her endless complaints and chatter with the noblest of patience. Which saves me from having to do the same.

Maybe it would not be such a bad thing to have a husband. After all, I've had to manage Mother all these years on my own after Father left us.

~~I do not want a husband. I want Mina.~~ I want Mina's happiness.

What is the opposite of a honeymoon? A vinegar sun, perhaps. Sour and stinging and harsh and burning. That's how I feel about our upcoming trip to Whitby. Mina is meeting Mother and me there; we will spend a few weeks together before Mina's wedding comes like an executioner for my heart.

I am resolved, then. I'll put on a good show, pretend to be happy and in love with Arthur. That way Mina will feel free to be happy, too. Is that not proof I'm capable of love, despite what Mother tells me when I question her?

Just yesterday, Mother wept and threw things and told me how cold and careless I am, how little I care for her and her sacrifices, how selfish and cruel I am, until I cried and promised to never leave her. I wonder how Arthur will feel when he discovers that marrying me means also marrying Mother. If only I could marry them to each other!

But Mother's wrong. I'm not entirely selfish. I can put aside what I want, all for Mina's sake. No matter what Mother says, I am not her heart walking free. Her heart could never love someone more than she loves herself. ~~Could anyone ever love me as much as I love Mina?~~

28

London, October 5, 2024

IRIS

The diary is better reading than I'd hoped. Lucy Westenra is seventeen, charming and witty and droll, perfect company for a lonely night. Her anecdotes give me context for this home and her life here. There's a small cast of characters, including her demanding-bordering-on-abusive hypochondriac mother, her hilariously inept art instructor (who's obviously in love with her), a nosy neighbor determined to catch her in some sort of misdeed, and a former governess named Mina (whom Lucy is obviously in love with).

Lucy's life seems relatively simple, despite the complications of her mother and her mysteriously absent father. She loves nothing more than going on walks with Mina, trying out new places for tea, and trading harmless pieces of gossip.

She's also viciously descriptive. I laughed so hard I almost cried over a description of a disastrous dinner party in which she compared her mother's would-be suitor to a flatulent octopus slowly deflating over the many courses.

But as the pages turn, so, too, does Lucy's story. Mina comes by less. I wonder if Lucy was even aware she was in love with Mina? That intensity wasn't just a schoolgirl crush. Their gradual drifting apart as Mina moves on to other young charges devastates Lucy. Whenever she tries to figure out a way to get Mina back in her life regularly, it ends in a fight, with Mina chiding Lucy that she's spoiled. Mina always harps on about how she has to struggle to make ends meet, but she certainly never says no to luxurious trips to the coast on Lucy's dime. Lucy doesn't see it. She has a huge heart, and it makes me sad.

She's also started editing her own thoughts. Sentences and paragraphs crossed out as though she can't even feel what she feels in private.

The next passage enrages me. "Oh, you motherfucker," I whisper. Lucy's much older art teacher just tried to kiss her during a lesson! When she tells him to stop, he insists it was her fault, that she tricked him, that she made him fall in love with her.

I want to reach through time and strangle that wretched man as poor, innocent Lucy, not even eighteen at this point, spends several pages wondering if it *was* her fault. As if losing her weekly art lessons wasn't bad enough, she overhears her neighbor conspiring with her mother. Proof that she actually *is* being spied on. Everything to make certain she stays in line, stays perfect wife material.

My mother didn't care if I was a wife, but the circumstances are so familiar it makes my chest ache. And it only gets worse. Lucy's already small world gets so much smaller and lonelier. She despairs over turning eighteen and the changes it brings. Now nearly every entry is about her mother sending her out to social events, to the opera, to high-class places to meet men of her own caliber. Lucy is uninterested in any of it, longing to return to the days when governess Mina was by her side. Because Lucy doesn't have the vocabulary or context to understand her feelings, she can't see a future for them and wants only the past.

Then I get to an entry that stops me cold. I read, then reread the opening paragraph.

> *Mother's been in my room again. I leave little traps for her everywhere, little ways that I'll know where she's been with her prying fingers and cutting eyes. But she didn't find my journal. Dear, dear Mother, who loves like a knife, slicing me into ever smaller pieces until I'm exactly the shape that pleases her the most.*

Love like a knife. I sit back, overwhelmed.

Sometimes I'll have a feeling, but I won't know how to express it until I find it captured in a poem or lyrics. Pulled straight out of my chest and put it into a form I can understand. If I can understand the feeling, then I can accept it and move on.

Here, in this journal kept by a girl at the end of the 1800s, is a perfect summation of my relationship with my mother: love like a knife.

I didn't weep when my mother died. I was relieved. I'm not stupid enough to think who she was and what she did can't still hurt me; I just know it won't be *her* doing the hurting anymore. I made sure of it.

But even knowing who my mother was, sometimes I doubt myself. Because she loved me, didn't she? She constantly reminded me about how she suffered and worked and bled to conceive me, to keep me, to bring me into the world. Her triumph, her gift, her heir. Hers. How could I turn my back on her? How could I reject her, after everything she did to create me? Didn't I owe her for my very existence?

Lucy's words explain it, though. It wasn't that my mother didn't love me. It was that her version of love was another form of violence.

I wipe under my eyes, careful not to let any tears drop on the diary. How can Lucy make me laugh in one paragraph and break my heart in the next? I swear we'd be best friends. We could make trauma bond besties bracelets.

But her emotionally abusive relationship with her mother is so woven into her daily life, Lucy doesn't dwell on it. Instead, she describes her newest torment. Gone is the disgusting art teacher, replaced by her mother's doctor, who seems far more interested in studying Lucy. I add him to my list of long-dead people I'd like to punch.

But then things get interesting. Lucy is in love! She has a secret darling she's writing to and planning on meeting.

I turn the page eagerly. Lucy hasn't been interested in any of the men who are courting her. Surely, it's not the art teacher returning. I'll scream if it's him. I'll invent time travel just to go back and kick him in the balls. Maybe Lucy has clued in on her queerness! Maybe she got a girlfriend!

A knock at the door startles me so badly I *actually* scream, dropping the diary. The light outside is hazy and soft. The overgrowth around the house obscures daytime cues; I thought it was still dawn, but when I check my nearly dead phone, it's 8 A.M. I read all night without meaning to.

I know I should share the diary with history buff Elle, but Lucy feels like a friend now that we've spent so many quiet hours together. I'm not ready to share her yet. Maybe I'll never share her. Her privacy was constantly invaded by her awful mother; how could I give her to a museum to be displayed for the whole world to look at? I put the diary back in the safe, then rush to make myself presentable.

I hurriedly wipe under my eyes, hoping I don't look like a total disaster. My makeup can best be described as casual goth; maybe the dark circles will seem deliberate?

"Coming!" I shout, not wanting Elle to leave. I apply a compensating-for-something amount of deodorant. My freshman lit professor warned our class that any guy who walks in wearing a hat and trailing cologne hasn't showered in at least two days. Am I that guy now? My mother would be so disappointed in me. That thought makes me feel a little better, at least. Any day I can disappoint her memory is a good one. I skip to the front door and fling it open.

Elle stands there, adorable in a pale blue men's button-up shirt. It's oversized, belted around the waist to make it a dress. An enormous tote is slung over her shoulder, but even more alluring than Elle herself is the fact that she's holding two takeaway coffee cups. She extends one to me, then digs a brown bag out of her tote and gives me that, too. "I figured you wouldn't have had breakfast yet."

"You're my actual hero." I take the coffee and put a hand over my heart.

Elle laughs. "Don't build me a monument yet. The coffee could be revolting. I'm a tea girl, myself."

There's a flash of orange from the hedge. A pair of baleful eyes glitter darkly, making certain I know I'm observed. I think of Lucy, constantly watched in this very house. We have so much in common, my journal friend and me. I hope she got out, like I'm going to. Hell, I hope she murdered her mom, like I did.

I usher Elle inside, flip off the fox, and slam the door.

29

Boston, September 25, 2024

CLIENT TRANSCRIPT

The Queen put me in a lightless cell, cut off from the sun and moon, even the passage of time denied me.

I don't know how long I lay motionless beneath the ground, as my body painstakingly healed itself aided only by the trickles of blood the Queen fed me. A second burial, one with a far more determined captor than my casket had been. Even after I could move again, I was trapped. I think I spent a few years in that cell, but who can say?

I wondered why she didn't simply destroy me, but I found the answer in the eagerness with which she studied my face during her visits. Perhaps it was my despair that felt like a mirror to the Queen. Or our shared connection to Dracula, the ways in which our lives and deaths still haunted us. Whatever it was, the Queen wouldn't keep me like one of her girls, but she couldn't get rid of me, either. And she didn't want to. She came to see me regularly.

I stayed sane waiting for her visits. Well, sane-ish. I think sanity is a strange concept, don't you? Maybe you don't, given your profession. But the idea that brains and thoughts should work a certain way, and if they don't, they're wrong? I have seen and lived too many lives to believe that.

Anyhow. She brought me enough blood to keep me conscious, but not enough to make me strong. She never left immediately, though. Because I already knew her secret, she felt safe enough to share more with me in the darkness. With an impenetrable wall of iron between us, she could be vulnerable. I got to see the bone beneath the gold.

Mortal experiences get hazy when you're on the other side of them, and she only had a few memories. She'd polished them like pieces of jade until they were smooth and easy to hold. Easy to give to someone else in the dark. A few were happy. Most were horrific. She gave me those memories like she gave me blood, and I fed on both of them.

She told me about her childhood, about her brief life before her endless one. As a young girl, she'd visited this palace with her mother. I liked to imagine her, wide-eyed and awed. And then coming back, red-eyed and awesome, claiming the palace for her own.

I'm not going to tell you about the other memories she shared. They were sacred. A shrine to the girl she had been, the one who had suffered so much. Whatever else has transpired between us—the captivity, the betrayal—I will always respect the secrets she told me in the dark.

At the end of every visit, when I could tell she was getting ready to become more statue than person again, I repeated the same thing:

"You deserved better. I love you."

I meant it, every time. I really did love her. My heart broke for what she had gone through. And at least her obsession took the form of stealing abused girls and giving them a new life rather than, say, eating children. She was downright noble for a vampire.

And every time after I said it, she growled at me and then left for another day or month or year.

Her visits stirred a painful hope in me: that she would let me go, or that she would decide to keep me. That she'd open the door and embrace me, and we'd be sisters or lovers or friends. We'd hold each other's pasts and be each other's futures.

I knew the truth, though. Neither of us was what the other wanted. She could never view me as an equal because I didn't see myself as one, either. And she could never love me as deeply as I needed.

And so I hatched my plan to get away.

She gave me enough blood to keep me functional and lucid, but I was still very weak. So I chewed up insects and sucked on their juices. I drained every rat I could get my hands on, every burrowing creature that dug too deep and fell into my cell.

You were probably hoping for something more dramatic. A vampire prison break! A golden-clawed battle! The violence comes later. This escape just involved swallowing my pride and picking bug legs out of my teeth.

Whenever I built up enough strength for it, I climbed the walls and clawed at the ceiling. I clawed and clawed and clawed, for months. Probably years. Eventually, I broke through to the tiniest sliver of moonlight. That was all I needed.

I had to escape. But I was leaving someone precious behind in that prison. Not just the girls trapped in the palace, but the Queen herself. She was never going to be free. I left her one last message, carved into the wall. *They deserve better. So do you.*

Then I became moonlight, and I left. But I hadn't factored in how weak I still was. Things were about to get much, much weirder, and much, much worse.

In my giddiness at freedom, I forgot to change back before dawn. Have you ever been moonlight in a sun-drenched world? Scattered and blown apart by light so much greater than your own? It took me ages to gather the particles of myself. I'd be so close, nearly there, and then the sun would be back in its merciless honesty. I nearly stopped existing then, I think. At least in any form recognizable as myself.

It was blood that saved me. One night in my infinite struggle to become corporeal, drifting slowly across the world, I smelled death. Not a single body, but countless. Whole fields soaked in blood, an entire land drenched and drowning in it. The smell of so much blood, the burning and chemical scents beneath and around it, was like smelling salts. Just like that, I was real and ravenous.

I was going to say I was whole again, but I don't know if I ever really was whole to begin with. Sometimes I wonder if I'm still moonlight, glowing everywhere but touching nothing. Perfectly lovely and perfectly useless. Maybe I was always moonlight. If moonlight can dream, maybe I dreamed Lucy. Maybe that's why she never mattered to anyone, why she never felt real. Maybe I'm dreaming this right now. Maybe I dreamed you. Can I feel your pulse? To make sure we're not both a dream of pale light washing across an infinite, cold wasteland?

Come closer.

Oh, Vanessa! I *am* sorry about that. Sometimes I forget how good I am at dazzling people. It rarely works on other vampires, alas. But don't look so alarmed. I never bite a woman without permission! Sometimes I just need to borrow a pulse, to anchor myself in the whoosh, whoosh, whoosh of life. Pull myself back into the regular flow of time.

Should we talk about something soothing? Or should we talk about war? Yes? All right then.

It doesn't really matter when the war was. They're all the same war. But I think this was the first World War. I made it back to Europe in time for the worst of it.

I joined the rats in the trenches, following the stench of decay and the sweet, spreading rot. But rats were never my friends, not the way they were his. Dracula could command them and bend them to his will. That's not a power I have. Nothing obeys me. Even the natural world recoils from my neediness.

Mina told me that once. That I was too needy and it made me look foolish. She suggested I hide it. Be aloof and untouchable, as my station demanded. I tried so hard, for her. I thought of her there, while I was in the trenches. I wondered if she was happy. If she had a child. If her child was down there in the gore with me, dying. I looked everywhere for her, in every face.

The blood was no good—too much infection and horror—but the sleep was divine. I curled up in abandoned trenches and was at last replenished. During the nights when I awoke, I walked among the dead and suffering. One night I was down in the blood-churned mud, cradling a young man. I sang to him as he approached the divide between life and death. He wouldn't be coming back from it, not the way I did. I wondered what would greet him on the other side. I hoped, for his sake, that it was nothing. No dreams. Only sleep, perfect and dark and eternal.

One should never let existential questions overtake them on a battlefield, though. There was more in the darkness than mustard gas and shells. The other vampire was on me before I realized she was there.

She threw me out of the trench, aimed straight at a rusted tangle of barbed wire. I turned into mist and moonlight on my way down, avoiding it. My vampire assailant hadn't counted on that. She leapt up after me, anticipating a soft landing on my body instead of the empty wire she'd sought to ensnare me in. She fell directly into her own trap.

I became Lucy once more, teeth bared. I wasn't going to be trapped again. Not ever.

She grunted in frustration, trying to disentangle herself. She was beautiful, skin a rich, dark brown, hair shorn close to her head, power and grace in her full, fat frame. But power and grace aren't a match against that much barbed wire. She continued to struggle, which gave me enough time to calm down. It felt impolite to attack her while she was stuck.

"Why don't you change into moonlight," I suggested, waiting.

She just kept thrashing. The barbed wire wrapped tighter, cutting her in a thousand places. She didn't bleed, which was curious. Even with this many bodies around, she hadn't been feeding much.

I crouched next to her. "Moonlight," I prodded again. "Or dust. Or mist."

"*What* are you talking about?" she asked, exasperated. She stopped trying to roll free, instead glaring at me.

"Shift your form so the wire isn't holding you anymore. And then we can have a proper fight, if you want."

Her tone dripped derision like her body wasn't dripping blood. "Why would I want that?"

"Well, I don't know!" I perched on a discarded helmet, watching as she tried to get free with more methodical efforts. "*You* attacked *me*. But I'm not going to let you drain that poor dying boy."

Disgust rippled through her, making the barbed wire quiver. "I'm not going to drain him! I was stopping you!"

I mirrored her disgust. "I would *never*." I paused, because it was obvious to both of us I was well-fed. A bit sheepish, I leaned forward and began slicing through the barbed wire. When I needed, I could make my fingers into claws to rival the Queen's. "I *did* bite a commanding officer. A few of them. All right, every officer I find, whenever I can. But only when they're comfortably far from the trenches, safe and cozy and well-fed. I would never attack these boys, though. They're children. I heard him dying and didn't want him to be alone. Oh, no!" I finished with the barbed wire and climbed back into the trench. He was gone. He'd died alone.

I sat in the muck and wept for him.

"Wasteful," the other vampire muttered, standing atop the lip of the trench. And then she tromped away.

But I wasn't finished with her yet. There was something familiar about her. Or maybe it was just that I hadn't had a conversation since the Queen, and I was desperate for company that wasn't dead or dying.

"You don't attack them, either?" I asked, scurrying after her. "How long have you been here? What's happening, anyway? This is ghastly."

I kicked a femur out of the way, then made myself a little less solid so I could walk without sinking into the mud. My companion was struggling with each step, using her strength to power through. "Why don't you turn into moonlight and float above everything? Where are you going?"

"Is this not bad enough without the torment of your questions?" she asked, gesturing to the cratered, corpse-littered battlefield around us. A string of barbed wire barred her way and I helpfully darted ahead, cutting a path.

She stepped through without a single thanks. Then, when it was clear I wasn't going to stop following her, she ticked off answers like she was checking them on a chart. "I don't attack soldiers. There are far more valuable uses for their suffering than sating my own base needs. I've been here since the first trench was dug in this pointless battle, which is a war being waged by most of Europe because someone was assassinated and every country had agreed to fight another country in such a circumstance and no one had the sense to say *Perhaps we shouldn't*. I don't turn into moonlight or dust because that's nonsense. And I'm returning to my field office so I can continue my studies."

"What are you studying? I was studying painting. I think. I remember paintbrushes, at least."

"Who are you?" she asked, looking at me in bewilderment.

"Lucy," I said brightly, holding out my hand. She ignored it.

"I'm a doctor," she said, leaving it at that.

I know what you're thinking. Hadn't I learned my lesson with Raven and then the Queen? But the answer is no. I hadn't learned my lesson. I was still desperate for companionship and connection. I didn't know why, but something about her was familiar, like she was humming a song I knew in my heart. It wasn't a song I liked, necessarily, but sometimes familiar is better than good.

She kept waving her hand at me like trying to shoo a fly, and I kept dodging it and peppering her with questions she ignored. We arrived, at last, at a factory. It was half caved in from a recent bombing. The side that still stood had been efficiently turned into a field hospital. There was an assembly line of beds. Each was occupied by soldiers in various states of catastrophic injury. There were tools, blades, bandages, bags of liquid suspended above the soldiers, and blood.

So much blood.

I got a little dizzy, my borders fuzzing.

"If you can't control yourself, I'll kill you," the Doctor snapped.

"I can!" I said, ever eager to please. I stood primly in the center of the room, hands clasped, idiotically angelic smile pasted on my face. "What exactly are you doing here?"

The Doctor was already moving from body to body, injecting things, checking pulses, frowning. "Studying all the ways humans can be broken."

"Oh, that's nice!" I paused. "Actually, that's not nice at all. Why are you studying that?"

"If I can examine enough dying and death, if I can map out all the ways in which mortal bodies fail, then I can protect them."

"Protect who?" I asked.

"Protect mortal bodies," she said, as though I should have known. "Are you really still here?"

I looked down to make certain I was. I was still a bit moonlight-traumatized. I never got over that, as you've seen. "Yes," I confirmed. "I'm still here."

"Well then, you may as well be useful. Smell this." She held up the arm of one of the soldiers. His other limbs were gone, though he'd been sewn up well.

"Laudanum," I said, wrinkling my nose. It reminded me of something. Some*one.* Mother. But something stronger, more recent. A trio of women, on the floor, unconscious. Who were they? What had happened? Everything from my life before was held at a remove, as ephemeral as a dream.

"Morphine," she corrected. "It's more efficient. But ignore that. Smell his blood, then go out and find someone with this exact type of blood. *Exact,*" she insisted. And then she turned her back on me and got to work.

That was how I became a blood and body parts courier, and how I inadvertently ended the war.

30

May 24, 1890

JOURNAL OF LUCY WESTENRA

I wrote of my sorrows too soon. To be fair, my sorrows never stop humming and buzzing around my head like a plague of flies. If I waited until they were over to write of them, I would never write at all. Though it is exhausting keeping up two journals, so perhaps I should stop. Let the fake Lucy be the only Lucy. Bury these truths in the floor forever.

I'm not ready for that yet, though. So, to my newest sorrows:

There I was, existing in a black miasma of restless despair (miasma is a word Mina taught me, and I always think of her when I use it~~, which isn't difficult because I'm always thinking of her anyway~~) when Doctor Seward knocked unannounced on our door. He does that more and more often now that Mother is dying.

(Mother's malady is strange. It comes and goes in waves. Doctor Seward always seems to visit as she has peaked in energy. Every time, I'm afraid he'll tell me he was mistaken and she's on the mend. But that is never the case. He assures me that such fluctuations in her health are normal for her condition. And he's never wrong—inevitably she sinks back into lethargy and takes to her bed for days at a time.)

I was surprised at his visit today, though. It was the hour after lunch, and Mother was abed, as she always is then regardless of how she's feeling. I tried to explain that she was sleeping, but he said he was there to see me. Fearing more medical news ~~(and hoping it was that Mother would die sooner rather than later, as my biggest fear is that this process will take years)~~ I sat and smiled at him as sweetly as I was able. I braced myself to properly demonstrate whatever emotions would be required of me.

Imagine my surprise when he proposed marriage!

I must have looked as shocked as I felt. He quickly began reciting his qualifications. ~~Running a sanitarium already qualifies him to care for me. A girl who dreams of marrying another girl. Who imagines such things?~~ He could not argue himself above his social status. If only he knew how little I care about that! But also how little I care for him. He could be as rich as the king and I would become a hermit in a cave before I would consent to a life at his side. ~~In his bed! Oh, I feel ill at the thought of it.~~

Too shocked to interject, I let him talk unhindered. Within five minutes he had proposed, justified the proposal, retracted the proposal, apologized, and vowed to remain my friend and caregiver. I may have cried at some point, it was all so horribly mortifying. He bowed stiffly to me, advised me to have some of my mother's brandy to calm my nerves, and left.

No sooner had he departed than another knock came at the door. I hadn't even had time to collect myself. I thought he had talked himself back into proposing. Would this be the rest of my life, hearing Doctor Seward propose and then un-propose and then re-propose until I really did need to be committed to the sanitarium?

But it was Quincey Morris. My relief was immediate, and I welcomed him gladly. I expected him to launch into a tale of American heroism and drama, but he was flushed and nervous. He was using such strange, unintelligible phrases (something about regulating the fixings of my shoes, a reference to lamps that might have been biblical, and, my favorite, "Won't you just hitch up alongside of me and let us go down the long road together, driving in double harness?") that it took me far too long to realize he, too, was proposing.

I laughed. It felt so absurd. Like an ad had been distributed in that morning's papers—"Lucy Westenra, Brokenhearted, Available for Marriage! Appointments start immediately after lunch!" I wondered how many would come.

His face fell when I laughed. Men hate to be laughed at by women. They usually become angry, as I learned when my art teacher tried to kiss me. To his credit, Quincey was merely sad. I reassured him that my laughter was because I was trying not to cry. He believed me, thankfully. And then I told him I could not accept his proposal—that the fault was not with him, I simply couldn't leave Mother, and so we would be chained to London for the rest of Mother's life.

"I could not bear to keep you from freedom and adventures in the wider world," I said, leaving out that I could not bear to be forever chained to his side ~~and sharing his bed. I must stop thinking of beds, it's unbecoming of a young woman, though I do wonder what happens in them, and why I have no desire to discover it at the side of any of these men. At least the idea of Quincey holding me feels only claustrophobic, not repulsive.~~

He accepted my reasoning and rescinded the proposal. I let him kiss my cheek; he declared us friends for life. Unlike with Doctor Seward, I believe him.

What an odd fellow. I half regretted turning him down as I bid him farewell. He's funny and dim and sweet. I would have to talk very little, which would ease some of my burden. I briefly considered running after him and asking him to whisk me away to America. Far from Mother, far from Mina. Maybe that would fix me.

Instead, I took Doctor Seward's advice for once and poured some of Mother's special brandy. I had a few sips to calm myself. It wouldn't do for Mother to wake and find out what had happened—two proposals rejected without consulting her!

I returned to the sofa. Soon I felt dizzy and strange, entirely tilted off my axis. I was half in tears, half laughing, which is where Arthur found me. And then he, too, proposed.

It was almost as if Mina were in the room with us. I knew what she would tell me to do. All I could think was how happy she'd be if I were engaged, too. How close it would bring us to be brides together. In my discombobulated state, it felt almost the same as being engaged to her. Before I knew what I was doing, I said yes.

Arthur embraced me, holding me up as the room spun around us. Perhaps that is love. Or merely our future: Arthur Holmwood, supporting spinning, silly, broken me.

And that was how I chose from three unexpected options. Sanitarium, America, or the future Lord Goldaming. The devil you know is better than the one you don't. And besides, Arthur is no devil. He's handsome and pleasant and kind enough. He's been helpful and courteous, and I will have exactly the life I'm already accustomed to. And his mustache will ensure I never have any crumbs on my face, sweeping them right off whenever he kisses me. ~~I do not want to kiss him.~~

Mother approves of him. She was thrilled with the news, flitting around the room, already making lists of what must be obtained, who must be informed, the wheres and whens and hows of it all that I cannot possibly be bothered to care about.

Perhaps Mother will turn her eye and all her suffocating attentions elsewhere. I have, at last, nearly fulfilled the purpose for which I was made. That is that. I am engaged to Arthur Holmwood. I will write all this in as charming a letter as I can to Mina, and she will be happy for me, and that will be enough.

It will have to be.

31

London, October 5, 2024

IRIS

I follow Elle back to the kitchen, breathing in the intoxicating steam from my drink. "You know what my mom always used to say about coffee?"

Elle puts her tote down by the stove and leans against the antique beast. "Do tell."

I pitch my voice colder and higher, tilt my chin up so even though we're the same height, I give the impression of looking down on Elle. "Caffeine is the refuge of the undisciplined." I soften my posture and my expression, slipping back into myself. "I worked as a barista to put myself through college. I loved that job. Plus, I always smelled like coffee, from my hair down to my bra. It drove her crazy when she'd show up and demand lunch together."

Which wasn't often, because I'd deliberately picked a school on the northeastern seaboard, with its frigid temperatures. Hastening my own decline, maybe, but definitely a barrier in the face of her imminent one.

Elle laughs. "What did you do after college?"

I take a sip of coffee to delay. It still hurts my pride to admit that, at twenty-five, I don't have the degree I deserved. The degree I was earning for myself, by myself, despite my mother and Goldaming Life. They took that from me, too. "Well, I was studying literature with an emphasis on poetry, so I continued to work as a barista."

This earns me another bright burst of laughter. I love making Elle laugh. I wish making her laugh could be my lifelong pursuit. I would throw myself into study for that degree, become the world's foremost authority. Her changeable face is maybe my favorite when she's laughing: a flash of deep dimples and her eyes nearly shut.

"Are you a poet then?" She pulls several neat lengths of firewood out of her tote bag and opens the stove.

"Oh god, no. I can't write." I think of Lucy and her shockingly incisive turns of phrases, her delightful descriptions, and wonder if she ever wrote poetry. I would read it. "Modern music was always off-limits in my house. I had to sneak it where I could. But my mother couldn't see how poetry might be dangerous. Little did she realize, poetry is just music someone whispers straight to your soul. It gave me such an escape. The way Louise Glück can write about a garden and gently unearth my own grubby dreams and delicate despair, or the way Gwendolyn Brooks gifts me a glimpse of someone else's life in a few perfect lines, or the way Amanda Gorman turns simple phrases into anthems of hope and power. Poetry makes the world bigger and smaller at the same time. Captures the unknowable and holds it in a form I can understand, even if it's only for a few precious seconds. Poetry helped me escape when I needed it most, and it still makes me feel less insane."

Elle pauses, looking back at me. "That's a strange way of putting it. Do you feel insane often?"

I give her a shrug of a grin, trying not to think of how my teen years ended with involuntary hospitalization. My junior year at university, too, which was also the end of my college attempt. I was a slow learner, but I *have* learned: There are some things I can't talk about, not ever, not to anyone.

I join her in front of the stove. "What are we doing here?"

"The present I promised! Even though this house was posh in its day, they hadn't yet adopted a gas stove range. This is a woodburning stove, which means we can heat water for you to take a bath. *I'm* your very own hot water heater."

I glance over at her perfect point of a chin, delicate swooping nose, and smooth forehead turned into a heart by a widow's peak hairline. "Elle, you've got to stop saving me. I don't like being in debt. Not even to my little butter chicken."

She laughs and nudges me with her shoulder and I want to wrap my arms around her. "There are some cleaning supplies in my tote," she says. "I'm assuming you'll want to scrub out the bath before you get in. There's also a smaller copper tub down here. They used to bring those into the kitchen to bathe in front of the stove in the winter." She points at the cupboards beneath the sink. I open the doors to find a narrow metal tub in there, barely big enough to fit in.

"I didn't even look through these cupboards yet."

"I looked yesterday, while you three were eating. It's mostly old dishes. We can take them out and evaluate them this afternoon. Nothing silver, though. Some porcelain that might be promising, but that's a trickier sell if it isn't from a specific line or artist."

"Is this worth anything?" I hold the tub up. It's dusty enough that my fingers are already coated. If I didn't need a bath before, I definitely do now.

Elle shrugs. "Maybe if it's real copper for the raw material. I'm not an expert in metals. I do want to get moving on the artwork, though. I'll sort through it while you're bathing."

I briefly debate trying to seduce Elle by bathing in the kitchen. But the copper tub is so small, I'd look more like a frog being prepared for boiling, all knees and elbows and awkward limbs. Plus, the level of scrubbing I need isn't sexy. Hard to be seductive when you're actually trying to get clean.

I leave the copper tub there and trek upstairs. How hard would it be to haul the clawfoot tub out of here? Surely anyone wanting to buy it could transport it, though. I mentally add it to my list of potential sales as I carefully rehome a few spiders out the window.

Fortunately, whoever left this house left it clean. The bath only has dust buildup, not mildew or mold. I scrub and scrub. By the time Elle hauls in a pot of water, everything's ready. In a minor miracle, the plug still works, and we add scalding water to cold.

After the flight, the stress of getting here, the fox and the photo, the mess and the dust and the sleeping on the floor and the not-sleeping the rest of the night? That steam curling up is the most alluring thing I've ever seen.

Second most alluring. First will probably always be Elle, on the doorstep, holding coffee.

"Have I mentioned you're the actual best person I know?" I ask.

"You must not know many people."

"Or I know a lot of genuinely horrendous people." I smile like I always do when I'm telling the truth, a crooked smile that implies I'm lying. It lets people off the hook, lets them dismiss what I'm saying as a joke. No one ever looks past it.

Elle hesitates, though. Like she believes my words, not my smile. She nods. "Me, too. Is it all right if I get to work without you?" She's so sincere, like she actually wants my permission to continue to do dull, dusty work for free. She's too good for this world. Definitely too good for *my* world.

"Knock yourself out. But not literally, because we have almost no cell reception here, so it'd be a whole hassle to call 911."

"999," she says, "which you didn't know, so I'll be extra careful not to get injured."

"Good idea. Don't forget to look right—that's my number one safety tip. Can't remember where I learned that one, though."

She laughs and leaves me to it, closing the door behind herself. I start stripping the second the latch clicks. The water's not quite as hot as I like it—if I don't leave a shower lobster red and parboiled, it's not even worth it—but after the last two days, it's a luxury. I use my tiny travel bottles of body wash and shampoo to scrub away the dust and sweat and bad memories.

Did Lucy use this tub? Did she come in here to escape her mother, to soak and dream? I have a nagging need to find out more about her life, her thoughts, her love. It's like being in the middle of a good book, only instead it's being in the middle of a good brain. A good life.

I hope she avoids those annoying men and defies her mother by marrying her secret paramour. I hope they lived to a ripe old age in this very house. No, that can't be right, given the dates. The last people to live here weren't long after Lucy's journal years.

I hope she and her darling ran away together. Explored Europe arm in arm. Kissed in front of the Eiffel Tower, unbothered by the cliché of it. Found an old villa in Italy and painstakingly restored it. Worshipped the sunset over the Aegean Sea, arm in arm.

But I'm not picturing Lucy and her mysterious lover anymore. I'm picturing Elle and me, in love, escaping into Europe. Which is impossible. Both because Europe isn't far away or remote enough to truly disappear into, and because I could never bring someone like Elle into my life. It would be cruel. To her, and to me, too. I know better.

Focus, Iris. At the end of two weeks, I'm gone, no matter what. That's my deadline, so I'd better have some cash by then. Today I'll go to a café to recharge my phone and portable battery and find some shops that might buy this house's crap.

My phone makes me think of Dad, though. I should call and check on him, after yesterday. I sink lower into the bath, resenting him, resenting having to run away when I'd love to stay and get to know Elle better, resenting my whole fucking life.

I freeze as claws slowly scrape down the window above my head. Dad was right. I left him alone, and I failed him, and I failed myself, too, by believing I could escape. He's probably dead already, and my desperate gamble for freedom is over before it ever started.

Because Mom's found me.

32

Boston, September 25, 2024

CLIENT TRANSCRIPT

It turns out I'm quite good at sniffing out blood type. For example, you're AB+, which makes you a universal recipient. I wasn't, and I speak from experience when I say you're fortunate, Vanessa.

The first time I brought back the blood the Doctor needed, still conveniently packaged within its original owner, who had, unfortunately, lost a good portion of the top of his head and wouldn't be needing his blood for much longer—

Sorry, are you all right? You look pale, Vanessa.

Anyhow, I was horrified, too. I dropped the body in outrage when I realized what the Doctor was doing.

"You can't put someone's blood into someone else!" I shouted, quivering with rage. There was a whisper of a memory, the details lost but the pain and fear remaining. I raked my fingernails down my arms, trying to claw out the sensation of my veins being on fire, but I couldn't, because it wasn't in my veins. The pain was somewhere deeper that I couldn't reach.

The Doctor inserted a needle without pause. "I use the same type of blood, so the body doesn't reject it. You did well. This is exactly what the patient needs. Now please go stand in the corner and calm down while I work, or I'll have to kill you."

I didn't think she could kill me, but I did as I was told. My shudders and shivers and flares of pain quieted. The man receiving an infusion of blood wasn't in any discomfort. A flush of life returned to his sallow skin, and he looked like he was sleeping, not dying.

"Good," the Doctor said, pleased. "Now he'll live long enough for me to trace the course of the infection through his body so I can determine the precise point at which it can no longer be treated. I was wasting so much time retrieving supplies. You can do that for me now. You're much more useful than I thought you would be."

With that dubious praise warming my own skin much like an infusion of blood, I agreed. What else did I have to do?

Besides, it was marvelous watching her work. She let me study what she was doing as she traced and tracked and cataloged every part of a human body. Those she could easily save were dropped off far away from the front—that was my job, since the Doctor didn't care about them once they were healed.

The Doctor preferred those she couldn't easily save, though, both for the challenge and for the opportunity to study life on its way into death.

You might think it would be difficult to move so many soldiers under the noses of all that military might, but it was bleakly easy. That's why the Doctor was there in the first place. An endless supply of broken bodies, and no one keeping track of where they went.

One night, months into my role as her courier, I was pulling a cart with two young men inside it. They were likely to make a full recovery, one without his right arm and one without his spleen. I didn't know exactly what a spleen did, but the Doctor assured me that the human body could compensate for the loss.

I myself felt as though I was missing something vital, something irreplaceable, something precious and lost forever. What had been cut out of me while I crossed from life to death? Was it my soul? My future? My humanity? All I knew was that there existed a pit inside me, a hole that no amount of blood could fill.

Lights ahead made me see I'd become dangerously distracted. I had nothing to fear from an active battlefield—you can't put a bullet in moonlight. The Doctor had to be much more careful. She couldn't change form at all except to shift her fingernails into precise scalpels.

Vampires are not all the same. Raven could shift into darkness and ride it like a current. The Queen was strong and a ruthlessly efficient fighter after permanently modifying her body. And the Doctor's senses were impossibly fine-tuned to be able to see, smell, and even hear the slightest changes in a human body. But none of them could change form as swiftly or easily as me—if they changed at all.

So it wasn't myself I was afraid for as I neared the front. It was these two boys in the cart. I already knew English, French, and Mandarin. I had been adding to them, though learning languages from soldiers left me with rather more profanity than anything else. I can say the most beautifully horrendous things in Italian, German, and Hungarian. But I was hearing German and English. Not close, but too close for comfort. I had no idea which side these boys had been fighting on. Their uniforms were bloody rags at this point, and sides mean less when they're represented by unconscious, bleeding teenagers dying for powerful men's stubborn avarice and pride.

One of the boys stirred. The morphine was nearly out of his system. I didn't have the heart to mesmerize him, not after what he'd been through. I pushed the cart closer to the English speakers.

But something gave me pause before I slipped back into the night. There was a train car surrounded by people in crisp, clean uniforms. Uniforms that hadn't seen so much as a day of combat, blood that was healthy, bodies that were well-fed.

My teeth were already sharper as I watched these old men who fought a war with young men's bodies, who counted them as supplies and weapons rather than people. They were German and English alike, and they entered the train car together.

I drifted inside, too, hovering in the moonlight near a window. I could taste the tension, smell all the chemicals and hormones and alcohol in these men. I watched as they sweated and swore and shouted over an armistice. It quickly became clear that whatever was supposed to happen in that train car was not going to.

I thought of those boys outside who had literally left pieces of themselves on the battlefield. I thought of the ones I hadn't saved. The ones I had held as they slipped past the divide between life and death that I had merely ricocheted off of.

"Absolutely not," I said, materializing in the middle of the train car. It was the only thing that could have gotten those men to shut up in unison. They stared at me, bewildered.

And then they all began shouting again, accusing the others of smuggling me in, questioning why they had smuggled me in, insinuating foul things about my presence there. So I bit them.

All.

Fortunately, they had been shouting so much already that the slight change in tone and tenor of the noise didn't alert any of the guards. And once bitten, twice shy. Or at least, twice as malleable.

"Shut up, all of you," I said, and they listened. I had never been listened to by men in my life, much less by a train car full of men convinced they were the most important people on earth.

"Sign." I pointed at the documents. "Sign at once, and when you leave here remember that it was like an angel descended from on high and appealed to your better natures, or some other nonsense like that. But forget me. Just remember how badly you wanted to sign this and how readily you agreed. And then get these boys out of the trenches, you fucking monsters." I said that last part in every language I knew so they'd all understand.

They signed. And, exactly as I had commanded, they were already forgetting me even while I was still there with them.

I was giddy. I'd done something good, something *real*. The Doctor wouldn't have to try and save a few souls here and there. I'd saved them all. I flew home, a jubilant moonbeam shimmering among the smoke, dancing along the flares. I burst into being right beside the Doctor, which made her drop the beaker she was holding, which made her swear as fervently as any soldier ever had.

"I did it!" I declared.

"Yes, fine, now go and get me—"

"No, I did it! I ended the war! They've just signed an armistice. It's over."

The Doctor frowned at me. I had expected to earn a smile, or at least less of a frown, which counted as a smile for the Doctor. Instead, her frown deepened.

"What do you mean?"

I told her the story, my words shooting out faster than a volley of bullets. But they didn't find the target I thought they would. She sighed and began carefully washing her instruments. "I wish you had consulted me first. It's very inconvenient."

"Inconvenient," I repeated with numb lips.

"Now we'll have to find another conflict somewhere else. This was such fertile ground for advancement of my work. It's disappointing, Lucy."

I wilted. I thought she'd be proud. I thought we wanted the same thing—to help these soldiers, these *children.* When we met, she'd been protecting them, too. Or so I thought.

I had to admit at last that, unlike me, she wasn't looking for the faces of those she'd loved. She wasn't looking at their faces at all. Only what was viscerally inside. What she could take apart and put back together to learn from. If she happened to fix them, fine. But healing had never been her main goal.

"I can't help you anymore," I said.

"Don't be silly."

My jaw clenched. It was not silly to protect the boys paying the price for this horrendous war. But I'd learn in a few years that she was right. I'd been very silly indeed, foolish and hopeful and shortsighted.

My time there was done in more ways than one. I had looked for Mina in every face of every boy I saw on the battlefields, but I hadn't found her. It was exhausting. I needed to stop looking for her, to let myself forget. I also needed to get the scent of blood and rot and terror out of my sinuses. That would never happen at the Doctor's side.

"Stay with me," the Doctor said. "You're useful. And we have so much more to do."

"No," I snapped. "You don't care about me. I've as much value to you as a scalpel or a needle."

The Doctor gave me her most withering glare. "Lucy, there is nothing you can do that is more important than helping me."

I nearly gave in and let her decide for both of us. Let her tell me who and what I should be. But the scent of morphine lingered, an itch in my soul. Once again something inside of me recoiled from a memory I couldn't find. A phantom scar on my perfect vampire body.

And just like that, I was moonlight. I fled the Doctor and the trenches once and for all. I didn't stop until I found so much light it shocked me back into my body.

Have you ever been to Paris in the frantic lull between wars? Everything building toward an inevitable, devastating climax, but oh, the pressure in that buildup! The ways people found to release it! I wandered the streets, lost among a populace raucous with joy over news of the armistice, drunk on the relief of it. I myself was dizzy with the heady triumph of knowing I had given this to them.

And then I was promptly murdered.

33

July 22, 1890

JOURNAL OF LUCY WESTENRA

Coming to Whitby was the right choice for Mother's health. Arthur was sad (he cannot visit us here often, due to his own father's poor health) and Doctor Seward cautioned against it, but Mother seems more herself than she has in months. For better and worse.

But not even being on her actual deathbed could have stopped Mother from making this trip. I have been dragged along on social call after social call, endless parades of tea and inanities as we bless distant acquaintances and local clergy with visits so Mother can tell them all about her greatest triumph: my engagement to the future Lord Godalming.

And Mother, unaware in the most morbidly hilarious way possible, always adds in a whisper that Arthur will be the lord sooner rather than later, owing to the poor health of his father. I do not add in my own whisper that I will also inherit everything sooner rather than later, owing to the poor health of my mother.

But it doesn't bother me. I feel more generous, knowing Mother's end is nearing. I can tolerate everything. I don't even mind smiling and feigning excitement over my wedding, demurring on taking a role in arranging the details because I cannot care about any of them.

My only focus is counting down the days until Mina's arrival. She's my lighthouse on the horizon, the fixed point I navigate by. Everything else is storm and tempest, confusion and despair, but Mina. Mina! Tomorrow the train delivers her to me, at last.

I've been sitting in front of the mirror, practicing my facial expressions. I must get them right so I don't disappoint Mina. Here, the rapturous smile when I talk about my engagement to Arthur. Here, the generous smile when she talks to me about dull-as-mushy-peas Jonathan. Here, the excited smile when we plan our weddings and futures as wives.

I'm so good at showing what I'm supposed to and nothing else. I'm a little mirror, reflecting back what others wish to see.

I snapped at the maid tonight, wanting to prepare Mina's bed myself. To make sure everything is perfect. ~~And then I sat on my own bed and cried because what am I doing? What am I hoping for? Why am I breaking my heart against Mina's shores, when they belong to someone else?~~

34

London, October 5, 2024

IRIS

Water sluicing off me, I stand and slowly turn to the window. "No, Mom. You're dead. I made sure of it."

Crouched on the ledge *isn't* my mother, red eyes glowing as she scrapes the glass with the blade I left in her heart.

It's a crow. It drags its beak down the window once more.

"Pervert." I cover my chest. You never know when it comes to animals. "Seriously, get a life."

Without drapes to close, bath time is officially ruined. I tug out the stopper and let the water drain away. I've long kept a catalog of trustworthy versus untrustworthy animals, but it's hard to be one hundred percent sure of most of them. Cats are the only species fully on the trustworthy side, mostly because they'd never follow a command they didn't want to. And pugs, because pugs are too stupid and adorable to be evil.

Good animals versus bad animals is one of those things I could never talk about. How do you explain that you're convinced your mother used various creatures to spy on you? That she was so insidiously controlling, so mind-bogglingly rich, even the natural world bent to her will?

Answer: You don't. At least not if you don't want to be involuntarily committed. The most dangerous thing I ever did was tell the truth.

Despite my earlier resolution to keep Elle out of all this, I take more time than usual getting ready. I brush my hair out so it will fall in loose black curls like a curtain around my face, then line my eyes and apply mascara. Finally, I add a healthy coat of tinted lip balm, just in case she finds my lips as potentially kissable as I find hers.

If nothing else, I feel human again. I love feeling human. Feeling human is the best. I pull on black jeans and a buttery soft, oversized gas station sweatshirt I've had since the first time I ran away. A chill clings to the house, and I don't want to feel cold. I'm already on edge enough without that fear tugging on me.

Downstairs, the sitting room is filled with all the paintings in the house. Their ghosts still hang on the sun-bleached wall in vivid wallpaper squares. Elle handles the paintings like vinyl in a record store, her fingers dancing over the frame tops as she flips through them one by one to give me a brief glimpse.

"Shite," she says, and I'm so shocked I laugh. She keeps going. "Shite, shite, shite that *might* be worth something because of the artist's relationship with someone who was actually talented, shite. Whoever decorated this house had both bad taste *and* bad investment sense. None of these artists are worth anything."

My heart sinks. "Oh. Okay."

Elle holds up a finger. "But! These frames are quite nice, so we should be able to sell them for at least a couple hundred pounds each."

"Oh! Okay!" My heart floats back up. There are easily twenty paintings here. That's a few thousand in my pocket. She lets the paintings rest against the wall again. I gesture at the nearest one, a bowl of the saddest, most repulsive fruit I've ever seen, complete with a kitten painted by someone who had evidently never seen a cat in their life. Its eyes gaze in both directions simultaneously from its eternal oil prison. "What is this one? *Still Life with Despair*?"

Elle nods somberly. "A stunning example of the Talentless movement, in which people with no talent were encouraged to create as much as possible to balance out the true masters. Their motto was 'Merit in Mediocrity.'"

I snort. "Wish I'd known that motto in school. I would have embroidered it on my jackets."

Elle points at another painting. "My favorite, though, is *Landscape with Absolutely Nothing Lovely*."

"I can feel myself becoming duller," I say. "A hallmark of the celebrated Ennui movement, which believed art had a moral responsibility to be so boring, people were forced to be industrious rather than creatively inspired. Heavily funded by the Fraternity of Factory Owners."

Elle laughs. "Are you sure you didn't get a degree in art history?"

"No, I went for the one even *less* useful in real-world job searches."

I want to keep at our game, and I suspect she does, too. But then she sighs and moves on. Unlike me, she *has* a real-world job, and probably can't devote too many days to this side project. I should be more anxious to get through everything anyway.

"Now, to the furnishings." Elle gestures around us. She's moved a few extra pieces of furniture into this room. "They weren't properly covered for long-term storage and aren't in the best shape. You'll need to have them restored by someone who knows what they're doing, which I'm guessing you aren't interested in."

I shake my head, glum.

"Don't worry. This was a fussy, pretentious house, so some of the pieces are worth money regardless of condition. A few of them are branded by the original makers, which is always a good sign." She lifts a chair covered in faded striped material to show me the bottom of the seat. Sure enough, there's a stamp. It means nothing to me, but she gestures excitedly at it. "I'll have to follow up with some contacts, but Hardy and Sons were local artisan woodworkers. There's almost certainly a market for Hardy originals."

"Oh good!" I want to stay in here and work alongside Elle. Unfortunately, it's not efficient. I can't really help her with any of this. Plus if I stay in here, I'll start asking her questions. I want to know about her life. How she ended up working for a museum. What her favorite movie is. Whether her family is populated by vicious predators. But I don't want to answer any questions about my own history, so I keep that door closed. "Okay, I'll be in the study, cataloging the books. Let me know if you need anything."

"I will." She tips another chair. "Oh, I meant to ask," she says, searching for a stamp or signature. "Did you find anything in the bedrooms upstairs or the locked room? Have you looked in all the drawers and nightstands? You'd be surprised what's worth something. Receipts, old recipes, that sort of thing."

The diary. I should tell her about the diary.

"No," I say. "I'll keep an eye out, though. Mostly I was hoping for jewelry, but there wasn't any."

Elle gives a thumbs-up, focused on the joints of the chair. I leave her to it and get to work on my own project. It takes less time than I thought to finish. Without internet access, all I can really do is write down the titles, authors, and publication dates.

Leaning against the entry to the sitting room, I watch as Elle examines the chandelier. She's standing on her tiptoes on one of the kitchen chairs, and I'm trying not to stare at the way her shirtdress is pulling up and exposing more of her legs. "It's good craftsmanship," she explains, "but I can't find a brand. I don't know if it's worth pulling down and selling."

"The bath upstairs also seems nice, if there's a market for old clawfoot tubs. I should take photos of both. Hey, I'm headed to a café. I need Wi-Fi to find out if any of these books are valuable. Plus my phone's almost dead and I can't charge it here. You want to come?"

"I'd rather keep going, if that's all right." Elle strains to reach the bottom of the chandelier, carefully turning it. The crystal decorations tinkle in delicate reproach over being moved after so long. Sensing my disappointment at being rebuffed, Elle flashes me a smile more brilliant than any chandelier could ever hope to compete with. "I get a little obsessive. Sorry."

"Please don't apologize. You're doing me such a favor." Besides, it's a better use of our time to work separately. It's just much less flirty.

"You want me to look at the bedroom furniture pieces when I finish in here? Or I could tackle the attic. Have you been up there yet?"

"No, I've been dreading it."

Elle steps down from the chair, wiping her hands on her dress. "Oh, let me! I *adore* attics."

"I can't tell if you're being sarcastic. The posh accent throws me."

"Absolutely sincere! Attics hold the things we don't want to see but don't want to get rid of, either. They're dreadfully sad. All those items that were once beautiful or beloved or useful, shoved up there and forgotten."

"I'll tell you what. You saved my life, gave me coffee and food and a hot bath, and offered expert evaluation of all this junk. In return, I'll let you explore a dusty old attic. Totally seems fair." I interrupt her laugh by holding up a hand and making my expression very serious. "But if you find a portrait of an evil, decrepit old gentleman, please wait until I get back. We'll stab it together and see if it was a whole Dorian Gray scenario."

"I promise, no portrait stabbing without you." She ties her shimmering hair back. It's the only vibrant thing in this weary space.

"Can I bring you anything from the café? Or pick up lunch?"

Elle gestures toward the kitchen, where she'd left her enormous tote. "Brought my own. Oh, but since we have the stove working, if you could pick up a kettle? That way we can make tea, and I'll never need to leave again."

If only keeping her forever were that simple. "Deal." I grab my purse from the den, then retrieve the journals from the safe. On alert for crows, foxes, and stray wolves, I head out for my coffee date with research and Lucy.

As soon as I leave the neighborhood, my phone blows up with notifications. A pit forms in my stomach as I see a missed call from my dad's assisted living center. And then an entire series of texted photos taken outside the house, plus an emailed invitation to join a brand-new Goldaming Life seminar in London.

The pit turns into a roiling maelstrom of dread and anger. They're here, and they want to make sure I know it.

35

Boston, September 25, 2024

CLIENT TRANSCRIPT

I had made it through most of World War One without so much as a scratch. And there I was, my very first night in Paris, lying in the street with my belly split open.

I wanted to change into moonlight, into mist, into dust. Anything to escape. But when pain is too overwhelming, it's nearly impossible to shift into another form. Nothing makes us so mortal and flesh-bound as pain.

Well, except pleasure.

But there was no pleasure in trying to hold my abdomen closed as someone dragged me through dirty alleys. Thanks to my time with the Doctor, I knew exactly how many precious things a torso contained. Would I die if I lost them? Or would I merely be in unfathomable pain until I healed? It had itched in the most agonizing way as my nerves and bones put themselves back together after the Queen snapped my neck. How much worse would it feel to regrow internal organs? I put all my focus and strength into holding them in, paying little attention to anything else until I was dumped somewhere. I fell immediately asleep, curled around my wound.

When I awoke, I had more or less healed. I was in a collapsed culvert at the edge of a cemetery, used for centuries to dispose of unwanted or unclaimed bodies. It was perfectly unhallowed, and my rest had been depthless and restorative.

I wasn't alone there, though. Lying beside me was a vampire. Her skin was white, her eyes were as colorless as the edge of the horizon on a sunny day, and her hair was a tangle of curls so matted with blood and gore that it was impossible to tell what color it actually was.

"You're awake!" She leaned forward and kissed the tip of my nose. "Ludicrously brave of you, trying to save me! You silly, sweet thing."

With pain no longer screaming for all my attention, I was able to sort through my memories of what had happened. I'd been wandering, enjoying the vitality and excitement of a city celebrating peace, when I heard a woman's scream. I ran toward the sound and saw a body crumpled on the pavement. But something was off. Nothing smelled like it should. I had been so puzzled by what was wrong, I didn't notice the ambush until I was stabbed from behind and then gutted.

"Were you the one who dragged me here?" I asked.

"It seemed only polite." She stretched and yawned, showing perfect, shiny white teeth and pale gums.

"*You* were the body on the ground!" *That* was what had been wrong. I had expected to smell fresh blood, and I didn't. She couldn't bleed properly, even after being split open by a blade.

"Frequently!" She bounced to her feet and shook out her hair, idly pulling the larger clots free. "You must have startled him. What a mess he left! Come on, I'll bet you're starving." She grabbed my hand and pulled me along after her. Though my dress was hopelessly destroyed, hers hung on her frame with jaunty playfulness, as though the blackened blood and smears of grave dirt were whimsical patterns. Strings of pearls around her neck, sticky and stained, clicked together like finger bones as she led me out of the cemetery and into an apartment abutting it. It was abandoned—one corner had fallen in from a bomb strike—but at the top a single apartment remained pristine.

She flung the door open and then flung herself onto a chaise longue, draping over it like the pearls draped over her breast.

"Pick anything you like, darling." She gestured toward the next room, which was filled to bursting with clothes. Dresses and coats and hats, gloves and stockings and shoes, furs and jewelry and scarves: enough to clothe a whole army of devastatingly stylish French women.

Fashion had shifted so much during my time away! First in captivity and moonlight, and then in the muck and mire of the trenches. I took my time marveling over the textures and cuts of the dresses, wondering how my hair should be done to match; primping gets difficult without mirrors. But when I slipped off my own dress and saw the gaping gash in it, as well as the angry red line on my stomach that hadn't yet fully healed, I remembered I had come here under rather odd circumstances.

You'd think it impossible to forget waking up in a bone-filled culvert, but it's not that unusual in my line of existence. And what can I say, I have a short attention span. Or an infinite one, depending. Things feel less urgent when time doesn't matter.

I was curious, however, as to why we'd been attacked, and who had done the attacking. I went back out to my new friend.

"What's your name?" I figured that was a polite place to start.

She waved breezily. "I can't remember, so I change it like I change my hairstyles: often and without reason."

Just like the Queen and the Doctor and the brides. Most vampires I met had no name. I wonder if that's part of why we become monstrous. It's hard to hold on to humanity when you can't see yourself reflected or even define yourself by something as simple as your own name. I owe my earnest would-be decapitator for that, at least. He gave me Lucy back.

My new friend gestured at her head. "Now, be a dear and describe my injuries to me. In detail, please. We have to be each other's mirrors, ma petite chou." It made sense. She wanted to know what had been done, so she could avoid it in the future. The back of her head had gotten the worst of it. I told her about the damage using all the correct anatomical terms, which delighted her to no end and made me miss the Doctor a bit.

The base of her skull had been smashed in—it was still a little concave, but I didn't want her to worry about it. Eventually it would even out, and in the meantime, I could fix her hair to cover it. She could see for herself the jagged knife mark in her belly, but not the wounds in her back. I traced them, detailing exactly which internal organs each stab would have hit.

"How did he sneak up on you?" I asked, curious. I had been distracted by her. What had she been distracted by?

"That's in the past, it already happened, why care? We have to move on to the next adventure!" She pulled me to the bathroom.

There are few pleasures that are the same in both mortal and immortal life, but a hot bath after you've been through something wretched? That's one.

It was strange, though. Raven had made everything physical, constantly pushing the limits of pleasure and pain. Sex, but no intimacy. The Queen shared her past with me, but our emotional connection was only on her terms and very one-sided. And the Doctor had neither the time nor the inclination for sex *or* intimacy. She was as utilitarian with our relationship as she was with life and death itself.

But with the Lover—that's how I came to think of her—our time together was oddly innocent. She was unconcerned with her own nakedness, oblivious to mine. There was a familiarity with her, a sort of recognition, that I couldn't explain. Like we had known each other for ages, instead of hours.

I washed her hair and she washed mine, and nothing was fraught or filled with any sort of tension, delicious or otherwise. It was . . . nice. It had been a long time since I'd had *any* experiences I would have described as "nice." Tenderness with nothing else attached.

When we were clean, we tried on dress after dress. We laughed and twirled and modeled for each other. I settled on a rose silk number, sleeveless—such a thrill; I'd never been allowed that before! It fell down my figure like a curtain meant to tease at what was behind it. I covered it with a shawl so sheer it might as well have been a rainbow. Stockings, soft and well-made, felt like heaven. And I wore the prettiest red heels, round-toed, with straps that buttoned across my foot. I loved those shoes. I wonder whatever happened to them.

The Lover wore a similarly cut dress, but in an indefinable color. Gray or blue or silver or white. It shifted with the light, like it was made of clouds, and rendered her nearly colorless. An artist's canvas, waiting for paint.

She had a collection of postcards and advertisements featuring women's fashions. Copying what I saw, I worked her hair in waves and pinned it to cover the damage to her skull. She fussed with my golden hair until she was satisfied, then colored my lips red, rubbed rouge onto my cheeks, and dabbed kohl above and beneath my eyes.

Such a small thrill, such a painfully sweet bit of normalcy, to feel *pretty* again.

The Lover danced and spun around our apartment, and with her, I felt lighter. She had a magnetically innocent charm, an eternal youth instead of just eternal life. After the trenches, after my captivity, after everything that had happened since I died, it turned out I needed to be nineteen again. A freer and happier and wilder nineteen than I could ever have been during my life, but still only nineteen.

We went out, arm in arm, and reveled among the revelers. She taught me to look for men and women drunk on champagne, because it made their blood fizzy and intoxicating.

It's adorable when you wrinkle your nose like that, Vanessa. It doesn't *really* change the blood. It was the Lover who was fizzy and intoxicating. I let myself be swept along with her through the glittering Paris nights. Everyone happy, everyone glutted on freedom, everyone exorcising the demons of the last few years. I was dizzy with the thrill of it all, alcoholic blood or not.

As for the attack, I forgot about it. I had come directly from the trenches; brutality and violence were hardly shocking. And besides, it hadn't mattered in the long run. In a way, I felt lucky. How would I have found the Lover otherwise?

I didn't know yet I would *always* have found her. And the Doctor. And countless others. But I hadn't figured it out. My attention was elsewhere. The women on stage— Oh, the women. They were a display case full of the most delectable pastries, confections of every flavor imaginable. They'd always invite us into their dressing rooms after, because everyone wanted to be near the Lover once they saw her. Everyone loves something precious and fragile. They loved me, too, because I was beautiful and happy and fun again.

They had no idea that we were the most dangerous things on the streets of Paris. It made me affectionate and protective. They didn't trust me because they were safe. They were safe *because* they trusted me.

I'd nearly always find someone to join me in a dark corner or costume closet. Sex, as frantic and hungry as it had been with Raven, but lacking the blood-soaked haze and confusion. I knew exactly what we were doing now, and how to do it. It was still without love, but at least it was with tenderness, with humor, with delight. Oh, French women.

French women.

Sometimes I think about them, my stages full of soft delights with their cupid lips, assured fingers, warm tongues. I wonder what happened to them. I hope they were happy. I hope life was one long thrilling jaunt from smoky club to brilliant spotlight to laughter-filled dressing room. I hope they aged joyfully, that they only got softer and warmer with time, that the lines of their faces told winking stories of pleasure and happiness, never want or fear or pain.

But this was Paris in the 1920s. None of that was in their futures.

Still, they didn't know what was coming, and neither did I. The Lover and I owned that brilliant city. We joined the dancers, performed on stages, drank our fill but never killed. The Lover was adamant about that, and I didn't mind. I only wanted to be full enough to take the edge off the infinite gnawing emptiness always stalking me. Blood did that. So did sex. If I ever got too empty, I remembered Mina. I remembered myself. And I didn't want to think about either of those things, so I made sure I was never thirsty and I was never alone.

Though I could have been happy at any of the clubs—they were all basically the same—we never danced on the same stage more than seven nights in a row. The Lover was searching for something, and when she didn't find it, we moved on.

On to the next club, the next dance hall, the next soirée. Every night was a bright burst of pleasure, every daytime rest an eternity, the only true marker of the passage of time the rotation of our dresses. I didn't pay much attention to the Lover. In all those arms, on all those stages, among all those frantic bursts of blood or pleasure, I wanted to be lost.

But I couldn't escape my past. Unlike in the trenches, Mina was everywhere. She always said Paris was for fools and dreamers, but I still found her constantly. Not in the mouths I kissed, the pleasure I gave and received, the audiences of adoring men. No, I found her in the narrowed eyes watching us as we laughed too loudly walking arm in arm down the streets. In the scandalized outrage of women tricked into coming to the clubs. In every pursed lip and judgmental gaze.

I knew exactly how Mina would feel about what I was doing, and I wished *desperately* to discover her watching me, horrified and disappointed. She'd cover my bare shoulders with a sensible coat and march me back home.

Every dance, every stage, every kiss was a dare for Mina to come find me.

I know it's not rational, but I felt close to Mina when I was in Paris. Like at any moment I would see her, and she would be the same, and then I could be the same, too.

So it wasn't just the Lover searching for something in every crowd.

We understood each other, though neither of us ever said what we were looking for.

Then one night, everything changed. I wore one of my favorite costumes: elastic bands with two strategically placed, enormous white feathers, and nothing else. At the door, the club owner charged for hand fans. Men and women crowded against the edge of the stage, waving their fans, trying to shift the feathers to get a glimpse of perfection. It was salacious and absurd, dirty and somehow innocent, too, because everyone was in on the joke. Everyone was playing. Sometimes Paris seemed like nothing but one big dare: to drink a little more, to kiss a little harder, to dance a little longer, to look into the dazzling lights and ignore the encroaching darkness for a few more hours, a few more days, a few more years.

As we took a bow and dropped our feathers—that always got a roar of playful anger from the crowd, who had paid for their useless fans—the Lover looked up into the audience and froze. A beatific smile crossed her face, so pure, so exultant, that I wondered what she had seen. In that moment, I loved her. In that moment, I would have done anything for her.

But the smile wasn't for me. The smile was for him, because *he* had found her again, and her favorite dance was about to start.

36

July 24, 1890

JOURNAL OF LUCY WESTENRA

Today Mina and I sat on a bench overlooking the ocean and talked as though we had no cares in the world. She took my hand as we walked~~, and I pretended the hand I was taking in marriage was the one I held then, the only one I ever wished to hold.~~

Mina's asleep in the bed next to mine. It's hard to focus. She told me something so funny today, though. She keeps a diary! One written in her own shorthand code so no one can understand it but her. When I asked her what she keeps a diary for, she laughed and said, "Evidence." I asked what kind of evidence, and she said, "That I am doing and feeling what I should be."

I was so relieved and excited that perhaps Mina, too, has an internal landscape of horrible secret longing. If we had been at the house, I would have shown her my journals on the spot. The journal filled with the fictional version of me, who thinks and feels only what she should, and this journal filled with the real version of me, who thinks and feels nothing that she should!

But then Mina immediately started talking about Jonathan. Missing him, wishing she knew how he was faring on his business trip into the mountains of Transylvania, wondering when he would return so they could be married. I barely know Jonathan. I doubt I could pick his bland face out of a crowd. So how is it that he creeps through my life like a thief, stealing everything I want?

I keep wondering, though: What is Mina doing and feeling that she shouldn't be? Why does she need to keep a journal as evidence? I don't dare hope, but looking over at her now, she's turned toward me. Her beloved eyes closed, those clever lips pursed even in sleep, as though she's hiding something. What are you really doing and feeling, Mina, my Mina? For the first time since she told me of her engagement, I dare to hope that maybe she feels as I do. That her engagement is a necessity and not what her heart wants.

But then why does she always tug our conversations back to my engagement to Arthur, no matter how I try to steer them away?

37

London, October 5, 2024

IRIS

"You do know the time difference between London and Salt Lake City, don't you?" Dickie asks as soon as he answers the phone.

"You do know what *Leave me the fuck alone or I'll never sign your fucking documents* means, don't you?" I snarl, prowling down the street.

"You're going to have to enlighten me about what I've done wrong."

"The photos. The ones you had taken of me outside the house. Could you at least try for a little subtlety when threatening me?"

"Are you perhaps still jet-lagged? Or you may want to have the house checked for gas leaks. Those photos aren't threats. Those photos are gifts. Gestures of goodwill. I had a photographer take a few exterior shots for when you list the house. If you'll check your email for once, you'll find I told you about it, and also asked you to schedule with the photographer so she can come back to get the interior."

I have no response to that. I move the phone away from my ear and check the email with the seminar invitation. Sure enough, Dickie told me about the photographer and asked when I think the house will be ready for staging.

No. No, he's gaslighting me. Or implying-gas-leaks-ing me. This is what they do. They threaten me, they hurt me, and then they have the most reasonable explanation possible. An explanation that makes *me* look crazy and paranoid.

As if we both don't know I have every reason in the world to be paranoid. It's not paranoia if it's based on fact and experience.

I put the phone back to my ear. "I flew across the ocean to get a little space to process everything. Do you know what space is? It's that thing where you leave someone alone. No more fun stalker photos, no invitations to soirées to show me how close the nearest cult members are, no *nothing* until I say so, do you understand?"

"I'm paid to care about your well-being, Iris. Whether either of us likes it, you're the heir to Goldaming Life. So much depends on you, which means—"

I hang up. I'm done with Dickie. It's still too early to call the nursing home back, though. I shouldn't call right now anyway. I'd probably be mean, and the employees there don't deserve it. I try to burn all my angry energy by speed-walking to the nearest street with a café. *Fucking Dickie. Fucking Goldaming Life. Fucking everything.*

The café has an open table near an outlet, at least. I wolf a sandwich but nurse my coffee slowly. While my phone charges, I search online. My collection of antique books is worth a few hundred pounds. It's not as much as I'd like, but I'll take what I can get.

I email a few rare-book dealers around London to get preliminary quotes. I don't want to waste my time visiting them in person if I'm not going to be paid. Then I check the time zone difference to see if it's okay to call Dad's nurses yet, since I can't once I get back to Hillingham.

A realization hits me like a bus: When my dad dies, I won't know. I'll be in hiding, with every line of communication cut. A scalpel dividing my life neatly in two, severing all that came before.

I honestly don't know how I feel about it, which somehow makes it all worse. My mom corrupted everything she touched, including my relationship with my dad. Maybe I should talk to him whenever I can over the next few days, but what would I say? I'd wish I hadn't called as soon as he picked up.

As always, when I start feeling like I'm a bad daughter, I slip my hand under the hem of my sweatshirt and trace the two tiny scars on either side of my abdomen.

No guilt, I remind myself.

Needing to kill some time and desperate to be anyone else for a while, I pull out Lucy's journal. The first line—*I cannot decide whether Quincey Morris is simple, or simply American*—makes me laugh out loud, which earns me puzzled looks from the other café patrons. I put my head down and keep reading.

"Lucy," I murmur, "I can't blame him. I think I'm in love with you, too."

I find myself rereading certain paragraphs. Lucy and I have so much in common. Both with terrible, controlling mothers pressuring us to have children. Both trapped in lives we can't extricate ourselves from despite all the privileges. Both practicing faces in front of a mirror so we can survive. I don't have three obnoxious suitors, so Lucy has me beat there. My mother certainly tried to force men on me, but even she quickly abandoned that pursuit and instead extolled the virtues of artificial insemination and unwed motherhood. As if I wanted that, either.

The next couple of entries are funny accounts of clumsy courting by the American cowboy. Lucy imagines a life of riding wild on the Texas frontier, unable to fathom why Quincey Morris would assume she'd be a good match for him. Even though she's still a teenager, barely nineteen at that point, Lucy was a good judge of character. She was keenly aware that when these men looked at her, they never saw *her,* merely whatever they wanted her to be to them.

After the cowboy interlude, there's a far more upsetting entry about the doctor. I've barely read anything about him, and he gives me the creeps.

"Girl," I mutter, "trust your gut." The doctor is every red flag that has ever existed. He tells Lucy that her mother's dying—I see myself in her mixed feelings, though mine are about my father—and then the creepy doctor straight up tries to drug Lucy. The tension of watching her carefully navigate his attempts to control her is making my stomach hurt.

"Mother is dying. I still cannot force my mind to accept the information. Mother is everywhere; Mother is infinite. Mother is the gravity of my whole life, keeping me chained to the earth, forever revolving around her. What will happen when gravity ceases its terrible tyranny? Will I float away? Will I shed my mortal coil and become nothing but light and happiness? Or will I be condemned to hell for these very thoughts?"

I trace her writing. It makes me impossibly sad for her, but also for myself. My own tyrannical mother's gravity is walled up now, and still I can't escape her. Not yet, at least. But soon. I hope Lucy escapes, too.

"Oh god," I mutter as I read what happens next. Lucy doesn't even get a chance to process her news. It's like the men are teaming up on her, making sure one always picks up where the other left off. Arthur is there waiting for her as soon as she gets home.

I know I'm a deeply suspicious person, and I've also read a *lot* of novels, but: Doctor Seward tells Lucy her mother is dying. Arthur's waiting for her as soon as she gets home. He suggests that they not only *don't* get a second opinion or a specialist to treat her, but that he should bring in his own solicitor to handle Lucy's estate.

"Lucy," I groan. I feel powerless. I know this all happened long ago, but Lucy's voice is so vibrant and real. I want to reach through the pages and save her.

My phone dings with a text, drawing my attention away from the journal. Thankfully it's Rahul, making sure I haven't been eaten by any foxes or wolves.

I have, actually, I text back. *But it's nice and warm in its stomach so I don't mind.*

Cozy, he responds, with a ball of yarn emoji.

My phone's fully charged now. Maybe it has been for a while; I've been lost in Lucy's words. Time to go. At least I have Elle to look forward to at the house. Except, *shit.* It's Friday. I can't expect her to work through the weekend. I'll make sure she knows I want her to come back on Monday, though. I get another coffee to go, then stop at a corner shop and buy a knife for my purse, plus a cute kettle. Not a wise investment for someone who plans on living in exile starting in a week, but it *is* a wise investment for someone who wants to keep Elle around as much as possible.

My phone rings with a London number. Hoping it's one of the bookshops, I answer.

"Miss Goldaming," says a pinching voice attached to a grasping crustacean of a man. I wish I hadn't answered. Mom's London solicitor continues without waiting for me to speak. "You asked me to inform you if the property in Whitby was open for viewing. I can confirm it isn't occupied this weekend."

"Oh." I'd totally forgotten about the other house. I doubt anything there is good for quick cash. But . . . it would be nice to get away from Hillingham for a day or two. Stay somewhere meant for human habitation. *And* it'll support my cover story that I'm checking out the properties here in order to list them. Might as well distract whoever is watching me from the fact that I'm essentially looting Hillingham. "Great! I'll head there this weekend."

"I can arrange transportation—" he starts, but I cut him off.

"Nope. Bye." I wouldn't get into a car arranged by that man if someone paid me. He'd probably be hiding in the trunk. In the middle of the night I'd waken to him sitting on my chest, pulling off little pieces of skin to shove in his mouth while talking about how long he's served my glorious family.

I look up transit options. I can get to Whitby via train. Another thing that'll eat into my dwindling funds. Maybe I shouldn't have splurged on such a pretty kettle, but I couldn't bear to buy Elle an ugly one.

When I get back to the house, she's tromping down the stairs, carrying a box. For the first time she looks disheveled, like she's in a mood as sour as the attic air probably is. Like she could use a weekend away, too.

"There's a leak in the roof," she says irritably. "Tons of water damage. This is all that's salvageable, and probably not even worth the effort it'll take to haul to a—"

She pauses, actually looking at me, and then sets the box down at the bottom of the stairs. "You're excited about something. Are any of the books winners?"

"No! Well, maybe. But the other property my family owns is available this weekend." Before I can talk myself out of it, I careen through the next sentences like they're a single thought. "If you aren't doing anything, do you want to come up with me, not as an appraiser or anything, just to get a break, because I don't know about you but I feel like this house is going to drive me crazy if I spend much more time here, plus the other house is a vacation rental so it will definitely have hot running water and a stove you don't need a PhD in history to start, plus I hear Whitby is really pretty?"

Elle's face had been increasingly amused until I got to the last sentence, at which point a cloud descends, cutting off the sunshine of her happiness.

"Oh. Whitby," she says. "That's a bad place."

38

Boston, September 26, 2024

CLIENT TRANSCRIPT

No, I didn't hear anything at the window, Vanessa. It's late, past midnight now. You're tired. Should we stop?

No? Then back to Paris.

There we were, on stage, and the Lover had just found what she was looking for. Instead of continuing our pattern of switching clubs almost as often as we switched hairstyles, the Lover insisted we go back to *that* one, every night.

I didn't mind. I wasn't paying much attention, fully besotted with a woman named Coral. Dimples everywhere: cheeks, wrists, elbows, knees. Dimples you could drown in. And her boyfriend, René, a perfect sprite of a man, lashes so long he looked sleepy all the time, jaw like he had been carved by the hands of the gods. I was besotted with him, too. Coral had a solo number each night where she slowly, luxuriously went from nude to clothed. I sat in the audience with René, clutching hands, both of us out of our minds with lust as we watched her.

Have you ever eaten the middle out of a fresh loaf of bread? Everything about it pleasurable, from reaching in and tearing a chunk free to chewing it? Coral was like that. René and I luxuriated in her, devoured her, lost ourselves in the pillowy, dense pleasure of her flesh.

So, as I said, I was distracted. One day as I was getting dressed, running my fingers along different material to see which felt most decadent, I noticed that our apartment was filled with flowers. They were all dried and dead, so there was no smell. That, and I didn't spend much time there, between the club and my various paramours and sleeping in the old culvert.

The flowers were everywhere. Bouquet after bouquet of them, all withered and desiccated. I asked the Lover where they had come from. She sighed dreamily, trailing a finger along one of the roses. Its petals fell, dark spots like dried blood on the floor.

"He leaves me gifts. Every night, a bouquet of flowers. And drawings. Look at his drawings of me!" She pointed to one of the tables haphazardly strewn around the space. The Lover and I were big on luxury—everything was silk and velvet, gilt and polished wood—but not big on cleaning, or on organizing.

I found a stack of drawings. My fingers twitched, remembering something lost long ago, but I didn't have time to think about it. I was looking at the Lover. Image after image of her, in every costume she'd worn since we'd started haunting that same club. Sometimes she was singing, sometimes she was dancing, but always, always, she looked *scared*. Her eyes never gazed directly out at the observer, cutting to the side instead. Like she couldn't see what was coming for her.

I had never seen the Lover look afraid. She was radiant on stage, a living smile. So why was this admirer drawing her that way?

"Who are these from?" I asked.

"Aren't they dreamy?" She took the drawings. "My face," she said, stroking them. "Me."

But it wasn't her real face. She had changed after that first time we woke up together. A rounder jaw, eyes tilted up at the corners instead of down, a slight swoop to the end of her nose. Like Dove, most vampires can change our appearance a little if we've had enough blood and enough rest, but the Lover was an artist at it.

Much more an artist than her admirer. I left her staring at his drawings and went back to choosing a dress. But the flowers bothered me. Had they been delivered dead, or did she leave them at the club until they were dried out and less noxious?

Unsettled and restless, I tore through the racks of clothes. I didn't want to wear anything I'd worn before. I wasn't even excited to see Coral and René. I wanted something new, something surprising, something to take my mind over. Behind the rows of hanging dresses were trunks I'd never looked in. I battled my way to them and opened the first.

The Lover stared up at me. I pulled out stacks and stacks of portraits, discarding papers like leaves falling from a dying tree. It was always the Lover, though her features were subtly changed in every set. To the unaware, she could have been a different girl each time. Just another beautiful face in a line of them, just another dancer on a stage.

No matter how the Lover's face changed, her expression never did. Always that fear. As I went down the stacks, the perspective got progressively closer. They always started as full-body portraits, the artist gazing from a distance. But the view crept up, eating the space around her, until at last it was only her eyes. Finally turned to look directly out, no longer terrified, but blank and lifeless.

There was a pattern. It had happened before, and it was happening again.

I was an idiot to have chalked up that first night to random violence. I rushed out to the sitting room, but the Lover was already gone. I grabbed the newest stack of art. There, at the bottom. Her dead, empty eyes.

Out in the night, the city didn't seem to gleam with twinkling lights and winking invitations. Every shadow held eyes, watching. Waiting. But I had an advantage. I might not have much sense, but I have excellent senses. The Lover's scent wasn't hard to find. All the vampires I'd met had a metallic *clang,* a smell like accidentally biting down on a fork.

The Lover's scent was softer than most, but I still caught it. I hurried through the night, afraid for her but also not quite sure *why* I was afraid. Maybe because I had too much information and not enough time to properly sort through it all.

She was being stalked. She had been stalked before. But it seemed like she knew her stalker, or at least knew when it was starting. So why did it keep happening?

I stopped so abruptly a couple behind me stumbled into my back. I didn't pay attention to their shock as they bounced off tiny me and I stayed ramrod straight. *Nearby.* There was a heart racing with pleasure, a cry of surprise, and—

Blood spilled. Old, borrowed blood.

Blurring with speed through the streets, I turned three more corners and found her. I should have known from the start. It was the same alley where he had gutted me my first night in Paris. And there was the Lover. Laid out on the ground like she was asleep, tucked into a ball with her hands beneath her chin. Three holes in her back. Her stomach split open like a smile. And her skull bashed in—except for her eyes. Those he had carefully left open, staring out lifelessly. Just like in the final drawing.

This time it was my turn to take her to unhallowed ground. Instead of dragging, I carried her as gently as I would a child. I laid her down in the culvert, packing the grave dirt around her. And then I waited.

It took several days, but at last she healed enough to wake up. She gazed into my eyes and sighed, a smile on her face. Like she'd been in the middle of the loveliest dream. Which I knew wasn't right, because we don't dream.

"Who is he?" I asked. "Who did this?"

She laughed. "I don't know. I never see his face. But I always know when he's found me again, when our dance is starting anew. I can hear his heart and the rush of his blood."

"How many times has he killed you?"

She laughed again, the sound as simple and charming as children at play. "Oh, ever so many! Think of all the girls I've saved, all the victims I've taken the place of. We've been dancing together for years. I become a new woman, I get on a stage, and I wait. He finds me, courts me from afar, and then kills me. It's like being in love, the way he watches me. The tender, obsessive care he devotes to following me, to getting closer and closer until, at last, he's right behind me. Then he takes me in his arms and carves his feelings into me."

Don't look at me like that, Vanessa. I'm just quoting her. I'm perfectly aware it's fucked up. Should I go on? Yes? Okay.

I made my voice as gentle as I could. "My darling, he isn't courting you. He's stalking and murdering you. Or at least, he thinks he's murdering you. That's not love."

"Isn't it? Doesn't love make us obsess? Doesn't love make us change ourselves to try and hold their attention? Doesn't love make them want to change us, want to make us theirs, forever? To put us out of reach of anyone else? Didn't it feel like love, when *he* made you his?"

If I'd had enough blood in me, it would have run cold. "Who?" I asked.

"Dracula, of course. I smelled him in you the moment we met. Didn't you smell him in me?"

That was what drew us together. That was the scent I could always find. Not just any vampire. One of *his* vampires. One of his girls.

Which meant the Doctor had been killed by him, too. How many of us were there, wandering the earth?

"I didn't know," I whispered. Was I still searching for him without realizing it, even knowing he was dead?

The Lover took my hands, holding my gaze with steadfast burning in her own. "Dracula saw me when no one else did. He remade me in his image, to his liking. He claimed me, and made it so he'd never have to let me go. It was like love. As close as I'd ever felt." Her eyes went far away and as blank as the dead. "But then he let me go. He let you go, too. And he still hasn't come back for us."

I wanted to tell her what the Queen's spies had discovered. Dracula was dead. He was never coming for either of us. But that hadn't stopped her from looking for him in the arms of a serial killer, and it hadn't stopped me from sniffing out the remains of his poison held in other vampires. We were both still desperate for answers he would never give us.

"I got lost," the Lover said. "The first time I visited that borderland between life and death. I got lost, and I never found my way out. Not fully into death, and not fully back into life. I've been between ever since. But my admirer, he lets me relive it. Lets me twirl closer to that border once again. Lets me claw through those shadows, trying to catch a glimpse of the other side. One of these times, I know it—one of these times, I'll see past the border. I'll know what's waiting for us. He'll show it to me. Because he sees me, and he cares. Because *he* keeps coming back for me, no matter what."

I had never noticed before, but the Lover was well and truly insane. With vampires, it's a fine line between reason and madness. We all tiptoe along it. She just tiptoed firmly on the wrong side *all* the time, rather than *some* of the time, like I do.

But what devastated me was that I really did understand her. The Lover desired above all else to be coveted and claimed.

I had let Raven touch me and control me. I had let the Queen hold me captive. I had let the Doctor use me as one of her tools. And I had let the Lover spin me into her glittering web of madness and hedonism.

What would I give, to be seen? To be carefully studied and perfectly understood? Would I let someone carve me up, if it meant feeling like

I was loved? I knew the answer was yes, because it had *always* been yes. I had let others bleed me dry for the sake of feeling wanted, even before Dracula came into my life. I wasn't any different from the Lover. Staring into a face I adored and finding only pathetic need and madness, my questions shifted. I no longer cared why Dracula had killed and changed me.

I wondered why I had let it happen.

39

August 7, 1890

JOURNAL OF LUCY WESTENRA

Mina nearly caught me hiding my journal the other night. I had just tucked it away beneath the window seat when she sat up. I pretended to be sleepwalking, and let her lead me back to bed. She sat next to me and petted my hair like she used to. I could have died, I was so happy.

But then she went to her own bed, and in the morning told my mother I'd begun sleepwalking. Which led Mother to fretting. My father used to wander in his sleep. He would leave the house and disappear for hours at a time. Until the night he never came back.

When I was younger, I believed that story. I believed that he would dream himself upright, dream himself dressed, dream himself unlocking the door and setting out on a regular errand. As though his sleeping body was merely pantomiming his waking one.

But that wasn't true. Awake or asleep—and I don't believe he was asleep—he was trying to escape. Was it desire that drove him out? Or was he simply eager to get as far away from Mother and me as he could?

~~It will be desire that drives me out. My soul itches, crawling with ants as I try to lie still with Mina so close. I want to go to her. Take her in my arms. Kiss her not like the kisses we shared when I was younger, but something deeper, hungrier, full of need and want and~~

I must get out of this house before I do something I cannot take back.

Arthur came to visit today. It was agony, pretending to be happy to see him, pretending to care about anything he had to say, pretending I was not counting down the seconds until he left once more. Mina excused herself to give us time alone. If she has nothing to say to him and is allowed to leave, why am I not?

I did see them speaking in the hallway right before he left, when I was supposed to be changing for a walk. They were standing close, their conversation hushed and intense. When I asked Mina about it, she laughed and said she was certain now that he loves me as well as I deserve to be loved. He had been asking about all my favorite things so that once we are wed he can make me happy.

Mina. Mina is my only favorite thing.

Now Arthur's gone again, but all Mina wants to do is talk about my wedding. She says I should wed as soon as possible, so that we can be married ladies together and plan our homes. Though she noted that my own future home prospects are much brighter than hers. She and Jonathan will be quite poor as he slowly takes on more of the duties of his employer.

I told her she can live with me and have anything of mine, hoping she would say yes. Hoping she would understand that when I say she can have anything of mine she wants, I mean me. She can have me. But she laughed and said the time for me to buy her lovely gifts has passed, as she is now my friend, not my governess. And then—

And then she said our time of being together like this is nearly at an end. She sighed and smiled and seemed perfectly content.

It was a knife to the heart. I recognized her tone and expression. Because it's the same way I feel about Mother dying. Mina's not upset by our impending separation. It will be a relief to her. She does not love me, not the way I love her. She never has, and she never will.

I panicked.

"Live with me," I insisted. "We'll keep house together. You can buy anything you need, anything you want. We don't have to get married! We can stay as we are forever." I grasped her hand, but she did not answer by squeezing my fingers back.

"You don't understand anything about me." Her voice was so cold I dropped her hand and wrapped my arms around myself. "I have no desire to stay as I am. You have no idea what it is to be poor. I don't want my comfort to depend on your affection for me. To be forever kept by you, subject to your whims, with no legal rights to anything. Can you not see how cruel that is, Lucy? How unfair? I'm going to make my own way. To make certain I'm never dependent on anyone. My fortune will be my own, and it will be a fortune I make for myself."

"I'm sorry," I gasped, doing my best not to cry, because then she would chide me for trying to manipulate her, as she always did when I cried over little things. "I was teasing, of course. Can you imagine such a thing, us keeping house together? I would drive you mad, always leaving my little paintings lying around, half finished. I suspect you would murder me."

Mina laughed. "I could never murder you, silly creature." Then she relaxed and held my hand once more as we walked.

I didn't say that she is going to be kept by Jonathan, subject to his whims, dependent forever on him. His whims have far less money behind them than mine do, and his odds of delivering her a fortune are minimal, while mine are guaranteed. I didn't say anything else on the subject, and I didn't cry, or beg, or confess my love.

But I can't stay in this room with her sleeping so nearby. ~~I want to tear out my hair, to fling myself onto her bed, into her arms, to beg her to make new secrets with me between the press of our lips. I want to devour her, and I want her to look at me and want me, and I want her to see that she has never really seen *me* at all, and I want her to *want* to see me. All of me.~~ I want and I want and I want and none of it matters. None of it changes anything.

I'll walk in the dark to the ocean, and maybe it—the ocean or the darkness, it matters not—will fill me.

40

Whitby, October 6, 2024

IRIS

Elle's so quiet and still the entire train ride, I worry she's gone catatonic or something.

I can't understand why she agreed to come at all, since clearly she hates Whitby. I might have jumped the gun by inviting her. *Wanting* to know someone and *actually* knowing them are very different things.

The train lasts forever. I left Lucy's journal in the safe out of fear that something might happen to it, and I miss her like she's my best friend.

I stare out the window as we pass an ancient viaduct. Lucy said something about Whitby in one of her entries, I think. I wonder what she thought of it. If she loved it there. If it felt like an escape from oppressive Hillingham.

If her traveling companion was so still and white she might as well have been carved from stone.

But as soon as we step off the train, something loosens in Elle. Her expression softens. She takes in the city, curled and sprawling along the coast. "It hasn't changed," she says. "I thought it would feel different, but it doesn't."

Given that she told me it was a bad place, I would have assumed that was a bad thing, but she laughs and links her arm through mine. I'm surprised, but also relieved. Maybe she gets trainsick, or maybe she was dealing with something I'm not privy to. But I no longer regret inviting her as she guides me out of the train station.

We aim for a narrow lane winding through the charming old harbor. The west side of Whitby is newer urban sprawl, but the east side looks frozen in time, and that's where we're headed.

Eastern Whitby is built into hills and cliffs overlooking the ocean, nestled in between lush grass, towering rock, and waiting ocean. The houses are mostly redbrick and whitewashed boards, all with the same reddish-orange roofs. They follow the organic lines of the land so well that they almost look natural. On a hill looming over everything is a weathered stone castle, or maybe a church. I didn't do any research before we came, which was probably a mistake. But so far, I'm charmed by Whitby. It doesn't strike me as a bad place at all.

The charm fades a bit when I check my phone's map. The house isn't along the harbor or beach walk, but rather in the hills. There are numerous walkways and infinite stairs winding up, so it won't be hard to get to. Just annoying.

"Tea!" Elle chirps. "I'll be right out." She darts into a tiny shop. I walk onto a pier and lean against the railing, staring down at the dark water. It's quiet here, a marked difference to the bustle of London. There's old and busy, and then there's old and sleepy. Whitby is the latter.

Elle returns and hands me a cup of coffee. There's a brisk wind coming off the ocean. Even though it's sunny, I wish I had brought a heavier jacket. At least Elle thoughtfully got me a hot drink. I hold the cup between my hands and breathe in the steam. Elle holds her tea the same way, staring down at it as though she can read her fortune through the lid.

"My dad died in Whitby," she says without preamble.

I choke on a mouthful of coffee. Once I have that under control, I turn to her. "Oh my god. What? I'm so sorry." No wonder she was distant and withdrawn on the train!

Elle's gaze shifts, sweeping over the harbor before resting on the cliffs in the distance. "It was a long time ago. I wasn't allowed to feel what I needed to feel about it, though. *Anger isn't a pretty emotion,* my mom always said. My grief became a wound that never healed. But now I know I'm allowed to feel what I need to. What I want to. And standing here, I can at last acknowledge my anger. He wasn't around to protect me from my mother anymore, and I resented him for abandoning me *and* for escaping. Which I know is an odd way to look at a tragic death, but that's what it felt like. That he got away, and I was stuck."

I don't want to be the person who answers someone's intimate emotional offering with my own trauma, but I do want Elle to know I understand. I lean a little closer so our arms are touching. "My dad didn't protect me from my mom, either. I'm sorry you went through that, and I'm especially sorry you weren't allowed to grieve how you needed to. Is it too hard for you to be here, though? You don't have to stay."

Elle's eyes find the building at the top of the cliff and linger there, like she's searching for something. She doesn't smile, but her face is open when she looks at me again. "No, this is good. It's good for me to be back here, to face the person I was when so much changed forever. I think part of me got stuck in those moments, you know what I mean? Like I'm still there. Like I never left. But standing here in the sunlight, I can finally forgive who I was then for everything that she did, and for everything that happened to her."

I squeeze her arm. I don't have anything to say, but I want her to know I support her, and I'm here for her. I have that same sense I get with poetry, that someone is saying something I've always felt but never been able to express. I'm a little choked up.

Then a smile as sly as a cat slinks across Elle's face. "Besides, I'm excited to see your disappointment when you figure out why Whitby is favored by the geriatric crowd. There's *nothing* to do here except walk around and say, 'Oh, this is nice,' and talk with people about the weather. It's windy. What else is there to talk about?"

I laugh and lean against the railing to look up at the cliffs. "It *is* nice, though."

"So nice."

"And windy."

"So windy!" Elle laughs, brushing her hair out of her face. My own curls are an impossible tangle already.

I'm relieved that Elle seems happy, and I'm quietly thrilled that I gave her this opportunity. Maybe this trip won't be the flirty diversion I had hoped for, but . . . this is better. I'm surprised to find I'd rather help Elle than spend a couple days looking for opportunities to make out with her. It's been so long since I connected with anyone on more than a safely superficial level. It feels nice. It also feels dangerous, but I ignore the warning bells in my head.

We stroll along the oceanfront, investigating various tourist-trap shops. I finish my coffee and throw the cup away, Elle tossing hers in after. She takes my hand, hers deliciously warm against my clammy skin, and pulls me toward an art shop.

"Look!" she says, pointing excitedly at the window.

"Mm." I put on my best museum face, where I pretend like I'm thoughtful and interested and have any idea what I'm looking at. I point to one particularly dull seascape, my gesture following the lines of the crudely painted sailboat. "You can really see the influences of the Ennui movement in the lack of any visual interest."

Elle laughs, the chiming tones bouncing off the stone street beneath us and the brick buildings around us. I'm surrounded in the best possible way.

"My little cabbage," she says, "I meant look at the *frames.* Seem familiar?"

"Oh! Yes. They look like the frames from the house."

"Exactly. That's why I'm sure I can sell them for a premium. That, and the very prestigious Ennui movement, of course."

"Of course." We grab fish and chips—just chips for poor allergy-prone Elle—and she sits on a bench to eat while I stand on the pier. I stare out past the protected harbor to the wild ocean beyond, wishing I could take a boat and disappear into the vast blue. Wondering where I'll disappear to, when I get the chance. It all depends on how much money I make.

Elle's already finished and waiting for me when I turn around. "You ready?" She points to the stairs leading up into the hills. "Race you!"

"Absolutely the fuck not." I laugh as she ignores me and darts up. I'm reminded again of a cat, the same way I was when she weaved through the crowd after saving me. I could watch her move for the rest of my life and never tire of her playful grace.

Calm your tits, Iris, I think. We only have a few more days together.

I navigate the stairs much more slowly than she does, eventually catching up to her on the hill immediately below the castle thing. "What is that?" I ask, pretending I'm not out of breath, because she isn't.

"A church and the ruins of an old abbey. We can go up there if you want?" She doesn't seem enthused by the idea, which is a relief. I don't want to climb any more stairs.

"Let's find the house so we can drop our stuff." As always, I brought everything with me in my trusty running-away backpack, and it isn't exactly light. Elle has a much slimmer backpack on.

She glances at the map on my phone and takes off down one of the narrow lanes branching away from the stairs. "Found it!" she calls.

The house, redbrick, white boards, and red roof, is at the end of the lane on the edge of the hill. The small back garden slopes down sharply, so that when you're standing where I am it looks like there's nothing beyond the yard but the infinite cold ocean. It's an absolutely killer view. I wish I could sell this house, or even move into it, because *damn.*

Did Lucy stand here and look out? Did it fill her heart and soul? It makes me feel closer to her, being here. Like I might open the door and hear her laughing, inviting me in for tea and gossip.

When I reach the front, though, I see they've cut the house in half to make it a duplex. I doubt it was that way when Lucy stayed here. I unlock the door on the near side first. I'm greeted with a hint of salt cut by filtered, circulated air. The narrow entryway has stairs leading to the second floor and a hallway back to the rest of the house. The floors are tasteful tile, the walls white, all charm and character smoothed out to make it as blandly appealing as possible. There are a few kitschy items—a glass table with driftwood legs and a mirror framed with shells—but nothing of the old owners remains. Lucy's definitely not waiting here for me.

I set the key down on the table. By design, nothing here will be easy to steal and sell. I'd expected as much, but I'm still a little disappointed. I glance over my shoulder to find Elle lingering on the doorstep, her back to me like she's considering continuing up the hill.

"You coming in?" I ask.

"Just thinking about what the sunset will look like from up there." She turns and steps inside, taking in the house with a single dismissive sweep. "This is dull."

"It really is, isn't it?"

"I hate it when they chop old houses in half like this. It kills the flow and the soul." She walks straight through. The kitchen is against the wall between the duplexes, probably to save on plumbing. It's all chrome and white, a small table crammed in next to the back windows. There's a family room, too, with stiff couches, a TV with laminated instructions on how to use the remotes, and a shelf with a handful of books doubtless left by previous vacationers. Sure enough, all I see are paperback thrillers and romance. I miss Lucy's journal.

All along the back of the house are windows that frame the ocean more beautifully than any of my antique gilded frames back at Hillingham. I can forgive the blank canvas of the remodel. The view is the point, anyway.

I follow Elle upstairs and resent the romance novels downstairs, which I'm sure feature the best trope: *Oh no, there's only one bed!* There are two main suites here. Elle leaves her stuff in one of the bedrooms and I take the other. There's nothing remarkable about either. They could be any bedroom anywhere, except for the views. I can see the abbey ruins from here.

"What happened to the abbey?" I shout.

Elle comes in, joining me at the window. "It burned down or something, I think. I don't know. It was too boring to pay attention to."

"I thought you were a historian," I tease.

"Well, I wasn't when I was a little girl. There's a graveyard up there, too."

"Ooh, I love old graveyards!"

Elle gives me a baffled look. "You say that with the excitement of a five-year-old being told they're visiting the zoo."

"It's just so fascinating, right? What we do with our dead says so much about us culturally. What we value. What we fear. So, like, in America we're not content with merely preying on people while they're alive by telling them they're not thin enough, pretty enough, rich enough, healthy enough, safe enough." My family is evidence of how lucrative that is. "No, we also have this predatory industry around funerals and death. When people are grieving and vulnerable, they're told that not only should they pick an expensive casket, but they should also pay for an outer casket, so that the thing designed to hold your body and go into the ground is protected from *the ground.* And you can't just cremate someone, they have to be in a casket in order to be cremated. Heaven forbid you leave this world without someone being able to cash in on it. And then just burial in general. Why are we filling bodies with chemicals and then sealing them away from the natural processes of decay? They're dead. Let them go back to the earth that nourished them. Instead, we preserve an already dead body—for what?—and then plant stones above them in a mockery of oh my god, I need to stop talking, don't I."

Elle's dimples betray her smile even if her lips are held perfectly neutral. "No, this is interesting. But don't you think there's meaning in remembering the dead?"

"Asks the historian! That's a trap of a question. Obviously there's meaning in it. When people die, they become memories. They become stories. And those have value. But their dead bodies? Not so much. But that's just my opinion. What do you think?"

"Honestly? I find graveyards quite uninspiring."

"So, you *don't* want to do a midnight tour." Normally I'd be up for one, but today I'm relieved. Last night I was so tired I slept ten hours straight. No moonlight interruptions, but my dreams were restless and upsetting. Nothing but being pursued by shadowy figures. I woke up feeling even worse.

"No, I definitely don't. I'm going to go for a walk now. You can join, if you want." The way Elle says it, I suspect she wants some time alone. She probably needs it, too, processing her feelings about Whitby and what happened here.

"Thanks, but I'm going to take the longest, hottest shower in the history of showers, and then I'm going to bed. I know that's boring."

"That's what Whitby's for! Being dull old ladies. I'll take a walk in the sea air for my health, and you can retire to bed before the sun sets. We'll blend right in. Just be sure to pay attention to the weather so we have something to talk about in the morning."

I laugh and remind her to take the keys so she doesn't have to worry about how long she stays out. And then I stay mostly true to my word. After my shower, my skin bright red from my attempt to steam myself alive, I investigate the house to see if there's an attic. Sure enough, I find an opening in my closet ceiling. My phone's meager light reveals that the attic extends the entire length of the pre–duplex remodel house. But it's empty. There's nothing to see, and nothing to sell.

Still, I can't regret this Whitby detour. It was good for Elle, and that has value for me. Plus, the shower was divine. Clean and exhausted and feeling like an ancient old crone going to bed with the sun, I lie down and close my eyes.

I open them. It feels like someone's weighted them with coins. My mother's outside the window, staring at me, silent and furious. Somewhere in the house I hear crying. They both want me to go to them, but I stay where I am, curled in the bed, trying to ignore it all. I have a book of poetry—no, it's Lucy's journal—but I can't read the words. They all blend and blur together. No matter how hard I try, I can't understand her.

"Lucy!" I shout. That's who's crying. She needs me. I have to find her; I have to help her.

I struggle so hard to move that I pull myself out of the dream. The room is dark around me, and I struggle to ground myself in reality. My mother's not outside the window, because it's the second story of the Whitby house. Lucy's not in danger. She's not alive anymore. And neither is my fucking mom.

I'm just on the edge of consciousness, about to slip back under, when something pounces on the end of my bed. My scream tears through the night as eyes flash at me in the dark.

41

August 8, 1890

JOURNAL OF LUCY WESTENRA

I never made it outside. The horizon roiled and crashed, reaching for us with foggy, clinging fingers. Even as high up on the hill as we are, I half wondered if the ocean would claim us. I half wanted it to. I was ready to greet it.

Mina caught me getting dressed to go out and stand in the chaos. The storm called to me. It felt familiar, the same as I feel inside with her so close and yet so far away. I pretended to be sleepwalking again and let her put me back to bed.

But I missed everything! Today on our walk to survey the damage, we heard tales of an enormous escaped dog, a ghost ship slamming into the harbor, and the death of one of the old men who pesters me whenever I'm out walking—he fell and broke his neck while sitting on my favorite bench! I'll be furious if he haunts it, though unsurprised he could find a way to make me listen to his stories even after death.

That's unkind of me. The poor man is dead.

But I don't care. I'm not feeling kind, or sweet, or happy. Mina wants to attend the funeral of the captain of the ghost ship (his dead body was found tied to the helm!), which will suit my mood as well as anything else. I'm tired of Whitby. I'm miserable, I want this to be over, and I also never want to leave. Is this how prisoners condemned to death feel?

Poor Arthur. I'm comparing our impending marriage to being condemned to death. He doesn't deserve me. What a wretched wife I will be.

We settled on September for the wedding. Next month! I can't breathe when I think about it too much, but I may as well get it over with.

Mina's cross, too, more worried each day she doesn't hear from Jonathan. She's received no letters from him, though she sends out ever so many. I've peeked over her shoulder. Most of her missives are written in her shorthand code. When I asked her why, she startled, then smoothed her face into a smile.

"Because it's faster," she said.

Mina's keeping secrets, and I cannot even be intrigued. She's keeping them from me, not with me. I can feel her getting farther away, like a storm receding. No amount of wishing will keep her here. I know she doesn't love me—I've given up that foolish dream. Could anyone ever love me as much as I love them?

Arthur was supposed to visit again, but his father is ill so he sent his regrets. Maybe his father will be ill on our wedding date, and Arthur will send his regrets, and I can—

I can what? Nothing. Mina will be married. It doesn't matter. Nothing matters. Mina is asleep. I'm going to walk in the night, where I can make whatever expressions I want, where I can be nothing because no one expects anything from me.

Except, there—

Out the window! I think I have just seen the missing dog. It looked more like a wolf, though, tremendous and frightening. Perhaps I won't go out tonight, either.

Boston, September 26, 2024

CLIENT TRANSCRIPT

Naturally you're questioning my phrasing when I say that I "let" Dracula kill me. After all, the Lucy that Dracula found was a child.

But she was also a fool. A sad, lost, confused little fool. When Dracula came to her, when he pursued her with relentless fixation, it really did seem like love. Or at least like being wanted. Not for money, or looks, or status. But for her whole self.

I speak of that Lucy in the third person because she *feels* like another person. Like a dream barely remembered. That Lucy, tragically young, had never been her whole self with anyone. That much I recall. But Dracula didn't care about any of it. He wanted me regardless.

It wasn't romantic. I never felt affection or attraction for Dracula. He terrified me. It's horrible in ways even now I can't let myself think about, lest I tip over that careful line of sanity and never come back.

I wonder, though. Whether I wanted what happened, one way or another. I hadn't wanted to *die,* but had I really wanted to keep living my life? Because Dracula didn't choose me, not at first. He wanted Mina.

I put myself in front of him on purpose. I offered myself up to him willingly. And I didn't fight tooth and nail to get away once he started, because by then it felt inevitable. I was always going to be devoured by an uncaring man; it was just a far quicker, more violent draining.

So, I couldn't judge the Lover for her choices. By being her stalker's victim over and over, she was saving countless Parisian dancers from the same fate. Did that make her noble? I thought it might.

And so I took the Lover home, and we kept dancing in circles. The same routines with different costumes and backdrops. Coral and René became Marie, then Adelaide and Pierre, then Josephine.

While I was finding beautiful women and men, trying not to feel so empty all the time, I watched the Lover's own endless cycle. She went through it four, five, a dozen more times. I tried to talk her out of it, tried to scare her—what if he decided to dump her body in the river? What if he decided to burn her? But she never listened.

Then one night I found a body in the familiar alley. Three stab wounds in the back. Gutted in the front. Her skull half smashed in, carefully leaving her eyes staring blank and unseeing. But the blood was fresh. It was a different girl, another dancer, an innocent who couldn't ever wake up again. And I was livid.

The Lover was a fool, just like I had been. I hadn't *saved* Mina by offering myself to Dracula. I died and left her alone, and he stalked her anyway. The only reason she survived was because the men in her life made the right choices to protect her. Because she was smarter and stronger and better than me. Because she deserved to survive in ways I never had.

I gently carried the dead dancer to our apartment and laid her on the chaise longue. The Lover, busy pinning up her hair, glanced over in confusion and disapproval.

"Lucy," she said, "we don't kill people!"

"We don't," I agreed. "But your paramour does. You aren't saving women by being his victim. You need to *stop* him, not pause him." I was angrier with myself than with her, really. I'd let myself be killed as though that was the only way I could protect Mina. It had been worthless. Meaningless. A sacrifice no one asked for or needed.

"Oh, Lucy," she said with a sigh, sitting next to the corpse and brushing the girl's hair back into place. "It doesn't matter, does it? None of it matters. Not really."

"It *has* to matter. *She* has to matter." Because if she didn't, nothing did. I walked out. I was never going back to that apartment. Paris was poisoned for me.

But I wouldn't simply disappear. I waited, and I watched. I stalked the Lover from audiences, just like he did. And the next time she went electric with anticipation, the next time she glowed with the thrill of being seen and desired, I paid attention.

He worked doing filing, paperwork, and the occasional suspect sketch art for the police. There was something dry and lifeless about him, skin flaking around his nostrils, scalp splotchy beneath his thinning hair. His eyes were his only lively feature. They had the intensity of a rodent, hyperalert, always watching. He didn't see me, though. Not until it was too late.

I wasn't like him. I didn't make a production of his death. I didn't even bite him; I wanted no part of him in me. I snapped his neck and then dumped his worthless body in the Seine.

I knew the Lover would be on stage, frantic with hope. I took away the one thing my friend looked forward to. The one thing that kept her going, that made her infinite afterlife worthwhile. And I didn't tell her I'd done it, because I *wanted* her to keep waiting and hoping. It was pathetic. I hated her for it, because I hated myself for the same thing.

We were fools, throwing our bodies in front of men because that was the only way we could ever feel like we mattered.

And so, having at least saved a few of the beautiful dancers who had distracted me in such lovely ways, I left Paris. I thought the Lover incapable of revenge; I was wrong about that.

Whitby, October 7, 2024

IRIS

"Iris, it's me!"

Elle's voice. Elle on my bed.

She scrambles off and hits the lights. There's no one else in here. My window's free of floating mothers, and no one is crying. No one needs me to find them and save them. Which is probably for the best, because I'm doing a shit job of saving myself at the moment.

Elle's flush with embarrassment. "I didn't mean to scare you! I thought you were awake. You said my name."

I put my hand over my still-racing heart. "It's okay. Actually, it's good that you woke me up. I was having a bad dream. What time is it?"

"Midnight." Elle grins at me, radiating mischief. "Do you trust me?"

"Yes." My lack of hesitation surprises me. I've learned not to trust anyone. But whether I actually trust her or I just want whatever she's about to offer with no questions asked, I mean it. "Wait, *are* we doing a midnight cemetery tour?"

"Better. I promise. Get dressed."

I do as I'm told, noting that she doesn't bother leaving the room as I pull off my oversized T-shirt and pull on ripped black jeans, a tank top, and the only jacket I packed, a black hoodie so old it feels like a friend. I want to check and see if she's watching me, but I also want to be cool and casual so it looks like I don't care either way.

God, Elle's turning me into a teenager again.

Elle and I stumble up the hilly stairs in the dark, laughing whenever we miss a step. She leads me higher and higher until we come to the top of the cliffs. In the distance is the ruined abbey, a darker smudge against the moonlit sky. And *inside* the ruined abbey are strobing lights.

"Secret midnight rave!" Elle declares, triumphant. "Whitby isn't as boring as it used to be!" She grabs my hand and we run along the path, heedless of rocks or tripping hazards. The wind is in a fury and storm clouds are massing on the horizon, but for now we have the light of the moon, and it's enough.

Something is missing as we get closer, though. Shouldn't we hear it by now? I want the thump of bass, the overwhelming vibration of the music. But the reason why is obvious when we arrive at the entrance to the abbey grounds. Not only are the lights all kept low to the floor so they're not visible from the houses below, but the music isn't going to attract any attention.

A young man made of nothing but bones and skin flicks his eyes at us. We must pass some test, because he gives us two sets of wireless headphones. "No noise, no cops," he says simply. Then he holds out his hand.

Elle covers me, for which I'm grateful. Then we're inside. It's surreal, watching all these bodies moving in silent coordination, dancing to a beat we don't hear. In a rush of bleakness so familiar it steals my breath, I feel lost and starkly alone.

Isn't this my whole life? Everyone else experiencing one reality, and me stuck on the outside of it?

I smash the headphones over my ears. Problem solved. Elle flashes me a giddy thumbs-up and we jump into the fray. I lose her for a bit in the press of bodies. When I find her again, she's dancing in a wild, frantic way. Still with her catlike grace, but with a borderless, uninhibited energy that I remember from my club days. She definitely took something. I've seen a few tablets passed around, small baggies exchanged.

I wish I could participate, could really let go. But I have to maintain absolute control at all times. If I don't, I'm afraid I'll never get it back.

I don't blame Elle, though. I hope it helps her work through her bad memories. I stay close, dancing and laughing and relishing the moments when our bodies are moving together. It's nice to see tea-loving historian Elle turn into a new version of herself. Her fluid movements, the sharp grace that makes it look like she's half dancing, half ready to attack whoever is near her, is entrancing. I've been into Elle since the moment we met, but tonight she's not just beautiful and charming. She's *devastatingly* sexy.

I shoulder aside a few people trying to take my place. I don't want to make a pass at her—it would be taking advantage, given how emotionally (and probably chemically) vulnerable Elle is right now—but I can't not be close to her. I *have* to be close to her. To keep an eye on her, yes, but also because it's a physical need. An ache inside me that promises it'll go away if I can just—

Just what? Seduce her? Make her love me? Make her mine? I can't do any of that. It would be unfair to her. She deserves better. And besides, I'll never treat a person like a goal. Or worse, like a vending machine for my own desires.

I'm returning from grabbing a water bottle for us when I see a guy, more muscle than man, grab Elle by the waist. He lifts her up like because she's small, he's entitled to do whatever he wants to her body.

"Hey!" I shout, but no one, including him, can hear me. I throw the water bottle at his face. It bounces off his forehead and he drops Elle.

Her pupils are dilated, eyes flashing with panic or fear or anger, I can't tell which. But I know what I'm feeling. I grab the guy by his enormous arms, pull him close, and knee him right between the legs.

He goes down with a howl loud enough that I hear it over the music. And then he glares at me with all the rage a shriveled soul in a muscled body can hold. Elle looks like she's about to do something crazy, too, so I rip off my headphones and chuck them at his face. Then I snag Elle's arm. This time I'm the one with catlike grace, tugging her along as I dodge between dancing bodies. I spy a passageway through a fallen wall. We duck in it, pressing our backs against the bricks, waiting.

Waiting.

I turn my face toward hers. She's watching me, expression unreadable.

"Sorry," I say. "I know you can handle yourself. I'm pretty sure you were about to royally fuck him up anyway. But in my defense, it was *my* turn to save *you*."

Her eyes are as dark as the night around us, but her smile is like starlight. "It's been a long time since anyone tried to defend my honor."

I bow. "M'lady, I solemnly swear I will knee every sack of balls that comes between your honor and me, forever."

"You are *so* strange." Her laughter is cut short by the roar of rage behind us in the abbey. The guy is shouting, demanding to know if anyone saw where we went.

I grab Elle's hand and we run into the graveyard, laughing as we weave among the headstones. We're both distracted, barely paying attention to where we are, constantly darting glances over our shoulders to check for pursuit. Half because we're scared, and half because it's hilarious.

A flash of lightning illuminates our path. "Stop!" I scream. I barely pull us to a halt at the cliff's edge, nothing between us and the ocean below but empty, cold air.

"Oh my god," Elle gasps. "Oh my god. I'm so sorry. I had no idea how far we'd gone." She turns to me, frantic, putting her hand on my cheek, on my chest, on my shoulder, checking to make certain I'm still beside her and not plummeting to my death. "Are you okay?"

"I'm okay. I'm okay! But it's about to start—"

The rain hits us with startling intensity, pouring down from the sky as the clouds move directly overhead. Elle stares upward, her face so white it glows, her expression horrified. I'm about to laugh when I realize there's something more to this. Either she's remembering something, or she has a genuine phobia about storms. *Or* the drugs have fully kicked in, and not in a good way.

I can't stay out in this rain either, though. It's already chilly enough that my heart rate is ticking up. I haven't been careful. I wasn't prepared for cold. Every time I experience it, I have to wonder: Is this it? The chill that will trigger my end?

Not tonight. I refuse to let it be tonight.

There's nothing around us but headstones, no shelter. I don't want to return to the abbey and risk running into our roided-out foe. The church isn't too far, though. I guide Elle in that direction. We run together, heads ducked against the lashing rain. The church is locked, but we find a deep doorway and huddle there, sheltered from the wind and the rain.

Elle's shaking like she's going to vibrate right out of her body. I put my arms around her, holding her close, stroking her hair. "It's just a storm," I tell her.

"I should never have come here," she says, teeth chattering. "I'll never find my way back out."

"It'll pass. We'll wait right here together, and it'll pass. I've got you. I promise."

She nods, burying her face in my shoulder. So she doesn't see what I do: a pair of glowing eyes among the gravestones, watching us.

I bare my teeth in defiance, daring it to show itself. There's a blinding flash of lightning. When my vision clears again, the eyes have disappeared. The night keeps its secrets. And I keep mine, too, as Elle trembles against me and I murmur soothing nonsense, knowing full well I'm putting us both in danger.

Tomorrow, I'll drive her away forever. It's the only way I can keep my promise to protect her.

44

August 10, 1890
JOURNAL OF LUCY WESTENRA

At the funeral today there was a dog.

Large and gray with eyes that looked ageless, twin dark pools of experience he didn't have the language to share. He was sitting, placid, as well-behaved as any dog. Then his owner decided he wanted him to move. The dog trembled and froze, staring ahead at nothing, or perhaps sensing something we lacked the ability to comprehend. The dog wasn't threatening, he was *threatened*. He refused to move. The owner, frustrated when his possession failed to respond to his every whim, got more and more abusive. At last, he struck the poor beast. He made the dog cower, broken, not even allowed to feel fear.

Mina could tell I was upset. She assumed I was saddened by the deaths of the ship captain, whom I didn't know, and the boring old man, whom I didn't like. Trying to cheer me up, she took me on a long walk. And it worked, for a while. We cut across a field and were chased by a bull, went for tea at the inn, and laughed until it almost felt like old times. Mother's dinner guest, a local curate, was impossibly tedious, but Mina and I kept joking, pretending to be afraid that the bull was still coming for us. And then we stayed up late, sitting on my bed with our knees pressed together, talking. Almost like old times, but I felt it as a goodbye. My own farewell to the Mina I'd hoped to someday find. I've been unfair. Looking for something in her that I have no right to demand.

Now Mina's asleep and I can't pretend I'm not alone. I'll always be alone in my head and my heart. And I can't stop thinking about that dog.

I'm going out now to find the yard he's kept in. I'm going to cut the rope that binds him, and I'm going to hold him and pet him and let him feel whatever he wishes to feel, all the time.

Or maybe we'll slip away and never come back.

45

Boston, September 26, 2024

CLIENT TRANSCRIPT

Don't look proud of me, Vanessa. Yes, I stopped a Parisian serial killer. But do you think I'm better than he was? You're assigning value and moral weight to different kinds of killing. Different kinds of being a predator. There is no right. There is no wrong. There is only life and death and the things that tip us from one to the other.

Do you remember the train car? The treaty I made everyone sign, congratulating myself on saving so many lives? It was a haphazard treaty, doomed to fail and tip the world directly into a new war. Directly into the same war.

All my false Parisian lightness shed, war once again raging, I felt the weight of hopelessness and failure dragging me closer and closer to the ground. How could I have thought I'd done some good? How could I make up for it?

It was one night, crying next to the dazed and still-bleeding spy I'd made a small meal of, that I understood: Wars were not won on battlefields. They weren't even won in treaties. Not when that treaty failed to take into account all the information possible. No, wars were won on intelligence. And hadn't Mina always chided me that I should be a better student?

"Where are all the spies going these days?" I asked the young man. He lay on his back and stared dizzily up at the stars. He was in no pain. My small meals left them wobbly but happy. He would remember this as a surprise tryst with a stunning beauty, and the scars on his neck wouldn't haunt him for the rest of his afterlife.

"Istanbul," he said, giggling. It was adorable. He had round black eyes and curly hair and looked so young I wanted to send him home to his mother. "It's neutral, so it's the best place to find, buy, trade, or steal information. Everyone wants to push Turkey to one side or the other."

Istanbul it was. I was tired of France, anyhow. The idea of being on the front lines again, of wading through that much suffering and devastation . . . Even I have my limits.

Istanbul was a dirt-crusted jewel, a glittering city built on so many layers of history they were indistinguishable. I was starving when I got there, nearly feral with—

No, I didn't hear anything. Would you like me to go out and look? No?

I was used to my teeth and throat aching, but Istanbul made my *soul* ache. I wanted to gorge myself on its sense of place and identity. I wanted to be swallowed by the stones, to become a theater or library or mosque, to plant myself there and let history move around me. Such a mixture of old and new, built out of and on top of and over each other. I could have wandered those streets forever.

Except, as I said, I was starving. I'd never minded powerlessness—being my default state, it held no terror for me, and so I didn't avoid it while traveling. *Some* might have to be coddled and tucked away into their own grave dirt simply to cross Europe, but I knew how long I could go without sating my thirst or resting my bones.

At a certain point, though, even I began to lose my mind to the drought clawing through me. Fortunately, I had scarcely set foot on the edges of the city when I smelled fresh blood, accompanied by a metal-edged scent I knew well: freezing and sharp, like a scalpel unearthed from snow. The Doctor was in Istanbul.

My nose wrinkled and my jaw ached. The Doctor's scent threw me back to the trenches. I felt the deaths of a thousand young men in my arms. I wanted to scream and run away. But I also wanted to weep and run toward her. Bad memories or not, the Doctor was my friend. Or at least, she knew I existed, which felt almost the same as friendship.

I needed to be at my best when I saw her, though. She didn't tolerate foolishness or weakness, and I've always been told I have a penchant for both. Also, she'd never forgive me if I showed up looking for a meal.

It was night in a big city, so a meal was easy enough to come by. I stumbled and weaved, projecting vulnerability. Three people tried to help me, which was sweet and reminded me why I wanted to cut this next war short. But the fourth had darker intentions. My would-be attacker followed me so clumsily I almost felt affection for the idiot. He didn't follow me back out of the alley. I don't always take small meals.

Happily fed, all I really wanted to do was sleep. But that was far trickier. Istanbul was so old, nearly every inch of it had been bathed in blood, but *also* consecrated by centuries of faith or love or belief. The ground held so much; even the stones were noisy. It would be a challenge to find anywhere to rest peacefully here.

With high hopes that the Doctor would have somewhere for me to sleep, I followed my nose and found her right away. I didn't need an invitation, since a laboratory is not a home. Much like a therapist's office isn't.

Home is a funny concept, isn't it? One that we hold sacred, whether we realize it or not. If a home was safe, we carry that feeling with us. And if a home wasn't safe, we can't shake the scars of that violation. We never forget the violence of losing a home, or the pain of never having been given one, or the comfort of having lived in one filled with love and community. The longing for home is a universal human experience; there are few of those.

I think that's why vampires carry both fear and awe of homes with us beyond the space between life and death. Entering one without an invitation is a line we cannot cross; *home* is sacred and traumatic on both sides of mortality.

I can see you puzzling it out. Is this restriction magic, or merely psychological? Who's to say what's magic and what's not? Stop trying to figure it out. You won't, and it'll drive you mad. And then who will you turn to? *My* therapist is quite busy.

You have such a nice smile, Vanessa. Warm and compassionate and knowing. If it were a home, I would love to live in it. Anyhow, I walked right into the Doctor's lab. Though "walked" isn't the right word. It was hidden beneath an old library, accessible only via a locked iron door set into the ground. But there were cracks, so I was moonlight, and then I was inside.

When I shifted back into myself, she didn't even glance up. Her hands spidered over a prone body, ruthlessly dexterous and relentlessly curious. I felt a flush of affection, seeing her again. Her frown made it clear it was not mutual.

"No," she said.

"But I haven't asked anything yet." I skipped toward her, delicately twirling past various body parts and a few bodies that were not yet parts but would be soon. I didn't want to get blood on my dress or shoes, not after working so hard in the alley to avoid it. I hate having to steal clothes. It feels cruel, especially back then when clothing was meant to last years. I only ever took from wealthy people, though, which soothed my conscience and suited my vanity at the same time.

Besides, I adored that dress. Blue silk draping down with a coy swish around my calves. It was from the Lover's collection in Paris, and it made me think of the smells of bread and blood and sex and her. I still think of it sometimes. The dress, not the smells of Paris or the Lover. Though I haven't forgotten those, either.

"You have that look," the Doctor told me. "You're going to make my life more difficult."

"How can you know what look I have when you haven't even greeted me properly?" I leaned on the table with my chin on my fist and batted my eyes at her. Flirting never worked on the Doctor, but it always entertained me. Maybe even more because it didn't work on her.

She didn't humor me. Her voice was like a door slamming in my face. "Because you *always* have that look. You're sad, and lost, and you think I can fix it. We both know I cannot. And even if I could, I wouldn't care. *You're* the one who left *me*. You criticized me and told me for all my claims of studying, I was never helping. As if you've done anything except flit about the world, inflicting yourself on others. Well, here I am. Understanding. And helping. I have a whole system in this city, and I share all my findings with doctors at the university, and I'm quite busy doing it."

I linked fingers with the body on the table. He was still warm, though he wouldn't be for long. The Doctor was doing something that couldn't be undone, rummaging around in the twists and loops and tubes of his abdomen. When insides become outsides, it never ends well.

"I'm busy, too," I told her.

"Really." It wasn't a question, because she wasn't curious.

I leaned closer, forcing her to meet my gaze at last. I loved looking at her. The Doctor was *beautiful*—rich black skin, obsidian eyes, cheeks as full as the moon, body all curves and soft folds. So many vampires become thin and rigid and sharp, outer reflections of insatiable, constant hunger. But not her.

I think it makes it a little easier, that she's the last thing so many dying people have seen. I wouldn't mind if she were the last thing I ever looked on. Though I *would* be dying in an unfathomably painful way if that were true.

Anyhow, she didn't believe me that I was in Istanbul to do something interesting. I pouted, a little. I'm not ashamed to admit it. I wanted her good opinion. "I really am here for an important reason," I insisted.

She let out a small scoffing noise. "You left me to carouse in Paris."

I lifted an eyebrow, surprised. "How do you know what I did?"

With a dismissive sniff, she continued her work. "I thought you might reconsider and join me here, once you knew what I was doing. But I saw that you were otherwise engaged."

The Doctor was *jealous.* It was adorable, but I couldn't press it or she'd shut me out. And I couldn't afford to lose this unexpected ally in a city I was determined to conquer. There was a war on again. I had to get it right this time. It felt as essential as blood, as imperative as sleep.

Have you ever held a child's body as they claw at their throat, choking, their own lungs drowning them? It changes even the unchangeable. I made the Doctor hold one of them, near the end of our time together before. I made her hold him and watch. Not study, not dissect, not assess. Just hold. Not so much as a hair on his chin. Soldier's uniform hanging on him like it was set there to dry. A child. Ended.

I held a lot of them, back then. Far from home and anyone who had ever loved them. It's a gasping, choking death, being gassed in a trench. Dying alongside so many anonymous brothers, so many other children. I held them, and promised them they would be okay, and then I snapped their necks to give them the gentle kindness of a swift ending.

It's the physicality of the snap that lingers. I've ushered many people across the divide, but that *snap.* I can still feel each and every one of them in my hands.

Look. Look at them. Look at my hands. People say they know things like the backs of their hands, but do they know their hands at all? Do they know what they're capable of? Do they take account of all the things those hands have done, all the things they could have done, all the things they didn't do?

The Doctor accused me of leaving because I wanted to have fun in Paris, but she never understood. I couldn't stop crying over those boys, and I couldn't protect them, and I couldn't save them.

Before I died, my fiancé and the cowboy and the doctor and the old Dutch pervert tried to save me. I know you only heard about their attempt to cut off my head, but they really did try to keep me alive. They failed. And they didn't give me the grace of a quick death. I lingered and suffered. No *snap* for poor young Lucy.

At least my sacrifice paved the way for Mina to be saved, though. But after Paris, I knew better than to throw my body in front of death and hope it was enough. This time, I was going to be clever and smart. I was going to keep so many lives from getting to the point where a quick death was the only thing I could give them.

"I'm not here for fun," I said to the Doctor as the man on the table's heart stopped. "I'm here because the war is back, and I have men to kill. I'm going to be a spy."

The Doctor at least had the decency not to laugh at me. She merely sighed. I think she breathed just to have the opportunity to sigh over me whenever possible. "You missed the real Istanbul, anyway. I was here, at the fall of Byzantium. When the city opened and scholars and teachers and students from all over the world were welcomed in. When it was a beacon of learning and progress. Built on a foundation of blood and horror, but all cities and empires are."

"You were here then? Tell me about it!" I hopped up on a clean table, kicking my legs, but she ignored me. She never did humor me with stories of her life, much as I wanted to know how she had become what she was.

It didn't matter. I still loved Istanbul. Even then, a city crushed between two wars, pinched and conquered and controlled, trapped in a long slow decline that would drive out so much of what made it vibrant, Istanbul was a wonder. And, like all wonders, it was equal parts incredible and terrible. Awe and horror are the same emotions, they just depend on the outcome.

I wanted to inspire awe and horror, and I knew who I wanted to inspire it in. Soldiers are just unfortunate children, but the machines behind them? The hands trading the information, moving the pieces? That's who I would take care of this time.

"It's pointless," the Doctor said.

"This?" I held up the scalpel I was toying with, which seemed quite pointed.

"Muddling around in the internal affairs of humans."

I waved at the man on the table. "You're muddling around in his internal affairs right now."

"This accomplishes something. He dies, I learn, lives are saved."

"My goal is saving lives, too! We're doing the same thing here."

"We are not." But she kept glancing over at me, and I could tell I wasn't being dismissed. "You look exhausted," she said, at last finishing her work. "I'll give you a place to sleep, and in return, you bring me any bodies you need to get rid of."

It was a good deal, and I took it.

46

London, October 7, 2024

IRIS

When we get on the train in the morning, something's shifted in Elle. Maybe it was the shock of the storm, or the aftereffects of whatever drugs she took at the rave. But she seems relaxed and happy. She points out various features of the landscape, telling me historical anecdotes. I love how much she loves history, how engaged she is in the world around us and everything that happened to make it what it is right now, today, this moment.

That's the strangest thing about her, I think. Because as much as she loves history, Elle is absolutely in the moment. *Every* moment. I wish I could be the same way, but I'm dreading what I have to do.

Before we part at the train station, just as I'm about to tell her not to bother coming over again because I've changed my mind about selling things in the house, she leans close. Voice heartbreakingly sultry, says, "Don't forget to look right."

My heart flutters. I reach into my pocket where—like a lovesick teenager—I've been carrying the backpack strap she ripped off when we met. "I swear I'll remember."

And instead of doing what I meant to and cutting her loose, I wave goodbye. I catch a cab back toward Hillingham. This driver is gruff and silent, radiating annoyance. I lucked out with Rahul my first day here. I get out at the nearby shops for more food and toiletries. Plus coffee. Always coffee.

My feet drag. When Elle comes over later today like we agreed, I'll fire her. Remove myself from her life before she gets hurt. Or, worse, before she willingly removes herself. Preemptive heartbreak.

I laugh darkly to myself as I carry my bags down the sidewalk. "Go on, girl," I say, thinking of every movie ever where a child has to drive away a beloved pet for their own good. "Get out of here! I don't want you anymore." I pantomime throwing a rock.

But Elle isn't a half wolf who belongs in the wild. She's the most beautiful, funny, intriguing person I've ever met. I've still got to set her free for her own good.

A huge hand grabs my arm. I'm yanked into a narrow alley and shoved up against a brick wall. My backpack digs into my back, my shopping bags drop.

It's both a shock and no surprise at all to find myself face-to-face—or at least face-to-chest, since she's easily a foot taller than I am—with Ford, my mother's favorite bodyguard. I stare up at her, instantly switching into the lazy smirk I know enrages her. If I could reach into my purse, I could take care of her. But she has me pinned. "Ford. What brings you to London?"

Her lips peel back from glimmering white teeth. I swear they're bigger than they should be, and that she has more than the average person. All her features are like that: Something is off, but you can't quite put your finger on it. And by the time you figure out whether she's beautiful or terrifying, it will already be too late.

"We're watching you," she growls.

"Boring. I'd tell you to get a life, but we both know that's not an option."

I'm sure she's about to hit me or break my neck. She'd probably be justified. It must take tremendous restraint to have a regular conversation with someone who ran over you with your own car. Twice.

But *also* to be fair, "Run over me once, shame on you. Run over me twice, shame on me," right? She should blame herself.

She gets her rage under control and takes a step back, shaking her head as though disappointed in me. "We're watching you for your own protection. It's not safe here."

"Yeah, craziest thing. Today as I was minding my own business, a woman attacked me from out of nowhere and dragged me into an alley," I say, dead-eyed and deadpan.

"You're a *child*." Another sneer distorts her features, making her look downright demonic before she smooths it away. Her face is once more vast empty planes broken by sharp lines. "You should come home, where you're protected. Where you belong."

I unclench my jaw and give what I hope is a convincingly sullen eye roll. "I'm going to, *god*. I just need a breather. Taking care of the properties here before I get buried with the avalanche of stuff waiting for me at home. Did you ever think maybe I'm dealing with, I don't know, the pain and trauma of losing my mother?"

Even Ford isn't stupid enough to buy that. She steps closer again, barely a breath between us. I have to crane my head all the way back to look at her. I can't hide the panic coursing through me. I know on an animal level that I should never, ever be this close to her.

A smile seeps across her face like pooling blood. "The lawyer said I have to give you to the end of the week, and then I can drag you home. I'll enjoy that."

"Yuck, Ford, keep it in your pants."

She lets out a low, disgusted grunt. But before she steps back, something snags her attention. "What is that? That scent." She leans even closer, putting her head down so her face is right against my neck. I twitch with revulsion, but I don't move. I don't show fear.

She breathes in deeply, then jerks away, wrinkling her nose in disgust. "You always reek of coffee." Without another word, she leaves.

I stay in the alley for a few minutes, trying to get my heart rate and breathing back under control. I knew they were watching me, but now they want me to know exactly who's here. The clock is ticking. My first impulse is to sink down to the dirty ground and sit in my despair. Give in to a good wallow.

Instead, I walk numbly back to the house, calling Rahul on my way. When I get to Hillingham, Elle's on the doorstep, her head tipped back to take in the sun. She has a to-go cup in her hand, and another for me on the step beside her.

"Elle, hi," I say.

Her smile shifts to concern. "Hey. You all right? I should have called first, sorry. Did you want to take the afternoon off instead?"

I shake my head. "It's not that. What would you do if someone offered you a hundred thousand dollars to never talk to me again?"

Elle's voice is perfectly cheery. "A hundred thousand before or after taxes?" Then she can't contain her teasing laughter. It's spilling out of the curve of her eyelids, her pursed lips. She shakes her head. "Iris, that's such a weirdly specific hypothetical question. Where did it come from?"

Experience, I think. But instead, I say, "Don't invite anyone in if they come knocking, okay? Even if they say they know me."

Before she can ask a follow-up question, I unlock the door and go into the den. I can't wait for the used bookshops to get back to me. I'll go to the nearest one and take what I can get. I start loading the worthwhile books into a box.

Elle puts a hand on my arm, stopping me. "Seriously, what's the matter? You were quiet the whole train ride back, and now you look like you've seen a ghost."

"My mother *is* haunting me. Not literally. But she keeps reaching out from the grave to drag me back home, and things are catching up faster than I'd wanted. Anyway. It doesn't matter. Point is, you should stop coming over. It's not safe."

She looks confused. "I've been in a lot worse places than a dusty old house, trust me."

"No, it's not that, it's—"

There's a honk from outside. "That's Rahul," I say. "Come with me to sell these books? I can explain on the way." I'll get her out of Hillingham and then make sure she never comes back.

"I've got this one." She takes the heavy box of books from me. "Why don't you grab a stack of paintings. We'll do as much on this run as we can." Elle heads out, leaving the front door ajar behind her.

Seized with paranoia now that I know Ford's in London, I open the safe and take out Lucy's two journals. The one I'm already reading, and the one I haven't started yet. If I have to run at a moment's notice, I don't want to leave Lucy behind. The diaries fit snugly into my purse. I should take my whole backpack with me, always, but I can't balance it right now. I awkwardly embrace several bad paintings and haul them outside, setting them down on the porch so I can lock up.

A rustling noise from the hedges announces the fox's appearance before it steps clear of the greenery. Its eyes are narrowed, its teeth bared. At the same moment, Ford appears from behind the house, running full speed toward me. So much for her deadline.

This time, I'm ready. I reach into my purse, whip out my spray bottle, and send a stream toward the fox. It yelps in pain and diverts, running blindly into the hedges with a crash. I turn just as Ford is leaping over the side of the porch. I give her several good sprays. She falls, legs caught in the railing. Her scream is anguished, and she leaves red gouge marks as she claws at her face.

I abandon the paintings and sprint for the street, spraying indiscriminately behind myself. Elle's waiting at Rahul's car with the passenger door open.

"Go!" I shout. "Get in and go!" I jump into the back and slam the door as Elle does the same.

Rahul looks out the window. His eyes widen, and he floors it. We peel away down the narrow street, tires screeching as Rahul takes several tight turns much too fast. "Who the hell was that woman?" he asks. "Why is she chasing you? And was that the *fox* again?"

Elle is turned around, watching for pursuit behind us. "Were they waiting for you to come out?"

"Yeah." I lean back in my seat and put my special spray back in my purse. My phone rings. Dickie. I silence it. "That's what I wanted to talk to you about, Elle. So. What do you two know about vampires?"

47

Boston, September 26, 2024

CLIENT TRANSCRIPT

The Doctor took me to a forgotten corner of the city, derelict and unusable between the rubble of old walls. In the chaos when Constantinople fell, bodies from both sides had rotted here, never found amidst so much carnage. A place of death without remembrance. A place where we could sleep and forget, too.

I was relieved to be in the same city as the Doctor. Being known made me feel like I had a stronger grasp on myself. And much as she insisted otherwise, the Doctor was glad I was there, too. I awoke the next night with her lying beside me, so close we could touch. There was a whole unhallowed plot of land, and she chose companionship. Solidarity in dreamless sleep.

"What are you doing today?" I asked as her eyes opened. She sat up, instantly alert and ready to get to work.

"You know what I'm doing."

I followed her back toward the heart of the city. "Why do you do it, though? Why are you so obsessed with mortal bodies? Have you ever thought about studying what happened to *us*? Why we are the way we are?"

She scoffed. "We make no sense. We shouldn't exist. Why study nightmares? Mortal bodies can be understood, which means they can be fixed. Perfected, even. And I'm determined to do just that."

I wondered if that was why she clung to her body, why she never changed form. But before I could ask her, she hurried away toward her laboratory. She had work to do, and so did I.

Fed and rested at last, I strode into the city properly, filling my eyes with the spires and the walls and the buildings and the people, the same way I'd filled my belly with blood the day before. A different kind of nourishment.

Did you know back then it was called Constantinople as often as it was called anything else? Names are funny things. I wonder who I would have become if I hadn't gotten my name back. A bride, or a queen, or a lover, or a doctor. I'll never know. I was still Lucy.

But I didn't want to be Lucy in Istanbul. I wanted to be someone else, someone capable of shifting the tides of war. The Spy. Being a spy was *exciting*, too. Nothing like it is now. I can't understand technology. If you think vampires make no sense, explain to me how you can push buttons that don't exist on a glass and metal rectangle to talk to someone on the other side of the world. If that isn't supernatural nonsense, I don't know what is.

No, back then spy work was about meeting people. Identifying targets and then convincing them to tell you things, give you access to information, trust you when they should know better.

I needed to be clever and resourceful and organized and capable. I never had been any of those things, but if I were pretending to be Mina, well, I could do it. I knew she'd be proud, seeing me there. So I styled myself Wilhelmina Vargasy. Depending on who was listening and what they wanted to hear, I was Hungarian, Swedish, British, or Moldovan. I spoke all those tongues, along with a few other languages. I forget which ones I know until I'm speaking them.

It wasn't hard to get a job at a bar near the square. All they required was a face and body that would attract men, and I've always had that. Add a little mesmerizing on top of it? I was the best barmaid in Istanbul.

When I served drinks and chatted with them, men forgot what they were supposed to be careful of. It wasn't only because I'm beautiful, or because I dazzled them as soon as the sun set. No, it was because I was nothing but a silly, pretty girl. What threat could I ever pose?

I hadn't understood what I was getting into, though. I had some hazy ideas about intercepting messages, preventing attacks, perhaps stopping the war with a cleverly timed assassination. But Istanbul was a hornet's nest. Spies upon spies, agents from every country imaginable, all cloak-and-daggering around the city, trying to outsmart one another.

It became very tedious and boring, figuring out who to seduce and what to steal and who needed helping versus who needed murdering. I've forgotten most of what I did, and certainly all the names of the men I did things to. They were small and arrogant people, scurrying around dealing lives for counterfeit money. All money is counterfeit. Useless, meaningless, imaginary.

I hated all of them, to be honest. All the men on every side, treating people like numbers, lives like gambling chips. But I hated the Nazis most, so that was where I focused my efforts.

It wasn't all bad. They had the loveliest tea in Istanbul. Have you ever had it? I couldn't drink it, but I could smell it. That part was nice. And the outfits! I had the most gorgeous evening gown, you should have seen it. As green as envy, as clinging as fear, as light as hope. I wore a diamond choker—I always like to cover my neck; old habits—and swept my hair back into an elegant chignon. The Lover taught me that one, too. She would have been fun in Istanbul, but also dangerous. She never did take sides. Only her own. And she would have hated the Doctor almost as much as the Doctor would have hated her.

I haven't forgotten everything, though. One story does come to mind. My first *triumph*. The biggest problem in Istanbul was that the Ottomans—sorry, Turks, I get confused about when I am. Turkey was politically neutral, which made no one happy. All sides were constantly jockeying and conspiring to push the Turkish president to their cause.

I met . . . I can't remember their names, let's call them Hans and Baris. I met Hans and Baris one night in the bar. Because anyone listening to me heard what they wanted to, for them I was Hungarian, and thus on their side. Or at least Hans's side. Baris was Turkish, and eager to be a wealthy man.

They picked me out almost immediately. They flattered me, bought me drinks, invited me to parties. Hans declared he loved me and wanted to free me from my life of drudgery serving drinks. There was just one snag—as long as Turkey was neutral, he would be stuck here. If we could tip things and make Turkey swing toward a German alliance, he'd be able to return home with me on his arm, where I could run his household and bear him many beautiful blond babies.

It was a good thing I'd had so much practice pretending to care when men were talking. He was insufferable.

Having "lured" me to their side, Hans and Baris gave me a task. All

I had to do was seduce a guard working at the presidential office. He'd let me in, and then I'd leave a package behind.

"Easy," Hans assured me. "And safe."

"But why?" I pressed. "What's in the package? Who's helping us, in case something goes wrong?" Thanks to my excellent nose, I already knew it was a smoke bomb. The smoke would drive the president out of his office. Once he was exposed in the street, doubtless Baris would shoot him with the Soviet sniper rifle he had leaning against the wall in his room. I would most likely be killed and left surrounded by "evidence" that I was a Soviet spy. Hans and Boris would pin the whole thing on the Soviets and push Turkey into Germany's waiting arms.

It was an obvious enough plan that I'd figured out all the details on my own. I just needed them to confirm there were no co-conspirators so I could make certain the entire plot was snuffed out.

Hans and Baris shared the long-suffering look they got whenever I hinted I had a working brain beneath my golden hair.

"Just trust me, liebchen," Hans insisted, pulling me close.

That was where my abilities as a spy fell apart, because rather than manipulating them for more information, I opted for the simplest possible solution. I turned into a demon.

48

August 11, 1890
JOURNAL OF LUCY WESTENRA

I don't know why I did what I did.

No. That's not true. I know why—to protect Mina. I'm not certain I know *what* I did, though.

I crept out of my bedroom, tucked a knife into my dressing gown, and stepped into the night. I was ready to look for my dog . . . but I was not alone. Standing in the darkness was a man, so still he seemed part of the rocks of Whitby. He stared, utterly fixed upon the bedroom window. The window behind which Mina was sleeping.

I froze. There was something wrong with him. The shadows hid his features, as though complicit in his disguise. My eyes told me he was an older gentleman, but my heart . . .

My heart knew it was false. Perhaps because I've spent so much time practicing expressions in the mirror so no one ever knows who I really am. Whatever the reason, I saw past what his face was telling me straight to what my heart was telling me:

He was not a man.

My first impulse was to hide. He hadn't noticed me yet. He took a step toward the house, eyes burning red, fixed on the window. Only a little glass between him and Mina, and I—fool that I am!—had left the window cracked open.

I know men's hunger. I have seen it in their faces my whole life, but the pure gnawing intensity of his expression made me cold all over.

As that cold washed over me, so, too, did calm. Because what did I care about a threat to myself? What hope did I have of future happiness? None. Without hope there is no fear, because there is nothing to lose. I only cared about Mina's safety.

I walked up to him, my nightdress white like moonlight winking behind the clouds of my dressing gown. The dressing gown that was hiding a knife. "Come with me," I said.

The ferocity in his face as he turned almost made me scream. But it shifted from pure predatory menace to the curiosity of the spider maintaining its web. He smiled, because he thought he had won, and I smiled, because he was going to follow me. And Mina would be safe.

I led him to the graveyard bench where so often I sat with Mina, looking out over this same view. But at night everything was shadow and mystery. The ruined abbey rose like the rotting ribs of some dread leviathan, the headstones around us flashes of pale, broken teeth. The wind dragged clouds across the moon, bathing us in sly, shuddering light.

I sat. It made me no more vulnerable than if I'd been standing. I longed to go and look down at the house in the hills beneath us, to gaze at where Mina was safe. But I needed this monster to stay focused on me.

"Why do you wander the night?" He leaned close. There was nothing lovely in his face, nothing heroic or handsome. Sharp lines and empty, burning pits for eyes. They expressed all the ravenous hunger his closed lips tried to hide. "Haven't you enough love? I have heard men's hearts race as they look on you."

I smiled prettily at him, a smile so blank and perfect that men could project whatever they wanted onto it. My former art teacher. The annoying old man who used to hassle me on this very bench. Doctor Seward, Quincey Morris, even Arthur. I wasn't a person to them, any more than I was a person to this monster.

"What love do I have?" I asked. "They look at me and want to possess me. They want to consume me. That's not love, no matter what they tell themselves. Why are you pretending to be like them? Show me the truth."

A low, urgent noise escaped him. He could barely hold himself in place here, something beneath his skin vibrating to be free. His animal moan of desire filled me with urgency to keep him here. Away from that window with the curtains drifting inward like fingers beckoning him toward Mina.

But his moan also filled me with a curiosity of my own. As the butterfly watches the spider approach, doesn't it wonder what it will be like? How it will feel?

He resumed his form as the stately old gentleman. It's such a flimsy disguise, I wondered how anyone ever believed it. Though most stately old gentlemen I know also hide fangs and claws. Perhaps that was the secret. People are used to looking away from what they're too polite to notice. The same way we all looked away from that man abusing his dog. The same way everyone looked away from who my father was. From who my mother is.

"She is waiting for him," he said. I felt another stab of cold dread. He was still thinking of Mina. I didn't know how to make him stop. I'd never been able to stop thinking of her, either.

"Waiting for who?" I asked.

"For her Jonathan." He smiled then, a smile as swift and brutal as an executioner's blade. "He will never come for her."

If he knew Jonathan, he knew exactly who Mina was. He had come here for *her.* It wasn't chance that brought him to our window.

But I had always been more desirable than Mina, hadn't I? She'd told me so enough times. "Perhaps that's for the best." I shrugged, letting my dressing gown slip off a shoulder, drawing his eyes there. "He could never have made her happy."

"How do you know?" he asked.

I laughed. I didn't mean to, but it was so hard to pretend with him. I wondered if I needed to pretend. Perhaps it was best to be my own broken, strange self. Who was he going to tell? "I *don't* know. I'm unhappy with my own fiancé, and I'm unhappy that Mina loves Jonathan, and so I search for signs that she's unhappy, too. We use other people like mirrors, projecting our feelings onto them, looking for our reflections."

He tilted his head. I don't think his face is capable of actual expressions, merely mockery of human emotion. But he almost looked thoughtful. "I never see myself reflected."

"Well, you're not a person. You're a monster." I felt a thrill of triumph as at last he focused completely on me. I had him then. Either I would kill him, or, more likely, he would kill me. But after he killed me, there would be an uproar. He would be caught, Mina would be safe. I laughed again, because men hate to be laughed at, and he was pretending to be a man. "Oh, don't be so surprised that I can tell. Of course you'll never see your reflection. You don't look at others and try to understand them, or try to understand yourself through them. You never could."

One dark eyebrow lifted above his bottomless eyes. "You know me so well, then."

I wished I did not. That I had searched his face and found nothing familiar. But maybe that was how I saw what he truly was. Because in him, I saw myself. "You are a gaping maw," I said. "An endless, insatiable hunger. There's not enough in this world to fill you, you can never have what you want, and yet you keep taking new forms, keep pretending, keep moving out of a desperate need to survive."

~~I recognized the sound of desire he made, the one that repulsed me and filled me with shame, because it was the sound my own soul made every day. The sound of my whole self when I looked at Mina and wanted to consume her and knew I could not.~~

I reached up with my free hand and drew him close, holding him there. Holding him to me, away from Mina. I didn't care if I couldn't have her—I would never let him hurt her. My other hand clutched the handle of my knife. "Look in my eyes, and I think you will, at last, see yourself."

He looked.

I was wrong. In his eyes, those pits of burning red, I saw *nothing* of myself. At last I was afraid. I drove my knife into his stomach.

It met no resistance. It was as though I had stabbed the mist. He pressed his dry lips to my neck. There was a bright burst of pain so sharp I felt myself erased by it, and then cold spread like poison, lancing from my throat toward my heart. My eyes closed and my soul fled.

The next thing I knew, Mina was shaking me. I put my hand to my throat with a cry of terror. Mina shouldn't have been out there! Everything was wasted if he found her! But my attacker was gone, as was my knife. Mina drew her cloak around me and guided me home. I could barely stand. I was so cold and dizzy that I was floating on the night air, part of it. Gravity had renounced its claim on me once and for all.

When we reached our room, Mina furiously berated me. I wept and hugged her, because it was so lovely to hear that she cared. That she came looking for me. She made me swear to tell no one I had been out, lest my reputation be ruined. I agreed.

I survived, somehow, against all odds. And Mina is safe. I saved her.

She can never know, because then she'd know such a creature exists out there. I wouldn't put Mina through that. Not for anything. Whether he was right about Jonathan or not, I cannot say and I do not care. I'll protect Mina, and take care of her, and stay at her side. She doesn't need to love me back. My love isn't contingent on that.

We are closer than ever, even if she has no idea what transpired. I know what I did for her, and my throat hurts, and I can't get warm, and there are shadows flitting on the edges of my vision, but I am happy.

49

London, October 7, 2024

IRIS

Judging by Rahul's incredulous gaze in the rearview mirror and Elle's total silence, I need to be less honest.

Honesty *really* isn't the best policy. Honesty gets you a schizotypal disorder diagnosis that makes it even easier for your mother to control your life. Honesty gets you involuntarily committed. Honesty gets you nowhere when Goldaming Life is involved, because the Goldaming lie is more powerful than any truth.

I take a breath and try again. *Tell all the truth but tell it slant.* My girl Emily Dickinson knew what she was talking about. "My family—my mother, until she died—runs a vast, predatory, multilevel marketing company. It basically exists to take advantage of people and drain them of everything they have."

Rahul lets out a relieved breath. "Okay. I see. Your vampires are metaphorical."

I give him my shrug of a smile. Elle relaxes a little, shifting in the passenger seat and turning toward me. She reaches out and squeezes my hand as I continue. It gives me a shiver of pleasure, which I don't deserve and can't indulge.

"Goldaming Life is a cult. It starts as health and wellness nonsense, drawing people in with promises of being beautiful and young and also making money off of being beautiful and young. The company's been around for a long time, but it was always regional and smaller. My mom took it to soaring new heights. Branding, merchandising, expansion. Always expansion. And thanks to influencers and social media, she's turned it into a whole lifestyle. People get *obsessed.* Goldaming Life is booming, getting even more hopeful dupes under its control every day. But I'm the sole inheritor, so now I'm the dupe Goldaming Life needs most."

Rahul frowns. "Goldaming Life. Aren't they those shiny-looking people pushing cleansing products that promise to restore youth? What's their slogan again . . . *The blood is life*?"

I startle. How does good, sweet Rahul know it? "Yeah, that's them."

"Bloody hell. They gave me a pamphlet in Piccadilly the other week. As if I need a more youthful glow. Have you *seen* my skin?"

"Your skin is the glowingest," I say, trying for a playful tone. But my stomach feels sick. My mother's next goal was expanding into Canada, Mexico, Brazil, and Europe. I didn't think she'd put any of that into motion yet. How far will I have to run to escape her reach?

"So why are they after you?" Rahul asks. "Can't you tell them you aren't interested in running things? Ask for a buyout?"

"If it were a normal company, sure. But you don't get bought out from a cult. They're obsessed with blood and bloodlines, which means I'm not only the sole inheritor, I'm, like, theirs. I'm a possession. And I'm legally the head of the company, so they can't make any business decisions or move significant amounts of money without my okay. They're desperate to get me back in the U.S. and under their thumb. By whatever means necessary."

Elle's voice is soft and sad. "Thus the need to sell everything for as much cash as quickly as possible. You're running."

I look down at my hand in hers. They fit so well. I wish we had time to discover the other ways we fit together. "My plan is to disappear forever. They're—the truth is . . ."

I lean my head forward against Elle's seat. I wish I could tell my new friends the truth. I wish I could tell *anyone* the truth and be believed. Sometimes I don't even believe myself. That's the worst thing my mother did to me in a lifetime of very bad things: plant a quiet voice in the back of my head telling me maybe I really *am* crazy.

I sit straight again. Not the full truth, but slant. "With Goldaming Life, the most awful secret organization–type things you can imagine aren't awful enough. I can't tell you the levels of abuse. Even I don't know the depths of it all, and I never want to."

"Can't you be a whistleblower?" Rahul asks, trying to be helpful. "Expose them?"

I want them to think I'm brave. Heroic. But I'm neither of those things. Not anymore. "I've tried. It's just—I mean, there are reasons why I'm not a credible source in the eyes of . . ." I trail off. "It's too much money and too much power to fight. I broke myself trying to bring them down when I was younger. All I can do now is get out and hope it hamstrings them."

"Well then. Getting you out it is." Elle sounds so calm and matter-of-fact I think she doesn't believe me. It hurts even more than I expected. But her next sentence makes me feel a little better. "Let's sell these musty old books for as much cash as possible."

Rahul navigates to the nearest bookshop on my list, a tiny place sandwiched between a café and a library. Before I can move to get out, Elle grabs the box. "Won't be a minute!" She closes the door and confidently strides into the store.

"I feel like I ought to say something encouraging here," Rahul says. "Or ask follow-up questions about your family's cult, or your future plans. But I'm stuck on the fox chasing you. Does it belong to that scary lady? Is it somehow, I dunno, trained? A sort of watchfox? Or do you just have genuinely shit luck and attracted the attention of a rabid wild animal in addition to all your other problems?"

I'd hoped dangling a shiny cult in front of him would make him forget about the fox. I don't have any explanation that will make his world make sense again. At least I know he and Anthony have seen the fox, too, and that it's definitely real. It's comforting. It helps quiet that voice in my head.

The best explanation I can give him is the one with the most room for him to interpret it however he wants. "Everything my family touches is cursed, including that house and its history. So maybe the fox is haunted. Or maybe it's rabid and I have the worst luck in the world, which I will also blame on my family."

Rahul frowns, tugging distractedly on his thick beard. He didn't take any of that as a joke. "After his mum died, Anthony broke out in hives. Came out of nowhere. Horrible red streaks, swollen and painful, all over his torso, back, and arms. We saw so many doctors and specialists, and no one could give us a reason they appeared like that, or a solution for treating them. Eventually the hives faded. I believe it was his mother, clawing at him on her way out of this life. Trying to make him suffer one last time. Causing him pain was her only way to be remembered. To matter."

I reach forward and squeeze his shoulder. He puts his hand over mine and shifts, turning around to smile at me. "Anthony's free of his mother now. You will be too, soon. And Anthony and I will help however we can. Including a call to Animal Care and Control."

I laugh. "You've already helped. Believe me. You don't need to do anything more." Plus, I need to keep him and Anthony out of harm's way, especially now that Ford is here. But I'm still determined to give them a gift. I don't think Dickie and the other monsters actually care about the properties here. Once I leave, they'll all be busy trying to find me anyway.

Still, maybe the impulse is selfish of me. Like Anthony's mom, I want to leave an impact as I disappear. A huge gesture so that I know at least somewhere in the world, two good people will think kindly of me. If I were really selfless, I'd cut Rahul off right now. Keep him out of my dangerous orbit entirely.

But the idea of Lucy's house—that's how I think of it now, as *hers*, no matter who else it belonged to—going to Goldaming Life makes me so angry I feel sick. No. I'm taking at least that small thing back on my way out.

Elle appears on the sidewalk, box gone. She climbs in the back of the car and hands me a shockingly full envelope. I peer inside and find it bursting with pounds.

"Holy shit." I thumb through the bills, doing a quick count. "This is so much more than I thought I'd get."

"You had some gems in there." Then she smiles, her dimples mischievous punctuation points on either side of her mouth. "*And* I'm extremely persuasive when I decide to be."

I don't realize I'm crying until she puts her arm around me. Then she gives Rahul a new address as our destination.

"Another shop?" I ask. "We didn't get the paintings, though."

"No. We're going to my flat," she says.

"We can't. It's not safe for you to be around me anymore. For either of you. I should—"

Elle interrupts. "You told me the truth and gave me the information I needed to make an informed decision. This is my decision."

Rahul turns onto the route that will take us to Elle's address. "I feel the same. I'll be your getaway driver for any and all cult rescues."

I don't know how to thank them. They've already done more for me than they know, just by listening and *believing* me. My throat tightens. Elle doesn't let go of me. I never want her to.

Rahul drops us off after making me promise to call him when I need a ride anywhere else. Elle's neighborhood is nothing like Hillingham's. Apartments squat above shops, half of which are vacant. It doesn't seem dangerous so much as stalled. Like people and industry had moved on, and these streets were left behind, waiting and hoping someday people would come back.

Elle's flat is above a chip shop, one of the only open businesses. The air outside smells warm with salt and grease. Normally that would entice me, but right now it makes me feel queasy.

She unlocks a faded red door on the street level. We walk up a narrow, utilitarian set of stairs to a second door, which reveals her surprising flat. I had hoped to get more insight into who Elle is, but it's so nondescript it could be anyone's. There's a sofa and a chair in neutral beige with a plain coffee table in the center of the living area. A small round dining table with two chairs nudges up against a clean but dated kitchen. A couple of paintings hang on the walls, but they have all the soul of something purchased at a discount bulk store.

"How long have you lived here?" I ask.

Elle pats the beige couch like she might pet a dog tied up in front of a store. "Since I got back to London. It came furnished. Doesn't make sense to invest in pieces I love until I'm settled. And I'm never settled." She doesn't laugh to turn it into a joke.

I put my bag down and cross the room to her, slipping my fingers around her wrist. I need to hold her in place. To anchor her and make certain she listens. And to watch her when I say this, so I can be sure she isn't just showing me what she thinks I want to see.

"It really is dangerous to associate with me. If the people in charge think you know where I am once I run, they might come after you. I want you to understand all the risks. They're rich beyond belief and have absolutely no morals."

"You don't want to lie to me so I won't be scared?" Her tone is teasing, but there's something there. Some history I'm not privy to.

"I wouldn't be lying to keep you from being scared, I'd be lying to keep you with me." I pause, my throat tight. "I *want* to keep you with me. But not if it gets you hurt. I meant what I said about Goldaming Life. They're monsters. Figurative and literal. I can't keep you safe from them."

Elle puts her free hand on my cheek. Her expression isn't what I expected. I was bracing for fear and alarm. Ready to watch in real time as she closed herself off from me. Instead, her face is impossibly tender. Tears pool in her eyes, such a dark blue in some lights they look almost black. The blue of the bottom of the sea, the blue of crushing depths and endless, blissful cold. "You really aren't going to lie to me for my own good? To protect me from things too awful for me to understand?"

"Lying about the existence of monsters never saved anyone from falling victim to them."

She lets out a surprised breath. I can't tell if it's half laugh or half cry. And then she kisses me.

50

Boston, September 26, 2024

CLIENT TRANSCRIPT

It's amazing how quickly men will confess when staring into the glowing red eyes and dripping fangs of death. That night, I delivered Hans, Baris, and four other Nazi spies to the Doctor.

"A little warning next time," she grumbled, hauling the unconscious bodies through the door. "The professors I work with prefer a *little* discretion."

"I saved the president from being assassinated and the Soviets from being framed for it."

The Doctor gave me a level stare with her depthless black eyes. "And is the war over?"

I didn't know what I'd expected. Praise? Excitement? I would get neither from her. So I went back to the bar, and I went back to work.

I prevented seventeen—*seventeen!*—more attempts to assassinate Turkey's president and blame one side or the other. I never even met the man, and yet it felt all I was ever doing was keeping him alive. In between killing everyone trying to kill the president, I made Italian fascists miss crucial meetings so the British could intercept their messages, passed Nazi secrets on to Greek operatives trying to liberate their country, and prevented my fellow barmaids from being assaulted more times than I could count.

One, Ingrid, was working extra shifts killing as many Nazis as she could. I adored Ingrid. She was loud and funny, quick with a knife, and an excellent kisser. She didn't know I knew about her after-work activities, which suited me fine, because I had no interest in involving her in mine.

Though there were rumors about me among every intelligence operation in the city, no one could figure out who I worked for, because I didn't work for anyone. No one could kill me, because I'd already been killed by something far worse than any of them. And no one could catch me, because they all saw a slightly different woman when they looked at me. Just a beauty behind a bar, pouring their drinks and listening.

The Doctor complained about the smell of alcohol every time I crawled into our sleeping space. She also asked the same question whenever I delivered new bodies to her: "And is the war over?"

The answer was always no. No matter what I did, the same plots popped back up. There was always another Hans, always another bomb, always another gun. And through it all, I had to smile and nod and giggle, pretending to be interested in dull men's dull machinations, pretending like I couldn't tell exactly what they were thinking, exactly what they wanted.

I often saw my fiancé sit on a stool at my bar, or a lecherous old Dutch man wink at me from across the room. I met all four of them in Istanbul, those men who had loved me and failed to save me. Sometimes they were the ones I was helping, and sometimes they were the ones I was killing.

It wasn't really them. But it was easy to get lost in time and see them in other people. It still is. One night I sat on the floor of a dark apartment, holding the Texan in my arms. "Why couldn't you have saved me?" I whispered. "How did you save Mina but not me?"

He didn't answer, because he wasn't *my* Texan. Also because he had been poisoned and was quite dead.

All that purpose and determination that had brought me to Istanbul was drying up and withering away. I had no roots to sustain myself. I got sloppy. I got careless. And I got Ingrid killed.

We often fell into her bed after a long shift if neither of us had somewhere to be. One night as she was getting dressed again, a bloody knife slipped out of her boot. She froze, unaware that I knew all about her activities *and* could smell the blood long before the knife was ever revealed.

It was my lack of reaction that gave her pause. She sat on the end of the bed. "Wilhelmina," she said, and I wished she could call me

Lucy. Maybe that was part of why I was getting so lost in my head. "I kill men."

I laughed. "Me, too."

"I kill Nazis," she clarified, mildly alarmed at how readily I'd volunteered my confession.

"I know, my pretty darling." I pulled her close between my legs and began braiding her hair. "I like that about you."

"How long have you known?" She was breathless with both fear and relief.

"Since we met. You always smell like blood." I remembered that was a strange thing to say, so I hurriedly added: "And I saw you dragging a body to the Bosporus the night before you started working at the bar. I would have helped, if I'd known you."

She laughed. "You're insane."

"Of course I am." I pressed a kiss to the neat part between her braids, then held her close. Ingrid was like unhallowed ground. A place I could rest and find some relief. I didn't love her, though. She didn't know me, and how can we love those who don't know us? "I'll always help you get rid of bodies. Just ask."

Her eyes brightened. "I have a list. And a plan."

I should have gotten more details, but I was always looking for someone to tell me what to do. Ingrid's plan would lead to my best and worst and last night in Istanbul.

Ingrid's plot was already nearly in full bloom. Seven Nazi and Italian operatives were targeting the British ambassador's secretary. He held the code to a safe in the ambassador's office. Inside were details of troop movements in Europe. That was where I came in. The seven men needed to isolate the secretary in a location where no one would look for him or notice he was missing. What better way than using their new friend Wilhelmina to attract his attention and lure him up to a hotel room?

They hadn't actually told me what they needed him for. Only that they needed him, and they'd buy me a pretty dress and pay me for my troubles. Ingrid had figured out all the rest.

I met one of the Nazis behind the hotel. He was a short man with a pleasant face and the clearest, most beautiful whistle. He gave me the key to the room I was going to use. "Once you get him alone, we'll follow," he said. "Leave the door unlocked. When we're inside, you can go and enjoy the rest of the gala."

I beamed like I had no thoughts in my head other than a good party. And then, on my way to the front stairs, I whispered the room number to Ingrid, waiting in the shadows just outside.

My entrance into the grand hotel ballroom was like an air raid siren: Everyone froze and looked. Including the British ambassador's secretary, who should have known better than to believe he was important enough to merit an invitation to this gala. And who *definitely* should have known he wasn't important or handsome enough to merit my attention.

The band was excellent. If you've never been to a wartime party, I recommend them. Bacchanals, always. The room glittered. Gilt walls, crystal chandeliers, tile like only the old Ottomans could do. Everyone was sumptuously dressed, reeking of secrets and violence and lust. I was drunk on them.

I knew my target on sight, but I couldn't be too obvious. I danced first with one of the Italians. Eyes like the sea, skin like honey. It was wasteful that I had to break his face later that night.

The secretary bumped into me near a champagne pyramid. I let him think it was his fault and laughed prettily at his attempts to apologize. He was as plain and unremarkable as mushy peas. *Jonathan Harker.* That was who he reminded me of. I'd forgotten Jonathan existed until then.

I fought the urge to kill the secretary.

"Make it up to me with a dance?" I asked instead of ripping out his heart for taking Mina from me. *Not Jonathan,* I reminded myself. I knew he wasn't Jonathan, obviously. But I was thrown off, unbalanced. Distracted. He sounded like home, and home was so far away. So long ago. Every time I looked at him, I imagined Mina living out her life with just such a dull, obliviously entitled man, claiming what he never could have deserved.

I didn't have to use any of my dazzling powers to get the secretary to follow me up to the room. He didn't even notice that I failed to lock the door behind us. He began pawing at me immediately, clumsy and eager.

His lust turned to fear as my seven co-conspirators slipped inside. "You can go now, Wilhelmina," said the beautiful Italian.

But I couldn't. I couldn't stop looking at the secretary, couldn't stop seeing Jonathan in his place. I didn't even remember what Jonathan looked like. Maybe it *was* him. Maybe I'd found him. The age was wrong, the eyes were wrong, everything was wrong, but he *felt* like Jonathan.

I pushed him to the floor and knelt over him, searching his face. Trying to find the memory of someone I had hated, someone who had taken something precious and perfect from me. But she had never been mine to take, had she?

"Where is she?" I demanded, crying. "Where's Mina? What happened to her?"

He blubbered desperately. The men shouted at me to leave. And I forgot what the next part of the plan was. Not even the sound of the closet door bursting open and the gun going off could distract me. I shook and shook Jonathan, demanding he tell me where Mina was, what her life had been like, whether he'd ever made her happy.

Ingrid's scream at last brought me to my senses. I turned to see her favorite knife sticking out of her chest. She looked over at me, devastated. The beautiful Italian turned, satisfied he had taken care of the threat. I smashed his face in, and then grabbed the next nearest man and broke him, too.

But Ingrid, beautiful Ingrid, Ingrid who had never really known me, wasn't aware I could do the rest all on my own. She had come prepared to finish it.

She reached into her coat, and then the whole room exploded.

51

August 14, 1890

JOURNAL OF LUCY WESTENRA

I'm feeling more at ease now. Though I'm up all hours of the night pacing, checking that the door is locked and the window latched—often until Mina awakes and guides me back to bed—I have seen no sign of the monster in the days since we met.

I don't know what he did to me or why. My throat still hurts, and sometimes where my pulse should be is an icy emptiness for a beat, two beats, long enough that I fear I'm dying until my heart once again stumbles into action. But I saved Mina from him.

She has had no word from Jonathan, and I'm sorry I ever wished our time in Whitby over. I was being a bad, selfish friend, too lost in my own misery. Now that I know what true misery and horror is, Mina's marrying someone else feels far less like life and death.

I can't write more now. She's returning from her visit to the church and we're going for a walk. But I'm nearly myself once more. My brush with death makes me all the hungrier for life now, I think! I will survive all of this. Mina, marriage, and monster.

I WROTE TOO SOON. Walking toward the abbey and churchyard, I saw him. On my bench, on *our* bench. His eyes flashed red. I couldn't tell whether he was looking at me or Mina. I don't remember what I babbled or how I swooned with fear, but Mina had to guide me home again. She fussed over me all afternoon and evening, worried about my nerves, reminding me that I had to stay calm so as not to upset Mother.

I fell asleep and woke in terror that Mina would be gone. That I had failed her. But she's asleep in the bed next to mine. I sit now writing at the window, on guard for those endless red eyes.

He wanted me to see him today at the abbey. To know he's still here, still watching, still—

52

London, October 7, 2024

IRIS

I kiss Elle back too fast, too hard.

It's been so long since I've felt anything like this. Since I've trusted that the person I was with wouldn't run, or take my mother's money, or betray me.

Elle dances like she's trying to exorcise a demon. She looks sad when she doesn't catch herself and school her expressions. She wrinkles her nose when she laughs. She's funny and smart and beautiful and kind, and she's here now, with me. By choice. Unlike in Whitby, I don't want to consume her. I don't want to use her to quiet that ache inside for a few stolen minutes. It's not about me and what I need. I want to *celebrate* her. To connect with her. To worship her.

I pull away and put my lips against her ear. Linger there for a few breaths to get myself steady. Then, keeping my voice as soft and low as a purr, I say, "Ask me to kiss you slowly."

Elle goes still against me, like a rabbit about to flee. I've ruined the moment. I've blown it.

Then she whispers, "Kiss me slowly. Please."

I trace my lips along her jaw, letting the magnetism of her mouth draw me back in. I wasn't wrong to compare her lips to a rosebud. They're velvet-soft, blooming beneath my own. I weave my fingers into her hair, cradling the back of her head, not grasping or grabbing. Careful, careful. Tender.

Forehead-to-forehead, we stop and breathe in sync. I'm about to brush her hair away and move to her neck, to capture her butterfly pulse in my mouth, but she puts a hand against my cheek, holding me there, keeping me still.

"Ask me to take my dress off," she says, her voice unsteady.

"Take your dress off . . . please," I add, the word curving out of my mouth like a smile.

Her fingers tremble as she undoes the buttons. I want to help her, but the waiting is delicious. The seconds stretch taut between us. She slides her dress off her shoulders and it falls to the floor around her feet, pooling there like she's a myth rising lovely and impossible from a pond.

I trail my hand down her throat, lingering at the place where neck becomes shoulder. Then I rest it, palm flat, in the center of her chest. I stretch my thumb and pinky, brushing the soft fullness of her on either side. She's so beautiful that looking at her is a hook in the center of my chest, tugging on something painful and yearning.

But still, I linger. I go slowly. I ask, and she asks, and we both answer.

It's a gentle, aching unearthing as we peel off layers. We experiment with touch and taste, pressed against the wall, then on the couch, eventually making it to the bed. Elle is a garden, subtle and beautiful and surprising, and I am as serious about making her bloom as I've ever been about anything in my life.

When she navigates my body, her lips against the curves of my breasts, her small hands somehow everywhere, it's like she knows what I'm responding to before I do. Like she can hear the swell of desire and instantly divert into the wave, riding it for as long as possible.

We move together until at last we're spent, lying diagonal across the bed, our legs still tangled. Elle turns on her side to look at me. For once I'm not self-conscious of how exposed I am. It was clear in the exploration of her hands and the press of her mouth that she loves the soft fullness of my belly, the place where my thighs kiss against each other. That in my softness she doesn't find weakness or failure, only pleasure. Only tenderness.

She cups one of my breasts, no urgency in the motion of her thumb brushing back and forth over my nipple, only idle enjoyment.

"Ask me," I say, trying to keep a straight face, "if my little butter chicken has replaced actual butter chicken as the best thing I've ever had in my mouth."

She snorts an inelegant explosion of laughter and grabs a pillow to throw at me. I take it and put it behind my head, absolutely spent and absolutely content.

"But seriously." I want to be sincere. I want to tell her what that meant to me, how it felt. "I—"

"Ask me if I know what you mean without you saying it," she whispers.

I lean my head close to hers and she brushes my curls away from my eyes. I close them, wanting to exist infinitely in this moment. No past, no future. A line of Emily Dickinson dances through my mind. *"Forever is composed of nows,"* I quote, needing only this *now* and nothing else.

But now can never last. The past is always with us. And on us, in my case, as Elle is discovering.

"These bumps are scars, aren't they?" Elle asks, running her fingers down my arms.

"I have an autoimmune disorder. It's similar to cold agglutinin disease, which you've never heard of because it's rare, and our version is even rarer. It's so unusual they nicknamed it after my family. Gold agglutinin disease. Cute, right? If I get too cold, my body starts attacking my blood cells. I'm mildly anemic on a good day, dangerously anemic on a bad one." I brush my arms where old IV scars linger. "When I was growing up, I had weekly blood transfusions. They'd pump out all my gold blood and pump in regular blood to replace it. But it never made me feel better, so as soon as I got away, I stopped doing it."

"Are you okay now?"

I shrug. "It'll kill me eventually. But not today, which is good enough for me."

She lets out a noncommittal noise. "And what happened here?" Elle traces the scars on both sides of my abdomen. I'm surprised she noticed them. They're little white crescents, like someone pressed a thumbnail too hard against the skin.

This time I'm tempted to lie, or kiss her, or deflect. But I told Elle I wouldn't try to protect her from monsters.

"My mother was obsessed with progeny," I say, using her word for it. Not "children." Not "families." *Progeny.* "She was always bitter she only had one child, angry with me for taking so long and 'ruining her' on my way out. Her phrase, not mine. I'm aware neither is my fault.

But she didn't feel that way. She made it clear she was owed more than she had been given, and it was my responsibility to pay that debt. I didn't think too much of it growing up, because it felt nebulous and far away."

I don't turn on my side, don't look at Elle. I need to say this part without watching her reaction, because it might break me. "When I was sixteen, she had me visit a special doctor. Even though I felt fine and had hit puberty like a lineman tackling an opponent—"

"What?" Elle asks.

"Sorry, American football reference. Hard. I hit it hard," I say, laughing. I squeeze my boobs. "These heavy babies were already D-cups by the time I was fourteen. Anyway, this special doctor told me I had a hormone imbalance that needed to be corrected. My mother gave me shots every day. Which was weird for many reasons, but mostly because she was doing it herself. Taking care of me with her own two hands, not via a nanny or tutor or any of the various employees she'd paid to raise me. Then my stomach got tender and swollen. I told her something was wrong. Like usual, I expected her to dismiss my pain. But she was gentle and attentive. And I gobbled it up. I reveled in it. At last, I'd cracked through her ice. She *loved* me. Appendicitis, she said. She took me to a private medical center. Held my hand as I was wheeled into an operating room.

"When I woke up in recovery, she was gone. She wasn't even waiting for me at home. No one would tell me how the surgery went, whether my appendix had burst, anything. So, I researched appendicitis. The symptoms didn't match up. I'd been lied to, and I didn't understand why, or what they were lying about.

"But my mother had made two very big mistakes in raising me. The first was assuming I wasn't paying attention when she entered passcodes into locks. And the second was giving me elocution, public speaking, and acting lessons so I could become charismatic and commanding like her. I broke into my mother's office and used her phone to call the doctor."

I hitch my voice up so it's higher, smoother, colder. I flatten my affect, every sentence delivered without life or inflection. "'*I'm calling to follow up about my daughter's procedure. She's complaining of pain in her shoulder. Are we concerned?*' The doctor reassured me that referred pain from the swelling was to be expected. And then he informed me that he had been correct—the procedure was a success. Six viable eggs retrieved."

"What the *fuck*?" Elle says.

"Yeah. That's what I thought, too. But this was my one chance. I stayed calm and told him, still in my mother's voice, that I had changed my mind. A surrogate couldn't be trusted. I wanted the eggs destroyed. He protested, but my mother never allowed anyone to question her decisions, so neither did I. I told him to call me back as soon as it was done. Then I sat in my mother's chair in her pristine office and waited until I had confirmation that what had been stolen was out of my mother's reach forever.

"They'd lied to me, drugged me, operated on me, and literally taken part of me away. That was when I knew: Everything I'd thought I'd seen and overheard over the years—the nightmare glimpses, the creeping suspicions? They were all correct. My mom was a monster, and so was everyone who worked for her.

"I ran to my dad. He'd been my ally sometimes, or at least a place where I could retreat for ice cream and movies and a few hours where nothing was expected of me. But when I told him what she'd done, he wasn't surprised. He told me it was best not to fight her. He wouldn't even—" My voice at last breaks.

Elle moves closer, draping an arm around my waist, holding me tight.

I clear my throat. "He wouldn't fight for me. He was old and tired and broken by her. That was the first time I ran away for more than just the night. It wouldn't be the last. It was an ongoing war where I lost every skirmish. I tried to tell the police what Goldaming Life was up to. She had me committed to an involuntary psychiatric hold. I tried to live on my own. She paid landlords to evict me, friends to throw me out, girlfriends to dump me. She even donated a new library building to my college so they'd disenroll me and all my student loans would come due at once. I did what I could to carve out independence, but it was impossible. She was inevitable. I knew one day she'd break me."

I sigh, running Elle's soft hair between my fingers, marveling at the shades of red. Elle is like light. Subtle and changeable depending on what she's filtered through. Right now, it's a bedroom haze of satisfaction and vulnerability, so she's all glowing gold.

"And then my mother died." I don't try to hide the smile in my voice. The truth of this next part I keep to myself, though. As much as I trust Elle, there are still some things I should never admit. Like how I knew that my mother used Ambien every night and slept like the dead. Like how I used her passwords to hack her home automation controls and set the middle-of-the-night thermostat as low as it would go. Like how I attacked her with cold, triggering her autoimmune reaction over and over again until her body couldn't make enough blood cells to replace what she was losing. I can't know for certain if it was what killed her, but I do believe it sped up the process, and I'm glad.

When she died, I flew with her body on the private jet. I threw a fit and demanded Dickie and the other Goldaming Life ghouls take a different one. For once I got my way. When the flight attendant was preparing my meal, I had a few precious moments alone. I lifted the lid of Mother's casket. There she was. As cold and lifeless in death as she had been in life. It was easy to imagine she might open her eyes. Easy to picture a red gleam in them.

I had a present for her. A piece I'd made in the metalworking class I'd taken before she got me expelled. I had to pick up so many extra shifts to buy that much silver, but it was worth it. It was surprisingly hard to drive my clumsy knife between her bones, and alarmingly loud. But it was worth it. She left permanent marks on me. I left one on her, too.

My mom is dead, and she's staying dead. I worked hard to create this shot at freedom, and I can't blow it.

"Anyway," I say, turning on my side to face Elle. "That's my mother. Who she was and what she represents. This is my one chance to get away forever." It's apology and explanation. I want to stay with Elle and get to know her better. To see if we have a chance. I hope she gets that in any reasonable world, she'd be enough to hold me here.

"Iris," Elle says. "Do you get seasick?"

It's so far from anything I expected her to say in response to all my trauma that I laugh, shocked out of my morose self-pity. "No, I don't get seasick."

"How would you feel about being on a boat for a long time? I mean a *long* time. A month and a half, maybe two months. Not a nice ship, either. A cargo ship."

"Am I in a box in this scenario?"

She smiles, dimples dipping into existence and then disappearing just as quickly, like a mirage of happiness. Then Elle gets serious. I don't think I've seen her deadly serious before. As petite and delicately beautiful as she is, there's something threatening in her narrowed eyes. Her voice lowers as she says, "Give me three days to arrange things, and I'll get you somewhere they can never touch you again."

I should ask how. Instead, the question that comes out of my mouth is, "Why?"

Why is she helping me? No one else ever has. Even when they believed me, they didn't dare go against the power of my mother and Goldaming Life.

Elle doesn't blink. She holds my gaze with her lightless ocean eyes. I could sink to the bottom of them and be secret and safe forever. "Because," she says, "so many girls deserve help, but I can't help them all. I can save you, though. Ask me to save you. Please."

I kiss the tip of her nose, then her forehead, then her chin. Her lips I merely brush, a promise. She takes it as me accepting her offer and buries her face in the curve of my neck.

I don't believe she can actually save me. It's cruel of me to let her think it's possible. But for today, in this precious, dreamy now, we can live in that fantasy.

53

August 17, 1890

JOURNAL OF LUCY WESTENRA

How many days has it been since I started that last entry? I haven't had the energy or will to finish it. I was correct to keep watch at the window. He came right to the glass. I don't know how—we're on the second story.

He scraped his nails down the window. I knew he would wake Mina, and once she was awake, he would have her. The only way to block his pathway to her was with myself. My body in place of hers. I undid the latch and offered my neck.

Mina found me there in the morning, unconscious, hanging half out the window. I wept as she chided me, so she became gentler and guided me to bed. I have tried to sleep as much as I can during the day since then. That way I can guard Mina against the hunger and the teeth that night brings.

What is he? My throat is icy cold all the time. The marks of his bite repulse me, yet I can't stop myself from touching them, exploring their edges. The wounds of my efforts to protect Mina. The proof that I love her, better than anyone else ever will, better than she can ever know. I'm not evil, I'm not selfish, I'm a creature of pure love. My love will keep her safe.

Mina knows I'm upset. I'm having a harder time hiding everything. She thinks my weeping and odd sleep habits are about Arthur and his absence, and assures me he's coming as soon as he can. She brushes my hair and tells me all the things Arthur loves about me. The lines that form between my brows when I'm puzzled or worried. The way I cover my mouth when I laugh, as though I can keep those peals from escaping. My delicate fingers, my golden waves of hair, my sparkling eyes. The ease with which I can converse with both lords and servants. My careless generosity.

But Mina and Arthur have barely spoken. Surely he hasn't told her all those things! I think she says them to make me feel certain Arthur loves me, but it only makes me hope that Mina's actually telling me all the things *she* loves about me. That I was wrong to fear she's looking forward to being rid of me.

I don't think she's in love with me, but I do know now that she loves me, and that's enough.

I have my own list. The collection of things about Mina that make my chilled heart swell and beat stronger. Her wit. Her fortitude. Her practical cleverness. The way certain light changes her eyes from plain brown to glowing amber. The way only I can make her lose her composure and laugh like we're the careless schoolgirls we never got to be. ~~The curve of her lower lip, the perfect dip in the center of her upper lip. The way she fits curled into me when she falls asleep in my bed. The way the blankets obscure and reveal as they drape over her form, and I~~

Or maybe she's reassuring me about Arthur's devotion because she's worried about Jonathan's. She's been rereading his letters, obsessing over them, quoting parts to me until I feign sleep just to stop hearing them. She claims the words don't sound like him, even though the writing is clearly his.

There's something else in her obsession besides worry, though. I have devoted my artist's eye to Mina's expressions, and I know when she's furious. She hides it well, but not well enough. Mina reads those letters and whatever she finds or doesn't find in them makes her angry.

Maybe my monster meant only that she's lost Jonathan's heart, not that he's perished. Either way, it doesn't matter. Mina has me. I'll keep her safe. I'll protect her. I'll stay awake here at the window, as the night flutters and swoops and presses close with hungry, sharp teeth.

54

Boston, September 26, 2024

CLIENT TRANSCRIPT

My green dress was black with blood.

I sat, soot-stained and reeking of smoke in the charred remains of so many men and one precious woman. I had ruined everything, yet again.

Ingrid had kissed me like she was dying, every time. Desperate and passionate and frantic. And now she was actually dead, because she trusted me. Because I couldn't tell her who I was. Because I was so distracted by the memory of Mina, driven mad by my questions of who she had become without me, that I'd failed everyone.

The secretary was dead, too, which meant he couldn't give up the information. But what did it matter? The Nazis and fascists would try again, or they'd try something else. Sometimes it would work, sometimes it wouldn't. And the monstrous machine of war would plow on, devouring youth.

What we'd done that night didn't matter. Ingrid was just another body, another woman broken and ended, and for what? The Doctor's question was eternal, and the only question that mattered: *And is the war over?*

It wasn't. It never has been. It never will be. All wars are the same war. Evil is banal, evil is boring, evil is predictable, and evil is everywhere. The heroes of that particular chapter, the liberators of Europe and Africa? Go backward or go forward, you'll find the same blood on their hands. The same violence and atrocities in their own lands, or in foreign lands under the banner of their flags. The same dark deals, the same sacrifices of young bodies in service of old money.

Though I understood at last in that room that I couldn't impact things in a way that would matter, I have no regrets about helping the sides I did. The Nazis were exceptionally good at evil. And still are. Different names, same agendas. Sometimes even the same name. Time really is a circle. No one ever learns, nothing changes, nothing matters.

I never did. Learn, or change, or matter.

I went back to the Doctor's lab that night. I slumped in the corner and wept, thinking of Ingrid, thinking of how poorly I'd done. To my surprise, the Doctor came and sat by me. She didn't hold me or comfort me, but her willingness to leave a man bleeding unobserved on her operating table for a few precious moments was a huge gesture.

"You were right," I said, miserable and lost. "I tried to be smart this time, and it still didn't fix things. I don't know what to do anymore. I don't know where to go or who to be. I don't know how to exist. How do we keep existing?"

"Stay here with me," she said. "Help me in my studies. The people I'm working with now are making so much progress. We'll do astonishing things. We'll defy mortality at every turn, we'll fix bodies, we'll . . ." She trailed off. "We'll steal back as many souls from death as we can."

But I didn't care about people the same way the Doctor did. She wanted to understand how they worked. To know all the ways they could break, rot from the inside, die. She wanted to save their bodies.

I just wanted to know how to make them love me. How to make myself someone worth loving. How to stop being a monster.

"You should study *us*," I said. "Figure out what's wrong with us, so you can fix it. So you can fix me."

She stood, all tenderness gone. "It's pointless, Lucy. There's nothing to figure out. We're abominations. Aberrations. It's best to focus on—"

"You're being intellectually uncurious." It was the meanest thing I could have possibly said to her. I wanted to hurt her. I began smashing bottles, throwing the Doctor's supplies across the lab. "You're the smartest woman on earth. Surely you can answer my questions. *Someone* has to answer my questions! You're the only one left, because he never came back for me!"

"Dracula never cares, afterward."

My tantrum immediately stopped. It was the first time she'd ever said his name. The first time she'd admitted our connection through him.

She stared past me. "I had been dying long before he killed me. Here in this very city. Sneaking into libraries and hospitals, researching. I was close to fixing myself. So close. And then Dracula found me. After what he did, I wasn't dying anymore, but I wasn't alive. He saved me and broke me at the same time."

Her eyes cut toward me, pinning me with her gaze. "I waited for him, too. I wanted answers, too. But when it became clear he didn't care about me anymore, I decided to never care about him, either. I focused on what I *could* do. What I could study and understand without anyone else. That meant researching bodies that still made sense. Exploring life and death in their proper, permanent order.

"But sometimes," she said, her voice very soft, "I still think he'll be there. In a dark corner. At a window. And at last I'll get to ask him my questions. It's been so long, though, I've forgotten what the questions were."

"It doesn't matter. He's dead," I said bluntly. "Killed by the men who couldn't save me."

The Doctor tilted her head, frowning. "Lucy," she said, about to upend my entire world. "That's not possible. I know for a fact Dracula is still alive."

55

London, October 7, 2024

IRIS

I wake up at twilight. I'm the good kind of sore, but I'm also alone. A note rests on the pillow next to me. Elle's handwriting is elegant cursive. Unsurprising that someone who loves history would value a dead art like handwriting. My own handwriting looks like notes sent to the FBI by a serial killer trying to taunt them.

"Going to see someone about buying the rest of the paintings. Be back soon. Sorry there's not much food in the kitchen, haven't had time to go to the shops. Met this incredible girl and have been too busy using my old stove lighting skills to seduce her before helping her flee her family's cult. Typical week around here. Chip place downstairs is nice if you're hungry. X."

I'm glad Elle's not there to hear the happy sound I make as I hug her note to my chest. I don't know if I'm "incredible," but she makes me feel that way.

I don't want to leave the flat. Not even for french fries. Opening a door to the outside world would puncture this bubble of happiness and safety. Temporary safety, sure, but I'll take what I can get.

Until she comes back, though, I have nothing to occupy myself with. Besides snooping, and I don't want to do that to Elle. That's when I remember the other woman in my life, tucked away in my bag. I can check in on Lucy. I hope she gets lucky like I did. I don't even mean it in a crude way. I genuinely feel lucky in the deepest sense of the word for what happened today with Elle. For having Elle in my life at all, however briefly.

I settle in with my last granola bar and Lucy's floor journal, determined to finish today so I can get to the next journal. Lucy's going on about plans for running away with her secret love. And then I sit up.

"Oh, shit!" I crow. Her secret crush is revealed to be none other than *Mina*.

It's been her best friend and former governess the whole time! No wonder I felt both affinity for and a slight crush on Lucy. She's confirmed sapphic, whether she has the vocabulary and context for it or not. My heart squeezes with tender affection, but also a foreshadowing of fear. Oh, Lucy. What's going to happen to you?

It's immediate heartbreak. Lucy's ready to inform Mina that once her mother dies, Lucy has all the money they could ever want. But before she can suggest they run away to Whitby together—my images of her in the city change, now putting a woman at her side—Mina announces she's engaged.

"Fucking Jonathan," I mutter. Ruining everything. Though Mina sounds a little like a bitch. I understand Lucy's crush-struck haze, but Mina's so dismissive of her. Cruel, even.

Lucy was so much more than a beautiful heiress. Which is even more evident when I read the next entry. She's keeping two journals—one as a fake record that she's feeling and thinking and doing only what she should. My clever girl, tricking her snooping mother!

I glance at my messenger bag containing the other journal. It must be the fake version of herself she used to keep her heart protected. No wonder that one was in the safe with other documents, and her real diary was hidden in the floor.

I wish I could hug her words close and whisper reassurances. Tell Lucy it's going to be all right. But the girl who wrote these things is long gone. I hate that she had to hide so much. And I understand why she did.

The next few entries are alternately sad, funny, and angry, as Lucy talks about how silly she was to imagine a life with Mina, mentions Arthur's increasing visits and all his help sorting out their estate and her mother's will, and writes a startlingly bleak detail about how her father died walking in his sleep.

I'm projecting again, but I hate Lucy's father for leaving her alone with her manipulative mother, surrounded by these men who insist they know how to help her but never actually listen to her.

The next notable entry has all three men—Doctor Seward, whom I'm convinced is evil, the dim but kind American cowboy Quincey Morris, and Arthur Holmwood—showing up on the same day within minutes of each other, each proposing to Lucy. Her details have me laughing so hard I'm tearing up. Oh, those poor idiots, thinking they had her figured out. Thinking she was a silly young thing they could own. She's delicately vicious in her summaries, though in person she behaved and let the first two down easily.

My laughter stops as she finishes her account of Arthur's proposal. Not just because Lucy accepts solely out of a desire to make Mina happy. But because of what she calls him. The future *Lord Goldaming.*

I don't know much about British gentry customs or why he has two names, but this is the first time I've seen that one. Which means Arthur Holmwood is also Lord Goldaming. My ancestor. And Lucy, the girl I've been relating to and feeling so much affection for—even crushing on—is my ancestor, too.

Feeling vaguely incestuous but also sad for how her bright, vivid life is going to be gradually worn down by being trapped in the closet, I close the diary.

I can't quite understand why the information that Lucy was a Goldaming is so disappointing. Obviously, I should have assumed she was related to me. But I hate my family and all their poisonous history so much. Knowing Lucy was part of it makes her feel tarnished. Tainted. Just like me.

I don't hear the door, so I jump like I've been caught doing something shameful when Elle says, "Where did you get that?"

56

Boston, September 26, 2024

CLIENT TRANSCRIPT

"Dracula is dead," I said. Though I don't need to breathe, it still felt like I wasn't getting any air. I grabbed the Doctor's arm. "Dracula is *dead*. He's dead. The Queen told me. She has spies all over. He tried to take a woman who people loved, and they saved her, and they killed him."

I needed him to be dead. If he wasn't gone, if he was out there somewhere? Mina had been in danger this whole time while I'd been lounging around Paris or trying to fix the world in small, stupid ways that never mattered.

If Dracula was still alive, then I'd failed Mina. My life and death and everything after were utterly meaningless, just as I'd always feared.

"Dracula can't be dead," the Doctor said, removing my hand from her arm. "If he were, every vampire he created would be dead, too. Which means you and I wouldn't be standing here having this conversation, interrupting my very critical task of slicing tumors out of this man." She turned back to her work. I wedged myself between her and the body.

"Explain it to me. Please. Make it make sense. If I kill the next vampire I meet, would dozens of other vampires cease to exist?"

Annoyance and eagerness warred on her face. The Doctor hated to be delayed in her work, but she loved explaining things she'd figured out, or things she knew that I didn't, which was a lot. I wish I could accurately capture what it felt like to be on the receiving end of one of the Doctor's lectures. Pretend I'm far taller and take up space like it exists for me to fill it, like I'm as beautiful and cold as an alpine mountain, like when I look at you I'm studying you for flaws down to your very genes, and I'm finding them all.

"Have you ever made another vampire?" she asked. "No? Neither have I. Have you met any other vampires creating more vampires?"

I had not. Not even the Queen had made any of her girls into vampires. Her infinite loneliness, longing for an equal but refusing to allow anyone to be that for her, hadn't been enough to make her cross that line. The Lover had strict rules about never killing anyone. And Raven only cared about Dracula and what he was doing.

The Doctor continued, hands behind her back, as still as a statue. Not calm, but rigid, holding herself as tightly as she could. "Dracula is the only vampire I'm aware of who creates new vampires. He's not content to consume. He wants to sow the whole world with his corrupted seed, plant us in the dirt like flags of conquest. Whatever we were, whatever we could have been: remade in his image. *His.*"

She paused, and for a moment I could see who the Doctor had been, before. Eager, inquisitive, yearning. Heartbroken by a world that rejected a genius mind in a woman's body. Desperate for a chance to do what she knew she could. Dying despite her abilities. That was who Dracula had found, who he had taken.

But then she snipped the thread of humanity away from herself and continued her lecture. "Besides, it takes so much patience. He bit you over and over again, yes? You remember that much, right?"

My hand went to my throat. Hers echoed the gesture, both of us lost in the memory of pain.

She recovered first. "My theory is that this method spreads out the blood loss, giving the infection time to take hold before the tissue dies. And he fed you his own blood, too, did he not? It's a tedious, involved process, bound to draw attention and expose the vampire to risk of discovery. So many nights returning to the same victim. Voluntary weakness by losing blood. Who would bother with it?"

"Maybe someone who doesn't want to be alone," I said. I knew what it was to want someone so much that you'd sacrifice everything for them. That you'd accept *their* sacrifice of everything, even if it was wrong. Even if it was selfish. Even if it would have destroyed you both.

It was exactly why I fled England to search for Dracula. To keep Mina safe—from Dracula, but also from me. We were the same monster.

The Doctor shook her head. "As we've both confirmed, Dracula was not there when you awoke. Your theory of his loneliness is disproved by our experience. Dracula doesn't care about being alone. He doesn't want companions, or relationships. He only wants control. And he still has it, doesn't he? Can't you feel him, somewhere out there? That shadow in your heart, that sting at your neck?"

She quieted, her eyes the empty black of the grave. Then she blinked it away. "Fortunately for us, he has a short attention span when it comes to his new toys."

"How does it work, though? Why are we connected to him? What happens when we change? Why can I—"

The doctor waved a dismissive hand, her fingernails sharp as scalpels. "I don't know, and I don't care. We're parasites. We aren't human, Lucy. We're just disease." She slit the man on her table from sternum to pubic bone. "*This* is what I care about, *this* is what I can learn with perfection, *this* is what matters. Stay here and help me, Lucy," she said, disproving her claim that she wasn't lonely.

I think she was the loneliest of all of us.

She held out her clean hand to me, the other sunk into the remains of a soul released at the end of his life. "Forget about Dracula, forget whatever connects you to him. We have all the time in the world. Let's spend it on things that can still be fixed."

Once again, the Doctor was proving that she cared about me. She wanted me to stay. But I was livid. I was *pointless,* and aimless, and I'd wasted so much time. I'd stayed away from London thinking it was keeping Mina safe, when this whole time Dracula was still out there. She'd been in danger. She might still be in danger. I had to find her.

The Doctor wanted me to forget about who I was, who I had been, who had made me this way. As though I could become like her, a swift scalpel to cut out all my feelings and emotions. As though she was somehow better than me.

"You're not doing anything people won't figure out on their own, eventually," I said. "This isn't noble. You're wasting time, exactly like I have been. You're ignoring what and who you are because you can't understand it, and so it scares you. But just because vampires shouldn't exist doesn't mean we don't. Why can't you care about us, too? Come with me, instead. Help me. Dracula is still out there, holding answers for us. Hurting women like us." I stumbled on the last word, because it wasn't true, was it? Those women weren't like us. Not anymore. But they would be, if Dracula found them.

My dead heart thudded dully to life. A poisonous hope spread through me. If Dracula was still alive, if he had gotten to Mina, then she'd be like me now. A vampire, lost and alone.

The Doctor was right. I could still feel him out there. I should have known he wasn't dead.

I'd never stopped looking for Mina in every face I saw, as though I expected to see her exactly as I'd left her. Maybe I'd stayed away for that exact reason. Part of me had wanted Dracula to find her, and turn her, and give her to me forever.

57

August 19, 1890

JOURNAL OF LUCY WESTENRA

I hate the monster. Not because of these holes in my throat, this exhausted stupor, these terrors and nightmares. But because he lied.

Jonathan is alive, and Mina is gone. I helped her pack and took her to the train station myself, clinging to her as I watched everyone else who got aboard. I made certain his red eyes were nowhere. Mina's heading for Jonathan, which is far away from me, but also far away from the monster. She's safe now. That's what I wanted, is it not?

It is. I do want that, more than anything. Mina's safe, and now I can sleep. She vowed to write and update me. She plans on marrying stale-pudding Jonathan as soon as they are reunited. Then they will travel back as husband and wife.

I can be selfless. I can be happy for my heart, my dearest, my best friend. ~~I can give up my dream of Mina, a Mina who would look back at me as she boarded the train, instead of staring resolutely ahead. A Mina who would choose me over everyone else, instead of only staying with me when she had no better use for her time. A Mina who would see how desperately I loved her, and welcome it, and love me back. I will bury that dream, and mourn it, and wear the black of a widow.~~

Arthur's here now. He arrived this evening, all smiles and calm solicitude. When I took his coat and hung it as an excuse to escape his small talk with Mother, I found a letter in his pocket. It was Mina's beloved handwriting, so I read it. She wrote him before she purchased her train ticket, before she even packed, telling him to come to me immediately and watch things here.

More happy proof that even if she doesn't love me how I wanted her to, she cares about me. I will hold on to that.

My time in Whitby is done. Arthur is escorting Mother and me back to London. In a month, I will marry him. I'm too tired to write more, and those wings are battering the window. I can sleep through it tonight.

"Fool!" I mock, smiling at my reflection in the glass. We have both lost her.

58

London, October 7, 2024

IRIS

"Oh! Hey!" I try to keep my tone easy. Maybe Elle won't notice the diary isn't a normal book. "How did it go? Do they want the paintings?"

Elle sets down a bag and walks to the bed but doesn't climb on. She looks *flat,* like a bottle of bubbly left out on the counter, all effervescence escaped.

"Is that a journal?" she asks.

I glance down at it and grimace. "Yeah. I found it hidden in the house."

"Why didn't you tell me about it?"

"Because," I start, and I can't help but grasp the diary tighter to my chest. "Because it doesn't belong in a museum. I knew this would be the thing you'd want in exchange for all the help. You can have anything else in the house. Hell, *everything* else in the house. But not this. Lucy, the girl who wrote it? Everyone around her told her who she was, who she had to be. She was constantly pretending, faking every feeling and smile and conversation, just to survive, because she was a teenage girl no one listened to. And because she was queer."

I lower the diary and look at the cover, trying to explain why it means so much to me. "I don't know if she even understood what she was feeling, but she was desperately in love with her governess. Writing in here was the only place she could ever be herself. I can't let her story go into a museum to become an object of interest. She'd be a novelty. I can't break her trust that way."

Elle's voice is surprisingly cold. "You're the one reading her diary.

You've already broken her trust. Besides, it was a long time ago. Just the scribblings of a silly, spoiled girl, right?"

Defensiveness rises around me like a flock of startled pigeons, flapping and clacking and clattering in my chest. I can feel my face turning red. "She was so much more than that. She was brilliant and funny and insightful and yes, also probably super rich, but that didn't help her! People always think being rich negates bad things or makes abuse somehow tolerable. I promise, it doesn't. It's just part of the cage they trap you in. And everyone in her life was using her—*everyone.* No one respected her or listened to her. No one really saw or understood her or even wanted to. I know I'm being irrational, Elle, I promise I know. And I'm sorry I didn't tell you about Lucy. But I *can't* let the museum have this. I know her better than maybe anyone else ever got to, and I love her."

Elle softens. Some of the life returns to her face. "She's that great, huh?"

"She really is. Here, come." I pat the space next to me. "You can read it."

Elle climbs into bed, sits between my legs, and leans back against me. She rests her head on my shoulder and snuggles in. "Read it out loud," she says. "Your favorite parts. Bring her to life for me, too."

Some of the tightness in my chest loosens. Elle's not mad, and she's not going to demand I give the diary to the museum. I knew she'd understand that teenage girls' feelings and heartbreaks and hopes matter, and they always have. Especially Lucy's.

I go back to the beginning and read all the funniest passages—particularly the vicious but fair mockery of Americans. But I also read the saddest sections—the descriptions of her mother, the way she's so desperate to be happy for Mina even though her heart is breaking. The full depth and breadth of Lucy. I breathe life into her so Elle understands.

Elle doesn't say anything, but she laughs at both Lucy's jokes and my horrendous attempt at an English accent to narrate her thoughts.

"Oh, oh," I say, excited. "Let me read you the triple-proposal scene. So awkward. All those idiots in love with her and refusing to notice that she wasn't attracted to any of them. Poor Lucy. First up is Doctor Seward." I pause and tap the page where Lucy describes how her mother always gets worse after he visits. "He's one hundred percent making Lucy's mother sick so he can have access to Lucy."

"What?" Elle asks, genuinely shocked.

"Oh, I have so many theories. But Doctor Seward is for sure a bad, bad dude. He's constantly trying to drug Lucy, too. Thank god she doesn't trust him. Anyway, where were we? So, he proposes, and she's shocked because she's always been polite but never given him *any* romantic encouragement. He basically treats it like a job interview, listing all his many qualifications." I switch back into my Lucy voice and read the rest.

Elle snorts a little laugh at Lucy's descriptions, and I laugh with her. "Right? She's hilarious. I wish I could have known her."

"Mm," Elle says. "You really think she was special." She traces a finger along the inside of my wrist, then up my palm and each of my fingers. Not touching the diary, just touching me where I'm touching it. "Should I be jealous?"

"Pretty sure she's my great-great-whatever, and also she was nineteen like a hundred and thirty years ago, so I think you're safe. But she was definitely special. And I care about her. So much in here is funny and charming, but also sad. See, look at this section. Things are crossed out. Even though her diary was private and hidden, she still felt the need to erase her own thoughts sometimes. She was trying to edit her feelings. It breaks my heart. I wish I could tell her there's nothing wrong with her."

When Elle doesn't immediately respond, I push on. I'm determined to win her over. She'll agree with me that Lucy was an incredible person, and that we need to protect her private thoughts from being put on display. I flip back to the proposal section. "But just wait. It gets worse for our girl. Because it's not Doctor Seward at the door next, it's the cowboy! Who has also showed up to, drumroll please . . . propose! But he uses super-weird turns of phrases and talks in circles like he's lassoing his thoughts. I swear he might not even have been American, his folksy sayings are so odd. He was definitely making them up to create an Ultra Cowboy persona and impress all the Brits. Anyway, he's so confusing, it takes Lucy a long time to figure out he's proposing, too. Here, I'll just read it, it's so funny, you'll—"

My phone rings from the nightstand. The number makes my heart sink. Dad's nursing home. I put my free arm across Elle's chest, holding her like a life preserver as I answer.

"Iris?" Dad's voice trembles with fear. "Iris! She was here again! She got into my room. I hid under the covers, but I could hear her, pacing around and laughing the whole night. She's going to come back tonight and—"

"Dad," I say. "She's dead. Mom's *dead*. She can't come back. I promise."

"But she is, she—"

"Call your nurse. Put them on the phone." I wait. There's some muted chatter in the background, and then a tired-sounding man answers.

"Hi, this is Greg."

"Hi, Greg. I left very specific instructions for my father's room. Have they been followed?"

The pause on the other end is all the answer I need. Bastards. As much money as we gave them, and they can't follow a few silly instructions?

"If my instructions are not followed to the letter, our contract is void. I'll move my father to another facility and sue for a full refund."

"That won't be necessary!" Greg understands how much my father is worth to them. "I've got the list right here. You're right, some of the items haven't been taken care of. I'll see to them personally."

"Thanks, Greg. I'm trusting you with this."

"Would you like me to put you back on with your dad?"

"Nope," I say, and hang up. Then I immediately dial another number.

"Is everything okay?" Elle asks.

"Nope," I answer. But before I can expound, Dickie picks up.

"Miss Goldaming," he says. He always emphasizes "Miss" so it's clear he's not saying "Ms."

"Dick," I say. I always inflect it so it's clear I'm being crudely offensive, not using his actual name. "Stop fucking with my dad."

"I don't know what you mean."

"Bullshit. You're terrorizing him so I'll come back."

"I'm doing no such thing."

I roll my eyes. "Right, sorry. You're delegating the task of terrorizing him to someone else. You have plausible deniability and an alibi, and I'm still forced to come back. And what's with sending Ford here to keep an eye on me? She about broke my arm threatening me."

"That seems excessive."

"It does, doesn't it? Listen." It's not a stretch to sound exhausted and pushed past my limit. "Just . . . leave my dad alone. Put Ford on a shorter leash. Preferably so short she chokes herself on it. Let me finish pretending like I'm a philanthropist, donating paintings and shit to museums so I can feel a little better about the piles of blood money I'm sitting on. Then I'll come home. Three days. You can even book my flight."

"The private jet will be available then. I'll make the arrangements."

"Great. Let's kill the environment while we're killing all my hopes and dreams. A clean sweep of destruction. Awesome. But when I get back, things are going to be different. Okay? I get a say. I get an actual voice on the board. If I'm doing this, I'm doing it my way."

"I'm looking forward to getting you settled where you belong. Where your blood is. Because—"

"The blood is bloody life, yup, got it, bye." I end the call and throw my phone across the bed in disgust.

Elle scoots around so we're facing each other. She takes my hands in hers. "We're running out of time," she says.

"We are, yeah. I've got to go back to the house tonight, sleep there so they don't suspect anything. We have to make it look like you're just working for me. Like I'm doing exactly what I've told them I'm doing. It's the only way to keep you safe."

"But—"

"Please trust me. Go to the museum tomorrow morning. Do your normal routine and job, like I'm not a priority. Sell the paintings if you can, but if not, don't worry about it. Come over tomorrow afternoon and we can plan more."

Elle looks torn, but she nods. "I have travel arrangements to make, and I can't risk being followed. Promise you'll be careful."

"They're not going to hurt me. Especially now that they think they're getting exactly what they want." And because I let them think they know how to control me. Threatening and harassing my dad won't change anything. I'm fully prepared to abandon him. It doesn't make me a good person, but I already know it's what he'd do in my shoes.

I climb reluctantly out of bed, then hesitate. "Do you want to keep the journal? Read it for yourself?" I don't want to leave Lucy here and stop reading, but I trust Elle with it.

Elle smiles and shakes her head. "I wouldn't be able to do Lucy's voice *nearly* as well as you."

I laugh and throw a pillow at her. "Mean."

"Bookmark more of your favorite parts for tomorrow. And maybe one of these days you can read the whole thing to me?"

I wish I could. "We won't have time before I run."

Elle bites her lip and looks to the side. The light seems to pass straight through her, rendering her nearly translucent. So fragile and vulnerable and breakable. "We will if I come on the boat with you."

My eyes close. I don't mean to close them, I just can't process everything I need to in this moment. None of it feels possible. Not after the life I've had, being shown time and again that *no one* puts being with me over what Goldaming Life offers them—or threatens them with.

"Are you sure?" I can barely force the words out, certain she'll laugh. That she's teasing or flirting, or that I somehow missed a cruel streak hidden by her sweet face.

"Ask me to come with you," she says.

I open my eyes, surprised to find her standing right in front of me. That sense of translucence is still there. It's not just vulnerability. It's sincerity. She's not hiding anything from me. Elle is the only truth I've ever found.

"Kiss me," I whisper, "and come with me. Please."

She presses her lips against mine, sealing our hope between the two of us. Because that's what Elle is: hope. That's what she feels like in my arms. I haven't had it for so long, I'd forgotten what it was.

Emily Dickinson is right. *Hope is the thing with feathers that perches in the soul.*

But things with feathers are always so fragile, and I can't help feeling afraid of what I'm asking Elle to take flight into alongside me.

59

August 30, 1890

JOURNAL OF LUCY WESTENRA

Mina found Jonathan. She's married.

I'm opening the latch on my window. We can be alone together, the darkness and me.

60

Boston, September 26, 2024

CLIENT TRANSCRIPT

I raced back to England, taking every form of transportation I could find. Motorcycles and ambulances and tanks and trains and boats and even an airplane. The only thing that mattered was speed. I had to see Mina. Just from a distance. If she was still alive, if she was happy, if she was thriving, then I wasn't pointless. I was worth something. My love had mattered, even if she never knew.

And if Dracula had gotten to her, well . . . I wouldn't be alone anymore, would I?

But when I arrived at last, London was different. My quiet city was an older, grizzled, scarred version of itself. It hummed with low, constant dread. Familiar sights were pocked from bombs and choked with smoke. Cars and ambulances and soldiers were everywhere. And Mina was gone.

I went to her house, but there was another family there and they had no idea who Mina Murray *or* Mina Harker were. The Harkers no doubt lived somewhere else together, but I'd never been there. Why hadn't I been there? It was odd that I'd never visited my closest friend after she returned to London a married woman. The end of my life was a pain-soaked haze I deliberately never thought of, but I knew Mina wasn't in it.

Sitting on a bench in a park—unsure why I was there, but drawn back to some of my old routes as a human—I puzzled through my options. Surely there were records that could tell me what had happened to Mina. But I had no idea where or even what those records were. I was a vampire, not a detective. And in life I had been a wealthy young heiress, so someone else always handled details.

Which left me with one other option. Treading the paths of my life had brought up additional memories. If I couldn't find Mina, then perhaps I could find some of my other old *friends.* Surely one of them would know what happened to Mina, since they were the ones who had hunted Dracula. They could help me, as long as they didn't know who they were helping.

Fortunately, finding directions to the sanitarium was easy. It had been turned into a hospital for wounded soldiers; everyone knew where it was, and it was busy enough that I was able to walk right in without anyone noticing me.

I did shift my appearance ever so slightly, though. I hadn't forgotten the sound of a saw cutting laboriously through Dove's spine.

"Excuse me," I asked one of the nurses. He had a body that spoke of past brawny health withered away. An old scar on his neck drew my eyes and for a moment I wondered if he, too, had been bitten. But instead of two points of pain that would never leave him, it looked like he had been ripped into. "Have you worked here long?"

He nodded, barely glancing at me.

"Do you know Doctor Seward?"

His eyes narrowed with suspicion. He stopped what he was doing and really looked at me. "Yes."

"Do you know where I could find him?"

He turned and spat on the floor, which hardly seemed sanitary. "He went to America, decades ago. Good riddance."

I hadn't been looking forward to a reunion with the man, but it was a blow. It not only took Doctor Seward off my list, it also took off the cowboy. I couldn't imagine Doctor Seward going to America without his Texan friend.

I wandered outside, walking as I thought. Who else could I look for? The third option was the lecherous old Dutch man, and I hoped he was dead by now, anyway. The idea of him still out there, looming and leering and holding young women's hands so they couldn't escape him, was so unfair it made my teeth grate against each other.

That was the worst part of trying to find Mina. It forced me to remember other things. I was digging around in the grave of my past, and I didn't enjoy what I was unearthing.

Arthur was the only option left to me. But that, too, proved impossible. Try as I might, I couldn't remember ever once visiting his family's estate. How had we been engaged and I never saw his home?

An older woman, with hair as white as fresh snow and joyful wrinkles around her eyes, took pity on me as I sat crying on the steps of an old tea shop Mina and I used to frequent.

"Are you lost, dear?" she asked.

"Yes," I sobbed. "I've been away so long, and now I can't find anyone. I need to see my friend, but no one knows where she is."

"Have you tried a directory?"

"I don't even know what that is."

She tutted and helped me stand, then guided me to a library. Inside, she sat me at a table and then brought over a bound book. It thudded down, heavy with the weight of souls. She tapped the cover. "If they live in London, they'll be in here. Or maybe someone you used to know will be. Would you like help looking up names?"

I stood and wrapped my arms around her, pressing a kiss to her cheek. "Thank you," I said. It was exactly what I needed. Both the directory, and the reminder that even in the worst of times, there's still kindness walking among us. "I can manage from here."

She bid me good luck and farewell. Honestly, if I were going to turn anyone besides Mina into a vampire, I think I would have chosen her. All the vampires I knew had been changed when we were young and impulsive and selfish. How much better to change when you've already grown fully into yourself, with all your wisdom and compassion and power?

But I let her go. And then I delved into the book. I looked for "Murray." "Harker." "Holmwood" and "Goldaming" both, since Arthur surely took his father's title at some point. I even looked for "Seward," just in case. I couldn't think of the cowboy's name, which was disappointing because he held slightly less dread for me than the others, but he was only "the cowboy" in my head. There was nothing. They had all disappeared. I couldn't find Mina. Was it because she was dead, or because the book was incomplete thanks to the chaos of war?

I wandered out of the library. The city churned and turned around me, and I stood in the center, unmoving. I didn't know how to find people, because I wasn't one. But I knew death, didn't I? And I had all the time in the world to search death for my beloved.

I went to the cemeteries. I worked methodically and intensively. Night after night, cemetery after cemetery, I read every single stone. Hundreds, then thousands, then tens of thousands of names. And then one night, I found a name I was looking for. *Jonathan Harker.* It was no wonder he hadn't been in any of the directories. He'd died only a couple of years after I did, still a young man.

There was no companion gravestone. No loving wife buried beside him. If Mina had been killed by Dracula, she would have been buried in a regular plot such as this before rising again as a vampire. But her grave wasn't here. I couldn't imagine Jonathan being buried anywhere but at her side. Which meant Mina had survived. Dracula hadn't won in the end.

I sat on Jonathan's grave and wept. I didn't know if it was from relief or disappointment.

Mina was still out there, alive. Not an old woman, but not a young one anymore. I was certain I would still know her, though. I would always know her. I'd stay as long as it took for a chance to see her.

I slept in my mausoleum, shoring up strength, drifting out to Jonathan's grave every night to search for evidence of Mina. No one left flowers, or visited, or so much as brushed the dirt from his name. I would have felt sorry for him if he hadn't been so *Jonathan.*

It was his fault I'd died. If he hadn't gone to Transylvania, if he hadn't been striving to deserve Mina, then my path, and more importantly Mina's path, never would have crossed with Dracula's.

I dreamed, lying on the uncut grass on top of his grave, of what that life might have been. A life without Dracula, a life without Jonathan. A life with Mina. But when I closed my eyes and slept, I found only darkness.

The stars wheeled overhead. Airplanes came and went, bombs fell, and then they stopped. A tree looming above me went from bare to tender green to droning with insects to brilliant orange and back to bare.

She wasn't coming. Mina was alive or she was dead, but she wasn't a vampire. Either way she was out of my reach. At last, I'd lost her forever.

It felt like a period at the end of a sentence I'd been whispering to myself for decades, a sentence of love and longing and the darkest glimmer of hope. And now I had to end it.

I wished then that Mina *was* dead. I wished that I'd found her grave. I would have burrowed beneath the ground, let the hallowed earth seep all my strength. Stayed forever in Mina's arms. But I was denied even that. There was no world in which Mina could be mine. There never had been. I'd always known it.

What point was there to anything after that? I went to my mausoleum, slipped inside, and slept. The earth spun, the years passed, and I sought to disappear from all of it. If I could not die, I could sleep. I could refuse to wake up.

I would have rested there forever, as close to peace as a creature like me can find, if not for the rat. The nearness of blood and heat at last pulled me from my deathly slumber.

As I was picking fur out of my teeth, barely lucid, all I could think of was Dracula and his rats. Disgust made me want to carve out my stomach the way I had carved out the stomach of his familiar in China.

But.

But.

If what we consume becomes part of us forever, then my world wasn't ended. Not yet. If Dracula was alive, and he had ever taken blood from Mina, then part of Mina was still here, too.

I burst from my mausoleum, barely more than moonlight and rage and desire. I was going to find Dracula. I was going to drain him. And then, with Mina at last part of me forever, I was going to go back to sleep and never wake up.

61

London, October 7, 2024

IRIS

"Pull over here," I say to Rahul, a block from the house. I don't want him driving all the way there. I trust that Ford will obey orders, but I don't want poor Rahul traumatized by rogue wildlife. "Do you know any lawyers? Solicitors, I mean. Good ones. Not pathetic, creepy little sycophants."

Rahul laughs. "I do, actually. One of my primary school mates, Levi Richardson. We still play cricket together. He'll do you right."

"Great. Can I have his contact info?"

Rahul gives it to me. I send a quick email while I still have access to a phone signal, then reluctantly open the door to get out.

"Hold up! Let me take you all the way home," Rahul offers. "I don't like you walking alone at night. Especially after what happened earlier."

"That's thoughtful of you, and I appreciate it. I resolved that situation through lying," I say. "As scary as my family's company is, they follow rules. If they think I'm following the rules, too, they'll leave me alone. Listen, though. Before I get things officially in motion, I should warn you: I'm going to give you and Anthony the house. Hillingham, I mean."

"What?" Rahul turns toward me, eyes wide.

"I know it's a mess. You two can sell it if you don't want to deal with it, then buy a nice place that isn't haunted by vengeful foxes. Or . . ." I pat my bag, where Lucy's journal sits, snug and safe. The house was hers once, too. Before she was a Goldaming. I'm clinging to that knowledge. There are plenty of good people I come from who *weren't* Goldamings. There's a chance for me to be good, too. "Or I don't know, maybe you could bring it back to life. Whatever you want. I just don't want it to stay in my family, where it'll sit empty and sad and useless for another century or two."

"No," he says, baffled. "No, you can't give us a house."

"I can, actually. I want to. It's not mine, not really. Please take it."

"But why us?" He's genuinely confused.

"Because you've been kind to me. Because I need to feel like my inheritance has done at least a little good. And because a girl who grew up in that house a long time ago dreamed of the kind of life you and Anthony have. It makes me happy to imagine how she would feel, knowing how much bigger the world got."

Rahul laughs, half delighted, half confused. "Thank you. Even the offer is the most generous thing imaginable. I'll talk with Anthony about it." He leans over and kisses my cheek. "You are the strangest person I've ever met."

"Good. Keep it that way. Any stranger than me, and things get sketchy." I get out of the car and stroll through the night toward the house. For once, it doesn't seem like a gaping maw waiting to swallow me alive. It still seems sad, yes. But not threatening. Maybe because I know it's just a house, whatever history it might hold.

I'm just a person, whatever history I might hold. I get to choose which parts I keep. And which I leave behind forever.

There's no sign of Ford or the fox as I pick up the discarded paintings from the porch, take them inside, and settle in the chilly den. I consider starting the stove, but I don't trust myself not to burn the house down. Fine gift that would make for my friends then.

I turn on my lantern and pull out the journal, then hesitate. I almost don't want to finish it. As long as I'm in the middle, I can imagine a reality where Mina came to her senses. Or better yet, where Lucy met another girl who loved her with her whole heart. Where that girl and Lucy ran off together and were happy forever. Where life didn't wear Lucy down, but instead gave her the happiness and love she deserved.

But I have to know. I open the journal where I left off. Lucy goes to Whitby for her mother's health. Mina meets them there. Lucy pines, and Mina constantly corrects her, tells her to be happy, reminds her of Arthur's love. It seems like she steers every conversation back to him.

There's also a paragraph about Mina keeping her own journal in shorthand, which is interesting. I once thought I knew shorthand, but what my mother taught me turned out to be some sort of weird code language. That was the only part of my education my mother personally oversaw, because no one else was allowed to know it. I'll never pass it on. Let those secret messages rot in my mother's safe. Let *all* the secrets rot with her.

I keep reading. Lucy gets more desperate as she feels Mina pulling away. Arthur visits and she catches him and Mina talking, wonders if Mina is giving Arthur tips on how to handle her. Because that's how she feels now—that Mina's getting ready to pass the burden of Lucy's love onto someone else.

I'm so angry and sad for Lucy, so annoyed at Mina. And also annoyed at Lucy, if I'm being honest. I understand her feelings for her friend, but it's clear they aren't reciprocated. Meanwhile Lucy is still bending her entire life around the shape of her unrequited love. She needed a good friend. Someone she could be honest with. Someone who would have gently forced her to face some truths. I wish I could have been that for her.

Lucy wants to go on walks at night. It's the only time she can be alone, the only time she can let her face show whatever she's feeling. I used to do the same thing. Though my walks were less about being alone with my feelings and more about being anywhere other than my own bedroom, with those closets storing existential dread.

An anecdote about a local funeral they attend makes it hard to breathe. Lucy sees a dog being mistreated just because it's scared and its owner is inconvenienced. She knows exactly how the dog feels, and I know exactly how she feels. I've never understood anyone as well as I understand Lucy.

She wants to save the dog. She even talks about running away. I want her to do it. I want her to get that dog and leave everything behind.

I know she won't, though, because I've already figured out how things are going to end, even if Lucy can't see it. I don't blame her. She's sweet and hopeful and innocent. She hasn't been properly introduced to how Goldamings work yet. But I have. Nothing that has happened has been by chance; not Doctor Seward's diagnosis of her mother, not the multiple proposals, not Arthur's romantic-hero role in her life. It's all part of a bigger plan.

Doctor Seward and Arthur Holmwood, aka the future Lord Goldaming, are well on their way to taking Lucy's inheritance.

Doctor Seward has been drugging Lucy's mother to keep her out of commission and sow the seeds of her impending death. He's also been courting Lucy to push her toward a better option—handsome and noble Arthur. Arthur, who conveniently swooped in with his own solicitor to "help" Lucy's mother get their estate in order. Doubtless the will was fixed so Lucy inherits everything.

After Arthur and Lucy are officially married, Lucy's mother will immediately die, thanks to Doctor Seward's expert care. That leaves young, vulnerable Lucy—and her vast financial resources—entirely in her husband's hands.

No one will help her. She has no one to turn to, thanks to her terrible mother and these terrible men. Mina won't notice Lucy's in trouble, because she was never the companion that Lucy saw her as. And the cowboy Quincey Morris is either a co-conspirator or just a hapless suitor with bad taste in friends, but either way he'll definitely be no help.

I know I'm right. I can't believe I'm getting an inside view of the first con on which the Goldaming Life empire was built. In a strange way, I wish I could share this with my mother. It's her legacy, after all. She really did Arthur and Doctor Seward proud.

But the next passage shows me I'm wrong. Not about the men, but about Lucy's fate. I was right that she'd fallen into a monster's trap. I just hadn't met the other monster yet.

62

August 31, 1890

JOURNAL OF LUCY WESTENRA

Home is the prison it has always been, but the bars feel closer now. I can't leave Mother's side. When we returned to London, I told Doctor Seward that the sea air had entirely revived Mother. (I know I've written such awful things, but I'm no longer ready for her to die. I don't want to be alone.) He examined her and cautioned against overexertion, then gave her his usual advice to drink her brandy to calm her nerves.

Once she had retired to her bedroom, he told me the truth. Often when nearing death, people will experience a sudden brief resurgence of vitality. Then a steep decline ensues. He was not wrong. Soon after his visit, Mother once again began slurring her speech and having difficulty walking.

I'm exhausted. My blood is sluggish, my skin pale, my temperature cold. How can I care for her, too? The maids are no help. Whenever Mother shouts for someone, they hide on the back staircase.

Doctor Seward calls on us every day now because she's so unwell. Arthur doesn't offer me relief from either of them; he's caring for his own ailing father. I wrote and offered to visit, desperate to leave this house.

"Your place is at your mother's side," he replied, "and I will not deny you a single one of your remaining days with her."

I wonder now how he actually feels about me. I thought him madly in love, but the closer we get to our wedding, the less I see him. He's been by only once since we got back home, accompanied by his two solicitors. The three of them locked themselves up in the sitting room with my mother. Fortunately, Quincey Morris accompanied them and saved me from having to sit in and listen. He regaled me with tales of Wild America as we walked the garden. Maybe I should have chosen Quincey, after all.

My only daily companion is Doctor Seward. This afternoon I caught him watching my breasts with clinical concentration. When he met my gaze, he claimed he was timing my breaths, because "they seem shallower than they ought to be."

He offered to listen more closely. I demurred and called one of the maids to bring us something to eat. It's my only strategy lately, though my own appetite has waned tremendously since Whitby. I do wish Arthur would return and bear some of the burden of Doctor Seward's company.

But . . . the doctor wasn't entirely wrong. My breathing does feel shallow and tight, my whole heart clenched with a low, vague fear. My days are haunted, and in my dreams something stalks me with relentless determination.

Doctor Seward is worried about me, and Arthur writes that he's worried now, too, thanks to Doctor Seward's reports. I wish they would leave me alone. Let me be sad and empty. Let me stop pretending. I do not want to pretend anymore.

I suppose I should make an entry in my other diary about being fitted for wedding dresses this afternoon. It's what the Lucy they all want would be excited about. But I cannot summon the energy for it.

LATER—
The monster is in London now. I didn't dream him. He's real, and he's here.

I knew he was coming, somehow. It's as though I've been waiting for him. When I saw him across the street, his red eyes burning through the shop window, it wasn't a surprise. It was almost a relief: I haven't lost my mind.

I returned his burning gaze with one of my own. Then I laughed and spun and pretended to be happy in my wedding dress. This is not the empty night in Whitby. This is my home. If he thinks I'm afraid, he does not know me.

And Mina's far away and safe. That made it easier to laugh with his wolf's gaze fixed on me.

I'm considering ending this diary. I do not care to have any feelings anymore, even secret ones and

There is something outside!

September 3

Doctor Seward found me pale and unresponsive.

(I am more relieved that my diary fell behind my window seat where they did not discover it than I was that I had survived the monster's latest attack.)

Once I revived enough, Doctor Seward insisted on examining me. Mother was fretting and he told me it was important to keep her calm, so I submitted. How is it that the doctor's examination felt more violating than whatever that other monster did to me? There is something about Doctor Seward's hands and eyes that make me feel naked even when I'm clothed.

Arthur is—allegedly, I have no proof myself—"very concerned," particularly that I be well enough for our impending wedding. He doesn't visit, though. And the doctor took it upon himself to bring *another* man into my home.

What can I say about Mister Van Helsing? He has eyebrows like two toxic caterpillars; he holds my hand too much and sits too close; he pats me like I'm a pet or a child; if I have to listen to him any longer I will throw myself to the mercy of the monster.

At least the monster has the decency not to speak to me anymore. With him, I don't have to smile and blush and pretend not to mind the horrible stink of alcohol and tobacco as he presses an unwelcome kiss to my cheek.

And the worst part is, I know exactly what happened to me. What *is* happening to me. But the men don't ask me, nor will they tell me anything about their own theories. I can see in their faces that they're alarmed, but it's all smiles for fragile, sweet Lucy.

But what would I tell them? A man who isn't a man visits me as moonlight and mist and bats, bites my neck and draws out my blood, leaves me trapped in nightmares waking and asleep?

I know what would happen if I told them the truth. Doctor Seward would claim me for his sanitarium, where he could examine me whenever he wished, however he wished. And as piercing as the pain at my throat is, as listless and cold as I am, I prefer this suffering to being under Doctor Seward's complete control.

I should run. I should flee. I should leave this house and everyone in it. But Mother won't give me money, and I have no one to turn to. Mina hasn't responded to my letters, and I can't put her back in the path of the monster anyway.

But it's fine. My brave, stalwart men are protecting me. Thanks to the advice of Mister Van Helsing, they have me surrounded with . . . garlic flowers. As though a flower ever held back a monster.

I cannot stand how small this house has become, with Doctor Seward and Mister Van Helsing and my mother and the maids. Surrounded at all times, alone at all times. I breathe in a miasma of lies, and I breathe out my own lies, and I'm so tired.

He's at the window again, and I don't care.

September 17?

I want to claw out my veins, find their ends, and tug them free like a poisonous weed's roots.

I can't account for the last few days. I would wake at strange times, free at last from my limbo of nightmares. But the nightmare followed me into the waking world. I was always wearing a different nightdress than before, knowing I hadn't put myself in bed. And one or more of the men were constantly here, watching me, so I had to pretend not to be terrified of what had happened while I was unconscious.

Today I woke not to the deep lethargy and listlessness I feel after a visit from my monster, but to violent illness all through my body. My organs themselves are rebelling against me. Everything hurts, everything is wrong, I can scarcely stand or breathe or think.

"Please," I begged Quincey when he sat with me while the others were conferring outside. "Please, tell me what happened. What is different? What changed?"

He looked torn, but then his face softened. "Swear you won't tell," he said. All performance was gone. No more nonsense sayings, no more exaggerated accent. Just the simple words of a simple man. "We've been putting blood in your veins. John—Doctor Seward—said you didn't have enough, though no one will tell me why, or where all your blood has gone."

"Whose blood?" I croaked through my tortured throat.

"Our own. Mine. Doctor Seward's. Arthur's."

I turned away so he wouldn't see my horror. They didn't ask me, they didn't tell me. They *drugged* me—made me sleep, when sleeping was the problem! And then they punctured me just like the monster did. Putting blood in instead of taking it out, but violating me all the same.

I wish the monster would come right now and take their blood! I feel dirty, corrupted. Doctor Seward must have loved seeing a blush in my cheeks and knowing he was responsible for it for once. And Arthur—how could he, without asking? Without telling?

I tried to hide my reaction from Quincey, but he could tell I was upset.

"We meant well," he said. "We're just trying to get you better. So you can marry Arthur."

So I can marry Arthur? Why not so I can be alive?

"I understand," I said, trying to reassure him even though I was the one lying in bed with my entire body burning from the inside out.

This blood crawling through my veins is *wrong*. I don't know how else to explain it. I have to get them away from me so I can open my window and pray my monster hasn't tired of me yet. Pray he will remove this blood so my suffering will end.

I want someone to hold me. To pet my hair and tell me it will be all right.

I wish Mina were here. I haven't seen her since the train station. I know I shouldn't wish her here, that she wouldn't be safe if she were, but I want—I want to see her. I don't have many days left in this life. I want them to be with her.

I broke down and wrote her again during one of my lucid days this week, asking her to come. I'm not proud of it. It puts her in danger, and I should know better. I'm selfish and weak.

Last night in my fevered dreams I thought I heard her. I tried to open my eyes and reach out for her, but I couldn't. It had to be a dream, though, because in the dream she was arguing with Arthur. When I asked my maids about it in the morning, they laughed and insisted no one had been to visit me in the middle of the night.

If only that were true.

Mother is furious. Not with me, for once, but *for* me. This morning I heard her tell Doctor Seward that the wedding would be postponed indefinitely, and that she was bringing the solicitors back to change the will. That it was time she took care of me. Could it be true?

I cannot write any more. I'm burning and freezing. My throat feels as though his teeth are in it even now, and my own teeth, oh, they ache. But it's nothing to how I feel inside, this sickness roiling in me. This is worse than anything he has done to me. I think I am dying. I need to open the window, I need

September 19

Not much time even less strength

Mother is dead

Someone drugged the maids I recognize the smell because it is how Mother smells when she is ill

Mother's papers are gone but the silver is all still here

I checked the doors and windows they are all locked so how did someone get in and why

My monster does not need doors but he also does not need to drug maids or my mother it makes no sense and he has not been here I am certain of it because my heart still beats with the blood that does not belong to me

Mother is dead she is finally dead and I am so sad why now when she has at last decided to be my mother instead of my burden my jailor my captor

Who will protect me now

He's close I can feel it

I've opened the window and will beg him to release me from this torment of poison in my veins

I will hide this journal one last time and then die with Mina's name on my lips

Mina I love you and I'm sorry I'm so sorry I can't protect you

63

London, October 8, 2024

IRIS

I can barely see through my tears. My breath hitches and my throat burns, in sympathy or because of my sobbing or both.

I was wrong about several things: Lucy isn't my ancestor. She didn't live long enough for that. And Mina wasn't uninterested in Lucy's fate. Quite the opposite.

But as much as I was wrong about, I was right about a lot. And now I'm certain of two things. The first of which is that Lucy was murdered in an elaborate scheme to take her inheritance—the very inheritance my family built their fortune on.

The second of which is that a vampire showed up and nearly ruined the entire plot.

And I have all the proof.

64

Boston, September 26, 2024

CLIENT TRANSCRIPT

The world had changed yet again during my time away. Remade not by war, but by new gods of technology. I felt about these things as the Doctor felt about vampirism: unfathomable nonsense not worth studying, best merely ignored.

It was both easier and more difficult to travel now. More options, but everyone wanted documents. Proof of identity and a quantifiable existence. Sometimes it wasn't enough to dazzle them with a smile and a gentle vampiric nudge. I crept onto ships, slipped onto trains, clung to ceilings and roofs, a tick hitching a ride on the edge of progress.

I didn't know where Dracula was, but I had a good idea of how to find someone who would.

Romania was beautiful in a way that made me feel less empty. My destination, Transylvania, had looming gray mountains cut by silvery serpentine rivers, dark green forests softened and hazy with clinging clouds. Quaint villages huddled around old fortified churches, nothing around but fields and hills for miles and miles in any direction.

I assumed my destination would be easy to find; it was a castle haunted by vampires, after all. But everywhere I asked—charming Braşov tucked into a valley, picturesque Sighişoara built on a hill, even chaotic and cramped Bucharest at last coming up for air in the aftermath of a dictator—no one knew what I was talking about. I visited Bran, Peleş, Hunedoara, and a dozen crumbling fortress foundations, but none were the right castle. None reeked of Dracula and his history.

How had Jonathan found it? He must have had a guide. But I wasn't giving up. I ventured to smaller villages, frozen in time. In places where a horse-drawn hay cart was as likely to be taking up the road as a modern car, where nights were still pitch-dark and winters deadly despite all the progress of the world, they remembered. And they refused to talk.

I used their reactions as my map. The more immediate the silence, the sharper the fear, the closer I was.

Eventually I caught that metal clang in my sinuses. The telltale scent of one of Dracula's vampires. I knew exactly who it was, too. I wandered over hills and through mountain passes, deep into land inhabited only by wild, creeping things, and at last found it.

My heart sank. The castle was in ruins. A repulsive heap of long-ago glory reduced to garbage. Dracula wouldn't stoop to live there, I was sure of it. But someone else would.

She was waiting for me as I picked my way over the debris. Her hair, once blacker than night, darker than shadow, had a dull quality to it. Her eyes were wide and red. Not the red of blood or frenzy, but the red of rust, of infection, of being slowly eaten away into nothing.

Raven. Ever the bride, loyally awaiting the return of her master.

Her voice was like the fluttering of a dying moth. "Have you seen him? Is he coming?"

All this time, she'd been here for him. And all this time, he'd stayed away. Even if she were to tell me Dracula's exact whereabouts, I wouldn't trust her. Not again. But my trip hadn't been a complete waste. I could still confirm something once and for all.

Slumped in the shadows of the castle was another of Dracula's vampires. A small, pathetic thing, half starved. Less than a shadow or a memory; a reflection in muddy water.

"You," I said, pointing to her. "When did you die?" No reaction. I tried again in several different languages. When I asked in Greek, she blinked at me with empty eyes.

"I'm dead?"

Resisting the urge to sigh, I crouched in front of her. "What do you remember, from your life?"

"I'm dead," she repeated, frowning.

"Don't bother," Raven said. "I found her on my journey back here. I thought she could be a bride, but she's worthless." She grabbed me, trying to slip her fingers somewhere they were no longer welcome.

I gripped her wrist, stopping her. "*When* did you find her? How long after I left you?"

Raven tilted her head in confusion. She'd been there for so long, the passage of time was meaningless. There were only two states of being for her: with Dracula, and waiting for Dracula.

I pushed her away and turned back to the other vampire. "What year is it?" I asked, keeping my voice soft and gentle.

Her eyes brightened a little at a question she could answer. "It's 1891! We just celebrated the new year."

She'd been killed after me—and *after* the Queen received her report of Dracula's death. I closed my eyes, relieved. He was out there. The four fools hadn't killed him. Which meant I could still find him and drain him.

I turned to leave, at a loss for where to look next, but at least hopeful that there was a goal at the end of all my journeying.

Raven threw herself at me, clawing, weeping without tears. "Please. Stay with me. If there are three of us, we can lure him back. He'll want us again, I know he will. I *know* he will."

Sickening as it was, I understood her desperation. He was my focus, too. I still wanted answers. I still needed to look him in the eyes and ask why he had turned me into this. What the point of it all had been. The idea that he might have tasted Mina's blood was just the excuse I needed to get back on this path. It was the same path I'd always been walking. The one that would take me back to him so I could understand myself.

"We need one more," Raven screeched.

"Two more," I corrected her. And then I killed the lost little Greek vampire. It was the only kindness I could think to give her.

Raven's howls of rage and despair echoed behind me as I walked away. She had welcomed me into this life, but she didn't have any power over me. And I wanted her to suffer.

I had few friends in the world—and "friend" was a stretch for some of them—but I tried them all. Revisiting Istanbul was surreal. The old buildings were still there, but everything was different. The same and yet irrevocably changed. It was beautiful, rich with history and people and tradition, but lessened. There were absences I didn't know how to explain, whole sections of the city that had been forcibly erased and changed to conform.

I wondered if I had remade myself so many times that I, too, would be recognizable but devastating to behold. No one lived who loved me, though. No one could trace the history of my gradual decline, because no one was left who knew where I started. Except Dracula, of course.

As soon as I arrived, I knew the Doctor was gone. Istanbul held no scent of her scalpel-sharp heart. I kept traveling east. The Queen had her network of spies. They had been wrong before, but perhaps they had unearthed new information.

Liaoning was unrecognizable. The harbor was bustling, the surrounding empty hills now filled with buildings and people. Though I remembered the way well enough, in place of her hidden sanctuary was a regular street lined with homes and businesses. No trace remained of her compound or her scent. All her work to build her gilded cage, to rescue and protect and trap her collection of girls, come to naught.

While I'd slept in my mausoleum, the world had gotten smaller. I hoped the Queen and the Doctor still existed somewhere, but I doubted it. I was beginning to suspect that only the solitary vampires like me, the ones who drifted along impacting no one, changing nothing, were safe. There were so few secret dark spaces anymore.

After that, I didn't bother with Paris. If the Lover was still there—I couldn't imagine her anywhere else—she wouldn't have information, and she certainly wouldn't be willing to help me. I was well and truly alone.

But thanks to the Lover, I was excellent at changing my face and blending in. Thanks to the Doctor, I knew how to obsessively apply myself to a difficult task. And thanks to the Queen, I knew exactly how to kill vampires.

I started hunting.

65

London, October 8, 2024

IRIS

By the time my doorbell rings, I've got it almost all laid out. The safe ended up being extremely helpful. Just not for my immediate financial needs.

I drag myself to the front door and find Albert Fallis standing there, looking disheveled and disgruntled like a crab caught mid-molt. He's holding a box of files.

"These are all originals," he says, "and I must insist that—"

I grab the box and slam the door in his face. I'm not proud of how I threatened him on the phone this morning, but manipulating the legal system is a long family tradition. One that his firm has been participating in the whole time.

The documents fill in the remaining gaps of the case I've been building. The entire den floor is papered in proof, arranged by type. Whoever decided to keep everything thought they were building an alibi, but it's so calculating, so conveniently tidy, it serves as condemnation. Even the shorthand journal tells me exactly what I need to know. Because it isn't regular shorthand, after all. It's a code. One that I was taught by my mother, who was taught by her mother, on and on back to none other than Mina Murray Harker *Goldaming.*

"You cunning little bitch," I mutter.

"Iris?" Elle sounds panicked as she rushes in. She stops on the room's threshold; there's very little space to walk anymore. "The front door was cracked open. I was worried."

"I forgot to lock it after the solicitor brought these documents." I wave dismissively. The lock doesn't matter. I'm not afraid of anyone who can walk in of their own free will.

"What's all this?" Elle carefully dances through the documents to perch on an armchair.

"I finished Lucy's journal."

"Oh? Any good stories? Is Lucy who you hoped she was, or did she disappoint you?" Her face is sad as she picks up the stack of watercolor paintings. I know now they were painted by Lucy. And I know now I should have looked through every single one that first night. It would have saved me so much time.

"They killed her," I say. "They fucking *killed* her."

Elle frowns. "Wait. *'They'*? Who's 'they'? Who killed her?"

"Everyone," I growl. I gesture at the case I've laid out. "You were right about the last inhabitants of the house. Father, dead. Mother, dead. Daughter, dead. But in the case of the last two, it was murder. I'm going to walk you through it, step-by-step. Please just trust me and listen to the whole thing."

"But shouldn't we—"

"I know this isn't what I'm supposed to be focused on." I can't even pace. I'm literally locked into place by the history around me, which feels so apt I want to laugh. "I *know.* But I need to tell you, because I finally have the whole story. And once you have it, too, then you'll understand what you're getting into if you run away with me. And you have to understand. Every part of it. Otherwise it's not fair to you."

"What does a girl's death over a century ago have to do with it?"

"*Everything.* Let me start at the beginning."

I narrate, Elle listens, and the past at last delivers its secrets, newly risen from the grave they tried to bury it in.

66

THE MURDER OF LUCY WESTENRA

Once upon a time, there was a girl named Lucy.

She grew up in a large, cold house, filling herself with as much love as she could. But she was always pretending, because she had to lie about who she really loved: her governess, Mina.

Mina was the most important person in Lucy's life, but there were other key figures. Her mother, a controlling, suspicious hypochondriac. Doctor Seward, director of a sanitarium making personal house calls to her mother. Arthur Holmwood, a dashing future lord courting Lucy. Quincey Morris, a bumbling but sweet American cowboy. Doctor Van Helsing, a Dutch acquaintance of Doctor Seward and expert in strange maladies.

And a monster cloaked in darkness and violence who crashed ashore at Whitby, where Lucy was staying with her mother and Mina.

The "truth" presented in Lucy's journals, the accounts of the men, and all the carefully collected and organized documents saved by Mina, is that Lucy—beloved by all, about to wed Arthur—was tragically killed by that dark figure, despite valiant efforts to save her. When that predator then turned his attentions to Mina, they were able to at last drive him out of London and heroically kill him in the Transylvanian mountains of Romania.

But the story underneath that story, woven through all the documents, clear enough to see if you look for it? It's still about murder. But there are no heroes.

Allow me to lay it out for you.

Mina was Lucy's governess, as evidenced by references in Lucy's journal. Lucy grew up with Mina as her most trusted confidante and companion, and Mina never hesitated to direct Lucy's thoughts, feelings, and behaviors.

In this letter to Lucy, kept among the many documents in the safe, Mina asks about Arthur Holmwood—aka Lord Goldaming—specifically. In Lucy's journals (both the real and the fake one), Lucy notes that Mina repeatedly asks about Arthur. Mina makes certain Lucy is focused on him over any other suitors or distractions. When Lucy expresses doubts or reservations about getting married, Mina always chides her and redirects her to Arthur.

Though Mina claims not to know Arthur, Lucy witnesses them having a conversation, and later finds a letter in Arthur's suit jacket pocket in Mina's handwriting.

We'll set Mina and Arthur's connection aside for now.

At exactly the same time Arthur appears in Lucy's life by introducing himself to her at the opera, Doctor Seward, his close friend and schoolmate, also begins visiting Lucy and her mother. There's no indication in Lucy's journals or in the safe documents that her mother sought out Doctor Seward or even paid him. He volunteered all his services, which coincided with a downward turn in Mrs. Westenra's health.

In fact, as Lucy clearly notes, her mother is always doing better *before* Doctor Seward visits, at which point she can barely function and takes to her room. Doctor Seward also tries to force laudanum and other drugs on Lucy and is generally a creep, though that's not evidence.

Putting a pin in Doctor Seward's activities, we move on to Arthur's courtship. According to Lucy's journals, she never meets his father or visits Arthur's home. Because Arthur introduced himself, rather than being introduced through other members of society who might have warned her, Lucy had no idea that the Goldaming estate was completely bankrupt. They were so deeply in debt that the family manor had been rented out. Fallis and Co. conveniently kept the rental documents, as well as Lord Goldaming's death certificate, which revealed he was living in a cheap boardinghouse.

So, we have two longtime friends descending on a wealthy heiress's life at the same time: a doctor who triggered a steep decline in Lucy's mother's health, and a bankrupt future lord presenting himself as a viable marriage candidate while keeping Lucy from discovering his dire financial straits.

Still circumstantial. Fortunately, Fallis and Co. is nothing if not fastidious about keeping documents. At the time of Lucy's engagement and subsequent death, they were a newly licensed solicitor's office with only two original clients: a penniless lord . . . and a governess from the lower classes, one Mina Murray. Why would Mina employ a solicitor at all, much less the *same* solicitor as a man she claimed not to know? More on Mina's use of the solicitor after we go through the Westenra documents.

Here, the original Westenra will. It leaves everything to Lucy, with the exception of a few pieces of land going to distant male cousins due to antiquated inheritance laws. But here, documented and signed by Fallis and Co., a new will naming Arthur *Fucking* Holmwood the sole beneficiary of the entire Westenra fortune.

Lucy died before they could wed. Engagements weren't legally binding. He had no relation to the Westenras, no claim, however tenuous, on their fortune. But Mrs. Westenra signed the new will, leaving everything to him *before the wedding.*

Notice how Mrs. Westenra's signature changes from the original will to the new will, drafted mere days before her death. What had been a fussy and elegant signature becomes practically illegible. The sad attempt of a dying woman . . . or a deeply drugged one.

Such a will was doubtless grounds for a legal fight, though. Who would believe Mrs. Westenra had consented to it? Contained within the safe as insurance were several written testimonies. Arthur Holmwood, John Seward, and Abraham Van Helsing all note in clear, precise detail that it was Mrs. Westenra's dying wish that Arthur inherit everything so he could take care of Lucy. Nowhere in the safe is Mrs. Westenra's written testimony to this same fact, nor Lucy's.

According to both Lucy's journals, when the new will was signed, she was in and out of consciousness. The men record that they were sedating her and performing transfusions and other procedures without her consent or knowledge in an effort to keep her alive.

Where was Lucy's best friend and dearest companion, Mina, when all this was happening? She was hard at work.

While her fiancé, Jonathan Harker, was in Transylvania on a business trip, Mina was negotiating her own business. She convinced his employer, the much older, extremely wealthy Mister Hawkins, to let them move into his house upon her marriage to Jonathan. The understanding was that Mina would care for him and manage the household.

Mina found and wed Jonathan in Europe. They returned, moved in with Mister Hawkins, and not two weeks later, Mister Hawkins died.

One week before his death, he, too, signed a new will. Though Mina and Jonathan had no relation to him or claim on his fortune, he left everything to the Harkers and their heirs. And even though Mister Hawkins himself was a well-respected solicitor with an entire office of solicitors to help him, the will was executed by . . . Fallis and Co.

We haven't forgotten about Doctor Seward, the sanitarium director so fond of making house calls to non-patients. Arthur and Doctor Seward both encouraged Lucy not to seek a second opinion on her mother's health issues. When Mrs. Westenra visited Whitby and was therefore removed from Doctor Seward's care, she improved dramatically. Only to slide back down as soon as Doctor Seward once again had access to her.

In Lucy's journal, her mother's special medicinal brandy is mentioned twice. On Doctor Seward's recommendation, Lucy takes a little to calm herself after two proposals and instead finds herself spinning and scarcely able to stand—and extremely pliable to Arthur's proposal.

Then, the night Mrs. Westenra dies, Lucy notes that the maids had gotten into the brandy. All three maids were unconscious on the floor, having consumed only a small amount of the liquid.

Whether Mrs. Westenra died of heart failure is impossible to determine. No one examined her other than Doctor Seward. This is something she had in common with several others, as indicated by this collection of death certificates declaring death by natural causes for her, the elder Lord Holmwood, Mister Hawkins, and Lucy herself. All signed by Doctor John Seward.

A collection of bodies tended to by Doctor Seward, a collection of inheritances legalized by Fallis and Co., and two clever con artists sitting atop both the bodies and the riches: Arthur and Mina.

They were quite the team. But they ran into an unexpected complication. While Mister Hawkins, the elder Lord Goldaming, and Mrs. Westenra were always going to die, *Lucy* wasn't supposed to. Arthur and Mina had successfully pressured her into a short engagement and quick wedding because she was crucial to their plot. With Lucy on

Arthur's arm, no one would look twice at his taking charge of his young wife's finances.

They can't be blamed for not anticipating what happened next, all because Mina's fiancé Jonathan had attracted the attention of a vampire.

67

London, October 8, 2024

IRIS

"Iris," Elle interrupts, her voice trembling.

I knew this was where I would lose her. Her eyes are so wide I can see the whites all around the stormy blue centers. She's crouched on the floor, searching through the various documents: the letters kept for no reason other than to provide alibis, the fake journal of Lucy's that unfortunately only praised her predators, the accounts of the men, meticulous in their details of trying desperately to save Lucy and yet somehow failing to prevent identical attack after identical attack.

There's even a letter in a careful imitation of Lucy's own hand, detailing the events of the night a "wolf" scared her mother to death, absolving anyone of guilt.

There was no wolf. There was never any wolf. Someone drugged the maids and killed her mother, and someone else—perhaps a clever governess who had so many loving letters from Lucy and a whole journal as handwriting references—forged a letter and broke a window to take advantage of the rumor of an escaped zoo animal.

"Look at this part," I say, pointing to Lucy's real journal, then to several of the men's accounts. "They knew she was being attacked. They scrambled to save her, even bringing in a doctor from Europe. They couldn't let Lucy die before everything was in order, and Mrs. Westenra hadn't signed the new will yet. Here, see, Lucy can't understand why she wakes up feeling so strange. Here, where she describes her blood feeling like shards of glass in her veins? Says it feels like everything inside her is on fire? Those fuckwits were giving her blood transfusions without her consent! They didn't even know what her blood type was. It was actually lucky that someone else was removing the blood before Lucy's body could destroy itself. It was probably too late for her anyway, but once they had the new will, Lucy's survival wasn't essential. Over and over, the same shit happened, and they let it. They 'fell asleep' or 'forgot to spend the night' or 'left her mother in charge.' Bullshit. They knew her mother was incompetent, because they were the ones drugging her!"

I'm ranting now, I can't help it. I'm so angry and sad. "Van Helsing saw immediately that they were dealing with a vampire, not some wasting sickness. They could have taken Lucy and run. Hidden her. *Actually* protected her. But they never did. When every legal document was in order, Lucy's inheritance secured, they let her die. They let the vampire have her, because they didn't need her for anything else."

"No, this is—this isn't right." Elle picks up various letters and documents, looking at them and then throwing them down. She doesn't touch the journals, doesn't even look at them. "This makes no sense."

"That letter, there. Van Helsing. He describes the vampire. I'm not making it up, I'm *not* crazy."

"But you read me her journal. Mina was her friend."

"Mina was a *monster.*" This is the part that makes me the sickest, that makes me wish someone would remove the blood of hers that flows in my own veins. "Two years after all this happened? Jonathan died. You guessed it—Doctor Seward signed the death certificate. Within a month, Mina and Arthur married. But they'd finally attracted too much attention, so they moved to America to avoid the press, with Doctor Seward in tow."

Elle sits right in the middle of all the papers, staring down at them. "This can't be right. It's absurd."

I crouch in front of her. "I know it sounds insane. But I read Lucy's journal. I read about what was hunting her. I read what the men said in their papers. I don't think Van Helsing was in on the inheritance scheme, he was just an old creep they brought in out of desperation to keep Lucy alive a little longer. I trust his account. Read it. Read it, please. He describes the vampire; he knows all about them." I push Van Helsing's papers toward Elle, but she doesn't take them. "The worst part is, they claimed they hunted down and ended the vampire who killed Lucy. There are all these receipts, tickets, travel itineraries, and diary entries. All about chasing Dracula back to Transylvania and destroying him there. But that was a lie, too."

Elle looks up at me, her face a mask of confusion. "What?"

I pick up the watercolors, toss aside portrait after portrait, most of which I'm sure are of Mina. Her eyes seem different to me now, not teasing or playful, but viciously knowing. She sat for this portrait; she looked right at Lucy, held her gaze, and *knew*. She knew what she was doing the whole time. The last painting is the one I'm after, though. It's done with a weaker hand, the strokes less confident, the color washed out except for a few details: the distinctive heavy brow, the aquiline nose, the upsettingly wet lips. But it's in the eyes. I'd know their hungry, soulless red gaze anywhere.

I hold it up. "This is the vampire who killed Lucy. This is Dracula. And I'm positive they didn't destroy him, because I fucking *know* him. When I was a kid, he almost killed my dad after I invited him in."

68

Boston, September 26, 2024

CLIENT TRANSCRIPT

I chased rumors, I followed ghosts, I stalked shadows, on the hunt for one thing: vampires.

I found them, too. That acrid metal sting was like a lighthouse in the dark, guiding me to them. Every time I met a new vampire, I asked if they knew where Dracula was. Every time they said no. Their stories were the same as mine. Young women, on the cusp of the rest of their lives, instead abandoned in this nightmare wasteland.

I killed most of them. Not out of any altruistic sense of purpose or a desire to protect humanity. Most didn't like being found and attacked me first. But also I was angry. The search was taking me *years*. Every vampire I found got my hopes up, and every vampire I found brought them crashing back down.

But no. It wasn't just anger. I let myself think that, before tonight. But now that you've had me lay my afterlife out in a neat pathway from beginning to end, I can see it was more than that. These vampires were mirrors. Bottomless pits of need, never sated, never happy. Living the same cycles, over and over, without hope of progression or change. I looked at them, and I saw myself, and I hated it. So I smashed a lot of mirrors.

The saner ones who didn't try to kill me I usually just fucked, though. Even an undead girl has needs.

I never found a vampire that predated Dracula, though. Not a single one that didn't smell like him. Was he the first? Or were there others out there, older and smarter than him, that I couldn't sniff out? But the Doctor proved right—none of the vampires I found had been making other vampires. We were monsters, all of us, but not like him. Never like him.

Eventually, I found myself in Lagos, Nigeria. If any city can be said to be living, Lagos is it. Everything is movement and chaos, all these intricate social systems balancing and striving and pushing and pulling. If I hadn't been so far into my search and so very tired, I think I could have stayed there for a long time, absorbing the sheer *life* of it all. I even liked the noise. The honking, the shouting, the constant, inescapable humanity. Overwhelming in the best way.

But I had caught my scent. This one was different. I was used to the thrill of the hunt, to the hope that even now stirred in my veins: *Maybe this time, maybe this time.* But I was possessed by this scent. I blurred through the night streets, dodging motorcycles and vendors, wishing I were electricity that could be carried along the wires strung everywhere like nerves in a body.

I arrived at a house clinging to the edge of the city. At last close enough to fill myself with the scent, I understood what it was that triggered such urgency. It wasn't just a vampire. It was a vampire I *knew.*

Two of them, in fact.

I didn't need to be invited in, but I knocked to be polite. The Lover opened the door, no surprise in her cloudy-day gray eyes. She took my hand the way she used to and led me inside.

Even if I couldn't smell her companion, I would have known the Lover wasn't living there by herself. The place was ruthlessly tidy. Floors swept clean, minimal furniture, clothes relegated to an actual closet. Several mugs were drying on the table, recently rinsed clean of blood because their owner still preferred to drink that way. The Queen stood perfectly still in the center of the kitchen, watching me.

"How did you two even meet?" I asked. Though they had been major figures in my history, I never imagined them together. Both geographically and temperamentally, they had been as far apart as possible. I turned to the Queen. "I looked for you in Liaoning, but everything was gone." I didn't add that I didn't look for the Lover. I didn't want to hurt her feelings.

The Queen's face was as unreadable as ever. "I lost a favorite companion. It made me realize all my girls deserved better. I let them go. Eventually the new government remembered the palace existed, and I was forced to wander."

"Someone ruined Paris for me," the Lover said, squeezing my hand a little too tight. "After that, I had to go out and find hungry men on my own, over and over. And I had to kill them instead of reusing them, because that same *someone* told me I was being selfish."

The Queen held my gaze as steadily and ready as she held herself, like a rabbit waiting to dart away . . . or a leopard waiting to pounce. "We heard whispers that someone was hunting down all of Dracula's vampires."

"Oh." I laughed. "Yes, that's me."

The Queen raised one eyebrow, the perfect smooth plains of her face untouched by the expression. She no longer wore silk robes, and her hair was pulled back into a ponytail, but her clothes were immaculate and regal nonetheless. "Eventually we found each other. Satisfied that neither of us was the hunter, we banded together. The world used to be a vast place, filled with secrets. Now it is too small for us to hide in. Too small to carve out our own domains. Even Lagos will not work for long." She cut her eyes toward the Lover. "Mostly because *she* cannot stop attracting and then killing murderers."

I didn't mention that the golden knives still fused to each of the Queen's fingers probably drew attention, too.

The Lover didn't react to the Queen's criticism. She watched me, curious. "I think I never understood you," she said.

"That makes two of us." I pulled her closer, surprisingly happy to see her. And happy that she seemed nearly sane at the moment. But she didn't wrap her arms around me, and the Queen seemed even tenser than usual. "I'm not going to kill either of you," I said, rushing to reassure them. "You're my friends."

After all, I'd shared more with them in the last hundred plus years than I had with anyone else. I wished the Doctor was there, too, but she was well and truly lost.

"As if you could kill us." The Queen waved dismissively. She did relax a little, though, softening from carved in stone to merely sculpted out of metal. "How *did* you kill so many?"

That was new. She had never asked me a question before without delivering it as a demand. Had she changed, or had I?

"I was trained by your girls, and they were the best. Besides, it isn't difficult." Part of it was the element of surprise. Vampires mostly avoid each other. So, at least at the beginning, no one was expecting an attack. The other part was the fact that I've never minded being vulnerable, which makes me better at surviving. Weakness is an old friend who holds no dread for me.

But the final and most obvious answer is that they *wanted* to die. Each of them was asking a question that would never be answered. I offered them an end, and they took it.

"This is nice." I sat on their sagging sofa. The material was coarse and cheap, not up to the standards of the Queen or the Lover. But they had covered it in pretty handwoven blankets. Even on the run, they still appreciated beauty. They were the only two vampires I ever met who tried to build homes wherever they were, rather than being satisfied with a patch of unhallowed ground to rest in.

The Lover sat curled against me, staring dreamily into a distance no one else could see. "We're going to America. I don't think they'll mind us there. They deal so much death and violence every day, no one will even notice us. And I'll find so many new murderous friends to love me before they die."

The Queen's posture shifted like a sigh. She sat on a rattan chair across from us. It was a far cry from her throne. "That is *not* why we're going."

"Then why?" I asked. America seemed so far away. Such an immature, new country. I'd held its dying soldiers, and I'd held children dying because of its soldiers. Its wars were the same war there ever was. It wasn't special or different, it was just too young to accept it yet.

"Because of the rumors," the Lover said, giggling.

The Queen clarified. "According to the whispers of those fleeing your campaign of terror, he's there."

I stood, as charged as if every wire in Lagos connected directly to my dead heart. "*Dracula?* Dracula is in America?"

The Queen shrugged irritably. "I still think he's dead. I had very good information that he was killed by a cowboy."

"Impossible," the Lover said, twisting a lock of hair around her finger. It was clear they'd had this argument dozens of times. The grooves of it were worn into them. "The cowboy carried a regular knife. A knife made of steel stuck into Dracula's chest would do nothing more than inconvenience him. Believe me, I know about being stabbed. He faked his death to escape pursuit. It's hard to survive once you've been noticed."

"Regardless," the Queen said, "there are rumors that whole vampire groups live together in America. Something strange is happening there. Maybe we can find safety in that strangeness."

Based on my extensive experience, large groups of vampires never banded together. Then again, here were two vampires, trying to survive through safety in numbers. Maybe my hunting had inspired a whole new form of vampire community living.

"And if Dracula's there," the Lover said, "he's been surviving in secret for more than a century. So we can, too. And I've never been shot before! Everyone gets shot in America. It'll be exciting."

It was all I could do to hold my form and not burst into moonlight, spreading myself so thin I'd cover the whole earth and find him. I didn't want to spend any more years looking. I didn't even want to spend days. Hours felt infinite. "Where is he, exactly? Do you have any idea?"

The Lover stroked my arm. "Do you know about the magic boxes?"

I looked to the Queen for clarification. She closed her eyes wearily. "She figured out how to use phones. It is *extremely* annoying."

The Lover beamed. "A birdie in my magic box told me Dracula was in a place called Boston."

Don't be frightened, Vanessa. He's not the one who attacked me tonight. Let me finish. You'll understand.

The Lover gave me an address from the little birdie inside her phone. I crossed the ocean clinging to the bottom of a plane, coated in ice and daring to hope. I found Boston. I found the address. It was a club, more frantic and violent than the clubs of my time in Paris. The beat pulsed so strongly it felt almost like my heart was working again. I wandered through the darkness and the smoke and the dancing, and then I smelled *them*. Everywhere. So many vampires.

I pressed close to one, luminous and gleaming in the darkness, and whispered my desperation in his ear. He nodded to the others, then took my hand and led me to a back room. It was quieter in there. Quiet enough to hear, and quiet enough to use my other senses. They smelled like him—*almost*. There was something different, something off. Maybe because they were young. Fresh. Maybe that's what I smelled like, so soon after waking. All the vampires I'd met were at least a hundred years old.

"I need to find Dracula," I said. "Do you know where he is?"

"Yes," said a woman, strung taut and deadly like a bowstring. I wanted to pluck her and listen to the vibration. "We can take you to him."

I'd done it. I'd found him, at last. I hummed with the knowledge that I was going to look Dracula in the eyes. I was going to make him give me answers. And then I was going to drain him.

"So pretty," the bowstring woman said, pressing her lips to my neck.

"So old," the first man said with a hungry laugh, running his hands down my back. The others, five, six, seven of them, pressed close, too, with lust and desire and the promise of borrowed heat.

I nearly wept. Being wanted, being touched? It reminded me I was real. I was real, and I was almost finished.

They tried to tear me apart.

I should have seen it coming. I practically invented this form of murdering other vampires. Though my method was always one on one, never seven on one. Hardly seems fair. They nearly killed me, but they're still so young. Tied to their forms in a way I never was. It's hard to murder moonlight, but do enough damage and even *I* can't shift anymore.

It was a setup. The Queen and the Lover figured out a way of killing me without getting their own hands dirty. I'm not even angry. I'm impressed with their organization and innovation.

So, here I am. I didn't find him, and I never will. I'm at the end of my search. Out of options, out of hope, out of reasons to keep existing. I was right about why it's easy to kill old vampires. We're so tired. We want someone to give us permission to sleep without the threat of waking.

You were right, too. There is something outside. Several somethings, now. It took them awhile to find me again and gather. I'm sorry I kept delaying you, but I wanted to finish my story before they finish me.

I think I'm ready to be finished. Telling you these stories, remembering everything I've done and everything I've failed at. I'm *pathetic.* So deeply pathetic, just like the rest of them. We were all mirrors to one another, all living the same story without end.

In her home, the Queen was trying to seize control from Dracula, who had never even set foot on her continent. He didn't have to, because he has all the power anyway.

On every operating table and in every body, the Doctor was looking for what Dracula took from us. But she couldn't find it, because it's his now.

On the stage, the gaze the Lover was really hoping for was Dracula's. The ending she craved was the one he denied her when he damned her to this endless mocking limbo.

We were, all of us, searching for Dracula. Reborn shaped around the horror of him, broken in the form he gave us. He claimed us and made us his own and tied us to him forever through violence. And then he never thought about us again.

Before you say anything else, Vanessa, I can smell the cancer eating away at you. I know you only listened to my story because you hoped I'd change you. You hoped I'd save you. But I would *never* do that to you. All I can offer is a swift, painless death right now, if you want. Or you can hide and pray the others pass you by. Not much of a choice, but few of us get any choice in the end.

At least we'll both get an end. Stories only have meaning if they end, don't they?

Lucy Westenra. Born in 1871, died in 1890. Forgotten, but not gone. At last about to rest in—

69

London, October 8, 2024

IRIS

I expect Elle to argue with me. To tell me why I'm wrong. To insist that I misread things, or that Lucy was writing fiction, or that I'm insane to believe the rambling diary entries of a dying girl. Instead, she stands and leaves. Just walks out without a word.

I sink down and sit among evidence of the truth. That's what always defeats me in the end, doesn't it? Anytime I tell the truth, I lose everything. But I couldn't keep it from Elle. Especially not after reading Lucy's journal.

Lucy died in part because no one in her life was honest with her. No one gave her the information she needed to keep herself safe. I won't do that to Elle. If I've driven her away forever, if she's out there counting her lucky stars that she saw how unhinged I am before it was too late, well. At least I saved her from being part of my life and everything that comes with it.

This one hurts more than any of the others, though. The way I feel about Elle is deeper and stranger and better than with anyone I've ever loved. There was a part of me—the fragile part with stupid, weak feathers still trying to fly me into a better reality—that hoped Elle would believe me. That she'd be so into history that she'd take historical records of vampires seriously. That maybe she wouldn't need evidence at all.

It feels like I've lost something irreplaceable.

I wipe away tears, shoving aside the painting of Dracula. At least I solved one of my own personal mysteries. Dracula has *always* been tied to my family. He's the reason vampires are part of my life; he's the reason I had to shove a silver dagger in my mother's corpse to make certain she never came back.

I didn't get to tell Elle the rest of the story, but it's so bleak I'm kind of glad. Dracula killed Lucy, those fucking men cut off Lucy's head, Mina pretended to kill Dracula, and he's been working with the Goldamings ever since. A literal deal with the devil.

Speaking of devils. I check to make sure my spray bottle is still nearly full. I've experimented with a lot of things over the years. Coffee leaves a scent strong enough to mess up my personal smell and throw vampires off, but simmering down garlic to a concentrated reduction hurts them the most. Van Helsing knew what to do. If only he'd told *Lucy* how to protect herself, instead of entrusting it to those useless, grasping men.

I take the key to Lucy's room and hang it from a silver chain around my neck, then let myself have a long cry over what I could have had with Elle. I cry for Lucy, too. I don't regret reading her journal or telling Elle about it. Lucy deserved someone to know the truth. Someone to care about what happened to her. I can't ever regret that.

And I don't regret the time I had with Elle, either. The intensity and depth of my connection to her doesn't make sense, but love rarely does. I'll miss her for the rest of my life. I hope I didn't hurt her as badly as this is hurting me. Who knows, maybe I saved her from joining Goldaming Life someday. She's certainly going to avoid Goldamings forever after me.

Oh god, *Elle.* I squeeze my eyes shut, pushing aside memories of our perfect hours together.

I can't wallow. I'm back on the hook for trying to find a way to disappear. For now, I need to get away from Hillingham and all its memories. Lucy was betrayed in this house; she died in this house. And then my family took it and left it to rot as a monument to their evil.

I take a walk to clear my head. I'm half tempted to cover the miles to Elle's flat and tell her I was kidding. Vampires aren't real, I just have a stupid American sense of humor. I can take it all back, beg her to take *me* back.

But I don't. If we can't really know each other, how can we really love each other? Instead, I walk until I have reception. Levi Richardson, Rahul's solicitor friend, has responded to my email. I pull myself together and we have a quick, productive call.

I keep walking until his follow-up emails and the documents come through. I don't even bother reviewing them, I just sign and return. I'm stealing something back from my family. Giving a gift to someone who deserves it, instead of taking everything I can from everyone around me.

That's assuming Rahul and Anthony are willing to sign, too. I hope they will be. I don't think getting the house will cause them any trouble, but I can't be certain. There's always a risk. Maybe they'll want to close the door on me forever, too. I wouldn't blame them.

When I finally loop back to Hillingham, trudging through the gloriously wealthy neighborhood, with its grand manors and ancient trees, someone is waiting on my doorstep. It's not Elle, but Anthony is almost as welcome a sight, sitting there surrounded by bags of takeout containers. He rushes to me and wraps me in a hug.

I lean in, loving the scents of garlic, onion, and ginger on him. He smells like life and nourishment and comfort. I needed this hug so badly.

"Are you certain?" he says as he lets me go. "*Really* certain? Because this is mental. You're giving us a house. A mansion. A mansion in a super-posh neighborhood."

"I'm one hundred percent certain. It's yours, whatever you want to do with it. Sell it, rent it, move into it. It's up to you."

Tears catch in the thick dark lashes around Anthony's eyes, glittering in the sunlight. He's beautiful, and so is Rahul, and they're beautiful together. "We've been wanting to start a family, but it hasn't felt possible. With this, though . . ." He trails off, looking up at the house with genuine love. I don't think anyone has looked at Hillingham that way in more than a century. Maybe ever.

I'm trying not to cry, too. "Honestly, you're doing me a favor. I'll get to feel good about this for so long. I don't have many things to feel good about lately."

"Well, I'm going to repay you. I made you everything on the menu, including a new tub of roasted garlic."

"See, and now I'm back in your debt again, because that's worth way more than this stupid old house." We walk arm in arm back inside and sit at the table. I expect Anthony to leave, but he's closed the restaurant for the rest of the afternoon. Both to bring me food and to make sure I'm serious.

"Rahul's on a shift, but he's coming by as soon as he's off."

"To double-check your assessment that I'm not out of my mind?"

"Always good to get a second opinion." He laughs and scoops more curry for me.

Anthony's phone dings just as we've finally finished eating. "More paperwork in from Levi. I think it's the last of it." He looks up at me, uncertain, but not in a pleading way. In a way that gives me an out if I want it.

I don't want it. "My phone has no signal here. Can I use yours as a hot spot?"

He sets it up. I download the documents and finish signing everything. It's done. The stolen house is stolen no longer. Whatever Rahul and Anthony do with Hillingham, it'll be better than Mina and Arthur making it a tomb of bad memories and deadly lies.

Thanks to Anthony's hot-spot connection, my phone rings. An unknown number. I brace myself for whatever new fuckery Goldaming Life is up to. It didn't take them long to figure out I was selling this property for a single pound, but they're too late. Dickie himself told me I could be a philanthropist here, and legally the house isn't mine anymore. Which means it's not theirs, either.

I hold up a finger to Anthony and walk down the hall to answer, not wanting him to overhear and worry.

"What?" I say.

"Oh, erm, hello. Is this Iris Goldaming?" The man on the other end of the line sounds old and kind and British, which unsettles me. It's not the type of voice I expected.

"Yes?"

"Hello, dear. My name is Tim Liu. I'm the director of the London Hills Museum of History. I apologize that we haven't gotten back to you sooner. Our administrative assistant is on maternity leave, and I'm afraid the messages have been allowed to pile up. I'm also sorry that I don't have better news."

My heart seizes. Something happened to Elle. No, he's probably calling on her behalf to tell me she's not coming back. That's it; that has to be it. "Is everything okay? Why are you calling?"

"As a courtesy to tell you that there's no one on our staff who can provide the appraisal services you need. I can recommend several trustworthy antiques dealers. And if you find anything of local historical value, we'd be happy to consider any donations to our collections."

"That's fine," I say, fighting my burning humiliation. "You don't need to recommend anyone. Don't worry about replacing Elle."

"Who's Elle?"

I speak slowly, worried my accent is throwing him. "You already sent one of your employees. Elle. She's been helping me, but she quit today."

"Oh, dear. This is— Oh, dear. I think you should ring the police. But no, let's get this sorted before we jump to conclusions. We don't have anyone on our staff by that name. Did you contact any other museums or stores? Is it possible she works for them? Because I'm afraid perhaps you're the victim of—"

"Thank you so much, I'll figure it out on my own." I end the call with numb fingers. I *am* figuring it out. Much, much too late.

That day, when Elle showed up on the doorstep. *I* was the one who said she'd come from the museum. I gave her the perfect cover story, wrapped up like a gift. She didn't even have to do anything to convince me to let her in. And because she's beautiful and I wanted her to like me, I never questioned it. I thought the coincidence of meeting her again was fate finally doing me a solid.

"Oh, Iris," I say, walking without thinking into the den. All this time in my family, all this time with my mother's vicious schemes, and I fell for such an obvious manipulation. Elle didn't save me from being hit by a car because she happened to be in the right place at the right time. She was there because she was following me.

And then I gave her access to this house, took her with me on a fucking weekend holiday, shared all my plans to run away. Which means Goldaming Life knows *everything*.

I'm such an idiot it's actually hilarious. I pick up Lucy's journal. I want to laugh because it's yet another thing we have in common: being so besotted with a woman that we let her destroy everything.

No. I can still salvage this. They don't know that I know about Elle. If she's been undermining me this whole time, then there are probably things in this house that *are* worthwhile. Things I wasn't supposed to find. I searched everything before she did, though, and she never left the house with anything I didn't give her.

Except . . . she went in the attic without me. The attic she told me had water damage and nothing worth looking at.

"Everything okay?" Anthony shouts. "Levi's calling in a moment to discuss how this affects us in terms of taxes and fees so there aren't any surprises. Rahul's heading over after his shift with some champagne, and we'll *really* celebrate!"

"Great," I say, hoping my voice sounds normal. "Just gonna go take a bath." I trudge upstairs, every step heavy with dread and pain.

I don't know how I looked at Elle and saw sincerity, even love, when there was only calculating manipulation. Of all the betrayals in my life, why does this one feel like the deepest?

Maybe it's what I deserve. I'm getting Mina and Arthur's karma. My own heart broken the way they broke Lucy's. I have three-fourths of a literature degree—enough to appreciate the elegantly cruel poetic parallel of it all.

On the third floor I pass the servants' quarters, then pause at the ladder leading up to the attic. Maybe I don't look. Maybe I turn around and run, right now. Leave it all behind. Never know what I wasn't supposed to find.

But I have to see what Elle was keeping from me. What Goldaming Life didn't want me to have. I climb up. The attic is dim, a long narrow room with a single round window letting in the last afternoon rays of sun. Crossbeams run everywhere; there's barely any room to navigate.

At first glance, there's nothing surprising. A jumble of old furniture, some trunks, a stack of paintings. But what's *not* here flashes like a neon sign declaring my stupidity. There's no water damage. Each new confirmation of her betrayal cuts a little deeper. I turn on my phone flashlight and sweep the area, no idea what I'm looking for. It's impossible to navigate. I trip, knocking over a stack of framed art.

My light catches on the painting at the bottom. Unlike the others, this one is free of dust. Someone pulled it out recently and spent time looking at it, then stuck it on the bottom of the pile. Why would Elle hide *this* from me?

I pick up the portrait and set it on a broken chair so I can take it in. Each feature of the subject registers individually, as though my brain can't process it as a whole yet.

Rich blond hair with a widow's peak hairline. Apple cheeks. A small, delicately pointed chin. Expressive eyebrows. A hint of dimples punctuating a rosebud mouth. And eyes so dark blue they could look brown or black, depending on the light. A beautiful portrait of the woman I've already fallen in love with through her writing, and was starting to fall in love with in real life.

"There you are," I whisper.

"Here I am," she says behind me.

70

Boston, September 26, 2024

CLIENT TRANSCRIPT

VANESSA: For fuck's sake, Lucy! You weren't looking for Dracula!

LUCY: What?

VANESSA: *You weren't looking for Dracula!* I know exactly what you're looking for, and I know where to find it. But I won't tell you unless you tear those other vampires to shreds.

LUCY: Vanessa, you—you don't want me to die?

VANESSA: Of *course* I don't want you to die! And I also don't want to be turned by you *or* killed by vampires tonight!

LUCY: *[sniffling]* Okay then. I'll need your help.

VANESSA: With wh—*[scream]*

[sound of clanging]

[muffled thumps]

[screaming]

[long gap]

VANESSA: Well, that was—that was—I don't know. I really don't know how to describe what just happened, Lucy.

LUCY: I do! That was surprisingly *tidy.* No blood on the carpet or chairs. Great teamwork!

VANESSA: Teamwork, huh. All *I* did was bleed.

LUCY: But you did it so well! I never could have lured them to the bathroom on my own.

So, we did it. We killed those poor stupid baby vampires. I gave up my ticket out of existence because you made me curious. Curiosity saved the cat, in this case.

A deal's a deal. What have I been looking for all this time? What did you hear in my stories that I didn't?

VANESSA: All these memories you've shared, all your adventures and detours. You aren't looking for Dracula. You never were. You're looking for *yourself.* You fixated on him as an answer, when really, you need to find someone else from your past.

And before you say it, no, not Mina. Aside from the fact that she's dead, Mina doesn't matter. I know she meant a lot to you, but she isn't the most important person in your past.

The person you need to find, the only person that matters, the only one who can answer your questions? It's you, Lucy.

You hate mirrors, but you need to find one. Not a warped one. A true one. A mirror that will help you reconnect with the girl you were. The girl who was murdered as a teenager and never able to properly mourn the loss of the life she should have had. The girl you've mocked and belittled and dismissed, because that's how you were taught to see her by everyone in your life, and everyone after your death.

I want you to notice how you've talked about yourself. The way you ignore how clever and capable you've been. You've survived, despite everything. You were turned into a monster, but you still showed mercy and tried to save other innocents from terrible fates.

You mattered to more than just the humans you helped, too. Think of the vampires you made part of your life. They were all trapped in their patterns before you. But after? The Queen released her prisoners, because of your compassion. The Lover stopped being an eternal victim and started hunting killers, because of your anger. And the Doctor gave up her obsessive individual study to work with human researchers and help them, because of your criticism.

And you— Sorry, let me get that box of tissues. You looked at me and saw me as a woman, treated me as a woman, acknowledged my existence when so many people in the real world refuse to.

Lucy, you're *not* a monster. I can say that with certainty. Even after what I just saw you do in the bathroom—and I will never, ever be able to forget that. Oh god, I can never forget that.

You were a nineteen-year-old girl who was stalked, manipulated, and murdered. You've told me almost nothing about your life before that, but I can connect the dots that you were never truly, selflessly loved. You've been looking outward for that love ever since, treasuring your idea of this Mina, desperate for validation from the monster who changed you, trying to find communion with other lost, desperate souls.

So. My official recommendation as your therapist is to stop looking outward. Reconnect with the girl you were. Grieve her death, and *forgive* her.

LUCY: But how do I do that? How do I find that Lucy again? I left her behind so long ago.

VANESSA: Go to the beginning. Try your best to remember. Give that history back to yourself.

LUCY: I don't know where to— Oh! I kept journals. I know exactly where my history has been hiding, safe and sound in the dark, all this time. I protected that Lucy, even before I knew what I was doing. I saved her for myself.

VANESSA: That's perfect. I'm so happy for you.

LUCY: Thank you. You're a good therapist. And I'm sorry about what I said before. If you really want me to change you, I can try.

VANESSA: No, thank you. As a very special girl once said: *You deserved better. I love you.* That's the reason why I listened to you. Because you do deserve better, and I do love you, simply for existing.

I'm going to hug you, if that's okay. There we go. You shared a lot with me here, and even though some of it will haunt me until I die, I'll genuinely treasure your trust and your stories. Your story matters because *you* matter.

And I'm not afraid of death. Or at least, natural death; I was definitely afraid of vampire attack death. As for my own story, I know what the ending will be. You're right about one thing: Endings aren't scary, they're beautiful. They have power and meaning.

Besides, I worked hard to be at peace with my body, to be exactly who I know I am. I have no desire to live as a vampire; I'm perfectly content to die as a woman.

No, don't cry. I'm so happy we had this time together. Oh, but one favor!

LUCY: Anything.

VANESSA: Can we stop by my transphobic brother's apartment and scare the shit out of him?

LUCY: *[laughing]* Absolutely.

VANESSA: Thank you. And then I want to see you off on your travels. What an adventure we've had together. And what an adventure you have ahead of you! Please find Lucy, and give her my love when you do.

LUCY: *[whispering]*

VANESSA: I know you will, sweetheart. I know. I'll make a special request to be buried in unhallowed ground without any chemicals in my body, so you can take naps with me if you ever make it back here. Send me a postcard when you get where you're going, though, so I know you made it. Where *are* you going?

LUCY: The house where I was born, the house where I died.

Hillingham.

71

London, October 8, 2024

IRIS

I turn around, the ground itself falling away beneath me. A new fault line cutting through my life. Everything I was, everything I will be. Before now, and after now.

When at last I see her, Elle—my Elle, my Lucy—looks empty. Her portrait behind me has more life to it. Whatever animated her face, those quick flashes of emotion that rendered her a different person from one moment to the next, a creature fully inhabited by whatever she was feeling at the time, it's all gone. It's like she's been emptied out.

I know she's still inside there, but she's retreating faster than I can catch her. Already running from whatever my reaction is going to be. I know exactly what she's doing, because I've done it, so many times. She's preemptively deadening herself to blunt the impact of what I say next. It breaks something inside me, seeing a perfect reflection of what it looks like to kill your heart before someone can do it for you.

She stays still and unmoving, so cold and lifeless she might as well be a statue left in the attic alongside her portrait. All those times she held a cup of hot tea between her hands, warming them. Her food allergies preventing her from eating with us. Pretending to eat on the move, or when I was distracted so I wouldn't notice nothing was going past her lips. The chill of her lips when we first kissed, the porcelain white of her body turning to a healthy flush after we'd moved together, after my heat became her heat.

I never even had to invite her in—this was her house to begin with. It's all so obvious. Elle is Lucy, and Lucy's a vampire.

And, to my infinite surprise, not only do I not care . . . I'm so, *so* glad. I step across the obstacles between us and wrap my arms around her. She doesn't move. No breath, no trembling, no heartbeat. But I don't care. It's *her,* and she's still here, and I have loved both the girl she was and the woman she is.

"Lucy." I hold her tighter, putting one hand on the back of her head and pressing her close as I stroke her hair. "I'm so sorry. I'm so, so sorry."

She twitches like her heart is being shocked back to life. The rigid lines of her body melt and meet mine with less resistance. "What?"

"I'm so sorry for everything that happened to you, and everything you've probably been through since. I have no idea what it's been like, but I'm so glad you're here."

"How can you say that?" she asks. "You know what I am. You *know.* Why aren't you scared? I'm a monster."

"You're not a monster. My mother was a monster. My father, too. And the people around you, the ones who let you be preyed on? You were a girl, Lucy. Practically still a child, and they devoured you. Your mother, those men, Mina. They were the monsters."

"Not Dracula?" she asks, disbelieving.

"Well, yes, obviously he's also a monster."

Lucy's shoulders shake. I wonder if she's crying, but when her voice finally breaks free, she's laughing. It's her real laugh, too. The chimes are older, worn with age and exposure to countless storms, but their sound is still beautiful.

I start laughing, too, because it's all so absurd. I laugh until I can't stand anymore, and then I sit, half on top of some old painting. Lucy sits far more elegantly on a chest, our knees pressed together. She's searching my face. Looking for fear, or rejection, or revulsion. She doesn't find any of it.

"You really don't hate me." Her eyes are wide with wonder. "You're not scared of me."

"Oh, my sweet butter chicken, you aren't my first vampire." I pause. "Okay, you're the first one I fell in love with both in person and in writing, and I'm almost positive you're the only one I've slept with, but still."

She raises a delicate eyebrow. "*Almost* positive?"

"Well, clearly my vampdar isn't what I thought it was. Knew you were gay from that first encounter, had no idea you were undead."

Her wickedly playful smile turns me on with a low, warm thrill. "Technically, I'm pan. All vampires are, since everyone we meet has at least one thing we desire."

I barely have a moment to worry that she only likes me for my blood before her smile drops. Her face becomes open and painfully earnest. It's like seeing her naked, truly, for the first time. Every part of her is exposed, and it's only Lucy in front of me. Desperately lonely, terminally hopeful, forever stopped at nineteen. "I came back here to reconnect with the girl I was. I didn't realize how badly I needed to forgive her for what happened to her. I tried to find my journal that first night—"

"Oh my god, were *you* the moonlight?"

Lucy's shocked. "You noticed?"

"Uh, yeah. Moonlight doesn't usually freeze when you see it."

She bites her lips and nods sheepishly. "It's been a long time since I had enough power to pull that trick well. I was a little rusty. Sorry. Anyway, I'm glad you found the journal first. I don't think I could have read it. Or at least, I couldn't have read it without hating the girl who wrote it for how vulnerable she was."

I open my mouth to argue in her defense, but Lucy holds up a hand to stop me. "I know. Hearing you talk about me, hearing you read the journal out loud, hearing the generous, adoring, protective way you took my worst and silliest thoughts? I could finally see *that* girl again. I could finally forgive her and accept that nothing that happened was her fault. She didn't deserve any of it. And all the pain and searching that came after was what I had to go through to get back here. To get back to that Lucy. To . . . find you, so you could help me see she deserved to be loved."

"She *still* deserves to be loved." I take Lucy's hand in mine, linking our fingers. "No matter what that bitch Mina—"

"No," Lucy says, the word sharp and fanged. Her eyes flash red, and for the first time I feel a spike of fear. She takes a moment to calm herself, then squeezes my hand. "I'm sorry. I've held Mina in my heart for so long. It's hard to explain, but when you become . . . *this,* everything crystallizes. Core beliefs—religion, fear, love—that you held most tightly in life become unbreakable chains in death. I always felt lucky that the only thing I believed in was Mina. It's hard to use a dead woman against someone."

She smiles wryly, but it's a performance. Her voice gets lower, more urgent. "Mina never hurt me. Mina *never* would have hurt me. She might not have loved me the way I loved her, but she did love me. Holding on to that, having that wrapped around me the last hundred and thirty years, I think it's helped me stay sane." She tilts her head. "Mostly sane. Okay, sometimes sane. I've had a lot of weird years. Okay, decades." She pauses. "Maybe we should get into that later."

I don't want to argue with her about Mina. I know she's wrong, but it doesn't matter now. I don't even feel jealous, only sad. Lucy loved someone who couldn't love her back. But maybe *that's* what I inherited. Not Mina's deserved retribution, but a chance to be the Murray-Goldaming who loves Lucy for exactly who she is.

As though keen to reassure me, Lucy says, "I think you're right about the men, though. I was too busy being repeatedly attacked by a vampire to notice they were preying on me, too. I'm glad Doctor Seward is dead. Wish I had been the one to do it."

"I wish you had, too," I say with a laugh.

"Quincey was sweet, though. In his own way. Obnoxious and rather dim, but sweet." She smiles at the memory, far away and sad. I wonder how many happy memories she has. I'd hope with as many years as she's lived it's a lot of them, but somehow I know it's not.

I frown, something new occurring to me. "Oh, wait. Which one of us is being inappropriate? Because I'm twenty-five, so does that mean I'm in a relationship with a nineteen-year-old? Or am I in a relationship with a one hundred and . . ." I pause, unable to do math quickly in my head even at the best of times.

Lucy leans dazzlingly close. She looks down at my lips, the sweep of her eyelashes like gold veins in the blush marble of her cheeks. "One hundred and fifty, give or take; I lose track. But the answer is both. Maiden and crone, but never mother. I'm an impulsive, emotional, infinitely hopeful nineteen-year-old and an ancient, exhausted, unfathomably wise old woman."

"Well, that's good, at least. We're *both* creeps, so we cancel each other out."

Lucy laughs and I press my lips to hers, desperate to taste that laugh, to swallow it, to make her part of me forever. Her mouth answers back hungrily. She tugs me forward with so much force I fall onto her. Gone is the tender consideration of our first explorations. It's obvious now how careful we were being with each other.

We are not careful now.

Lucy grabs her portrait and tosses it aside, lifting me onto the chair instead. As her mouth explores me I know, in the tiny part of my brain still capable of rational thought, that I should be concerned about that mouth and what it contains. But all I can think of is how much I want it on me. Where I want it on me. How I never want it to stop. Besides, isn't loving someone *always* giving them the power to destroy you?

I reach out to tug her shirt off, needing less between us, needing *nothing* between us, but my hand hits one of the beams. Then I stand, and my head hits another one.

"We need more space," Lucy says against the delicate skin of my collarbone. I've never felt fragile, but somehow knowing what she is makes everything heightened. Every part of me is aware of its vulnerability. Pleasure and pain are separated by the thinnest line. I'm trusting Lucy to navigate it.

We definitely need more space to do that navigation properly.

"Second floor," I gasp, her tongue dipping down between my breasts. It's still deliciously cool, but she's well on her way to warming up for the end target. "There are beds." I contradict myself by grabbing her and pulling her closer. My fingers slide up her thighs of their own accord, the space between her legs exerting an irresistible magnetism. I need to touch her, to feel her, to reassure myself that she, this, *us*—it's all real.

Lucy stumbles blindly backward, pulling me with her. She disappears and I let out a cry of dismay—both because she isn't touching me anymore and because she fell. But she smiles up at me from the third floor. She landed on her feet.

"Cat," I say, laughing. She holds out her arms. I don't even think about it—I drop. She catches me around the waist but doesn't set me down, stepping forward so the wall is holding me on one side and she's holding me on the other.

"Bedrooms are too far away," she says, desire making her voice thick and slow like honey.

I'm about to agree when I hear two things in quick succession. The first is a knock at the front door. And the second is Anthony, saying, "Yes, she's here. Come on in."

"No!" I scream, but it's too late. Lucy's already moving. I race down both flights of the narrow servants' staircase. Lucy leaps over my head, passing me. I burst out into the kitchen and grab the knife from my purse on the counter, barely slowing. I catch only a glimpse of Lucy in the hallway before a flash of orange leaps at her. They both wind up in the den, out of my sight.

"Help Anthony!" Lucy shouts. Something slams into the den wall so hard the whole house shakes. Plaster dust rains down on my head. I pull up short of the entry.

The front door gapes open like a wound. Beyond it, late afternoon calmly and quickly slips toward twilight. Next to it, Anthony lies unconscious on the floor. Ford is crouching over him, attention fixed on his neck with deadly intensity. Her mouth drops open, fangs extending.

Shit. I drag the knife across the top of my arm. Ford's head snaps up, frenzied black eyes fixed on my invitation.

I drop the knife—useless now; it's steel, not silver—and sprint back to the kitchen. My momentum slams me into the table so hard it scrapes across the floor. I scrabble for the dish I need, ripping off the lid just in time to turn around and fling Anthony's roasted garlic right in Ford's face.

She screams in agony, clawing at her eyes. I duck past her flailing limbs and back into the hall. The fox flies out in front of me, enormous and still in fighting form. I can't escape that way.

The locked room! I rip the key from the chain around my neck and unlock it, then dart inside. I slam the door and lock it once more. It's a flimsy defense, but I just need a few seconds to make a plan. To figure out what I can do to keep Ford's attention on me and away from Anthony.

That's when it hits me where I am. The boarded-up window cuts off most of the light, but I can still see the bed where Lucy's mother died. Where Lucy drew some of her last mortal breaths.

Brilliant. I locked myself in the death-by-vampire room. I'm not ready to join that club. I rush to the windows. The one that isn't broken is sealed shut. I move on to the boarded-up section, tugging on the lengths of wood. Of all the things in the house to be sturdy after this long, of *course* it's this.

I grab the little stool by the vanity and slam it against the intact window, closing my eyes against the anticipated shards of glass. The stool breaks instead.

"How fucking thick is this window?" I scream, incredulous.

The first blow hits the door. It won't hold for long.

Two of the stool legs broke off, forming perfect little stakes. Which would be awesome if it were possible to drive a wooden stake between ribs. But it's not, no matter how easy movies make it look. I tried to kill Ford that way once; she laughed at me. I hold on to one of the larger splinters, though, more for reassurance than anything else.

The door buckles, the frame half off. One more blow.

Think, think. Lucy said every vampire holds the same things holy in death that they did in life. What would Ford hold holy? What burrowed so deep that I can use it against her?

"Stop," I say, channeling my mother's voice in a pitch-perfect imitation.

Silence descends. The door stays still. This might work. Oh god, this might work.

"Bring a car around, Ford," I command. And then I use a phrase I heard so many times I could imitate it in my sleep. "We'll deal with this in private."

This being me.

"Ma'am?" It's the first time I've ever heard Ford sound uncertain.

"You're a silly, selfish girl, Iris," I say, and again, it's easy to mimic what I know. "You're embarrassing yourself. Why do you make me do this?"

I whimper a response in my own pathetic voice. "Mom, please. How are you here?"

My voice shifts up. "Stop asking stupid questions. Stand up straight, you look *poor* when you slouch like that."

"Ma'am?" Ford prompts once more.

"Ford, the car. Now, please," I say, and then I freeze. My mother never said "please" to anyone she considered beneath her, which was everyone. Maybe Ford didn't notice. Maybe—

The door explodes inward. I throw an arm over my face to protect myself. Ford takes my wrist in her hand. She yanks it up so hard my arm pops at the shoulder. Bright spots of pain dance in front of my eyes and I gasp for air.

Ford laughs. "Nice try. Seriously, I'm a little impressed." But she's not looking at me. She's looking at my extended arm. She twists it so the cut is facing her. Another burst of pain makes me afraid I'm going to pass out from shock.

"You can't touch me," I gasp. "It's against the rules."

"I'm tired of rules." Ford's bright red tongue darts out. I was right about her teeth: There are too many, and they're sharp. So sharp. "The rules exist so we can serve her. And that's what I'm doing. Serving her. Protecting her line. Bringing back her useless whelp. But." Her eyes go hazy, a red light kindling in them. Ford, or what's left of Ford, is quickly receding. "It would be like tasting her." There's a note of awe and worship in her voice. "I'd have part of her in me, always. I can stop. Just a taste, just a drop of her power, her legacy. That's all I'll take, that's all—"

I try to kick her between the legs, but Ford is too fast. Jarred from her blood-haze revery, she glares at me.

"She's *dead,*" I say. "My blood is mine, not hers."

"You sweet, sweet idiot." Ford pulls my arm closer to her. My toes are barely touching the floor, the pain in my shoulder unbearable. I must scream, because Ford laughs again, happier than ever.

"Since when does death matter?" She considers my arm, then shakes her head. "No, already old. Already ruined, scabbing and wretched. No beat, no rush, no life." She grabs me around the waist, lifting me in the air and crushing me to her as she nuzzles my neck. "You'll like it. I promise."

"Gross," I say. Then I jam the wooden splinter straight into her eye.

Ford screams, dropping me. I fall onto my ass, scooting backward on the floor to put as much distance between us as I can. I can't decide whether to vomit or laugh as Ford yanks the splinter free. Her eyeball comes out, too, with a wet *pop.*

Ford is gone. What's left of her is feral. This is it. This is how I die.

She screams in fury and charges toward me. Something big and orange bounces off the back of her head, stopping her in her tracks. Blinking in confusion, her eye socket leaking black sludge instead of blood, Ford turns and picks up the object.

It's a head. Full beard, unseeing eyes, red hair the exact tone of the fox that tried to kill Lucy.

"Vince?" The confusion in Ford's voice is adorable.

Lucy steps through the shattered doorframe. "I don't believe we've been introduced."

It's like a Viking warrior versus a porcelain doll. Ford tosses Vince aside, then holds her arms wide, each hand as big as Lucy's head. "You," she growls. "*That's* the stench I smelled on Iris. I'm going to tear you apart. I'll even make it fast, as thanks for stopping me before I did something regrettable to the bloodline." Ford takes a step toward Lucy, but stops, confused by Lucy's laugh.

It's a peal so silver I could stab Ford with it. And then it cuts off abruptly. Lucy's expression is oddly disappointed as she looks up at the deadliest creature in my mother's security force. "How long have you been a vampire?" Lucy asks.

"Not a vampire. I'm a living god. I went through the Celestial Gate five years ago." Ford's hand drifts to her eye socket like she wants to explore the damage. She makes a fist instead, taking another menacing step toward Lucy.

"Brand-new. I thought as much. If you were anything other than an infant, you would have been paying attention to the hour. You would have felt it in your bones. It's twilight, which means we can shape-shift again."

"I'll kill you in any shape," Ford sneers. Her hands change, fingers ending in razor claws. She lunges forward but Lucy is . . . gone. There's a blur of movement, a rush of air. Lucy is behind her. She jumps on Ford's back, wrapping her legs around Ford's waist and her hands around Ford's neck.

"You would *also* know that vampires are always strongest when they've been sleeping in their own burial ground," she says. Ford flails, trying to rip her off. Lucy ducks her head away from a deadly swipe. "My mausoleum's right down the street."

Lucy pushes a knee against Ford's back. The giant vampire's spine makes a popping noise, not unlike her eyeball. Ford collapses. Her legs flop in a stomach-turning way. Lucy picks her up by the now-useless limbs and flings her. The remaining window at last breaks as Ford slams into it.

Lucy's across the room in a blur, on top of Ford once more. "And you'd know that nothing is more powerful than a vampire in her own home. You should never have accepted an invitation into mine, and you should *never* have touched Iris."

Lucy punches her hand straight through Ford's throat. She grabs the spinal column and twists with a terrible series of snaps. Then she stands, taking Ford's head with her. The rest of Ford's body remains on the floor. It slowly slumps to the side, a pile of withered flesh in place of that unassailable mountain of a woman. Lucy drops the head with a sound of prim disgust.

She turns and sees the look on my face. "You're safe. I'm not going to hurt you." She moves to my side. Her expression is soft but also intense, like she's explaining something crucially important to a child or trying to soothe a frightened animal. "You told me the truth about yourself. You need the truth, too. The Lucy in the journal. Elle. The women you fell in love with—I'm both of them. Neither was a lie. But this is also the truth of me." She holds out her gore-covered hands, watching me. Waiting for me to scream or run. "I'm not going to hurt you," she says again, even softer.

I laugh.

Her expression shifts to alarm, worried I've lost it. Which, granted, I'm pretty close to. But not quite there yet. "Lucy. Babe. I know you're not going to hurt me. You just tore off the heads of not one but two vampires with your bare hands to protect me. And I've been trying to kill Ford for years, so this is awesome. We're good. I promise. Horrifying gore aside, I'm not *not* into this side of you."

Lucy's surprise is adorable, but I'm in too much pain to be horny right now. Lucy leans close, her breath cold and sweet on my neck as she puts her lips right next to my ear. I'm *not* in too much pain to be horny right now, apparently.

"Ask me," she murmurs, "to pop your arm back into its socket."

I laugh so hard there's barely a difference when it shifts to a scream as she does it without being asked. When I reclaim myself from the mindlessness of pain, I grit my teeth in my best attempt to smile at her. "Thanks. I'll unpack what my attraction to Terminator Lucy means later. Right now I need you to go make sure Anthony is okay."

She tilts her head to the side. "Heartbeat sounds good. No slowing or pooling anywhere in his pulse, so no internal bleeding or severe head trauma. I think he just got knocked out."

"Listening for injuries from a room away. That's a cool and not at all unnerving trick. But this is good. When he wakes up, we can tell him it was Animal Control at the door. Then the fox ran in and he jumped back and hit his head on the stair railing. That way we can explain that the fox is gone and never coming back, so he won't be scared to live here. Oh, uh. I gave Rahul and Anthony the house. I hope that's okay. I didn't know I should have asked your permission."

She smiles. "I think that's wonderful."

"Good, because we have work to do."

"Running away?"

I look up into her face. Lucy Westenra. Impossibly, improbably, imperfectly perfect and *here.* Which means my wish for vengeance—both for her sake and mine—is suddenly feasible.

"No. We're going to find Dracula, and we're going to make him pay for what he did to you. And burn my family's legacy to the ground while we're at it."

Lucy's smile spreads like a fever, barely noticeable and then inescapable. Her teeth are small and white and perfectly sharp, and I love fanged Lucy best of all, I think.

We're going to do great and terrible things, together.

72

THE STORY OF ALICIA DEL TORO

Alicia Del Toro wanted her life to feel different.

It wasn't that her life was *bad*. She didn't mind being a receptionist. She had health insurance and free dental work, and it was definitely better than the jobs her parents had taken to survive. She was bilingual and clever and personable in addition to being strikingly pretty—all qualities that got her the dentist office job despite her having had to drop out of high school.

Everyone who knew where she came from told her she was "lucky." They assumed her ambition had been adequately rewarded.

But a double-wide in the Nevada desert, always a little dusty no matter how much she cleaned, didn't feel "lucky" to her. It felt like a starting point, not the finish line her steadfast boyfriend, Ben, and their friends seemed to view it as. It wasn't until he started talking kids that she panicked, though. Kids were permanent. Kids were anchors. She loved Ben, she did, but.

But some nights—most nights—when she got home from work and made dinner that they then ate on the couch watching TV, she thought . . . *This can't be it.* This couldn't be everything the world had for her. She longed for excitement, for connection, for something bigger than herself. Something divine.

One day, a day like any other, a day like *all* the others, Alicia looked up from the reception desk and saw an angel.

The woman glowed. There was no other way to put it. Her clothes fit just right, her hair fell just right, her smile spread just right. There was something almost unhuman about her perfection.

That's what I want, Alicia thought. *That's who I want to be.*

As though aware of the effect she'd had, the woman paused and really *looked* at Alicia. Alicia was beautiful, and she knew it. But growing up without money had left its mark. Acne scars shadowed her cheeks. Her teeth weren't straight. She was still paying off medical debt from her parents' deaths, so her clothes were thrifted and her frizzy hair managed only with grocery store products. Alicia was real life; this woman was the movies.

The woman slid a card across the desk. "I'm having an I-Vee party," she said. "You should come. I think you'd really fit in."

Plenty of older men propositioned her, thinking they were entitled to her time or attention (they weren't, and she let them know it). Not a lot of women did, so this was new. She took the card, certain it was some sort of weird sex thing. What happens an hour from Vegas, etc. But when she searched for I-Vee that afternoon, the Goldaming Life website looked exactly the same as the woman: Polished. Beautiful. Glowing.

Alicia went to the party. She sampled products and listened attentively, but she'd already devoured everything on the website before she came. The party was a light introduction; she was ready to go all in on the patented Gold Path. A path that led members to bigger and better things, bigger and better selves, than they could ever have or be on their own.

Climbing the sales ladder at Goldaming Life felt equal parts attainable and aspirational. There were members—women like her, women who had nothing to recommend them but their intelligence and compassion and charisma—who were now top earners. They made hundreds of thousands of dollars in commissions, won all sorts of prizes for new membership sales, and changed their own lives by helping other people change theirs.

They'd gotten rich, yes. But more important, they were a community. A family. Goldaming Life was going to help her find the Alicia she was always meant to be, the one the universe had been waiting for.

Ben balked at the buy-in. They had bills to pay, and he wanted to save for a baby. So she did it without him. She had to use the products for two months before she could begin selling them—there were no false testimonials at Goldaming Life, only actual results from actual devotees—and she had no time to waste.

Everything exceeded her hopeful expectations. With just a few applications of the skin-rejuvenating cream, her acne scars were healed. But she didn't want to be limited to the creams. She sold her mother's family jewelry and subscribed to the nutrition shakes. Her metabolism sped up, so boosted that nothing seemed to stick to her belly or hips anymore.

She was a walking before-and-after. Everyone noticed. By the time she hit two months, she already had a waiting list of women eager to sign up under her. It wasn't hard to convince others to join. She loved everything about it, and her sincerity was the best sales tool possible. She sailed past the first goal points on the Gold Path in record time.

And the community! She was meeting people she never would have otherwise, people who saw her value and potential, people who recognized how much she had to offer the world.

No matter how Ben grimaced and complained that she was getting too skinny and too busy, Alicia couldn't be stopped. All her life she'd been working herself to the bone just to stay in the same place. And now? She was flying. Sprinting down the Gold Path. There was always a new level to attain, a new milestone to hit, a new goal just out of reach—for now.

Not only had she already earned back what she'd put in, she was bringing in enough money that she went part-time at the dental office. Even that seemed unnecessary, done to placate Ben and stay on the health insurance. She'd never felt this good, though.

But it wasn't all golden. Nothing ever is. She was bringing in five figures a month, breaking sign-up records for the region despite the sparse population, even invited to be the face of the greater Reno area I-Vee Center (which meant at last quitting her dental job, no great loss no matter how Ben fretted), but she *still* wasn't allowed into the exclusive back rooms.

All she could do was grit her teeth in a smile as yet another woman with deep pockets strolled right past her and through those sleek golden doors. Alicia didn't know what was behind them, but it made her blood boil that she had to earn admission when others just bought it. She was stuck in the central room, the one anyone could book for an I-Vee party. Standing on those polished floors with her polished skin and her polished teeth, waiting to welcome people. Still a receptionist.

"I hate her, too," another woman said, laughing.

Alicia turned and froze in surprised recognition. At the spring Goldaming Life Celebration—Alicia had live streamed it instead of going because Ben thought the airfare and hotel fees were too much even though it was obviously an investment in their future—Grace Ford had been named as a candidate to walk through the Celestial Gate during the next cycle. She was almost at the end of the Gold Path. The top.

It was like seeing a celebrity. Alicia's tongue went thick and dry. This close, Grace Ford reminded her of the villain in a Bond movie—tall and icy and powerful and beautiful. A little scary, but a lot sexy.

Grace Ford paused, standing next to her and taking in the sleek I-Vee showroom. Even though it wasn't *hers,* Alicia took great pride in it. She'd introduced so many women to the amazing products it held, and she was going to introduce so many more.

"Can I tell you a secret?" Grace Ford asked.

Alicia nodded. She wanted a secret. She wanted all the secrets.

"Women like her? Buying her way up is just another accessory. She hasn't worked for it or earned it. There's a limit to how far money alone will get you. Goldaming Life doesn't mind their cash—we can pass it along to members like you. But we also know the Gold Path only has whatever meaning devotees bring to it. She's never going to make it through the Celestial Gate."

Grace Ford looked at Alicia in a way that made her feel taller. Stronger. Valuable and valued. "I've seen your file, Alicia Del Toro. You're navigating the path step-by-step. Not through luck or money, but through sheer determination. Sheer *loyalty.* Same as me. Those of us who choose to be here, who earn our progress rather than buying it? We always go farther. We're the true Gold Lifers. You and me."

Alicia had never felt so seen. She threw herself in with renewed intensity. She'd be like Grace Ford. She'd walk every step of the way with her head held high, absolutely devoted, absolutely focused.

Ben tried to talk her out of investing more (of her money, of her time, of herself) into the Gold Path. She was earning more than she ever had as a receptionist—more in a month than she used to in a year—but maybe that was the problem.

He texted her constantly. Complained when she'd stay at the I-Vee Center for the weekend rush. He even brought her parents' priest in for an intervention, during which he cried and insisted she was being brainwashed.

Which was *exactly* what they told her he'd say. She was more disappointed than angry. It hurt that he couldn't see how important she was to them. They took her photo for their brochures, had her leading more exclusive I-Vee parties, and even put her in regular rotation at their massive I-Vee Vegas Information Center.

And it wasn't like it was costing her and Ben anything anymore. She wasn't spending any money on products; everything was complimentary now. When they asked her to begin serving at the Vegas location, they'd even given her a company car. No strings attached.

She and Ben came to an uneasy truce. He didn't complain about Goldaming Life, and she didn't try to get him to use the products. Neither of them brought up kids, because as long as they didn't talk about it, they didn't have to fight. He loved her, and she loved Goldaming Life, and surely he'd come around to seeing how good it was for them both.

Three years into Alicia's journey, Grace Ford visited her again. Alicia didn't recognize her at first. It was still Grace Ford, but *perfected.* The celestial version; that was the only way Alicia could think of it. The Vegas center, glimmering and brilliantly lit, seemed to dim as Grace Ford walked in, as though not even the Vegas lights could compete.

"Grace Ford!" Alicia said, immediately feeling foolish.

"Alicia," the other woman said with a laugh, "please just call me Ford. You use my whole name like I'm some sort of celebrity."

"What brings you to Vegas?" Alicia asked so she didn't have to admit that she absolutely thought of Ford as a celebrity.

"Blanche Goldaming." Ford smiled at Alicia's gobsmacked expression. The president and CEO of Goldaming Life herself. Alicia was desperate to meet her, but of course she wasn't going to ask.

She didn't need to. "Come on. I'm taking you with me."

Ford brought Alicia to a penthouse suite with floor-to-ceiling windows and art Alicia couldn't even begin to imagine the cost of. From up here, Vegas wasn't dirty and cigarette-stained and tacky. It was magical.

They snuck through a side door into a private donor meeting. Alicia leaned against the sleek mahogany-paneled wall and listened, awestruck, to Blanche Goldaming's stirring, inspirational, sparkling anecdotes.

Blanche Goldaming was a spiritual giant, fully committed to the

Gold Path and helping as many people as possible walk it. But she was also practical. Real in a way that shocked and inspired Alicia. At one point, she even made eye contact with Alicia, and smiled.

It was like falling in love. Not with a person, but with a concept. With a life.

After, Ford walked with her down the filthy Strip. Alicia loved this walk, with its foul smells, aggressive porn-pushers, and drunken tourists. She loved it because she always reached the I-Vee Center at the end. It was like stepping from the outskirts of hell to the front door of heaven.

Ford didn't go back inside with her. She handed Alicia a card with her cell number written on it. "We can cleanse your blood, but we can't cleanse your mind or your soul or your life. You're close. But only you can get yourself all the way there. When you're ready to cut away everything weighing you down and slowing your progress along the path, I'll be your personal sponsor through the next gates."

It was staggeringly generous, and a wake-up call. Ford was right. Only Alicia could do this next part. She'd been holding on to her old life. Telling herself she could keep both—where she had been, and where she was going. But it wasn't possible.

She changed her number, cut off contact with Ben and what was left of her family, moved out and on and into Goldaming Life Housing.

Her role changed, too. They transferred her from their Vegas center to their flagship Salt Lake City location. Everything she needed was provided; there was no push to bring in more money, because she was above all that.

Distraction was washed away. She devoted herself to the path with religious fervor. They used all of her: her beauty, her intelligence, her charm, her wit. *Everything* was valuable in helping others find their way onto the Gold Path, and they gave her opportunities beyond anything she could have dreamed. Not just modeling for their brochures and acting in their instructional videos. She even got to help in the lab beneath the Goldaming Life building. Alicia Del Toro, a girl with no high school education, a girl who was *lucky* to be a receptionist, processing serums and sorting biological samples!

The lab leader had obviously been through the Celestial Gate, too. Alicia struggled not to stare. She had Ford's otherworldly grace, her same aura of power and *perfection*.

Alicia didn't question miracles anymore. She'd seen too many of them with Goldaming Life. MS cured after switching to an all-shakes diet. Dementia reversed. Cancer spontaneously in remission. But more than that. She'd seen impossible change on a cellular level, in herself and others.

It was in the lab that Alicia figured out what the miracle of the Celestial Gate was. It was in the lab leader's movements, in the depthless quality of her eyes: even though she looked to be in her twenties, Alicia was certain she was decades older. Maybe even centuries.

That was the Celestial promise, if Alicia could earn it: *Perfection through immortality.* They were defeating death itself. When they whispered that Blanche Goldaming was living divinity, it was literal. And thanks to Goldaming Life, Alicia could become a god, too.

Alicia worked, and she worked, and she worked. She whittled herself down until she existed for a singular purpose: to perfectly walk the Gold Path.

And then one night, Ford was at the door of her company apartment. "It's time," she said.

Alicia burst into tears. Her heart was so full, her body so tired. She was ready. She was *ready.* She didn't know if she deserved it, but she trusted that what they saw in her was true. And she did believe she'd earned it.

When she entered the grand ballroom of the Salt Lake City Goldaming Life Center, she half expected a literal gate, shimmering and golden, with a rainbow haze beyond which immortality awaited.

Instead, Blanche Goldaming, smaller and older than she'd remembered, was sitting in a chair, supported on either side by people who didn't look like Ford, but *felt* like her.

"Come forward and kneel," Blanche said. She sounded tired. Alicia had a moment of confusion and doubt. Why would Blanche Goldaming look like that, when she held the secret of eternal health?

Alicia did as she was told, kneeling in front of the chair where Blanche sat. A hand rested lightly on top of her head, and Alicia struggled not to tremble. "Close your eyes," Blanche whispered. "Leave weakness behind, and become gold forever. Swear yourself to the Goldamings."

"I swear," Alicia said. Before she could wonder why she was swearing herself to the Goldamings and not to Goldaming Life, two points of ice stabbed into her neck. She tried to jerk away, but arms like chains wrapped around her, trapping her. Her face was tilted down; she couldn't see. Cold flesh was pressed against her lips. "Drink," someone commanded. She tasted blood. This was wrong. This wasn't what was supposed to happen. But she was so used to trusting and obeying. She swallowed.

"That's enough," a woman's voice said. "Snap it." Hands wrapped around her head. She heard and felt the pop as an atomic burst of color, and then everything was dark.

And then *nothing* was dark. She gasped back to life in an explosion of consciousness.

The higher connection she'd wanted with the universe descended on her like a mantle from heaven. She had senses and feelings and strength she never knew existed. She was also in a box, and had no idea who she was other than a desperate, terrible need.

"Open it up," a voice demanded. The lid was removed. "Welcome to the other side of the Celestial Gate, Alicia."

That's right. She was Alicia. She'd forgotten for a moment. And the woman who stood over her was Ford. Her sponsor. Her friend.

Ford escorted her to a small house in the middle of the desert. Alicia felt like a newborn deer, unsteady and baffled by the world around her.

Ford gave her a cup and commanded her to drink. "I've given you your name back, which will help. But you're here until you can control yourself," Ford said, all business. "Once you prove you can handle what you've become, we'll be able to use you. There are rules, and they must be followed with precision. Do you understand?"

Alicia nodded, desperate and eager.

"Good," Ford said. "First rule: We exist to protect the Gold Path."

"Yes," Alicia said automatically and eagerly. She understood that rule like it was woven into every cell in her body. She'd lived for the Gold Path for so long by then, it was instinctive.

"Second rule: Don't kill anyone. Once you have that down, you'll be ready to come back."

Alicia stared in confusion, but instead of clarifying, Ford left. Two employees showed up in her place, taking care of the house, watching Alicia, making sure she drank when she was told to.

Her teeth hurt—why did her teeth hurt?—and the boundaries of her body felt strange and unfamiliar. After the euphoria of waking wore off, she was thirsty all the time. Achingly, desperately thirsty. Worse, the people taking care of her scared her. Not because they were threats, but because they didn't feel *real*. They felt like . . . things.

She had wanted a greater connection with the universe, with herself. And even though she could hear and see and smell like never before, even though at night she could make herself go thin and flexible like she was about to become the air itself, she'd never felt more disconnected.

But she was going to do what she had to. She was going to get back to Goldaming Life. Ford would help her understand, and then Alicia would be an ambassador. Help women just like herself find this same strange new power. Maybe even work directly with Blanche.

When at last Ford was satisfied that Alicia could follow the rules, she was driven back to Salt Lake City. Alicia couldn't wait to find out what her role as a god on earth would be.

They assigned her to an elevator in an office building.

73

Salt Lake City, November 15, 2024

My Dear Butter Chicken,

I keep looking right, and you aren't there, and it makes me sad.

Are you in Boston yet? In my dreams—not the dreams you're in, but you know what those ones are like and I hardly think I can put them in writing, both because I'm not that good at description and it would make these letters X-rated and I don't know if your therapist (it still makes me laugh that you have a therapist, how human of you!) is going to be reading them before you visit her and pick them up—anyway, in my dreams you get to Boston and Dracula is just, like, hanging out. Outside MIT or something. I don't really know why he's there, maybe he's developed a taste for insufferable geniuses. And it turns out we don't need me to infiltrate Goldaming Life at all, because you make even quicker work of him than you did of Ford and whoever the ginger fox was. So I walk out in the morning, dreading my weekly torture sessions, but instead:

There you are. Radiant. Glorious. Dracula's desiccated head in your hand like the season's hottest accessory. I run to you and take you in my arms and you toss his head aside because who fucking cares about him, what a loser, and then we make all those dreams we've been sharing come true. Maybe even right there in the street, depending on whether I can stand to wait long enough to get into the house.

Who knows. We got lucky finding each other. We could get lucky again.

I know it's unlikely. I promise I'm doing my part here, getting in good with the powers at the top so I can access secret information and find him that way.

I'm so fucking scared. I want to admit that to you. Every time I get on that elevator, I'm terrified I'll never come out again. They'll hook me to machines, plug my blood right into a wall outlet Frankensteining me into the building itself, and use me to power their evil forever. The blood is life, and they want both from me. My blood and my whole life.

But the thing is, I'm so scared, but I'm also amped. Thrilled. Giddy. Because I never thought I'd be able to do anything to bring Goldaming Life down. I felt powerless. I was powerless. But now I have you.

And they have no idea. They're the ones not looking right. And when you come out of nowhere like a goddamn fucking nightmare superhero, I'll be ready to push them into harm's gorgeous arms.

XOXO

Iris

74

Salt Lake City, December 12, 2024

My Dear Butter Chicken,

You haven't written yet, but I thought of something else. While it's very charming that you don't know how to use a phone and are therefore blissfully unaddicted like the rest of us, it does make logistics difficult. Once you're done in Boston, I can't keep sending letters to your therapist's office.

How about this. There's a place here called City Creek Canyon Trail. It goes pretty deep into the hills and mountains. I walk there every night just to be alone. There's a big wooden post labeled "Bonneville Shoreline Trail." At the bottom of that post is a sign that says "Absolutely No Fireworks." Once I hear from you and know you're leaving Boston, I'll tuck my letters in the space behind that sign. Because without you, there are absolutely no fireworks.

You'll know it's the right post, because my backpack strap will be nailed to the top. Like a flag—the thing that started our romance. Yes, I kept it. It reminds me of you. But since I can't figure out a way to make it into some sort of bracelet, this is the next best use.

Anyway, remember the fantasy I told you about? The one where you show up with Dracula's head?

I've been dreaming about him lately.

I don't remember much about that night when I was a kid. Maybe I blocked it. Maybe I was just really young. Maybe what came after was so much worse that the first trauma sort of got swallowed up. The first rumblings of an avalanche of shit to follow.

Have I told you about the bedroom my mom made me switch to, after I invited Dracula into our house? Of all the bad things that happened to me, that bedroom was the worst, with its cathedral ceiling sloping down to a single round window—round and red like an eye watching me—surrounded on either side by these little closets set into the wall a couple feet above the floor. I honestly can't explain why those closets were so terrifying, why it felt like they were breathing, why they haunt my nightmares to this day.

Dracula was my first monster, and then the rest of my life became filled with them. I started running away just so I wouldn't have to sleep in that room anymore. I found girlfriends and begged them to let me stay over for as long as I could keep them hidden from my mom (who would then pay them off or threaten them so they'd kick me out). I moved as far away as I could, and it was never far enough.

Sometimes, when I'm stuck between sleeping and waking, I'm back there. That bedroom, those closets, that red window, waiting for me all this time. I don't move, but the window grows closer, and closer, so close I can't focus on it anymore, so close it blurs and doubles.

Two red eyes, looming over me, watching me, frozen between sleeping and waking.

I've had that dream since I was a kid. And it's getting worse now, slipping in whenever you don't take my dreams. It's him. I know it's him.

But as awful as the dreams are, I wake up feeling hopeful.

We're getting closer.

XOXO

Iris

75

Salt Lake City, December 20, 2024

My Dear Butter Chicken,

I know you're okay, because I feel you when I'm sleeping. But I'm worried, and I miss you, and I need to see you and touch you and remind myself that you're real.

XOXO

Iris

76

Boston, December 29, 2024

LUCY

At last, travel weary but humming with a body full of blood, I arrive outside the club. I want to visit Vanessa first and see if there are any letters for me, but I'm itching for progress. It's been too long already just getting here. I couldn't dazzle my way past airport security, so I had to take a boat. I thought the enormous yacht I climbed aboard would be faster than a bulky shipping container; I was wrong. At least I didn't feel bad taking a meal from the insufferable owner. Weeks I had to listen to him! Agonizing.

It would have been much simpler to get to Boston had I been able to hitch a ride on Iris's private jet. Unfortunately, given that her security team had at least one vampire who would sniff me out, that wasn't an option. Staying away while the Goldaming Life people took care of the bodies we hid in the locked room and then bundled Iris off was one of the hardest tasks of my entire vampiric life. I wanted to tear them apart. Just to have a few more moments, a few more infinite *nows* with Iris.

But I can live the rest of my life in the nows we had. In the look of love and wonder on her face when she realized what and who I was. In the way, at last, *at last,* someone saw every part of me and loved me.

Iris. My heart. My miracle. My wonder.

After making sure Rahul and Anthony were set with the house—Iris insisted, and I didn't mind because I agree that they deserve both the house and protection—I at last followed.

At least there was plenty of time to influence her dreams on the way over here. I'd had no idea exactly what giving her a taste of my blood before we parted would do. I only remembered that Dracula had done it to me and it had connected us. So it was a tremendously delightful surprise to find I could nudge her dreams in whatever direction I chose. Dracula chose terror. I chose something quite different.

We've had *such* a good time. It's not the same as being with her, but I'm with her all the time in my heart.

And thanks to her, I'm ready. The last time I entered this club, I was weary beyond belief. I was lost and alone and desperate. I'm none of those things now. My spirits soar as I stride back into the place where I was nearly destroyed. I'm going to show them what I can do. I'm going to make *such* an entrance. I'm going to—

There's a vampire brawl happening inside. It could almost be mistaken for a thrashing group dance, save the occasional limb that flies free of the melee. And in the center, pressed on all sides, about to be destroyed, are two familiar faces.

I had planned on killing the Queen and the Lover myself if I ever saw them again, but they're on the verge of being killed by the same vampire trap that nearly ended me. I don't think they set me up, after all. They must have made the mistake of listening to the Lover's little bird and coming here.

"Excuse me," I call out.

It's hard to be heard over the rumbling bass pumped through the sound system. Fine. At least it's after dark. I'll never understand other vampires' aversion to changing form. I let go of myself and I'm everywhere and I'm nowhere and they can't track me because who can see moonlight in the middle of flashing lasers?

There's nothing visceral or thrilling about what comes next. It's an efficient dismantling of bodies. Hand through a chest. Moonlight. Arms removed. Moonlight. Head torn off. Moonlight. I'm dizzy by the time there are only a few functioning vampire bodies left, unsure where I end and the night begins.

I'm going to kill and kill and never stop, I'll be doing this forever, I've always been doing this, body after body after—

"Lucy," a sweet voice says, like a bell calling me home. I shudder back into myself. The Lover and the Queen stand amidst a mound of bodies. A final vampire cowers behind them, too scared to fight for his unlife.

"It seems like you're about to kill us, too, and I'd rather you not," the Lover says, blinking slowly at me. Half her cheek is ripped off, skin dangling like fruit mid-peel. I press it back in place for her. Just like old times.

The Queen adjusts her clothes with a surly expression. Skirt and blouse back in her preferred neat order, she sets the broken bones in her arms. "Thank you for rescuing us."

"Wasn't my intention." I shrug, then peer around them. The vampire hiding there screams. His eyes are big and dark and panicked. He's brand-new, poor thing.

"You killed them," he gasps, looking around. "You killed them. You *killed* them."

"Killed them again," the Lover clarifies. She's dancing slowly through the remains, pausing birdlike now and again if a body's wearing something particularly shiny.

"I have some questions for—" I start, but he's insensible.

"You killed them!"

"Yes, you've established that," I say.

"But they told us—we went through the Celestial Gate! We're incorruptible! We're not bound by mortality anymore!"

"Who told you that?" I try to sound patient and supportive and nonthreatening. Which is difficult with my hands covered in the sticky remains of his friends.

"Goldaming Life. They gave us this gift. They rewarded us. They made us." He shakes his head so fast he's nearly blurring. Maybe he's about to figure out how to leave his human form. Good for him. A little too late, though.

"What does he smell like to you two?" I ask.

The Queen wrinkles her nose in distaste, but the Lover waltzes up to him and presses her face right against his neck. "He smells like—" She pulls back and sneezes, a tiny, precious sound. Her cheek skin dislodges again. I brush it back. She just laughs. "I didn't know I could sneeze anymore! He smells like Dracula. But not like you." She wraps her arms around me and rests her head against my chest. "No one smells like you, Lucy. Except the Queen. And me."

"Who turned you?" I ask the infant.

"I don't know what that means!"

"Who turned you into a vampire," the Queen clarifies, her question delivered like the falling of a blade.

"Vampire? What are you—I'm not—I'm purified. I'm a Golden

God. I'm divinity on earth. I'm not—I'm not a—oh god." He slumps to the floor, arms hugging his knees. He's on the verge of tears.

I spent so long not knowing who I was, but he doesn't even know *what* he is. I crouch in front of him. "Hey," I say, and this time my gentle voice isn't an act. "What's your name?"

"Ian," he says. "My name's Ian."

At least they gave him his name back. "Ian, I'm sorry to tell you this, but he killed you. He turned you into a vampire. Haven't you been sleeping in a casket, or dirt? And drinking blood instead of eating?"

"I have—we have cubbies. They only smell like dirt because of the organic, all-natural insulation they use. And we drink Goldaming Life supercharged, gold-infused liquid, which has everything we need to survive."

"And it's red?" the Lover asks, skipping around collecting arms and legs and heads, adding them to a quickly growing pile. "And it tastes like blood?"

He looks up at me. I like his face. He seems like he was a nice person, when he was a person. "I'm not a monster," he whispers. "I'm not."

"I know. Do you want to help us destroy Goldaming Life?"

He twitches. There's a familiar flash of instinctive fury. It's the way I must have looked when Iris accused Mina of betraying me. His expression is all I need to know. Whatever they did to Ian before they turned him, they made certain that loyalty to the Goldaming cause is the core of his existence.

Before he can lunge at me, the Queen's razor fingernails appear through his neck, neatly severing his head from his body. She glances at her claws with disdain as he slumps to the floor. "It will take forever to clean them, and no one does it for me now."

The Lover gently collects Ian's head and places it next to his shoulders. "Something's wrong."

"I know," I say, trying to be patient. "His head came off. You can't put it back on."

"No, ma petite chou. What's wrong is he's a him. Lots of them are hims. Or at least, they were."

I nearly dismiss her, focused on the next task, but—she's right. How did I not put that together before? I suppose last time I was distracted with trying not to die. But in America, Dracula has been turning *men*. I never found a male vampire in Europe. Only ever women. "Strange," I say, looking at the Queen for her opinion.

She shifts her shoulders, impassive. "We changed. So did Dracula."

The Lover pats Ian's cheek. "Poor little dear. I like him. We should keep him."

I guide her away from his body. "It would be very hard to do what we need to if we were lugging his corpse around with us."

"What exactly is it we are doing," the Queen says, raising a single imperious eyebrow.

I take her hand in one of mine, and the Lover's in the other. "I saw you two in the center of that circle. You weren't trying to survive. Not really. You were ready for an ending. It's okay. I was ready, too. But I have something better than being killed by a bunch of babies in an obnoxious club." I smile at them, my only friends, my oldest friends. The only two who will understand. "We're going to find Dracula, and we're going to stop him, once and for all. Together."

The Queen's fingers twitch around my own. I worry for a moment she's trying to cut me, but she's just holding my hand. Squeezing it back. She gives me a single, regal nod.

The Lover squeals in delight, letting go so she can clap. "Oh, yes, let's! It'll be a—what do they call them? Girls' trip! Girls' trip, girls' trip, girls' trip!" She twirls around the bodies, singing her song.

I came here to kill vampires and get information. I did both, with the bonus of securing two allies. It feels right, having them by my side for this. I only wish I'd managed to find the Doctor, too.

"You know where he is, then," the Queen says.

I begin pouring alcohol from the bar over the bodies. Wouldn't do for some poor hopeful dancers to come in here and find a massacre when all they need is a good night out.

"Not exactly," I answer, "but I know someone who will figure it out. First things first, though, we start this girls' trip the proper way: arson and then a visit to my therapist."

Boston, December 29, 2024

My Little Cabbage,

Thank you for your letters. I've read them so many times I know them by heart. I told Vanessa—my therapist—all about you. She's going to send this so you don't have to worry anymore. And the backpack strap is a great idea. It'll smell like you, so I'll find it anywhere.

I'm glad you can tell me you're scared. I'm scared, too, which I haven't been in ever so long. It's a novelty! Look at you, bringing even more sensations and emotions back into my life.

We can't be scared if we don't care what happens to or around us. Now we care. And because we care so very much, we're going to win. I know it.

So: I'll endeavor to take up all your dreaming time from now on, leaving Dracula no space in it. And I'll be there soon. Because I have news, too. Not "I'm showing up with Dracula's head as my new clutch" news, because it would be difficult to match to a dress and I'm still vain enough to be bothered by that, but "I officially know we're on his trail now" news. With bonus surprise allies! I saved a couple of old friends, and they're on our side.

My time in Boston proved you were correct: Dracula is behind Goldaming Life. All the vampires here are connected to the organization and also Dracula, and therefore violently invested in protecting him. Arthur and Doctor Seward must have worked with him back in my day, rather than kill him. Then they used Dracula's power and influence to amass a fortune while giving him a foothold in a new land. Our focus must stay on getting close to the top of the Goldaming Life pyramid. That's how we'll find him.

I know it's an unbearable burden on you. I wish Goldaming Life weren't involved. I want nothing more than to swoop in and rescue you from it all. Burn down your old home while we're at it.

But we're on our way to you now. Which is good. Being apart from you feels like going too long without rest—the borders of my self feel less solid.

You make me feel real.

See you in your dreams—

Lucy

P.S. The Lover—her name has nothing to do with our relationship, we're only friends and also she's not quite sane a majority of the time—wants me to tell you hello, and also wants to know if you're friends with any serial killers or know where she might find some. I told her it was unlikely, but promised to ask.

78

Salt Lake City, January 10, 2025

IRIS

Oh god. I'm going to die. I'll never get to tell Lucy I love her. Why was I writing about nightmares and my childhood bedroom when I could have been telling her how much I adore her? How it feels like I spent my whole life desperately hoping she was out there? How discovering her feels like an actual miracle?

"Miss Goldaming?" Dickie prompts.

I snap back to attention. The draining of my will to live must have shown in my glazed expression. "That's me," I chirp.

I know I can't actually die of boredom, but . . . *do* I know that for sure? Maybe this is Dickie's secret evil plan. Make me sit through so many financial disclosure meetings that I slowly wither and die, leaving him free to do whatever the hell he wants.

I remind myself that this suffering is for a reason. But with yet another infinite afternoon spent trapped in this soulless chrome and glass conference room, I'm regretting our decision to be big brave heroes instead of small happy hiders.

Dickie drones on. "If you'll turn to page 72, subsection 29a. The bylaws of the nonprofit branch of Goldaming Life, Inc. I'd like to draw your attention to . . ."

He keeps talking. How does he keep talking? Dickie is a naturally renewing energy source. I've found a grudging respect for him, with his cadaver hands and his sunken eyes and his bafflingly thick, lustrous hair. Maybe it's the hair that's leaching vitality from the rest of his body. Cracked and yellowing fingernails, bluish papery skin, near-purple lips, everything sacrificed to keep that hair vital and glorious.

My phone alarm goes off. I stand so fast, I feel a little dizzy. That could be from my treatment earlier, though. "Time's up! I get to go to the library now."

"It's heartening to see how much you value your education." Dickie's tone indicates otherwise, but he has to let me go. It's part of our deal. I go to an I-Vee Center near my school for treatments once a week, and then I pop into the office, where Dickie punishes me for refusing to just sign whatever they put in front of me by reading whole sections of company legal documents aloud. But in return, they let me live on my own and attend classes at the University of Utah. Not my first choice, but it's miles better than the other big college here where my sexuality could get me kicked out. Charming.

I fought *so hard* for these compromises, though. I bartered with Dickie on everything from how long our weekly meetings could last (two hours) to how often I'll see their private doctor for my gold agglutinin treatments (once a week) to whether or not I'd have my own security team (couldn't get out of it).

I don't care about any of it in the long run, but every concession I won made it look likelier that I was coming back of my own free will. The more they believe me a petulant but willing participant, the less they'll look at what I'm actually doing.

Which reminds me. Gotta pretend I'm getting more invested. "I have some ideas for how to expand our charitable giving."

Dickie's eyebrows rise. "Really?"

"Yeah. I'm excited. But not excited enough to stick around and listen to you for another hour, so I'll tell you next week. Bye."

I walk out of the conference room and stop at the third-floor reception desk. They still haven't let me past this floor. You'd think with my name on the building, nothing would be off-limits, but I'm watched constantly and I can't go up without someone noticing. Plus, every elevator has a guard I'm ninety percent certain is a vampire.

But the cutie at the third-floor desk is human. She perks up when she sees me, eager to get face time with the head of Goldaming Life. If only she knew how little power I actually have.

"Hey, Olivia!" I lean over the desk. "I love your nails." It's true. This week they're pearly pink with black tips, about as edgy as she can get away with here. The rest of her is perfectly highlighted hair and makeup so subtle it's an art form.

"Thank you! What can I do for you, Miss Goldaming?"

"You can start calling me Iris, like we've talked about."

She laughs. "Right. Sorry. Iris." She glances around surreptitiously, like she's engaging in clandestine behavior.

"Can I get all the Goldaming Life Path recruitment materials? I want to brush up on our talking points."

"Oh, sure!" Olivia practically skips down the hallway, leaving her desk unguarded and her laptop open and active—which I knew it was by checking out her nails.

Dickie's still in the conference room, Olivia's the only person out here, and security won't be back down this hallway for exactly three minutes. I slip around the desk and shove a thumb drive into her computer. I copy everything—her Outlook address book, calendars, every PDF and document and download.

By the time the security guard walks by on his patrol, I'm once more leaning against the desk, idly scrolling on my phone. Olivia returns and stacks several pounds' worth of binders, pamphlets, and glossy full-size brochures on the desk.

"Wow." I shove them into my bag, wishing I had asked for less weighty materials.

Olivia misses my sarcasm. "I know! It's all so exciting. I went through the Golden Gate two years ago. Here's my pin." She gestures proudly to a little gold pin on her collar. "I'm nearly qualified for the next stage! It's taken longer than I wanted since I started working here, because I just don't have much time to bring in new members." Her eyes go wide with muted internal alarm. "But obviously I know what a tremendous privilege it is to be here! I wouldn't trade this job for anything. It's amazing, getting to be a small part of what makes Goldaming Life work."

"We're lucky to have you," I say. "See you next week!"

And then my teeth clench and my fists clench and my stomach clenches—I'm just one big clench, really—as Olivia chirps back, "The blood is life!"

"Isn't it, though?" I unclench a fist to wave goodbye and push the button for the elevator.

Inside, as usual, is a security guard. This one is a stunning brunette, glossy hair done in a high ponytail, eyes dark and clever. Her name tag reads "Del Toro." She freezes with recognition—most everyone here knows who I am, even if they haven't met me. To my surprise, though, she doesn't step aside to let me in.

I squeeze in past her and stand pressed against the wall. At least it's only three floors. Or, it should be. She presses the hold button as soon as we start moving. The elevator grinds to a halt.

Can't kill me, I think. *Can't kill me, against the rules.* Doesn't make her any less terrifying.

She turns and fixes her gaze on me, her words so slow and measured it's clear she's holding back. "I'd like to know what happened to Grace Ford."

Shit. Leave it to Ford to find ways to ruin my life even after hers is over. "Car accident," I say, echoing the official Goldaming Life story. I still don't know if Dickie bought my thrilling tale. In that version, the one that leaves Lucy out, I cut my arm by accident. That led to the redheaded fox losing control and attacking me. *That* led to Ford bravely defending me, which led to their simultaneous deaths. It was hard to narrate with a straight face, but he didn't question it. Just sent a team to clean up their bodies. Which was nice, because I couldn't exactly bury them in Rahul and Anthony's new backyard.

Del Toro doesn't blink. "I'd like to know what really happened to her."

I smile, a smile that doesn't touch my eyes. A smile that bares my teeth. A smile I learned by growing up in this fucking cult of predators. "She died. It happens. Even to *people* like you."

I reach past her and push the button so we move again. The elevator dings cheerily at the lobby. I exit past Del Toro, who doesn't say another word.

I can breathe a little better once I'm free of that building. It's a twenty-minute drive to campus, and I use it to decompress with my favorite modern poets. Yesterday it was Halsey, but today I'm feeling Wolf Alice. They wanted to assign me a driver—aka a babysitter—but I refused.

Once I'm safely on campus, they leave me more or less alone. They're still watching, but I have the illusion of solitude. In the library, though, I can't concentrate on any of my homework. I'm tired and achy like always after treatments. Which is why I stopped doing them in the first place. Besides, they certainly didn't save my mother's life.

Giving up on homework, I pull out the Goldaming Life nonsense from Olivia, planning to recycle it. But a glance tells me she messed up. A lot of the documents are preliminary drafts, complete with margin notes from the muckety-mucks at the top. It's only a little gutting to see references to my mother, who must have been in the process of dying at the time these were made.

It's a surreal inside glimpse of how things really work at Goldaming Life: manipulation, inane influencer-speak, terms that sound desirable but are actually meaningless. I look up things I don't know about—free ultraradicals, nanoplastics—and find an avalanche of Goldaming Life member social media posts and testimonials. No actual science, but that never mattered. Not when so many beautiful, rich, glowing people are telling you this simple thing will fix everything you hate about yourself from the inside out.

I look up, surprised to discover night has fallen. I can't see through the window's reflection anymore. It's just my own face, thrown back at me. Under the direction of the Goldaming Life Image Consultants, I let them change my hair back to its natural light brown. My curls are healthy and shiny, my face is scrubbed and clean.

Do I look as hollow as I feel? Does it show, how much I miss Lucy?

The worst part is the uncertainty. How long will we have to be apart? Because even when she gets here, we can't be together. It was pure luck that Ford and the other vampire never figured out Lucy was around in London. With full-time security trailing me here, we can't risk it. I regret agreeing that we should re-hide her journal and all the other materials. At least if I had her journal, it would feel a little like spending time with her.

I get a notification for an email. My heart lifts when I see it's from Rahul. They sold the back half of the lot, which means he and Anthony have enough money to start a family *and* renovate the house. They're bickering about paint colors and want me as tiebreaker. Rahul also reminds me that the first space they've redone is a guest room: the Iris Suite, mine whenever I want or need. It's all so lovely and normal that it *hurts.*

"Excuse me. We're closing soon; do you need anything?"

I look up to find a guy in a U of U sweatshirt pushing a cart. I never know whether people here are actual students, or if they're Goldaming Life sycophants checking up on me. I can't trust anyone in the whole world except Lucy. And Rahul and Anthony, but they're far away and—

thanks to Dickie's expert body disposal team—still completely in the dark about vampires.

"Thanks, I'm fine." As soon as he turns, my smile drops away. I plug the thumb drive into my laptop and glance at the info I stole from Olivia's computer. A calendar of appointments, email addresses for the whole company, various directories and disclosures.

This is potentially juicy, though—Olivia's setting up meetings between the board of directors and a state senator named Harrell. I do a quick internet search and find out he's the nephew of a Supreme Court justice and head of a Senate committee for business protections. Utah is the worst state in the country for allowing multilevel marketing scams to pretend at legitimacy, the perfect example being my family's vampiric pyramid scheme.

Maybe I can get invited to the meeting and secretly record it. I'll also scan copies of the material notes Olivia accidentally gave me. If nothing else, I can leak them to show how insincere the people in charge are.

It's not enough—nothing short of finding and killing Dracula will be—but it's something.

The library flashes its lights as a warning. I pack up and leave, face burrowed into my scarf. It's freezing. I need to get inside. But once I'm past the main walkways, I pause. There aren't any lights around me, nothing but the dark and the night. I stop, tip my head up, and look at the stars.

I drink in their beauty, and I think of Lucy.

And then—it's all I can do to stay calm, all I can do to keep my breathing and heartbeat even—I *feel* it. I'm being watched. But this is different than the Goldaming Life goons. They linger close enough for me to see them. They want to make it clear I'm being observed.

I know exactly who this is. All these years later, awake or asleep, I haven't forgotten the weight of his eyes. It's *him*. All my searching and waiting, all Lucy's efforts, and this is how it happens. I don't find Dracula. He finds me.

"Got you, fucker," I whisper, smiling to myself.

79

Salt Lake City, January 10, 2025

DRACULA

Nothing about this feeding thrills him. It's merely the dull necessity of logistics. Preparing himself to have the patience necessary to claim you. He's doing this for *you.*

He sneers in disgust as a woman trembles under his fingers, bending her neck in invitation. There's no satisfaction in puncturing her fragile skin. When she faints in his arms, he drops her to the floor like a discarded tissue.

It served its purpose. He's not ravenous anymore. He can think clearly, make his plans for you. But maybe he should finish this woman, kill her rather than—

There's someone outside the door. This haze-choked city has become a cage. It's crawling with vampires; he finds them tedious and loathsome, like children. These new ones can't truly understand who or what he is. They assume he's the same thing they are. They're wrong. *No one* is the same as him.

The vampire outside, though—he catches the scent and knows it's *her.* She's not a child, she's a demon. Worse than a demon; a demon at least he would understand, he would relate to. She's like God. Distant, all-seeing, all-controlling, a force so powerful even Dracula cowers before the cross. God controlled him in life and holds sway over him still in death. Obedience and blessings and holy terror.

He cannot abide the demon vampire woman, hates the very thought of her existence. She's always watching him, inserting herself into his schemes, trying to control him. He's cleverer than she is, though. More vicious, more worthy. He'll make sure she doesn't notice what he's doing, and he'll do it right under her acolytes' noses.

There's a peaceful rapture that descends, one he's missed for so long. He can play at being God, too. He'll take you from them, and they won't know until it's too late.

The window provides a suitable exit. Theatrics have never been beneath him, and at last he feels a prick of excitement. This victim is a means to an end, and *you,* his end, are waiting.

As he slips free, there's no line between beast and man. He shifts without a thought, swooping into the darkness and fleeing the scene.

Bat, then wolf. Slinking low, wrapped in the night, because it loves him as he loves it. He pads toward your scent, confident and surefooted. You're waiting for him somewhere out there in the darkness, whether you know it or not. And now that he's sated, he has enough control—just *barely* enough, though, keeping the edge of hunger and violence that will thrill you as it does him.

He's ready to start your seduction. You aren't ready, you can never be ready, and that's exactly how he likes it.

80

Salt Lake City, January 11, 2025

My Butter Chicken,

I'll be on this path every evening, walking it, waiting for you, for as long as it takes. But I can't leave any more letters here for now, because people are always watching me. So know that this one contains my whole heart.

And you were right. We were both right. Dracula is here. We're closer than ever, and we're in more danger than ever, and I need you to stay safe. Which means you have to stay away from me. The only way this works is if we keep Terminator Lucy off Goldaming Life's radar. I'll only leave another letter when I have a solid plan ready to go.

I miss you. I wish I'd brought your journal. At least then I could have your words in my arms.

I never told you about the daydream I had when reading your journal. (We needed more time. We'll have more time, soon.) I read about you plotting to run away with your beloved, and in place of imagining you and this mystery person (I hadn't realized who it was yet), I imagined you and me. Even before I knew who you were, Lucy and Elle were already blending together in my head and my heart. I was always falling for every part of you.

It does feel like cheating that I got to know teen you, though. You've only known the current me, and she's a bit of a desperate mess. But here's a story from my childhood:

I went to summer camp when I was thirteen. My mother wanted me to do private tutelage straight through the summer, but Dickie suggested that giving me a summer away might cut back on the volume of runaway attempts. "An emotional reset," he called it. That's probably why he let me go to London, too. Sneaky bastard.

I didn't know what to expect from camp. I'd spent so little time around kids my own age. But it was magical. We were in the middle of nowhere, in a lush, dense forest. The air itself hummed with humidity and insects and life. I loved everything about it. The sunburns, the bug bites, the creaky bunks, the mediocre cafeteria food, the campfire singalongs. I painted and I learned ukulele and I excelled at archery. I made bracelets and lopsided ceramic pots and friends I was sure would last a lifetime.

I even had my first crush and my first kiss—the crush was on a counselor named Samira who was so cool I couldn't even function around her, and the kiss was with my bunk mate Alyssa, who just wanted to "practice" once, which turned into nightly practice sessions for the rest of camp. (I don't know if she wrote me after. If she did, my mother never let me have the letters. I looked Alyssa up a couple years ago, and she's lead singer in a lesbian punk band. Samira is married with two kids and writes critically acclaimed young adult novels. I've always had good taste, is what I'm saying.)

I'm thinking about that summer now, everything green-filtered woodsmoke scented sunshine, and how happy I was. How happy it was possible for me to be once I was away from my mother and my bedroom and everything being a Goldaming meant. It's a good reminder. I haven't always been miserable, and I know we can be not miserable together in the future.

Dreaming of that future (and also, always, of you),

XOXO

Iris

81

Salt Lake City, January 13, 2025

DRACULA

Somehow, you knew what he wanted. You're out, alone in the night that belongs to him, walking on a trail through the lonesome hills.

Tonight it begins, but he can feel the ending as if it's already happened. All your futures, all your potential, *his.* He's inevitable. The black drag of gravity, pulling you down to where you'll join the lives he's collected and become one of his secret safe graves. Unholy and perfect, pulsing across the globe like fireflies burning in a color only his eyes can see.

But you. You're all he thinks of tonight. His only *now* in an infinite expanse of *then.*

You walk down the wooded trail with confidence, warm brown curls bouncing defiantly. Such unjustified fearlessness. You don't realize yet how powerless you truly are. How easily the teeth of this world can pierce you.

That might be his favorite thing about this current age. Everything has been made so secure, so safe. People scurry about their short, empty lives, certain that they have death held at bay. But it's *always* waiting. He's always waiting. They've simply forgotten how to look for him.

He'll teach you. He'll catch your cry in his teeth and savor the taste of your surrender, that bitterest bite. That sweetest bite.

He reaches out into the night and finds the hungry, willing minds of feral beasts waiting for his call. It's time you felt the first wave of fear dragging you from everything you've hoped and planned into everything that's left for you in this world: only him.

The snarls of the stray dogs chase you, nipping at your heels but never quite connecting. He won't let them taste you. You belong to *him* that way. But dogs make excellent shepherds, guiding you into the wild. Just when it seems the whole world is fear and danger and death, you burst free of the scrub and hills. Onto the path and into his waiting arms.

He relishes your expression—fear and relief in one. You view him as your savior, and he is. Both your salvation and your damnation.

He sweeps you into his embrace, his the strength of generations, yours the weightlessness of mortality. You tremble against him. He can see the pulse pounding in your neck. He relishes the tantalizing agony of restraint as he sets you down next to the street. You eye the darkness warily, staying close to his side. He can still hear your rabbit's heart, scampering in your chest, looking for safety. He knows how your pulse would feel, flooding his mouth, coating his throat, and it's too much, you're ready, he's ready, he—

You look at him then, and something in your face stops him. Because it isn't gratitude or even fear in your expression. It's . . . a challenge. There's something indecent in your gaze, a bold defiance that makes him want to hurt you right now. Abandon the dance entirely and break you on the spot.

But no. He reminds himself to be patient. He needs to break your will, not your body. And to do that, he needs you to let him in. *Come with me,* he says. *You must recover from your fright. I live nearby.*

And then you laugh.

His fingers spasm, reaching toward you with animal urgency to silence that sound. But you're already stepping away from him. Rage boils, more than he's felt in ages. He'll show you, he'll teach you to be afraid, he'll—

You say you'll be walking again tomorrow, this same trail, this same time. He watches you leave, barely able to contain the storm in his chest.

He thought he wanted you the way he's wanted all the others, but *you.* You're something special, something new. The longer it takes to make you his, the more you'll pay for the privilege. This bubbling in his chest could be anger or lust or thirst, but it feels closest to something he lost so many lifetimes ago.

His own laughter.

82

Salt Lake City, January 14, 2025

IRIS

It's more than a little difficult to walk this trail knowing that the last time I was on it, I was chased by a pack of feral dogs into Dracula's waiting arms. Not exactly my ideal evening stroll scenario. When the dogs first showed up, I thought it was just my wretched luck. And then he was there, and I was so flooded with adrenaline I could barely process it.

I have to be on my guard tonight. At my best. And even though I'm expecting him, I still jump half a foot in the air when he appears next to me like he'd been there the whole time.

"Oh, hi," I blurt, trying not to let out a nervous laugh. I need to be someone he'll want to pursue, like Lucy. Or Mina, I guess, since he also went after her. Though I'd rather be like Lucy. Regular Iris with her donkey bray laugh and defiant attitude is definitely not someone most people would want. My mom taught me that much.

I keep walking, because I don't know what else to do. He matches my stride, his own steps silent whispers to my clomping trod. It's all I can do not to stare. There's something smudged about him, like I'm seeing him through dirty glass. He's more the impression of a man than an actual person. Maybe that's part of his vampire predator magic. People project what they want to see, but it doesn't quite work on me. My brain already knows something's wrong with him.

He's tall and gaunt, his hairline retreating steeply from harsh, haughty features. Even though we met on a hiking trail, he's wearing a suit tailored to emphasize the long, lean lines of his body. A cape wouldn't be out of place, but he's adapted enough to the times to leave that behind. In the lift of his eyebrow and a twist of his dark lips is a dare: *Make me care about you. Prove you're worth my time.*

I am. I have to be, so I can help Lucy destroy him.

"I love this trail; it's really nice," I babble. My nerves aren't an act. I'm walking side by side with the most dangerous creature I've ever met. "I'm sure it's crowded in the summer, but at night in the winter no one's out here. I can pretend I'm alone."

He tilts his head but doesn't respond.

I keep going, desperate to hear *anything* familiar and warm and human. Even if it's my own voice. "I'm a student. Studying literature. Which, don't tell me, I know won't ever get me a job. I've heard it many times. But I don't need a job. I'm already CEO of a wellness company, inherited from my mother. It's popular across the country, but especially here where they're headquartered. Maybe you're already walking the Gold Path?" I prod him with Goldaming Life terminology, trying to get a reaction. I want him to acknowledge that *he's* in charge, that we've met before, but he doesn't.

Actually, I'm not sure he's listening. He nods occasionally and has his head tilted toward me, but it's a pantomime. Just like my tutors when I tried to tell them about my mom, or the doctors when I insisted I wasn't crazy. He's fucking *humoring* me. He isn't paying attention to a single thing I'm saying.

I'm desperate to do something, anything, to make him really listen. To force him to hear me. What can I say that he'll like? How can I keep his interest and—

Oh god, I *get* it. I understand why so many young women fall under his thrall. We're trained to crave approval and acknowledgment, encouraged to force down our instinctive warning signals. Because what worth do we have if we're not desirable? Sexually, sure, but also on every other level. Be likable. Be pretty. Be pleasant. Be small enough not to threaten anyone, take up only as much space as you're given, be who and what they want you to be.

I know exactly what Dracula is, and I'm still trying to figure out how to bend myself into a shape he'll like enough to stick around. At least I know *why* I'm doing it.

But do I? What's the point of this? What's the point of any of this? Lucy and I could have run away. Between the two of us, we might have had a chance at disappearing. I hate Dracula, and I hate my family, and I want them both destroyed, but . . .

I'm tired. I'm so tired. It's been months here, alone, pretending my way through every single moment. And now I finally have Dracula at my side, and I'm terrified if I don't pretend well enough, he'll disappear.

Maybe Lucy would disappear then, too. That's my deepest fear since we parted ways: If we didn't have this goal keeping us together, would Lucy even still want me? Would I be anything more to her than a silly mortal fling? We had so little real time together. I probably feel more for her than she does for me. Maybe she's not even coming. She found her old vampire buddies and decided they're better company than I am. It's been so long since she wrote. *Too* long.

I'm flooded with all the relationships I've ever had, the people who said they loved me, but never enough to stay. Never enough to choose me. Not any of my friends or girlfriends, every single one of whom bailed when things got too hard or weird or when the money was better than me. Even my own parents never loved me as I am. My dad wanted me to be happy and easy, and my mom wanted me to be *her*.

"I feel so small," I say without meaning to. But I can't stop once I start. "It's too cold for me to be outside, but here I am anyway. Sometimes I wonder if I'm doing it on purpose. Hastening my end. Like maybe I should just give up and stop running from it. What am I trying to prolong, anyway? What is it about my life that makes me terrified to lose a few years of it? I walk through my days faking *everything*. Like I'm standing above myself, puppeteering my body through a dark stage for an audience I can't even see. Trying to fool everyone else, sure, but mostly trying to fool myself into believing that I'm real. That I matter. That any of this matters. Because it doesn't, does it? It's all fake. It's all make-believe. No one really knows how the world works, or why. Who we are, or why we're here. And the miracle of existence becomes absurd once you've seen what's beyond the 'real' world everyone else lives in."

His voice startles me, low and smooth and almost melodious. "You've touched the edges of the void and been contaminated by what you felt there."

"Yes," I gasp, both in surprise that he was listening, and that . . . he understands? I *have* been contaminated by knowing about the secret dark borders of reality. The ones no one else seems to recognize or care about.

"I see you." He pauses his steps, and I stop almost against my will. He leans close, forcing me to tip my head back to stare up into his face. I was wrong. It isn't smudged. It's clear. It's the clearest thing in the world, a perfect open expanse, brutal honesty in his two black pools of eyes. I can't quite look at them. I keep my gaze on his mouth instead, wondering what he'll say next.

"I'll save you," he says, long fingers brushing my elbow.

"From what?" I know I'm in danger, I feel it, I've always felt it. My whole life I've been on the edge of annihilation, but I've never known where the threat was coming from. He knows. He knows everything, and if I can just get him to like me, to want me, he'll share his secrets.

"From the delusion of self-determination. From the wretchedly small life you'll have here. From yourself. Look into my eyes, and I'll show you the eternity you seek."

His eyes. Someone described his eyes once. I know about them, they're a mirror into—

They're not a mirror. Lucy didn't see herself in them. Lucy! God, what am I doing? He fucking *thralled* me, and even knowing it's happening I can barely tear myself away! What was I thinking, meeting Dracula out here by myself?

I turn and hurry along the trail, rubbing my arms to imply I want to keep moving to stay warm. "I should—" I start, trying to think of some excuse, but he's right beside me again. I didn't even hear him move. He puts out a hand to stop me. His skin shimmers, like he can barely contain himself in the human guise he's wearing.

He's going to kill me. I was an idiot to believe I could ever take down my family or their founding monster. "Please," I whisper, and the worst part is I don't know what I'm asking for as his terribly dark lips part in a smile.

83

Salt Lake City, January 14, 2025

LUCY

We arrive at the foot of the mountains under cover of night. Again it took too long to get here. The Queen refuses to ride in a car, and this country's rail system is a disaster. I nearly left my companions behind several times on this journey. But I've left them before, and I'd rather not do it again, not when they want to be with me. And not when I might need them.

Salt Lake City stretches beneath us, a patchwork quilt of fireflies winking in the night. Iris is out there, so close, too far. I want to race along the moonlight to her.

I need to find her letters first. It will be a challenge, though. I thought I'd be able to smell her lingering scent, but because Iris drank some of my blood before we separated, I can actually *feel* her. A tug on my consciousness, like a string connecting us. No wonder Dracula found me so easily in London.

It's hard to ignore the pull of Iris herself and focus only on lingering traces of her scent. It's not the only surprising thing about being connected this way. I haven't dreamed in so long, I'd forgotten what it was like. Spending time in Iris's dreams is surreal and occasionally hard to control, but it means we have a way to see each other even when we can't see each other.

It also means after all this time I've found new pleasures. Not only having sex with someone I love who loves me, but having *dream* sex with her. The usual rules and processes don't apply. Last night all it took was whispering her name against her ear.

Iris, Iris, I want to be with you right now.

"Why are you smiling like that," the Queen demands. "It's upsetting."

The Lover sits on top of a rock, kicking her feet against it. "Lucy's thinking about sex."

"Easy guess," I respond. "Come on. We need to find Iris's letters."

We prowl through the night, three predators in search of ink on paper. I wish there were a better way. The Lover has her magic box, but she doesn't have Iris's phone number and none of us are tech-savvy enough to figure it out. Besides, Iris isn't in that little glowing screen. Iris is out there, in the night, waiting. She's been waiting too long.

What might have changed in our time apart? I try not to let fear claim me; Iris certainly hasn't grown tired of me in our dreams. Nor does she find me too needy. Our needs match up *quite* nicely.

But I want to do more than meet her in that hazy dreamscape. I want to talk to her. To hold her hand. To hear her abrupt burst of laughter that always seems to embarrass her. I want to just . . . exist with her. I wonder if we'll have another chance, or if what we've gotten is all we'll ever get. It's enough, but at the same time it will never be enough.

"Now Lucy's sad," the Lover says.

"I'm not sad, I—" I stop. I haven't been following a lingering trace of Iris's scent at all. The scent is moving. I'm following Iris herself. Before I can think better, I race closer. The closer I get, the more I can feel her, like déjà vu. Remembering something that hasn't happened yet. But she's nervous. No, more than that. She's *scared*. And she's not alone in the darkness.

"What is it?" the Queen asks.

"He's here." I scatter. I'm moonlight, I'm movement, I'm nothing but *need*. I need to get to Iris, I need to protect her, I need to stop him before he touches her. He can't touch her, he can't.

I corral the whirlwind of my desperation and coalesce into form once more. Everything is confusing, everything is raw, the night so bright, the trees so loud. I fling all my senses outward, not caring that it's too much, that I'm hurting myself.

And there—he was—

He isn't. He was there, and he's not anymore. But Iris is. I sprint down the path, blurring from darkest shadow to darkest shadow, until she's in my arms. Real. Alive. Here.

She goes rigid with fear and I'm sorry, I'm so sorry to have frightened her, but then she melts into me. The softness of her wraps me up, holding me as much as I'm holding her.

"Lucy!" she gasps. She's trembling, taking deep breaths as she calms down. "You're here. You're here."

"I smelled Dracula," I say.

"I know! I wrote you! I found him. Or I guess he found me, but he doesn't know I'm luring him on purpose. He thinks he's stalking me. He thinks I have no idea who or what he is." She pulls back to look at me, her beautiful forest-loam eyes, her nose turned up at the end as if to give full access to her bee-stung lips. I want to sting her lips, I want to turn back into moonlight and cover every inch of her, I want to—

"Wait," I say. "You've been *luring* Dracula? Alone?"

"I knew you were on your way."

"Iris!" All my lust evaporates, replaced by fear and anger. "He could have killed you! He could have taken you somewhere I can't find you! He could have—"

"I know! Trust me, I know. But he didn't. Twice now he could have. I think I'm off-limits. Even to him. I can tell he's holding back. He must be feeling me out on behalf of Goldaming Life. Trying to seduce me so I'm all in. That's it, that's got to be it."

Iris hums with excitement, flush with adrenaline. Because of *him.* For an instant I'm wretchedly jealous. I can't even say what I'm jealous of exactly, and I don't want to explore it.

"Lucy." Iris takes my hands in hers, holding me here. Grounding me in myself. "Lucy, this is it. This is what we were hoping for. And you're here now, you came for me just like you said you would, so I'm safe." She says it with such confidence it breaks my heart.

"We're never safe. Not with Dracula."

"But we are! You know all his tricks. He's a self-satisfied, arrogant old ass. He thinks I'm some easy mark." She pauses, her gaze going far away and blank for a moment before coming back to me. "But this time, *he's* the mark. I'm not just some useless iris anymore. I'm a Venus flytrap. I lure him. You and your friends destroy him. Yeah?" She shines with hope and determination.

It could work. For the first time since I died, I know exactly where Dracula will be. Exactly who he'll be stalking. Why did it have to be *Iris,* though?

"We've got this," she says. And when she kisses me, hungry and triumphant, I believe her.

She pulls back, staring at me like she's painting a picture in her mind. "This is awful, seeing you again and not getting to keep you. I have so much to tell you. The letters aren't enough. I've been going to school and have so many new poems memorized to whisper to you in the dark, and good *god,* Luce, the sex dreams are amazing but it's not the same. I miss you so much. I wish we could hang out in the dreams, too. Talk."

"I'm sorry," I say. "I've never done any of this before. I can only do feelings right now, and when I'm with you—"

"Arousal comes easily." She smiles wickedly at me. She makes me weak, and I'm so happy about it.

"Well, I was going to say I'm an absolute bucket of lust, but yes."

Iris laughs, that bright brassy bray. Something inside me breaks and heals at the same time, hearing it again. But then she shakes her head. "We don't have time for this. It's not safe for you to be with me. Here, memorize my phone number." She tells me a series of numbers, then lets go of my hands. "Hurry, go before anyone sees you. I don't know how often they're watching me, but I assume it's always. I'll keep walking this trail every night. He'll come again, and you'll kill him. I have some dirt on Goldaming Life now—enough to discredit them, and with their vampire CEO gone, it'll be over. It'll all be over, and we can be together."

I put my hand against Iris's cheek, lingering on every beloved detail of her face. I could drink in that face for a hundred more years, a thousand, and never get tired of it. How is it that after all these endless days, I'm running out *now*?

"It'll be over," I echo. I kiss her, and then I slip back into moonlight, because if I don't leave now, I never will.

84

Salt Lake City, January 15, 2025

My Little Cabbage,

Sorry to write this on the back of your letter. I had no other options. We're staying up in the mountains—the Queen has a hard time moving among regular people, on account of the gold blades fused to her fingertips—and stationery supplies are not really a priority. Which is very sad. I do love a crisp sheet of creamy paper and a pen full of ink.

But more than a piece of paper, I'd like to write my love on your body. Slip the words and the feelings beneath your skin where they'll never fade.

I left you a present under a rock next to the post. I don't know if you'll think to check this spot, now that the Lover has your phone number. But I want you to have proof. Proof you can hold in your hands, proof you can read over and over again, proof that can whisper to you in the dark when I can't:

Forever is composed of nows, and I've been unbound by time long enough to know our now was perfect. Imagine me living in it forever, and I'll imagine you the same way.

Thank you for at last answering the questions I feared I would die with—the reason, the purpose, the point of me? It was love.

It was you.

Lucy

85

Salt Lake City, January 20, 2025

DRACULA

You search the trees, walk slower and slower along the path. Lingering. Hoping. Already, your nighttime walks aren't yours. The space beside you and, soon, that space inside you, are his.

It's hard not to drag you into the dark crevices between the hills and give you what you need. But he wants to consume you entirely, to swallow the whole of you. He wants to luxuriate and linger.

Tonight, he'll follow you home. You'll invite him in. He won't bite you, though. Not yet. He'll show you the truth first: Nothing is yours. Your private, safe space is as open to him as your tender, chambered heart.

And then, once invited, he'll be at his leisure to—

There, again. A moth fluttering at the edge of his senses, a hint of movement that doesn't belong. Someone else is watching. He's not alone in the darkness, but whatever is out there hasn't sensed him yet. He's too experienced for that. All the vampires creeping around, watching him, studying him, are children. Infants. Idiots.

But this path isn't safe for him anymore. Maybe he was wrong to choose you. Maybe he was wrong to walk with you out in the open.

No. He refuses to blame himself. He never makes mistakes. Others merely fail to react how they should. It's inconvenient, not disastrous. And it will be all the more satisfying when you're his forever.

It's irritating that he can't follow you home tonight, though. Another step away from his patterns. He doesn't like altering his well-worn habits. It makes him agitated, prone to outbursts. He loves control, loves to have it over others, loves to lose it on his *own* terms. Never anyone else's.

But now he's cross *and* ravenous. He returns to the home of his most recent meal. He doesn't have the will to find something better to eat. He wants you, only you, but he needs blood. He pauses in his victim's yard. His aching teeth recoil from the prospect of listening to the woman again. Last time she clung to him, begging him to make her anew, to take her through the Celestial Gate.

He knows of no celestial realms. Only this flat, endless circle, where nothing is ever new or surprising.

It makes him want *you* even more. You, who have the will to resist him. Who dared defy him and say no. But you were close to accepting him before you were interrupted. He's nearly there.

Imagining the look on your face as you submit spikes his desire anew and he steps toward the door, but the stench of decay and confidence stops him short. *She's* inside, waiting for him. The demon, the only vampire he can't touch.

Rage consumes him. The demon's guards are nearby, but it's easy enough to find them and tear them into their composite pieces. To render them inert objects, which is better than what they were before. Servants to that abomination.

Called by his fury and drawn to the promise of death and rot, every rat in the neighborhood scurries near. Eyes beady points of malice, teeth dripping with anticipation. That is his dread gravity, his influence on the world around him. He didn't even need to will the rodents there; they obeyed without prompting.

He is power incarnate. He has absolute dominion over life and death. And he wants that wretched vampire bitch gone as much as he has ever wanted anything.

But he can't destroy her until he's dismantled her, until he's torn down the shield of absolute, damnable faith in *herself* that protects her wherever she is. Her belief in herself is like a cross, holy and unassailable. He always has to be invited in, and she remains a locked door he can't get past. The rats, however . . .

With a flick of his hand and a burst of malice, he surges them into the house like a tidal wave of pestilence. Then he shifts into a maelstrom of dark wings and flies toward his true target.

It used to be easy to get into a home. So many servants. Scared girls running a household, allowing anyone with a suit and an air of purpose inside. Now it's only you in there, with your precious rabbit's heart beating for him. Waiting for him. What a relief to see you through your window. He can fill his senses with the cleanness of you. The purity. The promise.

But it's agony to be trapped outside. Is it an invitation, that you don't close your curtains even though your light is like a beacon? Is it an invitation, that so much of your alabaster skin is bare, demanding he look, demanding he touch and taste and claim? Is it an invitation, that you're here, alone, with no one to come to the rescue if you scream?

But he knows the limits of his rules. And so he waits. He watches as the light goes out, as you climb into bed. As you stare at the ceiling, a small frown on your face. You didn't see him tonight, and you're afraid that you'll never see him again.

Afraid that you will.

At last, your frown smooths and sleep claims you. But then you begin shifting, restless in your dreams. He knows what you seek in the lawless landscapes of your sleeping mind. He can smell the sharp tang of arousal, and now—

No more waiting, no more planning. You need him. You need him to answer that arousal, to show you what happens when you *want.*

86

Salt Lake City, January 20, 2025

IRIS

I float in a haze of lust, anchored only by Lucy. I want to do things—to her, with her—but it feels like I'm moving through water. She *is* the water, though. Deliciously warm water, holding me up, buoying me. I'm nothing but nerve endings, every touch, every kiss, every whisper triggering so much pleasure it's overwhelming. I want more of her, more of us, more of everything. I can't focus past the sheer physicality of it all, can't find my voice to talk to her. And I want to talk to her, want to—

Oh god, I *want,* I only want.

A sharp sound cracks the world in half. I sit, heart racing, flush with feelings and full of Lucy, but . . .

I'm alone, in my lonely bed, in my empty, rented house. Lucy isn't here, because she can't be here. All my lingering warmth dissipates. We're still apart, and Dracula, *fucking Dracula,* hasn't visited me a single time since Lucy spooked him. Every night I'm out on that trail, cold, nervous because I'm cold, pacing back and forth, waiting. Tortured knowing Lucy is close but I can't see or hold or speak to her. And Dracula doesn't so much as show.

Maybe we scared him off for good. Maybe he decided he wasn't interested in me. It's weird that I'm offended by that, but—

A noise at the window. I startle in fright. Wings press close to the glass. They flap in a frenzy, darker than midnight, not velvet but veined and repulsive. I stare, wide-eyed, confused. A bat?

And then I realize: It's him.

He flings himself against the window, over and over, scrabbling at the glass. Does he really think I'm going to open it? Even if I didn't know it was Dracula, like I'd let some random, enormous bat inside! I'm also offended on behalf of bats everywhere. They're helpful, adorable creatures. They don't deserve to be mocked in this twisted and monstrous imitation.

He hits the window again. That's the sound that woke me. If he's going to be a creep, the least he can do is be a creep when we can kill him. Not when it pulls me from a Lucy dream. I raise a single eyebrow in annoyed defiance.

The bat hits the window so hard the glass shatters. I scream, throwing my hands over my face. I brace myself against the onslaught of wings and teeth.

It doesn't come. When at last I dare lower my arms, I'm alone again. A freezing breeze whips through my room. I think of another window, broken so long ago. Whether it was a wolf or not, that window symbolized the end of Lucy's first life.

If Dracula had been able to come in, I would have been powerless. Just like Lucy back then. God, no wonder she was so worried the other night on the trail. I was flippant and dismissive, high on seeing her again. And also so relieved that she'd come back for me, and desperate to forget how it had felt to be under Dracula's thrall. Embarrassed, too. I didn't want her to know that he'd affected me. I want to be stronger than that, and hate that I'm not.

I trudge downstairs to make some weak-ass tea. Of all the things Goldaming Life has taken from me, demanding I stop drinking coffee seems the most excessively cruel. It's "bad for my condition," puts too much strain on my heart and circulation, etc. All lies, just like their building-wide ban on perfume out of respect for "allergies." Heaven forbid we make it hard for the vampires to sniff out our blood type.

The tea's only tolerable because it reminds me of Lucy. As it steeps, I stew over why Dracula decided on a flyby. Does he know I know who he is? That I'm trying to set him up? Was tonight a warning, or was it just part of his whole deal?

It's 3 A.M., but I'm not going back to sleep. I read over more of the files I stole from Olivia's laptop. One of them is Dickie's official schedule. This morning he has a lab tour. Could be useful if I can sneak in a camera. I'm slowly but surely building a case to expose the entire organization as a fraud, so I'll take every chance I can get.

Yo Dick, I text, *I'm coming on the lab tour today and sitting in on the meeting with state senator Harrell next week.*

He responds almost immediately. *You should be sleeping. It's not good to strain your system.*

I flip off the phone screen. *Also can we stop pretending I don't know about the vampires it's tedious.*

Come on, Dickie. Admit something in text. But he disappoints me, as usual.

You have such a strange sense of humor. My car will stop by to pick you up at 8 AM sharp; please be ready. We'll discuss the Harrell meeting later.

What kind of sociopath texts with semicolons?

But at least I got my way. I regret it a little by the time the sleek black Goldaming car pulls up, though. I've been awake for hours and my attitude matches my face. Dickie takes great pleasure in the waves of surliness rolling off me. He talks the entire drive, a nonstop stream of legalese and corporate nonsense. I want to sink into the leather and never come out.

"As soon as you're officially sworn in as president, I'll have you sign off on our new agreement with Frye Technologies. I'm going to forward you the contract. Please read it all and let me know if you have any questions."

"My questions are usually just *Why* and *Will it ever end* and *Should I start day-drinking.*"

He doesn't look up from the sleek leather folio filled with papers. "I'd like you to pick some photos of your mother for the memorial charity auction next month."

"I don't care. I really don't. Put up a photo of her dead body."

Dickie sighs and at last sets down his folio. "I advised her against it, you know."

"Against dying? Was that your legal opinion, or just a general recommendation?"

"Against the egg retrieval."

All the air is sucked out of the car. No one's ever admitted that it actually happened. "What?" I croak.

"I advised her against a lot of things. This all should have been your choice. But she was always afraid."

"Blanche Goldaming, afraid? I think you're going senile, pal. If you'll recall, my mom was a terrifying bitch who never gave an inch on anything."

One of the things I remember best from when I accidentally invited a monster inside? While my dad bled unconscious on the floor and I cowered under the table, my mother stood in the dark in the next room and calmly talked to *Dracula himself* like he couldn't hurt her. Blanche Goldaming was many things, but afraid wasn't one of them.

Dickie stares out the window. "She worked hard to make herself essential. She worried you would jeopardize that, for her and for yourself. I didn't agree with her choices, but I can respect what she did with Goldaming Life. Under her ruthless direction, it flourished. But children shouldn't be raised like assets. I was rooting for you, you know. I wouldn't have looked that hard if you'd managed to follow through on your plan to run away in England."

I laugh. I can't help it. I don't know how to feel about this. Dickie knew I was trying to get away, and he was . . . on my side? Or maybe this is his way of getting on my side now. Pretending that he was always sympathetic to my plight. But he never helped, did he? No one did.

I'll keep playing my part. "Sucks to be you, Dickie, because I decided to stay and now you have to deal with me forever."

But when the car pulls to a stop in front of a building, all my confusion about Dickie's motivations evaporates. We're at corporate headquarters. He lied to me.

"What the fuck, *Dick*. You told me I could come on the lab tour."

Dickie exits and waits for me to climb out after him before answering. "You're welcome to use whatever colorful language you wish on your own time, but I recommend trying to eliminate the cursing habit entirely. You need to convey the correct level of warmth and gravitas befitting your role as president of the company, and habits at home have a way of seeping into work. Also, this is the location for the lab tour. Come along."

I drag my feet like the toddler he thinks I am. But once inside, we don't use the elevators in the lobby. Instead, he takes me down a hall to a nondescript door I've never noticed. It doesn't have any obvious security features. But something must happen, because there's a clicking noise and then the door opens. A guard is on the other side.

Dickie walks straight by. I follow. My lawyer's demonic grasshopper legs are so long I have to take a step and a half for every one of his. A glass door opens with a hiss of air. We step through and it seals again with an ominous sound. I'm already claustrophobic.

"I'm glad you suggested this," Dickie says, flashing a badge at the vampire standing between us and an elevator door at the end of the hallway. "It'll be much more efficient to do your treatments here, instead of at the I-Vee Center. We'll combine them with our weekly meetings. Less time away from your studies, and you can start today. You're looking unwell."

My breathing gets shallower and faster. The elevator in front of me is a gate straight to hell. This was their goal the whole time. Seal me in and drain me dry. They're finally going to finish what my mother started. They're going to take my blood and my eggs and my soul, and then—

"Iris?" The way Dickie says it makes it clear it's not the first time he's just said my name.

"What?" I snap.

He gestures. Hanging on the wall are several white jumpsuits made of thin, paper-like material. "To keep things sterile in the lab."

"Right. Yes." Surely they wouldn't have me dress up if I were a lamb being led to the slaughter. I awkwardly climb into my jumpsuit while Dickie puts his on with practiced ease. My curls are trapped beneath a humiliating hairnet, and, *damn them,* my phone is trapped beneath this suit. I can't reach into my pocket and surreptitiously record anything.

The elevator doors open. No fiery flames of hell, no straight drop into a pit, just a vampire standing there, which at this point I'm so used to he barely registers. For a brief moment I think I'm getting past the fourth floor at last, but the vampire guard pushes the down button.

We're going into a basement. The weight of the whole building is on top of us. I'm sweating with panic by the time we stop moving and the doors open.

I don't know what I was expecting to be revealed. A dungeon, maybe. Torture chambers. A vampire rave, complete with human victims suspended from the ceiling like blood piñatas. As a teen I was convinced Goldaming Life had a whole underground S&M ring, but the only latex in sight is medical-grade.

It looks like a regular lab, or at least what movies and television have taught me they look like. Machines buzz and whir, whole banks of them doing things I can't begin to guess at. Anonymously white-clad workers stare down at charts and tubes while others enter things into computers. The main area is huge and open, but at the end is a hallway. There are several curtained-off sections there, like you'd find in an emergency room. All the curtains are closed.

"Hello, welcome," a woman says. I've met her before. Susan something or other, high up in the corporate side of things. She has the sort of motionless face designed for photographs, not real life. Pretty, but nothing moves quite the way it should. "So happy to have you here, Miss Goldaming. Shall we get started?"

She efficiently escorts me from one thing to the next. I'm shown machines and given specs for them that mean nothing to me; I'm introduced to lab techs who tell me their roles in such specific jargon they could be building nuclear bombs and I'd have no idea; I'm taken down a row of newly developed products which all look like lotion to my eyes.

Everything is deliberately incomprehensible, all the lingo the same as in the brochures I've studied. They're feeding me total bullshittery.

Demanding to come on this visit was far from a coup on my part. It's clear in the way Susan keeps smiling, her eyes weighing and measuring me: I'm a harmless idiot, and we all know it.

"Right, I think that's everything," Susan says after a doctor or lab assistant or Vegas showgirl for all I know finishes "demonstrating" a new detoxifying patch by putting it on her arm and then taking it off.

"Do you feel less toxic?" I ask.

The assistant darts a puzzled, mildly panicked look at Dickie, who subtly shakes his head.

Susan gives me an imitation of a human smile. "You should join me tomorrow for the weekly branding meeting. We've nabbed the artisan who won the last season of that glassblowing show—I forget its name, very popular, Gwyneth was a judge but we got this one before Goop did, to design the jars for our new line of ultra-free radical combating creams, and she's giving us a demonstration of her techniques. A few of our top earners are coming, too, and I know they'd love to meet you."

"That sounds wonderful, Susan," Dickie says. One of his spider hands comes down on my shoulder, guiding me toward the curtain-lined hallway. "Now it's time for Miss Goldaming's treatments. She'll be doing them here now."

At last there's a hint of life in Susan's eyes. "Such a good decision to be proactive about your health. Your mother would be pleased."

Fuck that bitch, I think. "Yeah, it'll be more convenient," I say.

I want to believe coming down here more often will mean they won't watch me so closely. I'll be able to corner a chatty lab technician, or steal their formulas. Somehow, someway I'll spot a weakness I can exploit. Maybe find a big red button labeled "AUTO-DESTRUCT: NEVER PUSH."

But Susan is right. If my mother could see me, she really would be pleased. With that thought souring my stomach, I'm led to one of the curtained-off rooms. Inside is a chair that looks like it was designed for a Rolls-Royce. Which, knowing Goldaming Life, it probably was. The leather feels like it was molded to hold me. Which, knowing Goldaming Life, it also probably was. I half expect silver cuffs to come shooting out of the armrests, but nothing happens as I sit back. I keep my arms folded over my chest, just in case.

Susan and Dickie excuse themselves to go discuss important things about the company I ostensibly own. A young person, as weightless as a pop song, clips a monitor onto my finger. Beside me is a sleek white marble cube, three feet by three feet. Other than a tube going in and a tube coming out, it looks like a miniature tomb.

My heart rate spikes. I can't do this. I can't be trapped in the basement with them sticking needles in me. They could drug me. They could knock me out. They could finish the job I ruined when I was sixteen.

A woman yanks back the curtain. One hundred percent a vampire, obvious through her inhumanly graceful but powerfully efficient movements. But she's mismatched with the usual Goldaming brand of Instagram filter drones. Her goddess-like beauty is specific, not generic. She's tall and fat and Black, with hair cropped close to her scalp and no makeup at all.

And she's *pissed.* "Why is her heart rate so high?" she demands. The assistant mumbles something but the vampire doesn't even listen. She points toward the hallway. "Get out."

The assistant scurries away. The vampire frowns at her tablet, then finally looks me in the eyes. "Are you afraid of needles?"

"Sure. Needles," I say, on the verge of hyperventilating. How long will it take me to sprint to the elevator? What are my odds of overpowering the guard there?

"Your mother was never afraid of needles."

"Yeah, well, my mother didn't have her ovaries excavated without her permission when she was sixteen."

The frown doesn't move, but the doctor looks slightly less annoyed at me and more annoyed at the world in general. "I'll tell you everything I'm doing before I do it, and you'll calm down so you don't pass out during the procedure."

Oddly, I believe her. I can't imagine her lying; she seems too impatient for it. "Deal," I agree. I take deep breaths, trying to slow my heart.

"I'm going to insert a needle here," she says, pointing to my wrist, "and another one here." My elbow. "This one will draw your blood and send it to the machine next to you. And this one will replace it with standard O negative. The process will take approximately one hour. You may experience some lightheadedness. I'll have that useless assistant bring you apple juice and a cookie to jump-start your blood sugar afterward. Within a week, your body will have overcome the new blood and returned to its default state. At which point we'll do this all over again, over and over and over, and I'll have to be here every single time."

Her annoyance calms me. "You sound really put out about it, considering you aren't the one having your blood removed on a weekly basis."

She sterilizes my arm with practiced efficiency. "They didn't tell you who I am, did they."

"No, but I'd love to know."

One needle goes in. I'll give this to her—her bedside manor may suck, but her needle skills are beyond compare. She didn't even feel for a vein. Normally I'd be creeped out, but I've had enough blown veins to be grateful for vampiric precision.

"I," she says, inserting the second needle with ease, "am the genius who figured all this out. I'm the genius who identified the unique properties of your family's blood and pioneered these procedures. I'm the genius whose incredible, groundbreaking, world-changing work is being used for glorified *cosmetic procedures.* I'm the genius who has to sit here and babysit a simple blood exchange when I could be revolutionizing medical treatment. I'm the genius who figured out how to use vampiric blood to supplement—"

"Holy shit, you admit it!" I try to sit up, but she puts a hand on my shoulder and keeps me firmly in place. "Oh my god. Oh my *fucking* god. You admit that Goldaming Life uses vampires! Wait, are you all drinking my blood once it's out? Is that what it's for?"

Her eyes flick to the box, but she shakes her head. "I'd never be wasteful with such a limited resource. And yes, I'm a vampire, and I use the correct terminology," she says, her tone scathing. "Living gods, golden gates. It's absurd. Names matter, and proper terms should always be used. And yes again, I *am* more put out by this than you are, because they're taking your blood, but they took my freedom. It was my own fault, too, due to my own idealistic hubris, assuming we wanted the same things when I agreed to help them."

I'm horrified. I thought all the vampires were here because they drank the Goldaming Life Kool-Aid. "You're a *captive*? They're holding you hostage? I can help, I can—"

"You're a Goldaming," she says. It's not an accusation, it's a statement of truth. She finishes attaching the tubes and watches, transfixed, as my blood begins to flow. With a tremendous show of self-control, she drags her eyes away from the blood and checks my vitals before standing. "That's that, then. The worthless assistant can manage the rest. Please stop looking at me with that guilty expression. It's not *your* fault I'm here. If anything, I blame Lucy."

Her name jolts through me like an electric shock. Is this a trap? Have they known about Lucy this whole time? I lean forward, dropping my voice to a whisper. "How do you know Lucy?"

She looks up from her pad, puzzled. "How do *you* know Lucy? The last I heard, she was terrorizing Europe, killing vampires everywhere in her search for Dracula."

Footsteps are heading in our direction. Before I can ask her anything else, the doctor shakes her head. "I hope she finds him. I hope she kills him and puts us all out of our misery in one merciful strike. Susan," she says without turning around as the expressionless woman opens the curtain, "I'm going to sleep."

Without another word, the doctor turns and leaves.

"What the *fuck*," I whisper. I came down here hoping for solutions, and only found questions.

87

Salt Lake City, January 20, 2025

LUCY

I prowl the edges of the foothills, far enough away from the trail that I can't be detected, close enough to Iris that I can sense her heartbeat. I'll know if Dracula comes.

Like every other night this week, nothing happens.

It's agony, being so near Iris. Every time she has a spike of fear or anger, I want to go to her. Then it ebbs and I can only assume she's safe without ever knowing what triggered those feelings. I don't want to know what she's feeling, I want to know *how* she's feeling. *Why* she's feeling. She's barely sleeping, too, cutting our dream time together short.

The impulse to swoop in and take Iris in my arms so we can flee together is agonizing. I should have said yes to coffee, that very first meeting when she looked at me so full of hope and shy bravado after I'd pulled her to safety. I should have taken her hand and walked across the street to the café. I should have sat and talked with her, soaked up every perfectly human moment with such a perfectly human woman. I should have whisked her away on a giddily romantic European tour. I should have held her for hours, doing nothing. I should have hoarded every laugh, every smile, every touch.

But I couldn't have done any of that, because I didn't have myself back yet. I couldn't have fully loved Iris until she loved me, because I couldn't fully love myself until she showed me how.

It's all so breathtakingly unfair. I found myself again after so many lonely decades of searching, and I found Iris in the process, and now?

Now I have to do the only task left to me. The only one that matters. The only one that will take me away from her, forever.

"You're blurring," the Lover cheerfully declares. She's perched up in a tree for a better view of the hills and trail beneath us.

The Queen is still as stone, but she's watching me, not the trail. "You love that girl. Does this change the plan?"

"No," I snap. It's times like these I long for the existential flattening of being moonlight. No one can ask moonlight questions moonlight doesn't want to think about. "The plan is the same. No one's safe until we find Dracula and destroy him. Especially not Iris."

"You could make her a vampire. He can't kill what's already dead," the Lover says. As I watch her braid her hair, for a moment I'm back in Istanbul, braiding Ingrid's hair. Ingrid's dead, and I'm still here. I won't let that happen to Iris.

I look up at the Lover. "Would you do *this* to someone you cared about, if there were any other option?"

She blinks owl-wide eyes at me, then slowly shakes her head. "No. No, ma petite chou, I would not. But I've also never cared about any-one the way you do, so who can say?"

The Queen sounds tentative. She's *never* sounded tentative before. "We could bury him so deep he can't escape."

"You kept me somewhere deep. I got out anyway," I say.

The Lover jumps down between us. "Seal him in a cask and toss him in the ocean!"

"Casks break. Currents drift."

The Lover tries to fuss with the Queen's perfectly set hair. The Queen slaps her hands away, then makes another suggestion. "Stake him to the ground and cut off his limbs when they start to regrow. I would willingly sit sentinel and remove pieces of him long enough for you to have a life with Iris. A few decades is nothing to us."

I wrap my arms around them both in a hug, holding them close. The Lover lets out a small, happy noise, returning the hug. The Queen stands as still as marble, but she doesn't push me away.

"He *needs* to die," I whisper. "Doesn't he?"

At last the Queen moves. She pats my shoulder three times, care-fully keeping her blades from piercing me. "Yes. We were only being nice. I'll kill him no matter what."

The Lover squeezes my waist and kisses my cheek. "You taught me I have to kill the killers, not just distract them." She tilts her head to look up at the stars, smiling dreamily. "Besides, it's so exciting! Finally finishing the first song, the one that started me down this endless dance. At last I'll see what's on the other side of death. I hope it's nothing. Or I hope it's everything! I can't wait to find out."

Not so long ago, a lifetime ago, a heartbeat ago, I wouldn't have hesitated to kill Dracula and the rest of us alongside him. I was ready to be finished, too, because nothing ever changed, and I was tired.

Then I met Iris, and at last something changed. *I* changed. But if I choose myself over ending Dracula, I'm damning others to my own fate. Damning other innocent girls and women to this same torment.

The Queen and the Lover are right. The only way to truly be finished with him is to kill him. Anything less is selfish; anything less guarantees he'll escape and prowl the world once more. He'll find more desperately reckless Lucys. More lost girls like the Queen and the Lover, taken from trauma and pain and plunged into an endless nightmare. Countless lives, stolen and held forever in his limbo. All this misery, suffering, and death: a pyramid of it, with him at the top.

But it's not an unassailable stone edifice. It's a house of cards. I can knock it all down with a single blow.

He can't have anyone else, and he especially can't have Iris. Loving her makes me want to do anything but this; loving her makes it imperative I do exactly this. To save her from Dracula, and to save her from her family's legacy. If he dies, so does Goldaming Life. And Iris is truly free, once and for all.

"Will you tell her goodbye, before we do it?" the Lover asks.

As much as my infinite afterlife has tried to snuff it out, I still have a flicker of hope. A dream of love and happiness. The old Lucy, sparking somewhere inside me. I can't let that spark of hope turn into a flame. If I let myself, I would burn down the world to stay alive and keep Iris at my side.

"Killing him is the only way to save her." I love Iris. This is how I show it. This is how I live it. "She can't know."

And so, alongside the Queen and the Lover, I perch and watch and wait as Iris paces the trail, trying to lure an ending. She just doesn't know how final an ending it is.

88

Salt Lake City, January 20, 2025

My Little Cabbage,

She walks in beauty, like the night
Of cloudless climes and starry skies;
And all that's best of dark and bright
Meet in her aspect and her eyes.

Lord Byron wrote that. If you know the poem, or if you don't, don't bother with the rest. This is the part that matters, the part I hold in my heart and whisper to myself today, staring down at the valley that holds you, wishing I were the one holding you.

But you do walk in beauty. You're all that's best of dark and bright. The rest of the poem goes on to glorify innocence, but we both know innocence is wielded as a weapon against young women. A whip to wound us, ties to bind us. A commodity to be traded and sold. By the time we know what innocence truly is, it's been taken from us and we're shamed for its absence.

You're not innocent, and I'm sorry for everything that hurt you, but I'm so glad you've walked in enough darkness that your eyes adjusted. That you could see the subtle creeping moonlight, frozen under your gaze. That you could pin it in place long enough to give it form once more, to breathe life into the memory of the girl I'd lost long ago.

I'm sure you'll wonder, about that first moment. If I was following you. If there was a reason I was there at exactly the right time, if there was a motive behind saving you outside the train station. Because in your life—in my life—no one does anything without a motive.

I want you to know, you must know:

There was no reason. I was there to find myself, and I found you on the way.

It was luck, or fate, or the universe at last allowing us both a tiny triumph. I saw a beautiful woman. I wondered what made her eyebrows draw low like that, what she would look like if she were laughing. And then I saw her look left instead of right, and I knew I could save her.

All my countless years wandering, I fed on lives, I envied lives, I ended lives, but I think you're the first life I ever truly saved.

Even before I realized it, even before I knew you, you were changing me. And I am forever changed. Forever grateful for a universe with a sense of humor, determined to prove I could still be surprised. Forever yours, because as you said, forever is composed of nows. I'm yours now, I've been yours since that very first now, and that's an infinite collection of nows you can hold on to. Time isn't real, but moments are.

Don't forget.

If my heart beat, it would beat your name.

Lucy

89

Salt Lake City, January 21, 2025

Lucy—

He was at my house in the middle of the night. I'm going to pace the trail and hope you break the rules and come see me. This is a bad system. Tell your friend to call me or text me. Then I'll have her number and we can communicate faster.

Anyway. Dracula knows where I live, and he's swooping closer. There were also some developments at Goldaming Life. I think I met an old enemy of yours, but she hates Goldaming, so she might be an ally. She said something that's been bothering me. I need clarification.

I need you.

I hate this.

Iris

P.S. Adding this on now—I got your letters and found your gift. Thank you. It's around my wrist, and you're around my heart.

90

Salt Lake City, January 25, 2025

DRACULA

He retires to the dirt basement of his house. Beneath it lie graves of victims no one knows he's taken.

Time is a circle, and he's spun around it this long because he is vicious and bold, yes, but also cunning. His is a legacy spanning centuries and continents, an infinite cycle of obsession and death and rebirth. Wherever he has killed, he can dwell. His home is in the death of countless women, his bed in their resting places, final or otherwise.

The demon vampire woman has the dirt of his first home, the clotted and blood-soaked earth that renews him fastest. Because of that, she thinks she has some measure of control over him. She thinks him satisfied with her offerings and pathetic *protection*. But he's finished with the languorous stupor of ease that lulled him into this life. The idle curiosity of what it would be to merely consume, never hunt. The luxury of servants, of sycophants, of travel without fear or threat.

He is no useless noble, no pampered boyar. He is a warrior. A conqueror. He is death. The other vampires may have forgotten, but he'll remind them, before the end. And then he'll return at last to his castle, his first resting place, his place of greatest power. He'll take you with him, in his belly and his veins, sustaining him.

He sleeps, eyes open and dead to the world. He doesn't dream, and if he did dream, he would not dream of you. Only ever of himself.

He shores up strength, biding his time. The longer he's away, the more desperate to see him you'll be. And it works. When he awakes and searches, he sees you on the trail again. Pacing, afraid and upset. You're looking for him, as you've been looking for him—waiting for him, longing for him—your whole life. You're terrified you've lost him. Which means that, at last, you're ready to invite him in. To accept the gift of his blood, the blessing of his bite.

But he won't be caught off guard again. The other vampires believe him horrified by weakness, unwilling to be bound by the sun. Fools. He is *never* vulnerable. Even held in one form by the circle of the sun, he has more power and violence in him than the infant vampires could ever hope to.

And so, beneath the vicious light of day, he strolls along the streets and sidewalks that will take him to you when you least expect it.

91

Salt Lake City, January 25, 2025

IRIS

It's been days. No Dracula. And no Lucy. Hopefully she checks our post soon. I had two letters from her, which were lovely, but also left me feeling vaguely panicked in a way I can't put my finger on yet.

I'm still shaky, like a vague premonition of doom was pumped into my veins as a chaser to the O negative. The fateful backpack strap, elegantly sewn into a bracelet and left for me under a rock, circles my wrist. I twist it and twist it as I drink my morning tea and choke down some toast. Even my dreams have been hazy, like Lucy and I can't quite find each other anymore. I'm barely sleeping anyway.

At least a visit to my mailbox reveals a pleasant surprise: Two pieces of actual mail are waiting for me. The first is a package from Rahul and Anthony with spices and detailed instructions from Anthony on how to gradually raise my tolerance. I set it aside with an affectionate smile. The second is a heavy 8-by-12 envelope addressed to . . . Lucy. The return address is Lucy's therapist friend.

I can't imagine what it is. It's too big to leave for Lucy at our post, and I have no idea how soon she'll check there. Worried it might be something urgent, I open the package and find a letter on top.

Dear Lucy,

You inspired me to have a penultimate adventure before the final one! It was everything I hoped for. I felt so much hope and peace and joy, staring up at the northern lights. True magic. You were right. I don't have to understand it.

I wanted you to have copies of your stories, so I transcribed and printed them. I also put the audio files onto this thumb drive, but I suspect you won't know what that is or how to use it. Maybe your Iris will, though.

I don't think I'll see you again. It's nearly time. I'm going to be buried in the Hillside Memorial Cemetery outside of Boston. No chemicals or prayers, just like I promised. Come visit me sometime.

Love, Vanessa.

My fingers twitch over the papers beneath the letter. As much as I want to read them, they're not for me. I set the stack on the kitchen table with the thumb drive on top, and then I have a little cry. Lucy's nearby, but I'm still alone. There's no one I can talk to.

The doctor said my blood was a precious resource, which at last made such a crucial part of my life make sense: They aren't just replacing my blood. They're *taking* it. All those years as a kid, sitting in a chair with needles in my arms. It was never about trying to treat my disorder. It was always about taking something from me.

What is it about my family's self-destructing blood that's so useful? And who is that doctor? And how does she know Lucy? It's days until my next "treatment." That feels like an eternity, and even then I have no guarantees I'll get alone time with the doctor or that she'll be willing to talk to me.

I stare at Lucy's letters, but they hold no answers. I need her *here.* I need to talk to her, ask her questions, exhume her past in hopes of understanding our present a little better. Exhausted and sad, feeling helpless, I stand to finish getting ready for school. My hip catches the table and Lucy's transcript falls, scattering across the floor.

"Fuck," I mutter, kneeling to pick up the various pages. My eyes catch on a name. The Doctor.

Oh my god, the *Doctor*? I read her description. It has to be the same vampire. The papers in my hands feel like a gift. I can't talk to Lucy, but I can still hear from her. Until I have her permission to read everything, I'll just look at the sections that include the Doctor. For all I know, she's another huge threat and I should be on high alert.

It's tempting to get sucked into Lucy's voice and life, but I scan as rapidly and lightly as I can. I'm only looking for one word. I pull every page that mentions the Doctor, quickly shoving the rest of them into my bag to double-check later.

It takes all my willpower to attend class instead of holing up in the library and reading. But anyone watching on behalf of Goldaming Life will note if I'm deviating from my routine.

Between classes I rush outside and sit, pretending to do homework but actually reading through Lucy's experience in World War One. It's horrifying and sad and fascinating all at once. How did the Doctor go from the trenches to the Goldaming Life basement?

My phone dings with a text. I pick it up, expecting something annoying from Dickie. But the text is just a blurry photo of . . . a squirrel?

Who is this? I text back.

I wait for nearly a full minute with the little dots telling me someone is typing on the other end. Then it finally comes through.

You mean what is this it's a squirrel

I'm about to block the texts when I look closer at the photo. The squirrel is in the mountains behind me. I'd know that landscape anywhere after all my time spent on those stupid trails waiting for Dracula. Which means this text is from . . .

Are you Lucy's friend?

It takes another agonizing minute for the reply to come.

Am I? I can't ask her because she's sleeping

Did she get my letter last night? Is that why you're texting me?

I just thought you'd like the squirrel

My finger hovers over the screen. I have a way to contact Lucy now. *It's a very nice squirrel thanks. Tell Lucy to meet me on the trail tonight. We need to talk.*

Tonight. I'll talk to Lucy tonight. Which means I don't need to read these papers anymore. And I shouldn't. Not without her permission. Even though I'm totally invested. Now it's World War Two, and Lucy's in Istanbul to be a spy. Why does she even like me? She's so much more interesting than I could ever hope to be.

I lower the papers, staring down at them. Itching to devour every story Lucy's ever lived. But I don't want to read about them. I want her to tell them to me like she told this Vanessa. Missing her fiercely and feeling insecure, I pull out her two most recent letters.

I should feel better. I have a way to contact Lucy. I'll see her tonight. But there's still something about the letters that's bothering me. Unease whispering a threat in a language I don't understand, I just *feel*. I trace Lucy's handwriting. The ink fades in and out—I don't know where she got a pen, but it's not high-quality, which I'm sure bothers her. It's not just the ink, though. It's the words. It feels like—

Oh god, it feels like *she's* fading. These aren't love notes at the beginning of a relationship. They're love letters at the end of one. These letters are a goodbye.

Maybe I'm reading them wrong. Maybe I'm—

A shadow cuts off the sun. But the chill it brings is far deeper than it should be. I know before looking up who is looming above me.

Dracula wasn't supposed to find me during the day. I thought I was safe here, so I let my guard down. Idiot, idiot. I stand and start to stammer a suggestion that we go for a walk. Anything to delay so I can text Lucy's friend.

He grabs me and smashes his mouth against mine. I can't move. I'm too panicked. Then he bites my lip, and the pain shocks me out of my terror. I push against him, but I can't create any distance. His arms are like metal bars. He kisses me again. I try to scream but he swallows the sound, devours it. It doesn't matter that I'm on a college campus in broad daylight. No one notices he's a monster, because he looks just like them.

He angles his mouth toward my neck, and I can't stop him. I can't save myself. I can delay him, though. Give him something he wants even more: an invitation.

"Not here! Come to my house tomorrow."

His eyes turn from red flames to smoldering coals, and he smiles. It's the most stomach-turning thing I've ever seen. But he lets go of me, satisfied that I'm offering myself up to him.

I walk away. It's all I can do not to run, but I'm worried it will trigger some sort of predator instinct in him. I imagine him pouncing on my back, dragging me into the bushes and killing me mere feet from the sidewalk. It would be my own damn fault for being so confident I knew what I was doing.

How often will the monsters have to show me they always win before I finally get it through my thick skull?

I wipe my lip, disgust churning thick with shame inside me. Why did I freeze? Why didn't I scream sooner, or try to fight him off?

I've been used so much, my body drained and cut into and taken advantage of. Maybe I don't know how to do anything but accept it until the danger is past. To delay so I can find a way to fight after. But I *hate* it. I hate what he did, and I hate what I didn't do, and I hate everything.

At last I dare to glance over my shoulder. No sign of him. I lean against a building, hands trembling. I drop Lucy's pages on the ground and call her friend.

"It's chirping at me, like a little bird!" a voice says from too far away. She's not holding it to her ear.

I shout to be heard. "Tell Lucy that Dracula just showed up at my school. I need to see her!" Somewhere safe, though. Somewhere Dracula wouldn't go, somewhere any useless Goldaming guards trailing me wouldn't want to be, either. "I'll meet her at the big shopping center by the building with all the spires!" I don't know how else to describe the Mormon temple nearby.

"Oh, the strange castle with the golden man on top! Is that where Dracula is living? He does like castles."

"I really doubt it, but then again, who knows. There's a perfume store in the mall. Lucy will find me there. I'll wait as long as she needs." No other vampires will go inside. Ford couldn't even handle the smell of coffee; perfume is a full artillery barrage to vampire senses.

"I'll tell her! I'm glad you're not dead!" There's a clattering sound like she dropped the phone rather than ending the call. I give it a minute in case she picks it up again, then I hang up.

I crouch down to pick up the pages I dropped. They're out of order now, and my eyes catch on a sentence that casually destroys my life.

I read the entire Istanbul section. Then I pull the rest from my bag and skim to the end of the transcript. I put it together with what the Doctor told me, barely noted amidst so much other information. *I hope she kills him and puts us all out of our misery in one merciful strike.*

I was right about Lucy's letters. They aren't love notes. They're suicide notes.

I walk, numb, barely registering crosswalks and streets. At last, I drift like a bad dream into the perfume store. Lucy's already there, a frantic expression on her beloved face. Her beloved, lying face.

She rushes to me, inspecting my cut lip, checking me for other wounds. "Are you all right? I can't believe I let this happen. Iris, I'm so sorry, I—"

I hold up a hand to stop her. "If Dracula dies, *you* die. You didn't think I should know I'm helping you kill yourself?"

92

Salt Lake City, January 25, 2025

LUCY

The overwhelming scents bombard me like a thousand screaming detonations. It's hard to keep hold of myself with so much sensory input, but I try to focus on Iris's dark forest eyes. I want to make it better. I want to say something, anything, so she doesn't look this sad and angry. So I don't have to know that I'm the one who made her feel this way.

My old instinct seizes me. The one that let me survive my life at Hillingham. *Lie.* Divert her, distract her, say and do whatever I have to so she laughs and forgives me and we can move on. Nothing broken, nothing changed.

Nothing learned.

I grasp that instinct by the roots and tear it up. I won't lie to Iris, just like I'll try not to lie to myself. "Did Dracula tell you that?" I ask. If he knows I'm hunting him, things will be much more difficult.

Iris explodes. "No, he didn't tell me that! Not a lot of chatting between when he forced a kiss on me and then bit my lip. I was too busy scrambling to keep him from my neck!" Iris holds up a hand to cut off an employee approaching us with samples. He takes one look at her expression and turns on his heels. "God, I cannot *believe* we're having this conversation in a mall. Dracula didn't tell me anything, because he doesn't think I'm worth talking to. I met another one of your old friends. The Doctor."

"The *Doctor* is here?" There's a brief spinning moment where I wonder if I've gotten time wrong again. If I'm confused about where and when I am.

"Working for Goldaming Life. While she was taking my blood, she mentioned you and said something about how killing Dracula would end everyone's misery. And then your therapist sent transcripts of your life stories."

"You read them?"

She grimaces. "Some, yeah."

I don't consciously take a step back, but there's more distance between us now than there was a single moment ago. I need her to slow down. I need everything laid out more clearly. I need this wretched shop to stop assaulting me with perfume. "Those stories weren't for you. You know how others violated my privacy in the past, Iris. I can't believe you would do that."

Iris takes a step toward me, eyes blazing with anger. There's still blood on her lip. I want to kiss her so I can taste it. I hate that he touched her, that I wasn't there to stop it.

"I had no way of contacting you," she says. "I was only reading the sections that mentioned the Doctor, trying to find some clues. I was worried she was a new threat," Iris says. "Besides, I fell in love with you reading your journal. How is this different?"

There's a sound like wind as my vision narrows. I'm withdrawing, pulling deeper inside. I can't afford to shut down. I can't be anything less than fully invested in my body when I'm around Iris. But I don't want this to be happening. I don't want her to know what I've been. What I've done.

"You fell in love with an innocent nineteen-year-old," I say, my voice as hollow and empty as I am. "I don't want you to know the other me."

"I fell in love with *you*! Are you forgetting that I was fully into you in person, too? Not just the journal!" Iris grabs my hand, trying to draw me back to myself. She's still livid, but she's not leaving me. She's not running away. She should. Instead, she keeps talking. "Loving someone is being known. I thought that was what you wanted. I thought we'd have—god, I thought we'd have time. That we were doing all this so we could be together without fear. But you lied. You *never* wanted that. I read how often Mina came up. How desperate you were to be reunited with her. Your hunt for Dracula was about taking some of her back into yourself and then dying once and for all. God, did you ever even— Was I just the means to your end?"

"Oh. I forgot." I flinch.

"You forgot? About which part?"

"About how I hoped Dracula would have some of Mina's blood."

"You 'forgot' about that?" Iris looks aghast. "Seems like it motivated you to make your entire life about hunting vampires!"

"I never stopped being nineteen! *Every* feeling I have feels like the only feeling I'll ever have. But I've had about a hundred and thirty years of all-consuming feelings, so I'm sorry if sometimes I lose track of them. And yes, at the time, I was motivated by the idea of taking part of Mina with me. And yes, I forgot about it. I really did. I wasn't planning on draining Dracula anymore. Just killing him."

"That's not any better! Because you didn't tell me that killing him means you dying, too!"

"This was your idea, Iris. You couldn't have left all this behind any more than I could have." I don't want to be angry, though. I put my hand against her cheek, feeling the heat of her. I linger on every detail of her face. Her eyes are filled with tears, makeup smeared beneath them like bruises. I put those tears there. I bruised her heart. And there's nothing I can do to make it better.

"You don't understand," I say.

"Do I smell like Mina?" Iris asks, her bloodied lip trembling.

It stops me short. I have no answer for her. *Does* she?

"You didn't know who I was when you saved me. But if you can smell Dracula's blood in someone, surely you could smell Mina's blood in me. It wasn't fate or a miracle that you found me outside that train station, Lucy. You were still looking for Mina. You just want to be with her, however possible. Including by dying, since apparently I'm not close enough to the real thing for you to love me."

"No." I shake my head, try to pull her closer. I have to make her understand. I'm doing this for *her.* Not for Mina. "We have to kill Dracula, because that's how I keep you safe."

"You're doing it again and you can't even see it." She laughs darkly, no humor or joy in the sound. It's the laughter of the trenches, the laughter of the condemned, the laughter of the hopeless. "You're sacrificing yourself all over again to the memory of a woman who didn't even notice you died for her the first time around. Fuck this. I love you, Lucy. I'm not going to help you kill yourself."

Iris rips the backpack strap off her wrist and shoves it at me. Then she storms out. I stay where I am. The punishing, stinging stench of perfumes assaults my senses. I don't cry, because I can't. I don't deserve to. I found Iris, and I found myself again, and now I'm losing both.

All I can do for either one of us is finish what I started.

93

Salt Lake City, January 25, 2025

DRACULA

Satisfied with the taste of your blood on his lips, he watches as you scurry away, eager for your appointment with destiny tomorrow. You're his accomplice. A willing victim. Not because you hope for transformation or salvation, but because you understand: There is no salvation. There is no future. There is only him. His are the endlessly patient teeth of eternity, the ravenous, relentless passage of seconds into years into lifetimes. And when you are weeping and emptied at last of everything you thought was yours, he'll bind you to him, forever.

He licks his lips and shudders, bites his tongue so the traces of your blood mix with what's left of his. He follows, silently stalking. There is no tomorrow. There is only now.

But you don't go home.

His irritation flares. Were he not bound by the sun, he would shift into a bat or wolf—whatever pursued you the fastest, whatever drove you home with enough haste for his appetite.

You hurry instead to a shopping center. A tacky, teeming, distracting mass of people and stores. Everything is too loud, too chaotic, so many heartbeats and scents and noises. He misses the quiet of the old world, the pleasure of stalking a single pulse through the night.

Worse still, you enter a store with a riot of scents so violent he's forced to recoil and watch from a shadowed alcove.

Why are you there? Why does any girl wear perfume, though. You're unsure how to keep him, what to do to make yourself most appealing. You're in there, yearning for him and frightened by your yearning. He's tempted to follow you inside, but that *smell.* He can't abide it.

You usually have the good sense not to wear perfume. You don't cover the heady, perfect scent of your blood with anything that confuses or offends his senses. Even when you don't know you're doing it, you're making yourself available to him.

But *there,* under the barrage of man-made scents—a hint of something colder. His lips draw back in a snarl. He drops into a crouch, every sense on highest alert. There's a vampire nearby. He has to get you first.

Before he can tear through the store and kill everything in his path, you rush out. Tears blind you to everything. Your face is flush with emotion. The blood lingers at the surface, calling to him.

He follows at a careful distance, but you never turn around. You never so much as look over your shoulder. There's something wrong. Not just the hint of a chill scent clinging to you—did another vampire dare touch you when you belong to him?—but your blood.

There's a subtle difference between lust and fear, but also anger. He can't tell which is coursing through your veins. Those veins belong to him. That blood is *his.* No one else should be able to affect it.

Was it her? His demonic vampire foe? He can't kill her, but that shouldn't stop him. He's eternal, he's inevitable, he's the teeth in the night that always find their prey. A smile twists his full, sensual lips, revealing all the sharp teeth lurking beneath as an idea forms.

He can't kill her, but *you'll* be able to. Once he's finished. Once you're his.

You retreat inside your house and close your door. He should wait until nightfall, but he's waited too long already. He has you so close, and his vengeance even closer. Ecstasy and violence, control and satisfaction, and *revenge.*

His teeth ache. His fingers twitch. He lifts a fist to knock on the door. He knows exactly how it will go, because it's gone the same way countless times. The circle, always spinning back on itself. You, over and over, curious and excited and filled with potential, then scared and broken, yielding at last. Everything consumed by him. As is his right.

94

Salt Lake City, January 25, 2025

IRIS

"To what do I owe the pleasure, Miss Goldaming?" Dickie says.

I hold the phone against my ear as I throw my bag onto the kitchen table. "They're coming for him."

"For who?"

"For your vampire boss, that's who."

"Iris, slow down. I need you to tell me what you're talking about. Very clearly and specifically."

"Stop pretending!" I shout. "We both know I know about the vampires! Just tell him to get out of town. And to stay away from me. I'm done. I'm done with you, I'm done with Goldaming Life, and I'm sure as fuck done with Dracula."

There's a clattering sound on the other end of the line. "Tell me exactly where you are and—"

I hang up and put my phone on silent. It's not my problem anymore. It hurts, how stupid I am. I stare at my bag, with its devastating history of Lucy's only true love.

There's a knock on the front door. Lucy followed me. She's going to explain, apologize, fix this. I want her to. I want her to give me a reason why this was all a big misunderstanding. I open the door, ready to shout at her, ready to throw myself at her and beg, but—

He's on my doorstep. I've never gotten a good look at him in the daylight. All those sunken, bony, aggressive features, each more dominant than the other, not softened in the least by his sensual, full red lips. He smiles, the smile of every man who's ever looked at a woman and known he could do whatever he wanted and there was nothing she could do to stop him. Every man who assumed she secretly wanted that, too.

All he needs is an invitation.

"Well, come in," I snap, then turn and walk into the kitchen. Dracula hesitates. In all his endless days, has no one ever surprised him? What a mind-numbingly boring existence. I can't believe no one's managed to kill him before now. He's so predictable. So obvious.

"Well?" I demand, hand on the fridge. Between one breath and the next, he's beside me. I open the door and toss out containers of garlic and rotten food, everything foul, noxious, and overwhelmingly malodorous. He recoils as though struck, lifting one arm over his nose to physically block the assault. Funny how much he hates being forced to experience something he didn't consent to.

And he's so *shocked*. He really thought I didn't know what he is. I can't decide which is more offensive: that he believed my wide-eyed victim act, or that he doesn't even remember we've met before. Guess traumatized little girls aren't memorable.

I grab the bag I got from the Cathedral of the Madeleine the day I moved here and spread crumbs in a circle around myself. Lucy's idiot suitors weren't good for much, but their accounts of fighting Dracula did give me all the information I need on how to render him powerless.

"Communion wafers," I say, just in case Dracula hasn't noticed. "Ground up into powder." I wonder why only Christian religious iconography works on him. What it means, if anything, because it's meaningless to me. Doesn't matter how it works, though. Only that it does.

I give myself a moment to relish his look of disgust. "I know exactly who you are, fuckface."

He twitches, rage overtaking him. I'm not allowed to be crude, I'm not allowed to be bold. All those nights on the trail I played the lost girl. A demure, proper young woman, one whose future he could steal by corrupting her. Joke's on him. I don't have any future at all. I never did.

Lucy's face flashes in my memory. She was already pulling away from me during our fight. She's not coming for me, because it's not me she cares about. How could I have been so wrong? And why do I still love her?

Grief threatens to drown me. "If I kill you, do they all die?" I whisper. I need to know. Maybe the Doctor is wrong. But does it matter? Either way, it's what Lucy believes will happen. What she was willing to do without ever telling me.

Dracula just stares at me.

"Well?" I demand. "If I kill you, do all the other vampires you created die, too?"

I've heard terrible noises in my lifetime. The sound of my dad's head thunking against the wall like a melon dropped on the floor. The sound of my mother, ignoring my father's horrible moans, calmly telling Dracula she'd be happy to help him with whatever he needed. The sound of my silver knife cracking through my mother's ribs to make sure she stayed dead.

But *nothing* was as bad as the laugh that escapes Dracula's lips. It's discarded snakeskins rubbing against each other, dry and rasping cast-offs of life. "How," he says, the words so painstakingly formed it's like human speech itself is a foreign language to him, "could you ever kill me?"

I close my eyes. I don't want to look at what I'm willing to keep alive just so Lucy survives, even if she isn't mine anymore. I'm a selfish, evil person, and I don't care. "Just get out." I open my eyes, glaring at him. "Go! Get out!"

"But we aren't finished." He takes a step toward me. "We've barely begun."

I gesture to the circle at my feet. My survival instincts are all telling me to run, but I'm safe right here. "You can't touch me. And I can't— I can't lose her. I don't care. Get out, run away, slither back into hiding."

If he lives, so does Lucy. Maybe she'll never forgive me. But at least I won't be the reason she dies.

His smile spreads like blood seeping down a white tablecloth toward a little girl hiding underneath. My heart speeds up. I've missed something. I'm as stupid as Lucy's failed saviors, I just haven't figured out how yet. What did I do wrong? What did I fail to see?

He steps straight over my line of wafers.

I stumble back and he catches me, those iron arms pulling me close. I shove against him, I claw and punch, but it's useless. He's immovable. He's inevitable. He presses his cold lips to my ear, holding me so tightly now I can't even shudder away from the wet whisper of them.

"It doesn't work if you don't believe in it," he says.

95

Salt Lake City, January 25, 2025

DRACULA

Now you have the sense to be afraid. He's in control, and always has been, and always will be.

It's not the symbols themselves that hold power. It's that sacred space inside someone, that core of absolute faith no one can touch. That's what keeps him out. That's what refuses to invite him in. God or Jesus or even love. Hope. Whatever you hold sacred, whatever you know he can never take from you.

But *you*. You're nothing but a gaping wound of need and loneliness and pain. Life has taught you that faith in anything is weakness, that love is a step into the grave. That nothing and no one can be trusted, not even yourself. You've always been waiting to welcome him. Your very *existence* is an invitation.

Why are you crying?

He catches the tear on one long fingernail, lifts it to his lips and baptizes himself in your pain. He'll take it from you. All of it. The striving and the fighting and the fear. You're his. You were always meant to be his. He knows it, and now, so do you.

"Iris!" someone screams from the doorway. "Iris, invite me in!"

They're too late. He bites open his finger, pressing it to your lips. Then he grabs your curls and drags your head to the side, opening the white expanse of your throat.

His.

96

Salt Lake City, January 25, 2025

LUCY

I wander the same direction Iris left in. Not with any goal in mind, but in hopes of getting a few last stolen glimpses. I'm distracted, lost in my grief. My steps pick up, then get faster. I'm sprinting. I don't know why, only that something is wrong. Something is—

Dracula is nearby.

Iris. I have to get to her first.

I follow his rusted-blood scent, that horrible metallic clanging that fills my head, grinding like a tank crash, metal on metal, burning blood. Does he smell like burning blood, or do I, pushing the limits of the form holding me?

I skid to a stop outside a door. Iris is inside. *He's* inside. I don't know who's on the doorstep screaming Iris's name, begging to be invited in. She doesn't matter. Only Iris does. But I'm stopped at the threshold, the same as the mystery vampire.

I can't force my body past that line. I've never been to her house before, because I was hiding in the hills, lying to myself that it was the best way to keep her safe.

"Who are you? What are you doing here?" the other vampire demands. She has a phone out, mid-conversation. "No, I don't know who she is. Another vampire! Blond, small. I've never seen her before. How far is the team? I don't *know,* Susan! If I knew, I would tell you! No, she's stuck out here, too. She's never been invited in."

But that's not true, is it? Iris invited me into her memories. She invited me into her scars and her mind and her soul. She invited me into her *dreams.* Iris is a home, whole and complete, wherever she goes.

She's always had to be that for herself. She offered me a space in that home. She opened the door to me, without reservation or question.

I put one foot over the threshold. The other vampire stares in shock as I walk past her and inside. The interior is an assault of horrid scents. A flare of pride in my girl cuts through my mindless terror and rage.

And then I'm in the kitchen. With her. With him. He holds her, mouth against her neck. Her heart is still beating, but it's too slow.

He hasn't even noticed I'm here yet. I step behind him, yank his head back, and bite his neck. He drops Iris. Hissing, he launches himself backward. He slams me into the wall so hard the plaster cracks beneath me, but I don't stop. I drink and drink. He can't have her. He can't have any of her.

He grabs one of my arms and throws me across the kitchen. I land on all fours and skitter in front of Iris's prone body, putting myself between him and her.

And then I *understand*.

Time is a circle. I'm still spinning on my axis, with Dracula on one side and Mina on the other. Doing the same things all over again. Here I am, putting my own body between Iris and Dracula. Just like I did with Mina. I sacrificed myself for Mina, but I never told her what I was doing. I never gave her the chance to help me. To fight alongside me. To make a choice for herself.

Just like those four men did to me, taking it on themselves to prolong my life until they had what they needed. Never telling me what was happening or giving me the tools I needed to protect myself.

Iris was right. I was living the same pattern. Making my sacrifice without telling her or giving her a say.

But this time is different. This time, I know exactly what I'm choosing, and why. I'm not getting in his way because I think my life isn't worth living. I'm stopping him because I know Iris's life is worth protecting, just like mine was so long ago.

He's not going to kill me. *I'm* going to kill *him*.

I straighten. I've thought about this moment for more than a century. What I'd say to him. How I'd feel. I even practiced lines. But as I stare into the cold, dead eyes of my murderer, Iris unconscious on the floor behind me, there are no tears. There isn't even rage. There's only repulsion. Look at this small, pathetic man who thought he could end me. Who thought he could take Iris from me.

"'Sup, fucker," I say.

He tilts his head. "Who are you?"

One hundred and thirty years of pain and anger and longing come crashing down around me. I built my entire afterlife around him. I searched for him for *decades*. I promised myself that if I could just see him, if I could just speak to him, I'd understand why he chose me. Why he did this.

And he doesn't even remember me.

I laugh. It bursts out of me like a music box wound so tightly it's about to break. I cut it off, snap the music box shut. "I'm Lucy Westenra, and you should never have touched me." I leap at him, landing on his shoulders.

He's slow and confused. He's never fought other vampires. I have. My legs are around his neck, my hands under his chin. With my ankles locked around each other, he can't tug me off. He slams me into a wall. Another wall. Jumps straight up to smash me against the ceiling. I don't let go. I don't stop. I push down with my legs as I twist and pull up with my hands. His tendons pop. I feel the first hint of give in his spinal column. Only a little longer. I strain, pulling harder, wishing I could say goodbye to Iris. Hoping she understands. Dracula drops to his knees as he begins to lose motor control. I'm so close, it's almost—

Someone runs into the house. "Come in!" she shouts.

The kitchen floods with vampires. I hold on to Dracula with everything I am and scream. The sound bounces around the space like the scents of rotten food, overwhelming the vampires trying to pry me off my goal. But they're picking up Iris, my Iris. They're taking her.

I pitch my weight forward. Dracula crashes to the floor. I stomp on his head, then fly across the room, tearing at the vampires touching Iris.

Someone grabs me around the waist and throws me. I smash through a wall. Several things break inside me, but what is a wall, a wall is nothing, what is a body, a body is nothing. I am moonlight, I am death, the sun might bind me but it cannot stop me.

There are dead things between me and Iris. That's all they are, that's all they'll be. I tear off limbs, gouge eyes, bite and kick and move through the sea of vampires, swimming on a tide of violence and gore. They can't take Iris away from me.

But there are so many, too many arms grabbing me and trying to hold me down. I can't see anything but Iris, nothing exists but Iris. I'm almost to her. I'm almost—

A helmet is shoved over my head. The world explodes in noise and light, every sense filled until it bursts. I can't think

can't see

can't hear

can't do

anything.

97

TO SLEEP, PERCHANCE TO DREAM

The little doors are breathing.

In and out, in and out, soft, hungry exhalations. But my blanket is too small. I can't get all the way under it. If I'm not under it, whatever's waiting behind those closet doors—

Red eyes. Red eyes are waiting, and they're going to swallow me whole, and it's my fault. It's my fault.

A soft click. A hiss of something dragging itself along the floor. I squeeze my eyes shut but it doesn't matter, I can still see. I can always see. The red window gets smaller as it gets closer, blurs, becomes two burning points. Nothing can cover me, nothing can keep me safe, nothing can get between me and the teeth and the whispering, and—

SOFT ARMS CIRCLE MY waist. There are no teeth at my neck, no claws. A noise like the ocean in my ear, soothing, promising. I'm safe, I'm safe.

I'm safe.

But she's pulling me away so frantically. I want to ask what's wrong, what we're running from, but I can't talk. I can't move. All I can do is hope she's fast enough to get us—

MY FATHER FLIES ACROSS the dining room, slamming into the wall. Instead of a single percussive exclamation mark, the sound lingers, drawn out and extended until it fills the whole room. I try to scream but I can't. The burning red eyes are here, too, watching me.

There's no urgency in Dracula's movements. He knows exactly where I'm hiding under here. My father stumbles against the table, collapses against it. The white tablecloth slowly turns red beneath him.

I curl into a ball and press my eyes against my knees, but it doesn't matter. I can still see the monster, and he can still see me.

He can always see me. He was always going to find me again.

The waiting is agony. I need to open my eyes and look at him. Accept that he's there, accept that this is the end. Won't there be some relief in that? In not having to be scared of the unknown anymore? In seeing exactly what my fate is?

I lift my head, slowly, slowly, as though I'm not choosing to do it. As though the choice is being made for me. I can't stop, can't make my head go back down. My eyes are still closed, but they're going to open. I'll see him, and then—

A LOW GROWL RIPS through the darkness, but this growl is on my side. This one makes me feel safe. Her arms are back around me. I press my face against her neck. I want to stay here, I want to stay here, I want to stay here. Stay hidden in this darkness, alone with her.

Who—

How do I know her?

I try to drag my memories free of the sludge of dread and fear that has me trapped. I put my lips against her neck and beneath them I feel two small bumps, scars from a lifetime ago, scars from—

Lucy.

Lucy.

She's Lucy, and I'm Iris, and I'm not a little girl anymore.

I'M BACK IN MY bed, but I'm too big for it. It's a little girl's bed in a cold, empty room. I kick off the blankets and drag the bed across the floor as fast as I can, then shove it into the alcove against the hovering doors.

The eyes will get out again, they'll always get out again, but I don't have to lie in bed waiting. I leave my room.

I'm in the dining room. My father slams against the wall with that terrible thunk. He slumps against the table, head gushing blood.

But I don't pay attention to that. I pay attention to my mother, standing unseen in the darkness beyond the dining room. Not entering, not comforting or protecting her daughter hiding under the table, but calmly addressing the monstrous shadow looming on the edge of my vision.

She's not upset about my father. And she's not surprised by this visit. She *knows* Dracula.

It might have been my hand on the doorknob, my voice greeting him, but I didn't invite Dracula in. My mother did. My family did. They were the ones in business with monsters, in the business *of* monsters. I was just a child. I could never have protected my dad, but he should have protected me. He should have—

THE CHAIR IS LOWERED slowly, agonizingly, until I'm flat on my back. Exposed and vulnerable and unable to move. Then the needles come. Tiny metal fangs piercing me. Not just my wrist and my elbow, but my legs, behind my knees, my shoulders, my chest. And finally my abdomen, up and down the length of it, pulling everything out of me.

I scream but it doesn't matter. I'm not a person. I'm a body. Their body, to do whatever they want with. Figures bustle efficiently around me, unmoved by my suffering.

Two needles caress the skin at my neck. They're almost soft, almost tender. They're different. They would take me away from here, away from *this,* forever. I just have to let them. I just have to invite them in.

The tubes in me whoosh and whir. The machines around me beep, flashing red. Two lights, flashing red, burning red. Fixed on my neck. All I have to do is say yes. All I have to do is ask. Better to be his than theirs. Anything to escape this. Anything to be free of this nightmare.

I'm going to say yes.

A hand wraps around mine. I can't lift my head to see whose hand it is, but I don't have to. I know its cool contours, the fingers that slip so perfectly between mine. I squeeze and she squeezes back. Urgent. Afraid. But here with me, still.

"No," I say to the burning red eyes. "No, I think the fuck not."

MY CHILDHOOD BED, BUT it's not dark anymore. Dim light suffuses the room, giving shape to the cavernous contours of the ceiling, the slope angling sharply to the alcove, with its bloody window and those unnervingly suspended closet doors. The whole room points to them.

Everything is fuzzy and slow and painful. The little doors are there, closed tight. Not moving, not breathing, not doing anything except being stupid little doors set midway up the wall in an alcove. I sit up. I have to leave, again. Is this hell? Will I be trapped in this cycle forever?

"You're awake," my mother says. She's not hiding in the darkness beyond the dining room anymore. She's sitting at my bedside, face smooth and young once more, free of all the machines draining her and keeping her alive at the same time. Like she never aged. Like she never died. Like I never drove a silver dagger into her heart.

"Fucking nightmare," I mumble, my mouth so dry my gums ache.

"Watch your language," she snaps. Just like that I'm a little girl again. But nothing has changed. I'm not a little girl. I'm still me, and everything hurts because—

Oh god. I'm awake. And she's undead.

98

Moab, January 26, 2025

DRACULA

He seethes.

They interrupted his time with you. That first plunge of his fangs into your neck, that baptism of his teeth and tongue and throat in your blood. They *defiled* it. And now he finds out you've already been corrupted.

Someone got to you before him. Someone else's blood in your blood, someone else's presence in your dreams. This is when he takes control, when he takes everything you are. Your blood, your mind, your future.

But he can't do that, because *someone else* is already there. They're fighting him for control, blocking his unfettered crawl through your nightmares. Trying to make you feel strong and loved and supported. You aren't any of those things. You're his.

He doesn't know where he is, nor does he care. They carried him into a vehicle and transported him to another location while he healed. He hasn't felt pain in so long, and he flinches from the memory of the kitchen. It fills him with shame.

Someone is speaking to him, so he rips out their throat. The others freeze, unsure what to do as their friend gurgles and chokes, desperately trying to cover the gaping hole.

First, he'll find that other vampire, the small repulsive thing who thinks she can take you away from him. It has to be her in your dreams. He'll destroy her, and then you'll belong only to him. He'll get you back in his arms, under his thrall. Back in your place.

No one escapes him once he's started. He learned that lesson a long time ago.

A man calmly asks him to please stop hurting the others. He's ripped out every throat in the room. All the vampires writhe on the floor, trying to hold in their blood so they have enough left to heal.

They should understand not to speak to him. How could he have a conversation with an insect, an ant, a worm?

They are not the same as him. No one is. No one ever could be.

99

Salt Lake City, January 26, 2025

LUCY

I come back to myself slowly, like a fever breaking.

What did they put over my head? Flashing lights, blaring noise, and pressure strong enough to burst my eardrums. Every sense was overloaded to the breaking point. Whoever designed it knew exactly how to disarm a vampire. I'd admire it if it hadn't been used on *me*.

My head is free now, but I'm chained to a chair. I tug experimentally. The chains were also designed by someone familiar with vampires. I'm in a small room partitioned by a curtain. I'm not in Iris's house anymore, and Iris—

Iris.

I lose some time to a blackout moment of rage and panic. Eventually I shut that down, because it won't do me any good. I can't break out by brute force. That's never been my forte, anyway. I find a single link in the chain and begin working at it.

Then I close my eyes and search. *There.* A whisper on the edge of my thoughts. Iris is alive, but she's not awake. I try to wrap my consciousness around her to tug her free of whatever has ahold of her in her dreams, but there's so much resistance. It takes all my concentration.

If only I could *talk* to her. I'm getting more frantic, and my fear leaks through into the atmosphere of her dreams. I keep finding her and then losing her again. Dracula is fighting me for control, which means he's already started his final assault on her.

My stomach turns, sick at the thought. He has so much more experience. How can I win? How can I save Iris from this when I couldn't save myself?

"Where did you come from?" a man asks.

I open my eyes. He's tall and gaunt, with paper-thin skin and hooded eyes. A gloriously full head of hair sits atop his head like a leech feeding off the rest of him.

"That's a complicated question!" I give him my glassiest-eyed smile. "Where do any of us come from?"

He's not amused. He looks exhausted. I'd swear he'd been drained were he not clearly alive by the sound of his heart and breathing. "I just need to know when Dracula created you."

I drop my act, too angry to pretend. "He didn't create me. He *killed* me. Don't give him credit for anything else."

The gaunt man's eyebrows draw low. I've heard his voice before, but I can't place it. "You look young. I don't think you are. That's good. Both because I don't have to figure out when he slipped through our protective measures and killed you, and because older vampires are more valuable to harvest."

"*Dick!*" I declare, figuring it out.

Lawyer Dickie looks briefly offended, then sighs. "I'd ask how you know Iris, but it hardly matters now."

"Does he have her?" I ask, desperate. I'll tell Dickie anything he wants, I'll give him anything he needs. "Is she safe?"

He pauses, surprise at last shifting his features as he considers me. "The blood is life. She's a Goldaming. We'll always protect her."

I smile brightly once more. "Doing a brilliant job. Like when she was in London and your guard dogs didn't notice she was dating a vampire. Or here in your own territory, letting Dracula stalk her. He was going to kill her in the kitchen; I'm the one who stopped him. Let me go and I'll protect her myself. The blood might be your life, but Iris is mine. I'll keep her safe."

He walks out. I let my head fall back. It was worth a shot. The link I've been sawing at with my fingernail is starting to get warm. In another few hours I'll be through it. But I don't think I have another few hours.

"Full harvest," he says to someone outside. "Make it quick."

The curtain parts again and the Doctor walks in. My old friend, working for my enemies. That's who Iris met. That's why everything fell apart.

"I'm going to rip you into pieces and drop you in the ocean," I say.

"But I'll make certain the pieces are big enough that you can still think and hear and feel. I want you to experience every agonizingly powerless moment of your slow descent into starvation and madness."

"Hello, Lucy," the Doctor says, all business in her white lab coat. "You've changed. It's nice. Out of professional curiosity, what did you think of the sensory overload helmet? I never did try it on myself."

"You love your hands most, so I'm going to rip them off first."

"Stop being dramatic. We have work to do."

I'm tempted to plead, but I know it won't matter. How many men did I hear pleading on her operating tables? "Dracula's trying to kill someone I love," I say. "They've been working with him, protecting him this whole time, looking the other way while he stalks and kills women. It never stopped. It will never stop unless we stop it. You *have* to care about that. You can't be working for him, after what he did to us. You just can't. It's breaking my heart."

The Doctor's look is so withering it erases nearly a century and a half of life, reduces me to a girl once more. "*Lucy.* I said *we* have work to do. You and me. Together." She pulls a key out of her pocket and unlocks the chains.

"Oh." I brush them off me and stand, embarrassed. "Sorry. I saw you here and I assumed . . ."

"It was a mutual agreement at first," she says, unapologetic. "You inspired me to look into vampirism and its possible medical benefits, which eventually led me to the Goldamings. I assure you I was unaware of the connection to Dracula. They hid him quite tidily. And I liked my work, for a while. It was very promising. But they changed the terms, and I no longer wish to partner with them. Here, drink this." She reaches into a white box next to the bed and hands me a bag of blood.

"This is Iris's." I know the smell, and now I know the taste, because I already drank it as it pulsed through Dracula's veins.

"Better you consume it than they turn it into products to lure in new acolytes. Besides, Goldaming blood is special. You'll need your strength to break us out of here. I've tried, but fighting and fleeing are not my skill set."

All good points. It feels wrong to drink Iris's stolen blood, but I do understand a little more why she read the transcript of my life story.

She was desperate, and she needed me, and I wasn't there. I'm desperate, and I need Iris, and she's not here.

The scent of the plastic container lingers in my nose, and it's awkward to drink from. The blood is lukewarm. And still, it's *euphoric.* Iris's blood, her life, her taste, coating my tongue, rushing down my throat, filling my stomach and surging outward in waves of warmth and power.

She already had my heart, but now she powers it. Now she's part of me, down to my veins. And the Doctor is right: Iris's blood is different. I was too enraged to notice before when I drained Dracula. Blood is blood, despite what the Lover said about champagne blood, but this is . . .

This is so heady, so potent even one small bag has me feeling like I've been lit on fire. Like I'm *alive.*

"It feels like your whole body is an orgasm," the Doctor says bluntly. "I know. I've sampled Goldaming blood, out of scientific curiosity. Please focus, though. We have to get off this floor. There's an elevator, but I can't get it open on my own. Together, we might stand a chance."

Beyond the curtain, we're surrounded by heartbeats. Seven . . . eight. Eight people. "What about the—"

The Doctor moves faster than I've ever seen her. Before I can come out from behind the curtain, there are no more heartbeats.

"Can't have them tripping an alarm." She wipes the corner of her mouth, then sweeps her eyes over her carnage. "Wasteful," she mutters, stepping over the bodies on her way to the elevator.

I join her. I can feel the immovable boundaries of my body. It's not long before twilight, but not long is still too long. I can't change form until then, which means moonlight and mist aren't going to get us out of here.

"Are they keeping Iris in this building?" I ask, examining the door. It's solid metal. It would take me ages to punch my way through.

"I doubt it, but we can check. Assuming you can get us out of the basement."

"Put your fingers in the seam. We'll try pulling together."

Before we can, the doors slide open with a cheery ding. Inside is a young vampire with silky brunette hair, big brown eyes, and a haunted expression. She's wearing a security guard uniform, complete with a badge declaring her name Del Toro. "Come on." She holds the door for us.

"I know you," I say. "You were the vampire on Iris's doorstep." The first one there who was so desperate to get in and stop Dracula.

She nods. "I was following her. I wanted to talk to her. To ask about— It doesn't matter. I saw what I needed to in the kitchen." She pushes the button to take us up.

"Why are you helping?" the Doctor asks.

The elevator slows, then stops. Del Toro leads us out. We're trapped by several inches of clear plastic. But Del Toro solves that, too. She presses her palm to a pad and the sealed door opens. Beyond that is a plain wooden door, and beyond that, we're free in a hallway leading to a lobby.

"Because," Del Toro says, "they told me I would be a living god. They told me I would help people. That I was changing lives for the better. But they lied about everything. You tried to save Iris from that monster. They punished you, and whisked him away to safety. That's who I sold my soul to. I'm not a god, I'm just another vampire. Doesn't mean I have to be *their* vampire, though. Good luck."

She walks back through the wooden door toward the elevator.

"Where are you going?" I ask.

"To help people and change lives for the better. By destroying the lab." She smiles sadly over her shoulder, then the door closes.

"Come on. There might be alarms," the Doctor says. We race down the hallway to the main lobby. It's almost twilight. I can feel it creeping closer, the body around me less like a demand and more like a choice. I flex my fingers, ready. Waiting. I'm going to be unbound, and then everyone in this building will be—

"Everyone on this floor is already dead," the Doctor says, frowning. "No heartbeats at all."

"Oh, hi!" The Lover pops up from behind the reception desk. "We found you! Look, I found them!" She points excitedly.

The Queen steps out of a nearby hall, golden blades dripping blood. She nods regally at us.

"More friends of yours?" the Doctor asks.

I could swear she's jealous, but I don't have time to feel happy about it. I always knew she loved me, though. "I'm going to check all the floors. Where Iris is, we'll find Dracula, right? He's in charge here."

"Oh no, they took Iris?" The Lover's eyes get big and sad.

The Doctor answers me. "Dracula's not in charge."

"What? But all these vampires smell like him. I thought—"

The Queen shakes her head. "She's right. That devil could never run a billion-dollar company. All he's capable of are small, petty intrigues in pursuit of his next conquest. This requires vision. Determination. Clever industriousness. It has to be someone else's work."

"The Goldamings," the Doctor says. "They're the brains, and also the blood. It's their blood that hooks people. It gives them a flush of youth and a renewed hunger for life. I could have done such great things if I'd been given the chance." She looks longingly in the direction of the lab entrance, then shakes her head. "No matter. It's all meaningless in the end. They only turn the most loyal fools into vampires. I assume that's where Dracula comes in. He's their pet plague rat. They'll be keeping him hidden somewhere. If you get me upstairs, I can find out where he is."

I want the Doctor's help, but I want it freely given. I won't make the mistake I made with Iris. "We're going to kill Dracula," I tell her.

"Of course we are," she says, as simple as that. After several lifetimes of trying to beat disease and death, she's come to the same conclusion: The best thing we can do for humanity is end Dracula, once and for all. Even if it means ending ourselves, too.

My heart swells, both with Iris's blood and with pride in my friends. The Doctor, the Queen, and the Lover. We all changed, eventually. Together.

We prowl floor by floor, leaving the living intact, with some exceptions, accidental or otherwise. By the time we've cleared the fifth floor of everything undead, it's twilight. Things go much faster after that. I move from scent to scent, that metal clang calling me. No one can catch me, because there's nothing to catch until it's too late.

I don't even notice I'm on the seventeenth floor until the Lover sweetly calls my name, bringing me back to myself. There's some sobbing and a few small screams behind us. I remember nothing else about how I got here, and choose not to examine the evidence on my hands.

The Lover skips down the hall after the Doctor. "You're beautiful to watch at work, Lucy."

There's grudging respect in the Queen's voice. "'Beautiful' is not the word I would use."

"It's interesting to meet you both," the Doctor says. "Lucy told me about you before we last parted ways. Clearly, I'm not the only vampire she influenced. But Lucy, how did *you* change?" the Doctor asks me. "I thought you never would. This determined, fierce woman is not the girl who moped out of Istanbul."

"She forgave herself and fell in love," the Lover says.

I expect the Doctor to scoff, but to my surprise she nods like it explains everything. She stops outside an office door that reads "Kyle Palmer, CFO." She pushes it open. A man waits in the dark. Even though screams and sobbing drift down the hall, Kyle sits perfectly straight at his desk, an eager, almost beatific look on his face as he stares at the Doctor.

"Is he—" the Queen asks, horror cracking her serene expression.

The Doctor shrugs. "I was curious about familiars. I conducted some clandestine experiments. This one was successful."

"I knew you'd come." Kyle's eyes practically roll back in his head in ecstasy. "I can smell the blood on you. The blood is life, and you are life, and I will do whatever you need, my god, my mas—"

"That's enough of that," the Doctor says. "Tell us where they're keeping Dracula and Iris."

"There's a safe house in the desert. I can take you there myself!"

"The location is sufficient."

His whole face falls, like an infant on the verge of bawling. It's repulsive, but useful. "Let him take us," I say. The easier it is for us to get in the door, the sooner we can save Iris and end Dracula.

I don't have to think about what happens then. One step at a time.

100

Salt Lake City, January 26, 2025

IRIS

What do you say to the mother whose corpse you stabbed so you never had to talk to her again?

"My throat hurts," I croak.

"Yes, I would assume it does." Her gaze is flat and emotionless. I'd say it's because she's dead, but she's always looked at me like I'm a spreadsheet. Adding and subtracting in her mind, trying to find a way to make me worth her time. I never was worth her love.

I sit up a bit straighter. *Everything* hurts. Each muscle and tendon and bone, pieces of my body I never even knew existed making themselves known through sheer aching agony. I feel like I've been through an aggressive cycle in the dryer. "Can I have some water?"

"You don't need water, you need a transfusion."

I laugh, imagining Arthur Holmwood, Doctor Seward, Quincey Morris, and Van Helsing all lined up in the hallway, eager to make me theirs by filling my veins. Has there ever been a grosser analogue to sex? But I'd never have attracted their attention in the first place. I could never have played the survival game Lucy had to. They would have punted me straight into Dracula's arms just to get rid of me, inheritance be damned.

My mother flinches with the force of her distaste over my laugh. I study her. She looks young and not dead, but there's something off. Some lack. I never could explain it in a way that made sense, but growing up, that was how I figured out who was a vampire and who wasn't. Not fangs, not claws, not glowing red eyes. Just an uncanny valley of absence. Simulacrum of life. Almost there, but not quite.

Maybe that's why so many aspiring social media influencers, young moms desperate for validation and money, and aimless men who feel like they deserve more than they have are attracted to what Goldaming Life offers. It's real life with a filter. Everything smoothed and beautiful and *fake.*

That's why I didn't notice "Elle" was a vampire. Lucy's like them, but she's not. She still has something vibrant and living and authentic about her.

I lean my head back against the headboard. Even though this is my childhood room, nothing in it was ever mine. The bed frame is sleek and sophisticated and hard; the bed and a nightstand are the only furniture. My mom must have had a chair dragged in here so she could lurk in comfort. The walls are white, the ceiling black, the only notable features those two baffling closet doors and the round red window dominating the alcove between them.

"Well," I say, "I feel like we should address the undead elephant in the room."

She doesn't let out an annoyed sigh. I guess that's one big change. No more weary exhalations, no more sighs, no more hisses. So that's nice. But her expression conveys the sigh fairly well. "Yes, Iris, I'm not dead anymore," she snaps. "Though we prefer the term 'living goddess.' "

I snort. "Oh, that's *so* cringey. I'm embarrassed for you."

Her eyes narrow. I brace myself. Whatever she says next will hurt. Then one corner of her mouth hooks up in a smile. "It's going to happen to you, too."

My hand flies to my neck. It's bandaged, but I know what's underneath. Those twin points throb as if his teeth are still there. "Because of what he did to me?"

She has the decency to look cross. I'm glad she's annoyed that her pet vampire attacked me. Maybe she does have a single maternal bone in her body, after all. But one of the small, useless ones. Her coccyx, probably.

"No," she snaps. "We stopped that before it could progress past the point of no return."

That must have been who was shouting on the porch. Did I manage to squeak out an invite before I passed out? Doesn't matter. I'm alive. And Dracula is . . .

"Where is he now?"

"He doesn't matter." My mother's left eye twitches with the lie. She thinks she knows me, but I've made an art of studying her. He *does* matter to them. Which means they'll keep him safe. Which means Lucy will live.

I want him to suffer. I want him ended in agony. But not if it means Lucy dies, too. Even if she's not in my life, I want to know she's still out there, somewhere.

I put an arm over my forehead. "So, what? One of your cronies turns me before I die, like they did to you? Hard pass."

"No one 'turned' me. It was always going to happen. It's what's wrong with our—sorry, your blood. Mine's no longer a problem. Everyone in our family line is born infected."

"Because of Dracula," I say, feeling sick all over again. It makes a strange sort of sense. Dracula bit Mina and gave her his blood, but he never finished the job. And then she had a baby afterward. Born infected, then passing it down the line to us.

My mother keeps talking. "Our bodies fight back, trying to keep the vampirism dormant. That's why we're anemic, and why our immune systems attack our blood cells when our core temperature drops too low. But eventually our bodies lose the battle, and we die. Then our true nature can take over." For once, her smile isn't a performance. It's genuine.

"You're happy about it!"

"This is what I was born to be. What I'm meant to be. That other phase, that shadow of a life? It was nothing but suffering."

"Then why did you fight to stay alive? All those transfusions, all that medical care."

"It's our sacrifice. The price we pay to become this. To live forever under the protection and power and pride that the Goldaming family name offers. We might be born into it, but we still have to earn it."

Sounds like religious bullshittery to me. Like the churches that say God loves you unconditionally but then proceed to give you a bill you're expected to pay to stay in God's unconditional love, accompanied by all the many, many conditions under which God actually no longer unconditionally loves you.

"Either we're born to be vampires or we're not, Mom. Don't see why we have to earn it."

"*Living goddesses,*" she snaps. "Every new generation is required to give as much blood as they can, because the blood—"

"Is life?"

"No, the blood is worth a tremendous amount of money, you little brat. Stop interrupting me. Our empire was built on that blood and its unique properties. Do you think I wanted to be a mother?"

"Wow. *Wow.* We're just being fully honest now. Okay."

She shakes her head in disgust. "You act like you're the first woman who ever wanted to walk away from the responsibilities and demands on her body and life. Well, too bad, Iris. We have a legacy to uphold. We have a line to continue. And you're going to participate, whether you like it or not. I tried to help you have more children, earlier. Release you from some of the burden I felt so keenly."

"Oh fuck you forever, Mom." I try to get out of bed but I'm too weak to manage it. That's why she started this conversation before I got medical care. I literally can't leave. "You weren't trying to help me, you were trying to *breed* me. That wasn't kindness. That was straight-up evil, and we both know it."

She leans back in her chair. "Stop being petulant. This is what you were born into, and you'll contribute whether you want to or not. Don't make it harder on yourself than it has to be." She stands. I think I'm free, but then she reaches beneath her chair for something. "Then again, you never could take the easy path. I don't suppose this will be any different. And don't think I don't know about this."

She drops my precious silver dagger on the nightstand. "That was really hurtful, Iris. I also know all about your plan to escape, and that you don't care about your poor father. You only pretend to so we'll believe we can control you."

"Don't talk to me about Dad! He lived in absolute fear of you! He still does. Real mature, breaking into his room and scaring him."

She laughs. It's dainty, almost coquettish. I can't believe it's coming out of my frigid mother. "Can you blame me? It was funny!"

"You're a monster."

"No, dear. I'm a goddess. Branding matters. Get your terminology straight, or there will be consequences." She turns as if to leave, then pauses. "Oh, I meant to ask: Who is she? The vampire who tried to kill Dracula? She got inside your house before our security did. I thought you knew better than to invite people in."

"What?" My heart races with panic, but there's not enough blood in me to handle it. A wave of dizziness nearly pulls me under. "Where is she? Is she okay?"

My mother's eyes widen. Her nostrils flare and then her smile spreads. If I thought her laugh was bad, it's nothing compared to the triumph in her expression. "You *care* about her, after working so hard to make yourself untouchable. We have her in our lab. How does that make you feel?"

I lunge and grab her cold hands. She can literally smell how much Lucy means to me. As long as Lucy's safe, I don't care. "Don't hurt her. I'll do whatever you want. I'll have a baby, I'll have five babies, you can take my blood every day, I'll run the company and toe the line and wear a fucking pantsuit, anything. Just don't hurt her. Let her live."

My mother leans forward and brushes a kiss against my forehead. I try not to shudder at her touch. "Good girl," she says, the first and only time she's ever called me that. All it cost me was everything.

101

Moab, January 27, 2025

DRACULA

They have him hidden in a lifeless house in the lifeless desert. He hates this country and the western states more than anywhere he's ever been. Too much empty space. Bloodless and meaningless, any history deliberately destroyed.

But they have his own ancient grave dirt here. He needs to rest after what that *thing* did to him. His mind recoils from the memory of weakness, the knowledge of how close the small vampire was to—

No. She wasn't close. He was caught off guard because of his pleasure. He would have destroyed her, had they let him. Had they not interrupted him.

And now he's here, with talk of *keeping him safe.* As if he needs to be kept safe. As if he is not the thing that the world needs to be kept safe from!

As soon as he's regained his strength, he'll kill everything in this house and go back on the hunt. He'll find you once more and cleanse you. He'll make you worthy of him again. And then he'll set a plan in motion. He hasn't enacted a good plan in so long. He's gotten soft and lazy through the ease of his life here. That was the demon's trap, her brilliant ploy.

But he hasn't forgotten his old tricks. He can convince them he's nothing more than a sophisticated man. Convince them he's happy to be taken care of. After all, he once focused long enough and planned well enough to buy a new home in a foreign land.

Though that relocation *is* what got him here in the first place.

He cannot, will not dwell on it. His dirt calls to him. He'll sleep, and when he awakens, he'll begin his plot to find you and destroy the vampires here once and for all. Then he'll be finished with this loathsome country. He'll go home. He'll become himself once more. Grand and terrible, awe-inspiring, inescapably important.

One of the pathetic vampire servants is saying something at him. He makes an effort to pull the words out of the air and process them.

A visitor? he responds. Cold revulsion seizes him. It's the demon vampire, it has to be. He can't speak to her, not in this weakened state. But he can't let her know that. *Let her in,* he commands.

She'll see that he can barely hold interest where she's concerned. He goes back to his drink, focusing only on the blood and restoring what was stolen from him.

But instead of the demon, a human man walks through the door. There's something wrong inside him, an imperfect infection. Behind him are three women.

Not women. Three vampires. But still women, scarcely worth his attention. Why are they here? He waves to dismiss them, but he's not even through the gesture when he sees who's standing behind them. The small vampire, the *thing* that attacked him. Delivered right to him!

Hold her, he commands. But no servants come scurrying.

He blunted his senses by focusing on the blood. A frantic scan now reveals there's nothing else moving in the house. Nothing but these four vampires and their familiar. He can still feel the damage in his neck, slowly weaving itself back together. A reminder of how close she came to ending him. Closer than anyone ever has. He has to leave, has to—

He blurs, but is slammed back by an invisible barrier. The force of it makes him stagger and fall into his chair.

"Dawn," says one of the vampires, smiling at him like an old friend. "We waited, just for you."

Fools. They'll be weak, too. But they don't look weak as they file into the room, blocking all avenues of escape. He's never fought without the freedom to shift into untouchable forms. He's a predator and has a predator's fear of injury. Better to flee and fight on his own terms than risk being hurt again.

Besides, there's something repulsive in their faces. Not only the lack of vulnerability, the absence of soft life to sink his teeth into. But . . .

Confidence. They each move like they know exactly what the outcome of this will be.

No. He won't allow it. It's disgusting, they're disgusting, but *there*—that scent. He calms down, soothed. They're his. He made them. They already belong to him. He just needs to remind them.

He focuses on the small one who tried to kill him. He bends all his centuries of control and violence toward her, pinning her in place with his will. No matter what tricks or ploys other vampires might have, no one has taken as much as he has. And what he takes, he keeps.

The waves of his dominion flow out from him onto her. Her eyes go flat and distant, remembering some long-ago time when she answered that call and invited him in. Little does she know that, once invited, he can never be kept out. She's his. They all are. They want to be.

I am your master still.

Her eyes fill with tears as she gazes on him. He's won. He always wins. He is inevitable.

102

Moab, January 27, 2025

LUCY

Dracula, at last, *looks* at me.

I'm nineteen again. Real nineteen, new nineteen, raw and open and heartbroken nineteen. The whole world ahead of me, but a world so claustrophobic it feels as though my life has already ended. In love with someone who would never love me back, and lacking even the words to explain what I was feeling.

Waves of his will wash over me, and I understand why it happened. I see exactly the way he left me vulnerable and unable to fight back. The manipulation that had me questioning whether I somehow *wanted* that to happen, whether it was my fault, whether I deserved it. The way he turned my guilt and confusion back on me, making me feel complicit in my own assault.

I look in his eyes, and at last I find my answer. Why he took what he did, why he changed me forever. It had nothing to do with me. It wasn't my choice, or my fault, or even because I was somehow special. It was only ever about him.

That's the answer. The horrific, utterly banal answer. He did that to a nineteen-year-old girl *because he could.*

His power is still there. He's the same predator, the same elemental force with cunning violence behind his gaze. Waves of his compulsion begin to pull me under once more. They draw me into his thrall with promises that if I let him do what he wants, things will be easier. If I stay small and quiet, if I give in, he'll invite me into his world. I can be safe in his shadow. Iris will be safe there, too.

Through him is the only way we can ever be together. He's already started his dance with her. Nothing can stop him, so why try? This is how I save myself. This is how I keep going, keep living. And this is how I get Iris, forever. I missed my chance with Mina, but this is a new opportunity.

His power flows into me through those little points of pain in my throat. Those hooks left inside, tugging me through time ever since. *Iris,* he reminds me. He'll give her to me, after. When he's finished.

I smile.

He picked exactly the wrong pressure point. Iris is the reason I'm no longer the girl he left broken and lost and alone. I look away from his eyes. He lets out a small noise of disbelief that I could break the gravity of his existence, but I don't have time for his feelings. I'm worried about my friends. They all had the same hooks put into them when they were young, so very long ago.

The Doctor, the Queen, and the Lover each meet *my* gaze. Not his. My smile grows, because none of us are his victims. Not anymore. The suffering and the experiences and the growth we've gone through since? We're mausoleums, holding the girls we were with tenderness, and love, and strength. His violence turned us into our own unhallowed ground, our own safe spaces to rest, carried with us wherever we go. And he's no longer welcome.

He stands taller, glowering at us with a seductive twist of his lip. "Listen to me, my children of the—"

"You don't get to speak anymore." This time I don't go for his head, merely his jaw. I twist and pull. With a wet pop and a ripping noise, the entire thing comes off in my hands.

His scream is a keening knife, but it sounds like music to my ears. He flails, a gargling noise pouring out of him along with a sludge of inky black blood. We watch impassively as, with the frenzied violence of a cornered and injured animal, he climbs up and down the wall, looking for a way out.

He leaps at the Lover and she meets him midair, flinging him back into the wall. He crawls, darting across the floor toward the door. The Queen moves in, statue turned to lightning. She stomps on his spine with brutal efficiency. The screaming pitches higher and more pathetic.

He drags himself toward the Doctor, blood and drool draining from his useless fangs. She gazes disinterestedly down at him. "No," she says as he swipes at her ankle. She picks him up by the base of his neck, holding him away from herself like one might hold a leaking garbage bag.

"Iris isn't here," I say. "She's not safe yet. Not in the Goldamings' clutches." If she's right about what happened to me back when I was alive, Arthur Goldaming and his descendants have been perfecting the art of slowly draining women for several generations. That Iris is one of their own will make no difference. Not if they can profit off her. "Can you call your familiar?"

The Doctor lets out a sharp whistle. The familiar slinks into the room, eyes feverish and gleaming as he takes in the evidence of our violence.

"Yes, Master?"

The Doctor's nose wrinkles in distaste. "We've talked about that term."

He cringes, fawning, hands extended like he would pet her if he could, pull on her clothes and beg forgiveness. But there's a writhing, jawless vampire in the way, so Kyle stays where he is. "Yes, Goddess?"

"Not much better," she says wearily. "Do you know where Iris Goldaming is?"

"Yes!"

My hopes rise, but then he flinches and corrects himself. "No. But I know where she will be! Tonight! They're having a gala for the Celestial Circle in the Goldaming Life Center. Iris is going to be inducted, and her mother will reveal herself in her final, glorious form."

"Her *mother*?" I ask, shocked. "Her mother is still alive?"

"Alive again, yes. A living goddess, like the four of you." He gazes at the Doctor, rapt.

"Can I kill him?" the Lover asks. "Please? Even if he hasn't murdered anyone yet, he's definitely done it in his heart."

"Oh, but I have! I've killed several people, to prepare! To show my devotion!" Kyle turns to the Lover, a smile like a child's asking for an allowance.

Dracula tries to claw the Doctor's arm. She shakes him until he goes back to screaming and writhing. We should kill him now. I know we should.

But.

"I'm going to ask for a favor, and you each have to agree. If even one of you doesn't, I'll accept it. But the Doctor and the Queen are right: Dracula was never in charge here. It's Iris's mother pulling the strings. Keeping Dracula as a pampered pet, letting him prowl unhindered and protected as she took her family's empire to new heights. She's in charge of all of this. And she's got Iris. She'll use her up and drain her dry. I can't leave existence until I know Iris is free."

"But all their vampires smell like Dracula. When we kill him," the Queen says, "they all die. She'll be safe."

"Vampires aren't the only monsters." The Lover crouches in front of Dracula, hitting his legs so he swings wildly back and forth. He hisses and spits and she hits his legs again.

"A lot of Goldaming Life leadership is human," the Doctor admits. "If you use the term 'human' loosely. Even if they lose all the vampires, they'll still have Iris and her blood. Which will be even more valuable then. They'll never let her go, not willingly. What are you proposing, Lucy?"

"Can you take Dracula somewhere? Keep him hidden until I get Iris out? And then, once she's safe, you kill him."

The Doctor nods. The Lover looks up from where she's breaking Dracula's fingers as he tries to claw at her. She shrugs. "Oui."

But the Queen hasn't said anything. I look to her. I know her story best of all. I know what she went through, what was done to her, what Dracula represents. She's going to say no, and I'll accept it. Iris is brave and tough and clever. I have to believe she'll be able to save herself after we do our part.

"We deserve better," the Queen says, so softly I can barely hear her. Then she looks at me, chin held high, as regal as the day we met despite her lack of silk and jewels. "You changed our lives. We can keep hold of those lives long enough for you to save the girl."

"Yay!" The Lover claps. "This is exciting!"

Dracula swings at her, raking his remaining nails down her arm. She hisses and breaks his wrists as if she were snapping pencils. She looks down at the damage to her arm, thoughtful and concerned. "How do we transport him? He's dangerous."

The Doctor, still holding Dracula suspended by the back of his neck, twists. With a crack, the rest of his body goes limp. "Internal decapitation. Not permanent like the external variety. We'll have to redo it every few hours, but we'll be fine."

"What about when it gets dark?" I ask. "I don't know when I'll be back."

"Look." The Doctor points to Dracula's jaw, or lack thereof. When none of us understand what she's pointing to, she closes her eyes, nostrils flaring with irritation. "The blood."

"There *is* no blood," the Lover says, slowly and sweetly, as though talking to someone who has lost all connection to reality. I know, because it's how I talk to her.

"Exactly. He's already spent it all bleeding from this wound and trying to heal. He has none in reserve, and we aren't going to put him in unhallowed ground or allow him to drink. He can't finish healing if I keep breaking his neck, and he can't shift without any blood in his system. Honestly, Lucy, you're the one who told me to study vampires." She's disappointed in me, but I can't even care, I'm so relieved.

"Where will you go? How will I tell you when I have Iris?"

"Iris can call me on my little birdie box!" The Lover pulls a phone out of one of her many pockets. She's wearing enormous jeans, but only a bra on top. I hadn't noticed before now. Apparently her fashion sense has deteriorated over the decades. That, or I'm the one who's out of touch.

"You can come to my house!" Kyle, whom I had happily forgotten existed for a few brief minutes, skips toward the front of the building. "They'll never look for you there!"

The Doctor shrugs. "I'd rather not, but we know he's loyal."

The Queen smiles. "Dracula's final moments, spent in the soulless home of someone else's familiar. No dignity, no grandeur, no gravitas."

He snarls and glares, tongue lolling, eyes rolling madly in his head. The overall effect is deeply pathetic. I don't know if I have a soul, but whatever's still inside me is nourished by the sight.

We toss Dracula into the trunk of Kyle's car. I grab keys for another vehicle off one of the headless vampire guards. Then I pause and take in my three friends. The Queen who held me captive because she was so lonely, the Lover who let herself be murdered just to feel something, and the Doctor who dismantled countless humans trying to find humanity.

"My friends," I say. Each of them were vital parts of my journey.

I'm glad they're here as we near the final steps. "It's been an honor knowing you. I love you all, and if there *is* anything waiting for us beyond this, I'll—"

Kyle interrupts. "I can give you detailed instructions on how to drive to the Goldaming Life Center! All the best routes and exactly how much time each will take you, as well as—"

"Shut the fuck up, Kyle," I say. "No one needs travel itineraries."

"I'm so excited to kill him," the Lover sings to herself.

With one final shared look of understanding between us, I leave my friends and head toward the last, best, most important thing I'll ever do. I defeated Dracula; now I'm going to save Iris, and there's no force in the world that can stop me.

103

Salt Lake City, January 27, 2025

IRIS

"I always knew she was evil, but I never understood how evil until now," I mutter as I sign yet another piece of paper in an infinite stack of pieces of paper. My mother is a vampire. She's an actual undead creature of the night, I've sold my soul to her, and she's making me do *paperwork*. Again.

People keep knocking on the door, summoning her out for terse conversations I'm not part of, but she never leaves me unattended.

"And sign here." Dickie taps with one unsettlingly long finger. I swear he has more knuckle joints than he should. "And here. And here."

I'm still exhausted and aching. They gave me what my mom referred to as a "mini transfusion." Enough to keep me upright without diluting my own remaining blood. She wants me weak. Not that it matters. I'm literally signing away the rights to my own life.

"That should do it. Congratulations, Iris." Dickie smiles at me, an expression as dry and joyless as a three-hour corporate training session on sexual harassment. "I look forward to working together."

"Me too." I smile at him, a smile as fake and lifeless as his much younger wife. But now I'm thinking about her and him and wondering if their foreplay involves reading company bylaws. I hope she murders him for the life insurance.

It's baffling to me that the most vampiric person at the company is human. I wonder what's holding him back. "Why haven't you taken the old fang plunge yet?" I ask. "Why's your cold dead heart still technically beating?"

He lifts an eyebrow at me, then closes the leather folio containing the rights to everything I am or will be. "That's an inappropriately personal question, Miss Goldaming."

"Please don't call HR on me. I missed the form detailing the don't-ask-don't-tell policy regarding vampirism."

"Iris," my mother says as a warning from the doorway. She doesn't even have to raise her voice. She's got all the leverage she'll ever need. I saw the video footage of Lucy in their lab, chained to a chair. As long as I behave, she'll be transported back to England and then released. I wish I could talk to her, tell her why I'm doing this, but it would break me. I'll write her a letter that she can open when she gets there.

Part of me wants to doubt my mother's word. But if Lucy dies, so does Goldaming Life's leverage over me. That alone will keep Lucy safe forever. And my betrayal will keep Lucy away from me. She'll probably be glad to be free.

I close my eyes. It's early afternoon. Surely I can be done for the day and go back to bed. Preferably in a different bedroom.

Instead, a flurry of Goldaming Life drones come in. They're too flushed and excited to be vampires, but they've got that look. Perfect hair, perfect skin, perfect nails. A veneer of unreality about them, walking advertisements for wholesome, aspirational lives.

Under my mother's guidance, they spackle concealer and foundation and highlights onto my face, airbrushing over the damage done by Dracula. My lips are painted just-bitten red, my newly false-lashed eyelids lined with liquid gold. When they get near my eyebrows with tweezers, I give them a death glare so intense they immediately alter course and brush them into place with gel.

Face done, they buff and trim and paint my nails pearly pink even though I request black. My mother watches over everything, directing them when necessary.

"At least you finally got rid of that horrendous dye job," she says, eyeing my loose, wild curls as the women paste and pin them into submission.

"Yeah, I was trying to seduce Dracula." I give her my most placid, Goldaming Life–approved expression. "Worked, too. I can give you some pointers if you want to bone him. Or I guess bite him? I don't know what you're into anymore."

Her own expression flattens with menace. She snaps her fingers and the drones scurry from the room. "You represent the whole company now. Don't forget. We can do worse things to Lucy than kill her, believe me."

I believe her. Even the careful makeup work can't cover the ghastly pallor of my face as I fight my sick dread. "Sorry."

"Don't ever mention Dracula again. He's not your concern. And never, ever speak of the particulars of my condition, or the condition of anyone within Goldaming Life who has gone through the Celestial Gate."

"I'll do better."

"I know you will." Her hand comes down on my shoulder and squeezes tightly enough to be painful without leaving marks. "I know you hate me. I'm fine with that. My own mother failed me by hating what we are and trying to get out of it. I won't make the same mistake. I've made myself invaluable, and you'll do the same whether you like it or not. Now go get changed."

"For bed? Thanks for noticing how drained I am." I wait a beat. She doesn't so much as smile. "But seriously, can I rest for a while? Please?" Asking permission to sleep. This is going to be the rest of my life. Part of me wants to ask more about her mother—my grandma died before I was born, and Mom never talks about her—but I don't actually want to have a conversation with her right now. Or ever.

"No, for the gala."

"The what?"

"The dress is in your room." She glides down the echoingly empty halls of home sweet home. It looks like a museum—arched pillars, marble floors, and blisteringly white light. It's a hollow house, a structure of bleached bones. The only thing that can be said for it is that it's not cold. I laugh dryly to myself, thinking of my stupid trick. Thinking of my stupid self, imagining I was hastening my mother's death and my own freedom. As if something as simple as dying could ever stop her. The silver dagger she carelessly left in my bedroom is proof enough of that.

We take the stairs to the second level. I'm so much slower than her right now that by the time I get to my bedroom, she's already holding my dress.

It's ghastly. White and shimmering and poofy, complete with a bow over my boobs to wrap me up like the world's weirdest wedding gift. "Mom," I say, because honestly.

She rolls her eyes. "I knew you'd reject that one, because it was my favorite. Here." She sets it down and picks up another from the window seat between the closets. I've never once sat in that seat, never gotten closer to that side of the room than the end of my bed.

Shocked at her concession, I take the new dress. It's still too clingy and feminine for my tastes, but at least it's cooler. Metallic gold with a structured bustier that can actually contain me. The same metallic material is shredded in strips over a pitch-black underskirt slit to my thigh.

"Can I wear boots?" I ask, daring to hope.

"Absolutely not."

I wait for her to leave. She doesn't, so I turn around and change as fast as I can. Credit where credit is due, it fits. "What exactly is the gala? What do I need to do?" If I'm giving a speech or something, I'll need time to practice without grimacing. Maybe that's why my mother has such a flat, affected mannerism. It makes it easier to lie.

"It's to honor my transformation and acknowledge your new role as figurehead." She pauses, and there's a flicker of uncertainty on her face, like a cloud passing the sun. Or a bat flickering across the face of the moon, in her case. Then a smile slides into place, the smile that launched millions of memberships, that inspired so many sad, lonely, hopeful people to join her multilevel marketing vampire cult.

"You're finally ready to go through the Celestial Gate," she says. "But first, you'll meet the divine wellspring. And then you can read the story, and understand."

"We can talk honestly when it's the two of us, can't we? Just because I'm going to be in charge of your cult doesn't mean I have to believe in any of its nonsense."

"Oh, Iris," she says, in a tone like a pat on the head. "You're not in charge. You'll never be in charge."

"Right. Because you still are." I'm the puppet.

My mother's eye twitches, but her smile stays in place. "I was never in charge, either." She turns away from me and walks to the closet alcove. My chest tightens. I can't get enough air. Not those doors. Never those doors.

"Mom, what are you doing? What are you doing? Don't open those. Don't—"

But she doesn't open them. She does something far worse. She *knocks* on one.

The door swings outward. A scent of rich, newly turned earth floods my bedroom. The scent of my nightmares, the scent of my deepest childhood fears. A figure in white crawls free, then stands, pristine and radiant, framed by the red window. A window designed to make a perfect halo for a head at that exact height. *No no no,* I think or moan or pray, but I'm frozen in place. I can't move. I'm a little girl again, trying to sleep in this room, knowing without knowing that those doors hid absolute evil. I was right. I was always right, about so many things.

The figure moves across the room with dizzying grace and speed, stopping before me.

"I know you," I whisper. Then I stagger back and collapse, falling onto the nightstand before slumping to the floor.

104

Salt Lake City, January 27, 2025

Dear Lucy,

They said they'll give this to you. I hope they do.

Run. Run and never look back. Promise me. If any part of you loved me, if any part of you still cares, run and never, ever come back here. Be free for both of us. Please.

I'm sorry for everything. I was right from the start, I shouldn't have brought you into my life.

Stay away.

Iris

105

Salt Lake City, January 27, 2025

LUCY

I wish Vanessa could see my dress. It's not quite my Istanbul gown—and offers more coverage than my Paris feathers—but oh, I feel pretty. It's slinky and clinging, a perfect sunset lavender. The color of transformation. The color of freedom.

Doubtless Mina would have chided me for my frivolity in stopping for a costume change, but I had a few hours to kill before the gala started. And besides, it's a gala. I have to blend in. I can't wreck my chances of finding Iris by showing up early or looking out of place.

My accessories are a precious backpack strap bracelet and a black handbag. The bag doesn't match at all, but I needed something big enough for my invitation. I hold it casually at my side as I saunter up the walkway to the entrance of the flagship Goldaming Life Center.

Unlike their utilitarian, brutally modern chrome office building, this feels more like a house of worship. There's an elegant grandeur to the masonry. It's meant to inspire awe, but also intimidate. The stone is a forbidding gray punctuated by arched windows set with reflective stained glass that makes it impossible to see inside from the front. A gold-tipped spire reaches up to pierce the skies.

Arthur would no doubt approve of his name being slapped on this building. He always did dress to impress and intimidate. It worked, too. No one looked under the façade, including my mother. I still can't believe he was penniless. Until my postmortem donation, at least.

I suppose that makes *me* the true founder of Goldaming Life. Their first conned fortune, their original unwilling and unwitting donor. I'm their past, which has a nice parallelism, since I'm here to take their future.

I'd hoped to mingle and work my way inside, but there's no crowd. What kind of gala is this? It's just me and the front entrance guard, a life-size slab of butcher meat packaged in a tuxedo. He frowns, unable to place me. I *look* like I belong, though, which gives him pause.

"Invitation?" he asks.

"I have it right here." I reach into my handbag and retrieve Dracula's jaw. Iris was right. It's a tough accessory to work around.

He blinks down at it, frowning as his marbled-beef brain tries to process what he's seeing.

"You can smell who this belongs to, can't you?" I prod. "Oh dear, you're a very dull boy. I see why they make you stand at the door." I laugh, because men hate to be laughed at, even after they've died. "Go find someone with authority and tell them I've got Dracula. Unless they give me Iris Goldaming, I'll destroy every single one of us."

"Let her in," a voice crackles over a radio. The meatsack looks up at the doorframe. I follow his gaze to see a lens. Some little spy, watching us. I wave a cheery hello with Dracula's jaw.

"You can go in now," he says, still not sure what just happened.

I prance past him. I'm not letting myself think about anything except how pretty my dress is, and how soon I'm going to see Iris, and how after I get her out of here, she'll be free. They'll think it's a bluff and let her go, assuming they can kill me after Dracula is safe again. They've been packaging and selling vampirism as a lifestyle for so long, they can't imagine someone would reject it. That lack of imagination will be why I win.

The long hallway is arched like a headstone. I twirl down the shiny marble floors toward an open door. A towering blond vampire steps aside to let me pass into the ballroom. This one holds no Nazis, no champagne towers, no orchestra. Just a dozen vampires circled tightly together in the center.

On the far end are two massive doors with an actual throne in front of them. They've not opted for subtlety. A glittering chandelier hangs overhead, throwing thousands of lights like a constellation across the mirrored ceiling. That ceiling fails to reflect everyone in the room beneath it, except the person who matters the most. Inside the circle of vampires, Iris is dazzlingly beautiful in a golden dress. Though they've done a wretched thing in covering up her skin with makeup to hide all the imperfections and subtle shades of life.

My whole body's a smile. I win. I save the girl this time, on my own terms. It feels like saving myself, too. I beat Dracula, and I beat the Goldaming machinations, and I'm giving Iris the wide-open future she deserves. The one I deserved, too. The Queen was right. We deserved better, and we never got it, but we're giving it to Iris.

"My little cabbage," I say. "Let's go."

The vampire circle shifts, opening. The vampire next to Iris is clearly her mother, like a colder, cruel, bleached-of-life version of her. I want to kill her, but I don't have time. We have to get moving.

But Iris doesn't run to me. Even when Ford nearly ripped her arm off, she didn't look like this. Iris is *terrified.*

"No!" she shouts. "Lucy, run! Go! Get out of here, now!"

The golden doors open.

Like an impossible vision, a dream held so long it has lost all details and meaning and become only feelings, *she* walks through.

The woman I loved so much I shaped my entire afterlife around the idea of her. The woman who was my core of belief and hope and want, so unshakable that not even death could kill it. She renders me powerless, even now.

"Mina," I whisper.

106

THE TESTAMENT OF MINA

I create this record so my descendants can understand where they come from and to whom they owe their life and legacy. Explaining it over and over is tedious, and I intend to have descendants for the rest of human civilization.

My name is Mina Murray Harker Holmwood, though when Arthur and I married, I adopted the title of Lady Goldaming. Upon moving to America, we chose to keep the Goldaming name. I always liked the shine and weight of it.

I will not bother detailing the circumstances of my youth. I was always fiercely bright and determined to make my own way in the world. I had no advantages through birth, no way to cross the great gulf that separated me from those who had everything through no skill or effort of their own. I found work teaching exactly that type of girl, the spoiled, empty-headed, thoughtless daughters of spoiled, empty-headed, thoughtless wealth. It was around this time I met Arthur. We could never be married—his father had squandered his fortune, and neither of us wished to be poor—but we formed an alliance. Together, we would move upward.

We were well on our way. We both secured engagements with promises of good fortune. An heiress for Arthur, a solicitor with excellent prospects and connections for me. Then disaster struck: My fiancé attracted the attention of a vampire named Dracula.

Normally, this is the part in the story where one would gasp. But as you have been raised a Goldaming, I'm certain you have your suspicions. Allow me to get this out of the way: Vampires are real. Loathsome, grasping, tiresome creatures. I am not a vampire, and neither are you.

After traveling to the continent to retrieve my fiancé, whose encounter with Dracula had left him quite enfeebled, I returned to London. My friends Arthur and Doctor John Seward had encountered Dracula as well, alongside their American cowboy friend Quincey—M? I forget—and an old Dutch doctor, Van Helsing.

As is so often the case, my fiancé had made a mess but I was the one punished for it. No sooner had we settled into our newly inherited home and business than Dracula came to me.

I will not supply the lurid details, but when Dracula bit me, I felt different. There was something special in his bite. I was frightened, but also curious. I'd always had a finer, sharper mind than anyone around me. I wasn't going to let pain and fear get in the way of opportunity.

Dracula's goal was to feed on and eventually kill me so I would turn into a vampire under his control. The men's goal was to find and eradicate him before he could succeed. I had a different idea, though.

I could not speak of it with my fiancé—my husband. I forgot, we had married by then. He was too weak from his experiences to contemplate anything greater than mere survival. The old Dutch doctor and American cowboy couldn't be trusted either; they were too fixated on killing Dracula. The American, especially, was a devoted hunter and seemed to take Dracula's activities personally. He vowed never to stop until the vampire was dead.

But Arthur and John listened to me. Dracula had power, which meant we could have it, too. The vampire was yet another example of someone squandering privilege they hadn't earned. Flitting about Europe buying houses, stalking pretty girls, always looking for the next thing to consume. Never building, never striving, never working toward something greater, because why would he?

Arthur and John agreed that my husband, Van Helsing, and the ghastly American were never going to let Dracula live. Plus, we needed a convincing paper trail should anyone look more closely into Arthur's inheriting his fiancée's fortune. We settled on a plan. Pretending to work as a team with the others, we drove the vampire out of London. After pushing Dracula to the brink of panic, we proved to him that we could and would kill him at our leisure. That was important. He needed to understand his life was in our hands.

Arthur was ready to step in when needed, but things lined up perfectly for once. The American stabbed Dracula with a steel knife but was injured in the process. Van Helsing was distracted trying to keep the silly cowboy alive, and Arthur and John kept my husband out of the way.

I crouched beside the coffin where Dracula lay and had a frank conversation with him. I knew he was faking, waiting until he could flee and rebuild his power. Twisting the knife as I spoke, I told Dracula in no uncertain terms that the men I was with and the record we'd left would ensure that he'd never know peace again. He would be hunted to the ends of the earth. No rest, no conquest . . . unless he let me help him.

I alone could take care of him and make certain he was never in danger. That was the life he deserved, I said. Not luring solicitors across Europe in an effort to find a new home and hunting grounds, not hounded back to the castle he was so desperate to leave.

If he allowed me to see to the details, I would plan his transportation and find him homes and victims, all without consequences or risk. In short, security and ease and luxury in addition to not being summarily beheaded.

It wasn't difficult to convince him. Despite his trappings of nobility, I've always been certain his name and title were stolen. I knew a fake when I saw one. Still, I appealed to his vanity, pretending he deserved my attention and help.

He agreed. He was under my control, as much as any wild thing ever could be.

We went back to London, transporting Dracula under my husband's very nose. John set Dracula up in a home attached to the sanitarium. It was a tidy situation. Lost souls no one missed served a higher purpose in keeping Dracula fed, and we looked the other way when he dabbled in stalking pretty young women. Thus we kept him satisfied and held in reserve while I worked to secure my legacy.

I had a baby not a year later. It became clear no other babies would be coming. My own body was slowly shifting and changing as Dracula's infection spread at a creeping pace. No one had ever survived long enough to experience this type of transformation, and I documented it with great detail and interest.

Meanwhile, my first husband died. Jonathan had grown very tiresome. Incessant chatter and complaints about his health and remarks about how the baby looked nothing like him. Everywhere he ate, he'd ask for the recipe and bring it home like a prize. As though I was sitting in the kitchen, longing, hoping for some new task to be dropped in my lap. As though I hadn't given him everything he had, as though I hadn't tamed death itself, as though I didn't regularly visit death to make certain he was still under my control.

Anyhow, Jonathan died. I married Arthur, but London society made it clear they would never accept me. Rumors and petty gossip swirled, and the wrong sort of people began to take interest in the number of unexpected deaths and inheritances we had collected between us. They didn't think I deserved my place among them.

I was tired of London. I knew I could do very well in America. There, they were not so fixated on who did and did not deserve a fortune; if you had one, you were respected. Arthur and I, along with Doctor Seward, brought Dracula across the ocean to settle in a new home with us.

The child was sickly, which worried me, since I could not have another. I found his very presence draining. Children are much like vampires that way. Doctor Seward was interested in him, though, and found odd properties in his blood. His theory was that since I had conceived after being infected by Dracula, some of the infection passed through me into the child. Not vampire, but not entirely human.

I couldn't invest too much time or thought in the child, though. I became ill. I was cold all the time. My appetite died. I could sense Dracula nearby, always lurking, waiting to kill me. Despite everything I had done for him. Everything I continued to do for him.

He never got the chance. I died in my sleep, and then I awoke. I was not a vampire, but something new. Exactly who and what I was meant to be. I had always had a superior mind, and now I had a superior body. A superior existence. I was a goddess.

Arthur didn't even wait until after the funeral to begin spending my carefully earned fortune. He didn't expect me to come back for it. When I visited him after my death, he died.

Unfortunately, my passing had been common knowledge. I was forced to remain in hiding. With Doctor Seward's loyal help, I continued investing, growing my wealth and power. And I kept Dracula on an ever-shorter leash. Before, we had controlled him by limiting access to his grave dirt. But something changed when I was reborn: He was afraid of me. Afraid of my divine strength, unassailable and unbreakable. I knew Dracula could not harm me, and because I knew it, he knew it, too.

My son was sickly and unimpressive, but we found him a good enough match. He fathered a single child before dying. In a surprise, he, too, awoke after death. But his weakness in life followed him. He was forever weeping and moaning about the noises and thirst and overwhelming scents. He begged me to end his torment, and as his mother I could not refuse.

That's important to remember: Just because you are a Goldaming does not mean you deserve your place here.

Fortunately, we had a new Goldaming. Doctor Seward found the same properties in my grandchild's blood. He assured me we had something special and miraculous. He began publishing papers, hinting about what he'd discovered. His goal was to lure the right minds to participate in our research.

Doctor Seward did eventually find such a mind, belonging to a vampire woman of all things. As soon as we had secured her services, he died. This new doctor knew so much more than Doctor Seward had about the secrets of life after death. I had considered killing Dracula and being done with him, since it was now apparent that my condition would be inherited. But she warned me my life was tied to Dracula's. Keeping Dracula safe became the burden I had to bear. It was no small price to pay, but I've always been willing to do the hard things and sacrifice what I needed to.

Even with the disappointment of the necessity of Dracula, my empire grew in new and exciting ways. We explored the unique properties of Goldaming blood, and I realized we could package and sell renewed vitality. Doses of youth. Health from our death-touched cells.

I could even dole out the ultimate boon: eternal life. But only to those who deserved it. To those who understood that they owed everything to me and me alone. Loyal in life, and loyal forever after.

Everything you have is because of my sacrifice, vision, and determination. As my blood, you're allowed to share in the rewards.

You have sacred duties. Continue our family line and honor me by keeping the name Goldaming. Play your role as Goldaming heir, and pay your dues by giving your blood for as long as you can. And when your body succumbs, be buried in a new place so I can rest all over the country and eventually the world.

Remember, always: Everyone useful will be protected and taken care of. Everyone loyal will have wealth, security, and power. And everyone who remains faithful and obedient will have eternal life at my side. But only because of me, and through me, and in support of me.

Never forget where you came from. I'll always be here to remind you.

107

Salt Lake City, January 27, 2025

IRIS

I can't look away from Lucy.

She can't look away from Mina.

Dracula's words in my kitchen come back to haunt me. *It doesn't work if you don't believe in it.* He can't touch belief, can't attack faith. Maybe it was the core of who he was when he was alive. I can't dredge up any curiosity for what made him into the monster he is.

But according to the manifesto they made me read, Mina's strongest belief was in herself. How wonderful and smart she was, how much she deserved everyone else's money and lives.

I know exactly what Lucy believed in most. I read it, in her journal and afterlife story. I saw it when I tried to tell her that Mina had been in on the plot to take her inheritance. And I see it now. Lucy's been walking in the darkness for over a century, and, at last, she's found the sun.

My mother's phone rings. It feels out of place in this glittering, vampire-filled ballroom where the love of my life has just discovered that the love of hers never died. Mom steps out of the circle to take her call. "Yes? Mmm hmm. I see."

I'd like to strangle her. It wouldn't do any good, but it might make me feel better.

"Mina?" Lucy says again, this time a question, not a statement. There's so much contained in that question. I want to drag Lucy away. I want to read Mina's manifesto to Lucy, show her the truth, but it doesn't matter.

It doesn't matter, because Mina is what Lucy believed in. The core of her soul. And vampires can't change that.

Mina knows it, too. "Lucy," she says, holding out her arms. Lucy steps to her like she's not in control of her body. Gone is the cat's grace, the joyful bounce in her step. She stumbles forward and rests her head against Mina's shoulder. Mina puts one arm around her, the other on the back of Lucy's head. She pats her, a maternally condescending gesture, then releases her. She decided when the embrace started, she decided when it ended, and Lucy? Lucy obeyed.

"Little Lucy Westenra." Mina looks down at Lucy. Lucy's hopeful smile is crushed like a bug under Mina's heel. "Is this it? This is all you have to show for eternal life? A pretty dress and a new crush." Mina laughs. The edge of mockery in her tone cuts me straight through. "Nothing changes, does it? You never could see past the next outfit and the next object of obsession."

"Mina, I—" Lucy searches her face, devouring it with her eyes. "I did my best to keep you safe. To keep Dracula away from you. But I failed." Tears fill her eyes.

Mina watches as the tears stream down Lucy's face. She doesn't wipe them away, doesn't draw Lucy closer like she should.

"You didn't fail," I say. "Mina made a *deal* with Dracula. She saw him as an opportunity, and she took it. She wrote all about it, and she never so much as mentioned your name. You were nothing to her. Not even a footnote."

Lucy doesn't glance at me. I don't know if she heard me. My mother brushes past and whispers something in Mina's ear. Her smile grows, satisfied and smug.

"Speaking of Dracula, your little jawbone joke is over. There's an army of my acolytes on the way to him right now. We have to protect him. Even Iris agrees with me on that."

Mina cuts her eyes in my direction. I want to rip her throat out with my teeth. She's already won, and she knows it. "Anyhow, let's not dwell on that," she says, her tone practical and efficient, as though she's issuing cleanup instructions to young charges after a long afternoon of study.

"Fuck me," I whisper as something long lost is unlocked in my head. The night Dracula got into the house. I thought my mother wasn't home, but then she spoke to him from the dark stairs. She's always had a peculiar way of speaking, almost like someone with a British accent trying to hide all traces of their roots. It's the voice I learned and perfected to imitate her.

It's the voice *she* learned and perfected to imitate Mina.

It was *Mina* that night, greeting her old pet Dracula. Not caring that I was cowering and traumatized under the table. It was Mina who decided I was ready to be moved into her room. Mina who crept out of that closet at night to traumatize me. To make certain that her voice, her eyes, her presence were so scarred into my psyche that I'd fall into line, that I'd be powerless to defy or reject her, just like my mother was.

Mina's been feeding off me my entire life, shaping me in a careful, decades-long campaign of terror and control. Just as she has all her descendants. But looking around, I don't see anyone else who could be part of our family. Mina, my mother, and me. Mina's not only been demanding new Goldamings every generation, she's also been getting rid of them when they no longer suit her.

Unaware of the explosion of revelations happening in my head, Mina's still talking to Lucy. "Your friends holding Dracula won't be spared. Except the doctor, because she's useful. But I think you knew the others would be lost when you sent him with them. You didn't want him to die. Not really. Because part of you . . ." She puts one elegant finger beneath Lucy's chin. "Part of you knew I was still here, didn't you? Part of you has always known. You never stopped looking for me, and now you've found me. Oh! I've realized who you are. The scourge of Europe. The slayer of countless vampires. I'll bet you're the same little minx who sprang our Boston enclave trap by asking about Dracula. You killed so many of my servants! Lucy, *honestly.*"

Mina laughs again. Lucy drinks it up, the smallest, most heartbreakingly hopeful smile tugging at the corners of her lips.

Mina smooths Lucy's hair. "But this is nice, seeing you again. And I was wrong, wasn't I? You aren't just a pretty face in a pretty dress obsessed with someone new. You're a pretty face in a pretty dress, still loyal to me. Still my best, my dearest. And you'd never let anything happen to me."

Lucy shakes her head. I feel sick to my stomach. What can I do? How can I stop this?

"That settles it, then. You can stay. Loyalty is the one thing we require from all our initiates before I make them anew. And who could be more loyal than you, a vampire whose entire core is made up of her love for me?" She pats Lucy's head once more, like she might a puppy or a child.

Fuck. *Fuck.* Dracula didn't make the Goldaming Life vampires. *Mina* did. They only smell like him because *she* smells like him. So much for the Doctor's belief that no one else would ever dedicate the time and attention and creepy possessiveness required for creating new vampires. I thought I couldn't hate her more, but Mina is nothing if not ambitious—she's going to keep finding new ways to outdo herself in the category of "bitches I want dead."

But then—

Then—

Lucy turns her head. Mina's right there. Mina, the object of her deepest desire and hope and shame and fear. Mina, the core of her soul. And still, Lucy turns her head, and she finds me. She blinks, and something clears in her eyes. Like a veil beginning to part. She touches her fingers to her wrist, where she's wearing my backpack strap bracelet.

"Lucy," Mina commands.

Lucy keeps her eyes on me for a few heartbeats longer. And that's when I know. Lucy might not even know it yet, but I do. I laugh.

Mina flinches and glares at my mother, like my donkey bray laugh is her fault. "We're finished here. You can take Iris back to—"

"You're not her core, you pathetic narcissist."

Mina raises an eyebrow at me. She puts a hand on Lucy's shoulder and strokes her neck with a quick flick that makes Lucy shudder. "Oh? I'm not?"

"No. You were never her core. You were just the symbol of it. Everything she wanted, and everything she couldn't have. Hope and torment in one. Lucy didn't want *you,* she wanted the idea of you."

"Lucy has always wanted me. And now she can be by my side forever." Mina tugs Lucy's delicately pointed chin, forcing her to look away from me. "That's what you want. What you've always wanted."

I roll my eyes. "She wanted the freedom to be herself—truly herself—with someone. That's what her core was. But she knew even back then that you weren't the answer. You didn't love her the way she loved you, and she was ready to leave you."

Lucy's eyebrows flicker into a frown.

"You *were,* Lucy," I insist, desperate to keep her lucid and connected to me. "You knew Mina would never answer your heart, that she would never be the mirror you wanted. The one that reflected the same wild and open and true love you were brimming with. The night you met Dracula, remember? You were going to free that poor neglected dog. And then you were going to walk away. Choose yourself over all the greedy hands pawing at you, the eyes watching you, the people who said they loved you but only with conditions. Always so many conditions." I hold out my hand to Lucy. An offering. A question. "Ask me if I love you without conditions," I whisper.

"Iris," Lucy says, and she's so sad, so far away. She tips her head and looks straight up instead of at me. "I wasn't going to run away that night. I was going to do what my father did and walk off a cliff. That was why I wasn't afraid of Dracula. Why I went with him. I was ready to die anyway, so I decided to die in Mina's place."

"Oh, pet," Mina coos. "You silly little thing. Mine then, mine now."

My hand is still out, but Lucy doesn't step toward me. She's motionless, her eyes on the ceiling.

How many times can my heart break? I don't blame Lucy. Not after everything she's been through. I do blame Mina, though. Mina and my mother and this whole bloody cult. And I can still hurt them. What have I got to lose?

I walk, dejected, toward the door. It's the single greatest act I've ever put on. My steps are heavy, my shoulders stooped, my hands pressed over my heart. Then I pause and turn around.

"Since you're claiming Lucy," I say, my tone light and cheery, "I'm going to take what you love most, Mina."

"Iris," my mother hisses. There's a reason we aren't surrounded by Mina's other descendants. Each of them eventually failed her, or annoyed her, or ceased to be useful. My mother's eyes are filled with dread that I'm going to get her permanently killed, one way or another. I wink at her.

Mina barely deigns to glance at me. "I love nothing. That's the secret to legacy and power. The reason why I'm still here and why all this will always be mine."

For someone convinced she's better and smarter than anyone she's ever met, Mina's an idiot. "Legacy and power," I say. "That's what you believe in. What you believed in so much during your life that you set up Lucy—a nineteen-year-old girl, a girl who *loved* you, who would have *given* you anything you asked for! You set her up and then let her die. Then you killed Jonathan's boss, and then killed Jonathan, and eventually killed Arthur Goldaming and Doctor Seward. Anything to make certain no one had power over you or your bank account."

I shake my head, disgusted. "You've always been a vampire. You've always looked at the world around you and wanted to take *everything*. You drained innocents dry again and again, then moved on to the next conquest. No wonder Dracula saw a kindred spirit in you. He had no idea what he was getting into, though. I almost feel sorry for him. I feel sorry for everyone in your orbit. For myself. For my stupid mom. And most of all, for Lucy." I look at her, but she's still staring at the ceiling. Lost. That's okay. It's not her fault, and it doesn't change my feelings. I love her without conditions.

"Are you finished?" The cold, carefully contained fury in Mina's voice drops the temperature in the room enough that I should worry about my health, but I'm not worried about anything. Not anymore. Dracula's going to be freed, again. Mina has Lucy in her grasp, again. Goldaming Life will continue flourishing, draining money and hope and futures from everyone it touches. I'm not strong enough to beat any of them.

But I can still hurt them.

"Almost finished! Power and legacy, right? That's your core. That's what gives you strength, but also weakness. Well, guess what? Without me, you've got nothing." My hands, pressed so delicately over my heart, reach into my structured bodice and retrieve my silver dagger. The one my mom thought was such a joke that she left it on my nightstand, where I conveniently fainted so I could stash it between my glorious breasts.

I stab deep into my palm, then drag the blade up the full length of my forearm. Wrist to elbow, opened. "Blood bank's closing, bitch."

Then I sit on the floor and laugh, because there's nothing else to do now.

108

Salt Lake City, January 27, 2025

DRACULA

He plays dead. The three disgusting vampire women know he's not dead, but if they think him weak, they won't pay enough attention.

Just like he didn't pay enough attention. Anger courses through him, a live wire of rage burning so brilliantly he can barely see. Which is a problem, because his senses are all that are left to him at this point. No jaw. Barely any movement or control of his limbs. More than he lets on, though.

He's been rendered powerless, and he will never forgive them. He'll never forgive anyone, not a single creature in this entire world. He'll make them all suffer, he'll make them all pay, for eternity.

Due to his miserable state, he doesn't notice at first when the vampire women, those three wretched, worthless creatures, go tense and still with waiting.

He does his best to actually listen to them. He hates them even more for forcing him to act as though they're worth any space at all in his miraculous, unparalleled mind.

"I smell them, too," one says.

"Oh! Twenty! Maybe thirty!" That one claps her hands in excitement.

"We can't win. Not without Lucy. We have two options. Kill him now and solve all the problems in one fell swoop, or—"

"We promised Lucy," the clapping one says. "We *promised* her."

"Or we stay and fight. All my time studying death, dissecting it, trying to find ways for humans to delay it. And now it's arrived for me, at last. I don't know how to feel about that. I wish Lucy were here to tell me how I ought to feel."

The third shakes her head. "No. Those are not our only options. This creature, this monster—" She kicks at him. He tries to snap, forgetting yet again he has no lower jaw. "This pathetic *parasite* is not worth our lives. He never was. We leave him here. Lucy will find him again. As for myself, I cannot waste another moment on him. Not if I have only a handful of moments more or an eternity of them. I have realized at last that he doesn't matter at all."

The clapping one laughs. She leans close, breath sweet and soft against his face, eyes like chips of ice sharp enough to cut. "Did you hear that? You aren't worth anything. You're not worth dying for. You're not even worth killing. We don't care about you."

He wants to annihilate them. He wants to rip them into pieces. He wants to gather up those pieces and spit on them, grind them beneath his heel, teach them to fear him. Teach them to respect him. Teach them that he is the *only* thing that matters. The only thing that's worth anything.

They walk away.

Come back! he screams, but he has no jaw. It's a garbled, pathetic, meaningless noise. They don't get to reject him! *They* don't get to leave *him*! It's worse, somehow, than being captured, than being injured and defanged and broken.

He writhes on the floor, willing the bones and nerves in his neck to stitch themselves together.

New vampires come pouring in. They're too late. They're worthless, they're pathetic, they make him sick. Finding no fight or threat, most of them leave. The handful that remain prop him up against the wall like he's a child's plaything left broken and discarded on the floor. They dump blood into his exposed throat, spilling it everywhere. He chokes and sputters as it slides down his gullet.

One of the vampires promises they're going to get him somewhere safe. Says that Mina wants to talk to him.

His hands can move again, and move they do. He rips out that vampire's throat. Tears his head off. The others can fight, but not to kill. Never to kill him. He destroys them. Everything is red, but it's a new red. It's not the red of lust, or desire, or even rage. It's the red of despair.

When their bodies are mounded around him, he staggers into the night. No one will ever have power over him again. No one will ever humiliate him again. He'll remind them all that he matters. *Only he matters.* His demon wants to talk to him? Very well. He'll find her, and kill her, and kill *you,* too. You never deserved his time. You were never worthy of him. No one is.

He will kill everyone and everything, and the carnage will stand as a monument to how much he matters.

109

Salt Lake City, January 27, 2025

LUCY

I go away for a while.

There's a maelstrom inside me. Mina is here, Mina is alive, Mina has *always* been alive. Which means that Iris was right: Mina never loved me. If she had, she would have looked for me. She would have known I was still out there. She would never have stopped looking, like I never stopped looking. But Iris is right about that, too. Just like Vanessa was. I wasn't looking for Mina or even for Dracula. I was looking for myself. For a way to feel all that love, burning bright and eternally hopeful inside me.

Mina and Iris are talking. I keep my head up, staring. The chandelier sparkles like starlight. Between those dots of light, I can't see myself. I *can* see Iris.

I watch her, alone in that mirrored reflection. Angry and sad and defiant. If hope is the thing with feathers, Iris's hope is a talon. Her hope is a weapon. But no, that's not right. Her hope is a fortress, keeping her safe all these years. Her hope is a home. My home.

Iris isn't the answer, because I know another person never can be. But Iris is the reflection I need. The mirror to show me the answer. That's how I do it. That's how I free myself. That's how I keep moving and living:

Love.

Love for myself, and love for the person who showed me how to love myself through how fiercely she loves me.

I'm caught in a flood of freedom. At last, I'm releasing the dreams that trapped me as a girl. The ones that told me if I waited just a little longer, if I performed just a little better, if I pretended just a little more, I could be loved by the people who never saw *me.* Who never wanted to.

They don't matter anymore. They have no power over me. I'm in complete control of myself and my fate and my heart, for the first time in my endless life.

But—

There's *blood.* Blood more precious than any other blood in the world. I turn in a daze. What happened while my entire inner landscape shifted so seismically?

Iris is on the floor, laughing. Her face is pale. Too pale, ghastly and ghostly. "No more Goldamings!" she trills in a singsong voice.

A vampire lunges toward her, unable to resist the siren song of that blood. Mina jumps onto his back, grabbing his head and tugging. Her attempt at decapitation leaves something to be desired; I could give her pointers, but Mina never liked it when I corrected her.

"No one touches her!" she screams. "Get out, all of you! Now!"

Her other vampire minions scuttle uncertainly from the room. They leave the door cracked open, waiting and ready to answer Mina's call.

Iris keeps going in her teasing tone. She's lying on the floor, knife abandoned beside her, blood spurting out of her arm as though it can't wait to be free, either. "No more blood to sell! No more brand-new resting places across the country where you can recharge at your leisure! No more lurking in my life or my closet, you goddamn creepy grasping vicious *boring* coward!"

"Fix her!" Mina screams as she at last finishes tugging off the head of the vampire who couldn't resist Iris's blood. Iris's mother scrambles to her daughter's side. She tries to pinch the skin closed, as though that will help. I'm frozen. What do I do?

"I'll fix her!" Iris's mother says, her tone wheedling. "I'm so sorry! I'll fix it, I'll fix it, don't—"

Iris slaps her mother's hands away, rolling out of her grasp. "She's gonna kill you for this," she taunts. "How does it feel, Mom? How does it feel having a cold, ruthless, utterly uncaring monster in charge of your safety and well-being? I gotta say, I'm having a schadenfreude field day!"

"Get back!" Mina throws Iris's mother across the room. The vampire stays where she falls, either too broken or too afraid to so much as move.

Mina and Iris, Iris and Mina. My head is swirling, my body numb. Am I here? Have I become moonlight? Did I dream this?

Mina kneels over Iris, pinning her in place. She tears a strip from Iris's skirt and ties it tightly around Iris's upper arm. Then she rips off another strip and begins wrapping the wound. Always efficient and practical. As she works at the business of keeping Iris's blood contained, Mina speaks.

"I'm going to lock you up," she says. "Keep you drugged enough that you can't move, but make sure you're aware of what's happening to you, every minute of every day. I'll harvest you for parts—first, I'll take every last egg to make an army of Goldamings. I'll drain your blood as fast as you can make it, and when you beg me for death, I'll smile and tell you the same thing every day." Mina leans close to Iris's ear, dropping her voice to a whisper. "*Not yet.* I'm not going to let you die, Iris. You don't get to choose that. I do. I'm life. I'm death. And you're *mine.*"

With Mina's eyes glowing red, her teeth brushing Iris's neck, her fingers grasping Iris's body while clutching at her soul, I realize what Iris already figured out:

Mina is Dracula. She always was. They're soulmates, a matching pair. I could never see it before, but Iris showed me. I drift across the ballroom floor and kneel beside Mina.

I look at Mina, but I say, "My little cabbage."

Iris's skin is pallid, her lips almost white. But she smiles and her fear fades. Because she *knows.* She knows I'm back.

"I'm not sure if I can do it alone," I say. I died to protect Mina because I loved her. Even seeing what she truly is, there's part of me that loves her still. That always will. "I'll need help."

"What are you talking about?" Mina snaps.

Iris's lips split into a bloodless smile. "Ask me to help you," she whispers.

Mina turns her head toward me with a baffled expression. I devoted so much energy and study to that face—its subtleties, its secrets. But I wasn't looking for the truth. Only for what I hoped to find there and never did.

"You always were a little fool," Mina says.

"Let's kiss like we used to, Mina." I lean close.

Mina laughs in my face. And because she's laughing in my face, she doesn't see Iris's hand close over the knife.

"Shoulda looked right." Iris stabs straight into Mina's chest.

Mina screams. It's a scream of lifetimes dealing death to others while hiding from it herself. A scream of, at last, being truly seen. She scrabbles back on the floor, staring at the silver knife piercing her long-dead heart.

"I did it," Iris gasps. "Guess I just needed the right inspiration."

"Mistress?" a vampire calls at the door.

Iris lifts her voice a few notes higher and flattens the tone to a cold command. A perfect imitation of her unconscious mother, who crafted a perfect imitation of Mina. "Close the door," Iris says. "Wait outside the building."

The door closes. Iris lies back, giggling. "What a bunch of chumps."

I walk to Mina. She's not my Mina anymore. She never was. I straddle her, pinning her to the floor like she pinned Iris.

"Lucy," she whines, the red light dying in her eyes. They're brown again. The eyes I painted over and over, desperate to re-create them. I pull the knife free.

She gasps with relief. "I knew you would never, I knew you could never—"

I slip my hand into the hole made by Iris's silver blade. My fingers find Mina's heart. The heart I'd hoped so desperately she would give to me. Instead, I follow Mina's example and take it for myself.

It's so small, freed from its cage of bone. I wonder why I let it have power over me for so long. I gently insert the silver knife back into it, just in case, but Mina isn't here anymore. Her corpse is already drying beneath me.

Iris coughs a laugh. I stand and see the reason. Her mother, slumped against the wall, is *actually* dead now. Dead for real, dead forever.

"Mina made them," Iris says. "Mina made all of them. Every Goldaming Life vampire is now a Goldaming Death vampire. Including me, probably. No get-out-of-jail-free card when I die, since it was her blood infection that turned us. Oh well."

I'm next to Iris in a heartbeat. I know, because I can hear her heartbeats. They're struggling. Too shallow, too slow. She's lost so much blood.

Iris puts a hand on my cheek, drawing my attention from her arm to her face. "Hey. It's okay. I promise. I'm happy. God, I'm so happy, and I'm so fucking proud of you. You freed yourself. You're *free.* We both are. We did this, Lucy. For ourselves, and for each other. And don't you dare say that none of it matters if I die. It matters. I promise. We have right now, and I love you right now. And my now is an eternity."

I open my mouth to say I can't lose her, but the truth is, I can. I can lose Iris and still love myself. But that doesn't mean I have to lose her without a fight.

"I have an idea," I say, running my thumb along her bottom lip. "I don't know if it will work. And I won't do it unless you want me to. But if you want to try to stay, I want that, too." I pause, knowing the full weight of what I'm offering her. Knowing she understands it, too. At least as well as anyone still human can. "Ask me to change you."

Her eyelids flutter as she struggles to stay conscious, but her smile is still the sexiest thing I've ever seen. "Lucy," she whispers, "*bite* me." Then she giggles, because even while dying she's a little shit. I love her so much.

I bite my lips and press them to hers, giving her more of my blood just in case. And then I pierce the cool skin of her neck with infinite tenderness. I take what little remains of her blood, every drop holy, every drop perfect, every drop Iris.

She dies.

I wait, content to sit here forever with my love in my arms.

110

Salt Lake City, January 28, 2025

DRACULA

He knows where they'll be. His demon loves to surround herself with finery and flattery. He loathes her for it, even though he took someone else's name because his own never merited so much as a scratch on the great scroll of history.

But he has gouged himself into history. Punctured and drained and terrorized his way across the ages. *He's* important. She'll be no more than a footnote in his story after this. Less than a footnote. He'll forget her as soon as it's over. He'll forget all of them.

No animals have heeded his call, though. He notices it only now, as he nears the building holding *her,* holding you. Why have none come to him? He brings them without a thought, without effort, but tonight—

He cannot muster the blade of demand to cut through the natural world.

He's just tired. He needs more blood. Besides, he doesn't want animals to do this for him. He wants to do it himself. That's the real reason. But clambering gracelessly over the fence, crawling like a beast on his belly toward the ballroom windows, he realizes that something else is wrong.

He doesn't smell his demon or her servants. There's some fresh blood, but mostly rot. Death, *final* death, long delayed and at last come to call. Only, there—

One vital scent left. One foe remaining.

He presses a red eye against one of the windowpanes. He sees her. His demon. Mina. The only one who ever forced him to learn her name. The only one who ever tricked him, who ever manipulated him, who ever wielded power over him. The only one he ever feared. He knows, now, that he feared her. There are no more lies, not even to himself. Because he *was* afraid of Mina, afraid of her confidence and her cleverness, afraid of the core of absolute self-belief that rendered her holy and impossible for him to touch.

Someone else was powerful enough to kill her, though.

His fear swells and grows. Sitting in the middle of the room, clutching your lifeless, useless body, is . . .

What was her name? He forgot it as soon as she said it. But her face. Her face, he will never forget. It's blazed on his mind, branded there. Eyes like the ocean, hair like gold flame, face like an avenging angel.

She nearly killed him. She tore his jaw off. She took you when even he couldn't. And she ended Mina, once and for all, without a plan. Without decades of preparation. Without his infinite lifetimes of strength and darkness and cunning.

His borders shimmer and quiver. He tries to shift into a bat, but he can't change. Fear holds him like a lover whispering in his ear, saying that she'll find him again, and she'll end him.

No. No, he's not afraid. He's slinking away into the night because it's what he wants to do. Because she's not worth his time. Because he doesn't need or even want to kill her. It's beneath him. He'll feed, he'll rest, he'll build up his strength once more.

And then he'll take care of her, once and for all. He can be patient. He can wait as long as it takes for her to drop her guard. Years. Decades. Centuries. He'll disappear, and then, when he's ready, when he *chooses* to, he'll find her. He's not fleeing. He doesn't run from anyone or anything.

But he can't stop looking over his shoulder as he goes.

111

Salt Lake City, January 28, 2025

IRIS

Everything is too bright, too loud. The air moves in ways I can see now, smell, even *hear,* it's all too much and not enough and I'm so thirsty, so aching and raw that I feel every nerve in my entire body, which is being cradled by a stunningly beautiful woman. She gazes down at me and then shoves something plastic into my mouth and squeezes. By the time I've swallowed it all, I'm coherent enough to realize she's been happily chattering this whole time.

". . . a whole supply of it back there, like juice pouches. But now you won't be out of your mind with thirst, so even if it takes you awhile to come back to yourself, I've got you. You're not alone. I'll take care of you, Iris, for as long as—"

Iris. My name floods into me with more power than the blood, filling me up, reconnecting those pathways in my brain. A link to who I was before I became . . . whatever I am now. Iris. I'm *Iris.* And she's Lucy.

I pull her down to my lips. Her lips aren't cool anymore; they're the same temperature as mine. I can feel her and smell her and she's real and I'm real and everything is too much but just enough. I laugh against her mouth and she smiles, so big we can't kiss anymore, and that's okay, too, because *Lucy.*

Lucy, and me.

"I've been saying your name over and over," she says. "I hoped if I gave it back to you as soon as you woke up, it would help. It made a difference for me."

"It did help. It made me remember, who I was and— Oh my god, it worked. I'm a vampire. I *am* a vampire, right?" I look down at my hands. They're still just hands. My body seems like my body. But my senses—I have a hundred where I used to have a handful.

Lucy's eyebrows knit close together as if to reassure each other. "Is that—is that okay?"

I nod, but there's one detail bothering me. It will always bother me if I don't know. "Do I smell like him? Was it his blood that changed me, or yours?"

Lucy presses her face against my neck, lingering there. Then she leans back and shrugs. "I don't know. And I don't care. I'm not his because he changed me, am I?"

I shake my head rapidly.

"So, you aren't, either. And you're not mine because I changed you. You belong to yourself, complete and whole and beloved. But for the record, I think you smell *delicious.*"

I laugh and pull her close. "Likewise. So. What now?"

"Well, first I'm going to teach you how to be a vampire so you don't go out of your mind and do things you might regret. Though no judgment here if you do."

"Right, yes, good. I'd like to stay in my mind. And then?"

"And then, if you want, I thought we could go kill Dracula." Lucy is both hopeful and tentative as she searches my face for my reaction. "I promised my friends I would, and I'd like to keep that promise. That would mean an ending for us, too. But you should know, I spent decades searching for him, and that was *before* I ripped his jaw off—"

"You *what*?" I'm delighted. "Is that what you were holding when you came in here? I couldn't see it!"

She beams proudly. "He was so pathetic, drooling impotently, tongue lolling. You would have laughed."

"I definitely would have. I also might have vomited, but that's neither here nor there."

"Anyhow, he was hard to find *before* I nearly killed him. I suspect he'll be even harder to find now. It could take ages. A lifetime. Two or three lifetimes, even." She's soft and hesitant again, like she's reaching out to take my hand for the first time. Unsure if I'll accept the offering of her fingers in mine.

I don't know what my core is yet, what defining thing I brought back over that line between life and death. I don't know what will give me strength and purpose and also weakness in equal measure.

I suspect I'm looking at her, though. Loving someone is always giving them the power to destroy you. But I trust both of us enough to know it's worth it.

"Well," I say, "if it's going to take awhile, good thing I'm immortal *and* rich now." Even with the family pyramid-scheme cult destroyed. The obscenely rich never actually lose their money, and I'm the only Goldaming left. No one needs to know that I'm also technically dead until I've cashed out.

Lucy isn't working alone now. I have resources she never could have. All the access and connections money can buy. This time used not to hide Dracula, but to hunt him. We'll find him together, sooner or later.

I might prefer later, though. I lean my forehead against Lucy's and close my eyes, letting all my miraculous senses explore her in new ways. "Ask me to spend my afterlife with you," I whisper.

She kisses me, and I'm free. We both are.

112

THE PRESIDENT IS DEAD, LONG LIVE THE PRESIDENT!

Subject: Goldaming Death

Hey, fuckos!

I'm sure you noticed a big change when all your vampire lackeys and hapless cult members dropped dead. Actually dead this time. Bad news, good news? Bad news is we killed Mina Goldaming and everyone she turned into a vampire. Good news is we killed Mina Goldaming and everyone she turned into a vampire.

I'm in charge now. And thanks to Dickie (Hi, Dick!), I've learned how to be ruthlessly meticulous when it comes to paperwork and legalities. My grasp on the company and the funds thereof is iron-clad and unassailable. (And before you get cute, I moved my dad to another location. You'll never find him. Don't try.)

Here's the fun part: Turns out my mother kept detailed tabs on each one of you. I know all your bank account information, I know your investments, I know where your properties and offshore accounts are, I know about your affairs, I know about your bribes, I know about the not insignificant amount of straight-up murder you've all committed, and I have a paper trail for everything. Neat, right?

Here's what you're going to do. You're going to figure out a way to explain why so many members of Goldaming Life are no longer life-ing. You've all got experience with creative ways of reframing suspicious deaths. Put that practice to good use. Once you've done that, you're going to give insurance payouts to the families of the poor dupes you conned into becoming vampire servants. Not from Goldaming funds, but from your own personal savings. I think a million bucks per vampire is fair. If you run out of money, no, you didn't. I know exactly how much you're all worth.

Whatever remains of the fortunes you built by draining innocent people in so many ways? I'm attaching a list of charities I've personally vetted. You're not going to make donations in the name of Goldaming Life, or in your own names. Anonymous, every single one of them.

And then, finally, I give Dickie the honor of liquidating Goldaming Life on my behalf. Shut it all down without explanation or warning. Donate the properties to the charities I've listed, under the condition that the Goldaming name is utterly erased and never credited.

Once you've done all that, you're free to slink into the pathetic remains of your penniless lives. And know that I'm watching. If any of you so much as sniff in the direction of vampirism or multilevel marketing pyramid schemes again, I'll be on your doorstep. And I won't need an invitation inside, because as far as I'm concerned, everything you are and have and own already belongs to me. You bought it with my blood, after all.

I think that's it! Hope you do exactly as instructed. Then again, I've found a brand-new thirst for life, and I won't hesitate to show you exactly what that means if you try to cross me.

Kisses!

Iris

113

Hillside Memorial Cemetery, January 30, 2025

VOICE MEMO OF LUCY WESTENRA

LUCY: So, now you've heard the rest of it. Or at least, the rest of it so far. I'm going to disagree with you, though, Vanessa. Which I know is unfair since you aren't here to argue your point, but I think you'll like mine.

You were wrong. Not about what I was searching for, or that I deserved to mourn myself, or that I was actually making a difference all those lonely decades when I felt so lost.

But you were wrong about endings. It's not endings that give stories meaning. It's the forever-full-of-nows. Every step, every choice, every feeling: That's what holds meaning. For a story, for a life. I'm happy to not be at the end just yet. I'll take an eternity more of nows.

But if you do want an ending, because I know you love a good story, I've got one for you. I found the girl I was, and I forgave her, and I even managed to save her.

IRIS: Ahem. With help.

LUCY: Okay, yes, Iris notes that I saved her "with help." Thank you for listening, and for showing me the way.

IRIS: Wait, you're done? You're just going to leave the phone on her headstone?

LUCY: Yes. It's got my story on it. I told the story for her, so I'm leaving it here.

IRIS: That's not—that's not how recordings work, that's— You know what, sure. It's fine. We'll get you a new phone. But I'm keeping you as Butter Chicken in my contacts.

LUCY: I don't know what that sentence even means.

IRIS: I know. Oh, Anthony and Rahul texted. They're expecting us next week and I still have no idea how to explain my new lack of appetite.

LUCY: I gave you my allergies?

IRIS: *[laughing] There's* an odd euphemism for vampirism. We'll figure it out later. Come on, it's getting dark. We have work to do.

LUCY: We do. Goodbye, Vanessa. Sleep well. If there's anything beyond that last strange border, my love and I will meet you there someday, with even more stories to tell.

ACKNOWLEDGMENTS

If you read *Hide* and *Mister Magic,* you've probably come to this page ready for me to give you a deeply personal story about why I chose to write this book.

Here it is:

Lucy deserved a girlfriend.

That's it. Really. I first read Bram Stoker's brilliant (and infuriating) classic in college. It's alternately scary and funny and boring and delightful. He has turns of phrases so good they take my breath away, and then he has entire chapters that make me want to gouge my eyes out. (My favorite detail is how, as the book progresses, Quincey Morris talks less and less. He's ultimately relegated to single-word answers delivered "laconically." I relate to an author who sets out with high ambitions—in this case, to make up a baffling American cowboy dialect—and then gets tired and gives up.)

I love *Dracula,* and it makes me angry, particularly in its treatment of Lucy. The agonizingly drawn-out suffering, the infantilizing, the lack of consent and bodily autonomy, and especially the shaming of sexuality and equating it with monstrousness in a young woman—all this from the heroes, mind you, not the vampire. And while I absolutely believe my own theory that Mina, Arthur, and Doctor Seward were running an inheritance scam (so many conveniently dead people, so many wills giving them everything!), I also absolutely, one hundred percent, down to my very soul believe Lucy is queer.

Okay, so it turns out that wasn't *entirely* it, after all. As someone who wasn't able to embrace parts of myself until my thirties, who was taught that natural feelings inside me were inherently monstrous and evil, it meant the world to me to write Lucy's journey of self-acceptance and love. I love her, and I love myself, and I love you, too, if you're reading this and need to hear that.

(Also, Utah, I wasn't planning to set another horror novel in you, but when considering where a vampiric pyramid scheme cosplaying as a multilevel marketing company would flourish, the predatory MLM capital of the world just made sense. Someday I'll set a happy novel in you, Utah!) (Just kidding, I won't; the next one's even worse. I still think you're really pretty, though?)

On to actually acknowledging some wonderful people who make all this possible:

My brilliant editor, Tricia Narwani, has been all in on this idea from day one. The book wouldn't exist without her enthusiasm, incredible insight, and editorial guidance. It's a joy to make books with Del Rey: Ayesha Shibli, David Moench, Scott Shannon, Keith Clayton, Alex Larned, Julie Leung, Meghan O'Shaughnessy, Craig Adams, Debbie Glasserman, Ashleigh Heaton, Tori Henson, Sabrina Shen, Ada Maduka, Marcelle Iten Busto, and every other person I have the privilege to work with there are so smart and dedicated and excellent at what they do. And a huge shout-out to Regina Flath and Rachel Ake, cover designer extraordinaire: reunited, and it feels so good! I love reclaiming literary women with you. Audrey Benjaminsen gave me the luscious goth cover of my dreams, and I feel so lucky to have her art bringing Lucy to life. Thomas Cherwin, thanks for the valiant copyedit. This hyphen is for you as a reminder that you understand how to use it correctly even if I don't, and I'm grateful: -

Michelle Wolfson and I have worked together for more than fifteen years, on dozens of books, and I couldn't ask for a better agent or friend. One of these days I'll write a romcom so you don't have to read with the lights on. (Just kidding, I don't think I'm capable of that.)

I remain supported by two of the smartest, most compassionate, best women I've ever known. Stephanie Perkins and Natalie Whipple show up in all my acknowledgments ever. They've seen me through so many drafts, but also so many versions of myself, and they've shown up with love for all of them.

The earliest versions of this book were scribbled in a notebook overlooking a glorious pool and the glorious ocean. Thank you, Cassie and Josh, for your generosity in inviting me to run away to a villa and dream gothic dreams in the least gothic setting ever, and thank you to everyone at the retreat for inspiring me. Especially you, Holly Black. Who would have ever guessed you'd be good at brainstorming vampire stories?

A special note to my friend Ian Carlos Crawford and his inimitable force of a mother, the real Alicia Del Toro. Thank you for sharing her with me, Ian. She was truly one of a kind and I'm grateful I got to know her through you. (And thanks for letting me kill you, again. Besties!)

Music was crucial in bringing this book to life. Halsey, boygenius, Wolf Alice, In This Moment, Radiohead, The Cure, Everything Everything, and Hozier all kept me company, provided inspiration, and pointed my focus where it needed to be.

I'm going to specifically, clearly note that, whatever you might interpret based on my last several books, I have a wise, loving, generous mom. Mom, I love you. And my dad is the kindest, warmest, most supportive man you'll ever meet. Sometimes we *don't* write what we know. And to Erin, Lindsey, Lauren, and Matt, thanks for being my siblings and perma-best friends. I'm also lucky to have phenomenal in-laws. So many of them. So, so many of them. I'm surrounded by tremendous love and support, which allows me to safely go to dark places in my books.

Noah, you remain the best decision I ever made. If I was forever stuck at nineteen, I'd be fine because that's when I knew you were it for me. And to our three delightful children, you won't read this because you never read my books, which is totally okay. I'd rather be your mom than your favorite author.

And finally, to Bram Stoker: Sorry. But also thanks. But also sorry. But mostly thanks.

ABOUT THE AUTHOR

KIERSTEN WHITE is the #1 *New York Times* bestselling, Bram Stoker Award–winning, and critically acclaimed author of many books, including *Hide, Mister Magic, The Dark Descent of Elizabeth Frankenstein,* the And I Darken trilogy, the Camelot Rising trilogy, and *Star Wars: Padawan*. She lives with her family in San Diego, where they obsessively care for their deeply ambivalent tortoise, Kimberly.

kierstenwhite.com
Instagram: @authorkierstenwhite

ABOUT THE TYPE

This book was set in Dante, a typeface designed by Giovanni Mardersteig (1892–1977). Conceived as a private type for the Officina Bodoni in Verona, Italy, Dante was originally cut only for hand composition by Charles Malin, the famous Parisian punch cutter, between 1946 and 1952. Its first use was in an edition of Boccaccio's *Trattatello in laude di Dante* that appeared in 1954. The Monotype Corporation's version of Dante followed in 1957. Though modeled on the Aldine type used for Pietro Cardinal Bembo's treatise *De Aetna* in 1495, Dante is a thoroughly modern interpretation of that venerable face.